Praise for Harbour Street

'Cleeves, a master storyteller with a forensic eye for small detail, is fast becoming the new Agatha Christie with her fiendishly clever plotting, compelling characterization and earthy, authentic dialogue . . . A perfectly crafted murder mystery . . . don't miss it!'
Lancashire Evening Post

'A gripping novel, told with piercing prose and a forensic eye, from the award-winning writer of ITV's *Vera* and BBC's *Shetland*'
My Weekly

'Ann Cleeves excels in writing about the day-to-day, the familiar, the normal – and turning it into the foundations of a cracking crime novel . . . Those cleverly disguised dead ends had me completely fooled, which is just the way I like it. *Harbour Street* is one of those books that you don't want to finish, because the journey has been so engrossing and enjoyable, and I was sorry to say goodbye to Mardle'
CrimeFicLover.com

'There is no shirking of the miseries and cruelties of real life in this series, but Cleeves displays them without resorting to any graphic violence. She has always rendered the landscape and inhabitants of the North East of England with a quiet skill but there is a sense of expansion in the writing of *Harbour Street* and a confidence that make it even more appealing than its predecessors'
BookOxygen.com

Praise for the Vera Stanhope series

'Cleeves brings a large cast to life, shifting points of view between bereaved relatives, victims and suspects in a straightforward, satisfyingly traditional detective novel'
Literary Review

'Ann Cleeves, winner of last year's inaugural Duncan Lawrie Dagger, is another fine author with a strong, credible female protagonist . . . It's a dark, interesting novel with considerable emotional force behind it'
Spectator

'Stepping into *The Glass Room* is a little like being transported back to the golden age of mystery stories: a windswept landscape, isolated country house, disparate people thrown together, crime scenes mimicking their fictional counterparts and a plot liberally strewn with blind alleys, red herrings and misdirections. This book has all the elements of Agatha Christie at her best'
S. J. Bolton

'Cleeves is excellent not only on the main character but on the mixture of exasperation and respect that she provokes in others. Combined with the intricate plotting, this makes for a compulsive read'
Independent

'Ann Cleeves is a skilful technician. Her easy use of language and clever story construction make her one of the best natural writers of detective fiction'
Sunday Express

'Cleeves has a way of making unlikely murders plausible by grounding them in recognizable communities. In this world, neighbours are close-knit, and close ranks'
Financial Times

'The latest novel is as smoothly written and entertaining as anything Ann has ever produced . . . I'd rank this as one of the best books she's written . . . Her mastery of technique, developed over more than two decades, would be worthy of study by anyone starting out as a writer of popular fiction . . . An excellent balance of puzzle, character and setting that makes for first rate entertainment'
Martin Edwards

'This novel has all Ann Cleeves' trademarks – great timing, strong characters, lots of tension and plenty of red herrings to keep the reader hooked. The setting of the murder in an isolated house with its mysterious guests also gives it a distinct and satisfying Agatha Christie-esque feel. If you like the TV series, you're in for a treat – because the atmospheric but realistic books are even better'
Press Association

Praise for the Shetland series

'*Raven Black* breaks the conventional mould of British crime-writing, while retaining the traditional virtues of strong narrative and careful plotting'
Independent

'Like a smoky Shetland peat fire, this elegantly written, slow-burning intrigue shrouds you in mystery and crackles with inner heat'
Peter James

'Beautifully constructed . . . a lively and surprising addition to a genre that once seemed moribund'
Times Literary Supplement

'*Raven Black* shows what a fine writer Cleeves is . . . an accomplished and thoughtful book'
Sunday Telegraph

'Ann's characterization is worthy of the best writers in the field . . . Rarely has a sense of place been so evocatively conveyed in a crime novel'
Daily Express

'In true Agatha Christie style, Cleeves once again pulls the wool over our eyes with cunning and conviction'
Colin Dexter

'It delivers the unexpected: a fully satisfying novel, rather than a genre formula'
Judith Flanders, *Times Literary Supplement*

'A most satisfying mystery set in an isolated and intriguing location. Jimmy Perez is a fine creation, and I hope Ann Cleeves' Shetland series will be with us for a long time to come'
Peter Robinson

'A carefully constructed, atmospheric and interesting mystery'
Literary Review

'Cunning character-play and deception play their part in this satisfying tale, bringing about a denouement that turns everything in the plot neatly and bewilderingly on its head'
Scotsman

'Ann Cleeves' fellow crime fiction practitioners (from Colin Dexter to Peter Robinson) have been lining up to sing her praises, and it's unlikely that there will be any blip in that chorus of praise on the evidence of *Red Bones*, which is quite as assured and entertaining as its predecessors'
Barry Forshaw

'This is a real, page-turning thriller. It is beautifully crafted, belonging to the golden age of well-fashioned detective fiction. Clues, red herrings, isolation, birds, wings, feathers, unusual passions made understood. I simply could not put it down . . . a terrific, atmospheric novel'
Frances Fyfield

HARBOUR STREET

Ann Cleeves is the author behind ITV's *Vera* and BBC One's *Shetland*. She has written over twenty-five novels, and is the creator of detectives Vera Stanhope and Jimmy Perez – characters loved both on screen and in print. Both series are international bestsellers.

In 2006 Ann was awarded the Duncan Lawrie Dagger (CWA Gold Dagger) for Best Crime Novel, for *Raven Black*, the first book in her Shetland series. In 2012 she was inducted into the CWA Crime Thriller Awards Hall of Fame. Ann lives in North Tyneside.

www.anncleeves.com
@anncleeves
facebook.com/anncleeves

By Ann Cleeves

A Bird in the Hand   Come Death and High Water

Murder in Paradise   A Prey to Murder

A Lesson in Dying   Murder in My Back Yard

A Day in the Death of Dorothea Cassidy

Another Man's Poison   Killjoy

The Mill on the Shore   Sea Fever

The Healers   High Island Blues

The Baby-Snatcher   The Sleeping and the Dead

Burial of Ghosts

Vera Stanhope series

The Crow Trap   Telling Tales   Hidden Depths

Silent Voices   The Glass Room   Harbour Street

The Moth Catcher

The Shetland series

Raven Black   White Nights   Red Bones

Blue Lightning   Dead Water

Thin Air

Ann Cleeves

HARBOUR STREET

PAN BOOKS

First published 2014 by Macmillan

This edition published 2014 by Pan Books
an imprint of Pan Macmillan
The Smithson, 6 Briset Street, London EC1M 5NR
EU representative: Macmillan Publishers Ireland Ltd, 1st Floor,
The Liffey Trust Centre, 117–126 Sheriff Street Upper,
Dublin 1, D01 YC43
Associated companies throughout the world
www.panmacmillan.com

ISBN 978-1-4472-0209-7

17

A CIP catalogue record for this book is available from the British Library.

Typeset by Ellipsis Digital Limited, Glasgow
Printed and bound by CPI Group (UK) Ltd, Croydon, CR0 4YY

To Oliver Clarke and Arthur Raynor

Chapter One

Joe pushed through the crowd. It was just before Christmas and the Metro trains were full of shoppers clutching carrier bags stuffed with useless presents. Babies were left to scream in expensive buggies. People who'd been drinking early spilled out from office parties, stumbling down the escalators and onto the trains. Youths used language Joe wouldn't want his children to hear. Today, though, he'd had no option about using the Metro. Sal had been adamant that she needed the car.

It was just him and his daughter. She was in the school choir and there'd been a performance in Newcastle Cathedral. Carols by candlelight, because even at four o'clock it was dark in the building. Beautiful singing that made him feel like crying. His boss, Vera Stanhope, always said that he was a romantic fool. Then out into the rush-hour evening, and it was just starting to snow, so Jessie was excited all over again. She was a soloist and had hit all the right notes, so the choirmaster had given her a special mention at the end. Christmas was only ten days away, though she was too old now to believe in Santa. But there was snow. Tiny little flakes twisting in the gusty wind like mini-tornadoes.

In the Metro he held her hand. They were standing, because all the seats were taken. In the space by the door stood two young girls, hardly older than Jessie, but their faces orange with make-up and their eyes black with liner and mascara. Squashed beside them, two lads. He watched what was going on there and hated what he saw, the pawing and the groping. Vera also called him a prude. He wouldn't have minded so much if the encounter had been affectionate, but there was something unpleasant about the way the boys spoke to the lasses. Putting them down for their lack of street cred, mocking. Joe thought he'd like to bring the girls into the police station. Let Vera give them a pep talk about feminism – a woman's right to respect. The thought made him smile. He looked at the badge on the girls' blazers. One of the private schools in town. He and Sal had wondered about sending Jessie private. She was as bright as a button and they had high hopes for her. Certainly university. Maybe one of the grand ones. Watching the simpering and defensive girls, he wasn't so sure about the posh school now.

The train pulled into a station. In the lights on the platform he saw that it was snowing even more heavily, the flakes bigger, settling on the terraced roofs. A woman with a long coat got on and took a recently vacated seat further down the carriage. Joe had been eyeing it up for Jessie and felt an irrational antipathy towards the woman. She had silver hair and discreet make-up, the fitted coat reaching almost to the ground. Despite her age – she must be seventy – there was something elegant about her. He thought she had money and wondered why she hadn't called a taxi, instead of squashing into the Metro with the rest of them. At the next station a group of men filled the carriage. Suits and ties, briefcases. Loud voices talking about some sales conference. The mood he was in, Joe hated them too, for their brashness. The showing-off. Every station, a shifting tide of people, but he and Jessie were squashed into a corner by the door now, and he could see nothing but the back of a fat man wearing a Newcastle United sweatshirt. No jacket. A Geordie hard man.

The lights in the carriage flickered, and there was a moment of complete darkness. Somewhere a young woman gave a small scream. The lights came back on and the train pulled into a station. Partington, nearly the end of the line. The snow was an inch deep on the platform. Joe hoped Sal was home, the central heating on and tea nearly ready. She'd talked about getting a tree. He'd have been happy with an artificial one – his mam had never bothered with the real thing – but Sal was like a kid at Christmas, buzzing with preparations and excitement. He imagined walking into the house and the smell of pine and something cooking. Wondered again why he'd thought this marriage – this family – might not be enough for him.

He decided that they'd get a taxi home from Mardle Metro. Sal had said she'd come to pick them up, but he didn't want her driving in this weather. A taxi would cost a fortune all the way home, but it'd be worth it. The Metro doors were still open and he caught a brief glimpse of the passengers sitting opposite, saw that the cold air had blown in a flurry of snowflakes that clung to their hair. He'd dressed smartly for the cathedral, and Jessie was only wearing her school coat over her uniform. He put his arm around her, hoping to keep her warm.

The tannoy buzzed and the driver spoke.

'Sorry, folk. There's a problem on the line. Wrong sort of snow.' Muffled laughter from the passengers, too full of seasonal cheer and strong lager to be irritated by the disruption. 'This is where we stop. A bus will be along shortly to continue the journey, if you follow one of my colleagues to the main road.' A good-natured groan. The passengers stumbled out, complaining about the cold, but rather enjoying the drama. It would be a good story to tell in the pub that night. Ashworth held on to Jessie. Let the drunks and the weirdos get off first. He was feeling in his pocket for his mobile, to call a taxi, as he stepped onto the platform. They were only one stop from Mardle. Really this was no big deal, and again he thought there was no need to drag Sal out. He tucked Jessie under his overcoat, held her close to his body, as he searched for the number. The other passengers were following a Metro guy in a green jacket; they were drifting away, invisible already in the falling snow.

In the train the lights were still on, but they were faint. There was no sign of the driver. Jessie nudged Joe in the ribs.

'Look. That lady hasn't moved.'

'Don't worry.' Joe had the phone to his ear. The number was ringing. 'She'll be asleep. Had too much to drink at lunchtime maybe.' Then he saw that Jessie was pointing to the elderly woman in the long coat.

He was about to say that the driver wouldn't drive off without checking that all the carriages were clear when Jessie slipped out from under his arm and ran through the open Metro door. She shook the woman gently by the shoulder. She'd always been a kind lass and Joe was proud of her, but sometimes he wished she wouldn't interfere.

The taxi firm answered his phone call at the same time as Jessie screamed.

Chapter Two

There was only one house on Harbour Street; the other buildings were businesses. It was tall and grey, almost black with the coal dust that also coloured the little beach on the other side of the harbour wall. Three storeys, a basement and an attic. Imposing. Carved above the door, a date: 1885. There was a light in the basement window and inside a woman was taking sheets from a drying rack that had been suspended over the stove. She folded them expertly, held them corner-to-corner and stretched them, before putting them on the table. Upstairs other windows were lit too, but from the pavement there was no way of seeing who was inside.

Next to the house was Malcolm Kerr's yard, separated from the road by a rusting metal fence topped with ferocious spikes, the gates fastened with a huge chain and giant padlock. A couple of elderly boats, bits of engine, odd bulbous shapes covered by tarpaulin – it had the feel of a scrapyard. Malcolm ran the seabird trips out to Coquet Island and in the winter, when the *Lucy-May* attracted fewer charters, he worked in the yard, making repairs to his neighbours' boats. The snow had started to soften the harsh silhouettes in the yard, making them mysterious and hardly recognizable. In one corner stood a shed, built from corrugated iron and wood. Malcolm often worked there all night, drinking cans of beer, but this evening the place was dark and quiet and there were no footmarks in the snow.

Next door to the yard was the lifeboat station, housing the inshore lifeboat, and outside it, to the seaward side, sat the tractor and trailer that would carry the vessel to the water in emergencies or on exercise. Then came the Mardle Fisheries: alive, buzzing with sound, background music from the telly on the wall, laughter from the people in the queue. During the day the fisheries sold wet fish, much of it locally caught, retail and wholesale from a long, low building at the back. In the evening it was a fish-and-chip shop, with a sit-in restaurant by the side. Behind the fryers two women dressed in white were flushed with heat, despite the snowflakes blowing in through the open door. There was a line of people spilling onto the street. All local. Mardle wasn't a place for tourists, even in the summer. There was nothing beyond the fisheries except the harbour, enclosed by the wall. The boats there were dark shadows, half-hidden by the drifting flakes.

On the other side of the road stood the Coble pub, and already the snow was flattened and hard where people had crossed between it and the chip shop. Outside, a couple of hardy smokers leaned against the wall for shelter from the worst of the weather. Next to the pub was the low, squat building of the harbourmaster's office; beyond that some rough ground that was used as a car park, and then, opposite the big residential house with the brightly lit basement, stood

St Bartholomew's Church. Victorian Gothic, a church built for seamen and pitmen, now regularly attended by a handful of elderly women. At the end of the street, like a beacon or a square glowing moon, shone the yellow cube with the black M that marked the Metro station. The end of the line. People waited on the platform to get into town for Friday-night partying, but no trains came.

This was Harbour Street.

In the big house Kate Dewar carried the linen up the stairs to the airing cupboard, pausing briefly outside the numbered doors. Not listening. Kate would never eavesdrop on her guests. But this was her territory and she liked to know who was at home. The house seemed quiet. Perhaps the snow was causing travel problems. She was glad her kids were already in; she'd heard them arrive earlier and imagined them slouched on the couch in the basement flat, watching TV. She had a rule about finishing homework before switching on the set, but it was nearly the end of term and today she wasn't going to push it.

Climbing the stairs, she thought she heard the front door opening, but, stopping to listen, there was no other sound. It must be the wind, rattling the letter box. She could always tell when the wind was northerly because of that particular noise. The airing cupboard was on the attic landing, between Margaret's room and the shelf where she placed extra sachets of coffee and tea, a tin of home-made biscuits. Beside the shelf was a small fridge with a carton of fresh milk inside. There were hospitality trays in each of the rooms, but she liked her guests to feel welcome. It was the small touches that brought them back. They certainly didn't come for the location; there was little that was attractive about Harbour Street. An arched window looked out across Malcolm's yard and beyond the fisheries to the sea. It was still snowing. She saw the flakes billow in a triangle of light shed by a street lamp. Out at sea a light buoy flashed red. Her husband had worked on the rigs and she still felt a mixture of guilt and grief when she thought of the vast space beyond her doorstep.

Kate stood for a moment and listened to the music in her head. She coaxed the tune to life, hummed it. A song for winter, clear and spare. For love in winter. And again she thought of Stuart and the unlikely infatuation that had hit her in middle age; she was breathless and astounded, aware that at this moment she'd sacrifice everything for her new man. He was more important than Ryan's nightmares, his prowling through the neighbourhood at night like a feral animal, unable to sleep, his occasional outbursts of temper. More important than Chloe's exam results and her terrifying ambition. Stuart, old and wiry, more like a mountaineer than a musician, had brought Kate back to life.

On her way back to the flat she bumped into George Enderby by the front door. He had snowflakes clinging to his woollen overcoat and his big, good-natured face beamed down at her. 'What do you think, Kate? Snow for Christmas. The kids will be excited.' He had one of those rich, posh, southern voices that made her think of a politician or an actor.

Kate thought that *her* kids were super-cool these

days, and they'd consider building snowmen to be beneath them. But George was so innocent with this fantasy of a perfect family life that she couldn't disabuse him.

'Yeah,' she said.

George worked as a publisher's rep and he travelled with a big wheelie suitcase full of books. Often he left copies for her children. Chloe liked some of them, the thick ones about other worlds, but although Ryan pretended to be interested he wasn't a great reader. He took the books in order to please. At the back of Kate's mind there was always a niggle of anxiety about Ryan. He was no real trouble, but despite his easy smile she suspected he was unhappy and she wasn't sure what she could do about it. And there were occasional flashes of temper that reminded her of Rob. But Harbour Street took up all her time and her energy, and Stuart took up all of her dreams. Ryan had stopped talking to her years before. She told herself that the boy was still young, and that kids were complicated and never confided in their parents.

George had a wife, but they'd never had any children. He'd told her that once. He'd told her a lot of things during late nights, as he took his usual nightcap in the visitors' lounge. He'd sip whisky and she'd look at her watch and wonder when he'd go to bed. She ran the guest house pretty much by herself. There was only Margaret to help in the kitchen, and the last few days she hadn't been much use.

'Have you had a good day, George?'

She knew that business was tough for him. He'd confided that too. 'I wouldn't know what to do, Kate, without my work. Books are what I live and breathe.'

She'd sensed that he didn't need to work to earn a living. He had that laid-back confidence and careless attitude to money that comes with being born rich. She thought he wasn't happily married, though even when he was very drunk he was never unpleasant about his wife. 'My Diana is a marvel,' he'd say, 'a wonderful woman.'

Now he was shaking himself out of his overcoat. 'Usual room, Kate?'

'Of course.' George liked the big room at the back of the house looking out over the sea and didn't mind that it was the most expensive in the place. *My bosses are used to London prices, Kate. They never quibble about my expenses.*

'I'm just here for a couple of days this time. Then on my way south again. Unless the snow is as heavy as the forecast. Then you might have an unexpected guest for Christmas dinner.' He smiled sadly and she thought he'd love that. A proper family Christmas lunch with her and the kids, sitting around the table in the basement, him carving the turkey. But this year there would be Stuart too, and she wasn't sure what George would make of that. She had a sneaky suspicion that George Enderby fancied her rotten.

'I'll put a pot of tea in the lounge.' This was a ritual too. He'd sit in the lounge with his laptop and his books, drinking tea and eating Margaret's biscuits. Then, because she didn't provide evening meals, he'd go out into the street – either to the fish shop or the Coble – for his supper and come back with a few pints inside him, to sit up drinking whisky until midnight.

As she entered the basement she saw the kids were watching telly. She thought perhaps there'd been something else on and they'd changed channel when they'd heard her on the stairs. Something unsuitable. She was a control freak and wanted to know what they were watching. Sometimes she wondered if she was too strict with them. Perhaps that was why they didn't talk to her any more. They were almost grown-up, after all. She saw the way other kids behaved, what they got away with. But she knew what *she'd* been like when she was young: sex and drugs and the music scene. She'd never finished her exams and she wanted better for them.

They were still in their school uniform and Kate was going to send them to change, but then she held her tongue. No sense starting an argument. *Choose your battles.* She'd seen that in a women's magazine and thought it made sense.

'Okay?'

The reply was a muffled grunt from Chloe. Then Ryan turned and gave one of his smiles that always reminded her of his father and made her stomach flip because it was like looking at a ghost.

In the kitchen Kate prepared George's tray. A cloth, leaf tea in the pot, a cup and a strainer. Milk in a jug. Sometimes Ryan laughed at her efforts. 'This is Mardle, Mam! You're not in charge of the Ritz.' And Kate knew that the kids got teased for her attempt to maintain standards – the cloth napkins at the tea table even though they were just eating pizza, her insistence on manners. But she was sure that the small things mattered, and she wanted to prepare them for the future. She wanted more for them than life in a rundown street in a rundown town. She'd known better than that herself once – her father had been an accountant with his own business, until it had fallen apart in the recession – and it still rankled that she'd ended up like this.

The lounge was empty. George would still be in his room. Kate set down the tray, switched on the gas fire and drew the curtains. The snow had blown into a small drift against the window.

She was thinking that she'd get a casserole out of the freezer for their supper, when the doorbell rang. If it was another visitor, trapped in the town by the weather, she could put them in room six. She opened the door.

Outside there was an enormous woman. She wore a shapeless anorak over a tweed skirt. A wide face and small brown eyes. Her hair was covered by the anorak hood. On her feet, wellingtons. Her hair and her body were covered in snow. Behind her another figure, but hidden by her bulk, so that it was impossible to make out any detail.

The abominable snow-woman, Kate thought.

The woman spoke. 'Let us in, pet, will you? It's freezing out here. My name's Stanhope. Inspector Vera Stanhope.'

Chapter Three

Vera got the call while she was shopping and, when her mobile buzzed in her pocket, she felt a joyous sense of relief. She rarely ventured into Newcastle except for work and this was a nightmare. Christmas shopping: hordes of fraught people with a kind of mad panic in their eyes. Like the rabbits, when her father Hector had gone lamping for meat. Hector had died years ago and Vera had no other family to buy for. Christmas Day she'd go to her hippy neighbours for dinner and they'd all get drunk as skunks, but Jack and Joanna wouldn't expect presents – except perhaps a decent bottle of whisky – and neither would she.

Then Holly, one of her team, had devised this scheme. Secret Santa: names in a hat and pull out the name of the person who'd receive your gift. Vera had been hoping for Charlie. A bottle of whisky would have suited him fine too. Vera had picked Holly from the hat, though. Holly wore perfume and make-up and smart clothes, even to work. What could Vera possibly choose for her? So here she was in Fenwick's department store, sweating because she was still in her outdoor clothes, surrounded by smart and shiny people, just wanting to do a runner, when her phone rang. Joe Ashworth on the other end. If he'd been there she would have kissed him.

'What have you got for me, Joe?' her voice sang. A sales assistant in a white tunic, who was plastering foundation onto a middle-aged woman perched in a chair like you'd see at the dentist's, was staring at her.

'Murder,' he said and her heart lifted again, before the guilt set in and she told herself that the victim would be someone's relative and friend. They hadn't died for her entertainment. 'A stabbing on the Metro.'

'Bit of a scuffle got out of hand?' That seemed odd. It was the sort of thing you might get late at night, but not in the early afternoon.

'No.' She knew him well enough to sense that this wasn't going to be straightforward, and that pleased her too. She liked a bit of complication. A challenge. 'It's an elderly lady. I was first on the scene. The CSIs are on their way.'

'Give Holly a shout too.' Vera was more careful these days to include Holly, who could strop for England if she felt she was missing out. She paused for breath, already pushing her way through the crowds to get to the exit, feeling in her coat pocket for her keys. 'And dig Charlie from his hole. Who found the body?'

'Jessie,' Joe Ashworth replied. 'My daughter Jessie.'

It took Vera longer than she'd expected to get to Partington Metro station. A couple of inches of snow and the world went mad. A car had slipped across the road in Benton, blocking one lane of traffic. She was in Hector's Land Rover, which was against all the police authority rules because it was so old, but today she was glad of it. The station was closed, marked by crime-scene tape and protected by a couple of Metro inspectors, enjoying every minute of their moment of glory. On the platform in the distance she saw Joe Ashworth. Her sergeant and her surrogate son, her protégé. And her conscience. The snow was falling around him and he had his back to her. He wore a black overcoat and was speaking into a mobile. No sign of the daughter. Sal would have whipped her away. Both parents were protective of their bairns. Vera thought Jessie would probably have preferred to stay and watch the action. There was something sparky about the girl that gave Vera hope.

She'd pulled on the wellies that she kept in the Land Rover. It had taken an effort – her legs only just squeezed inside. She'd lost weight, though. The boots were new, and a year ago she wouldn't have fitted into them at all. The platform was slippery and she walked carefully. If she fell over, it would take a crane to get her to her feet. In the brightly lit train compartment she saw white-suited figures at work. She hoped Billy Wainwright would be heading up the team of CSIs. She couldn't see the body and wouldn't be allowed in now until they'd finished.

'Joe!' He turned to look at her and started to walk her way, finishing the call and putting his hands in his pockets.

As he approached, Vera saw that he was frowning. He would have had other plans for this evening. A night in with Sal and the bairns. Maybe wrapping the presents when the kids were in bed. Sal would be the organized type; she wouldn't leave her Christmas shopping until the last minute. But Vera knew that Joe got bored with the perfect domestic life, although he'd never admit it, even to himself. Perhaps this murder had come as a lifesaver for him too.

'What have you got for me, Joe?' They moved into the shelter of the station concourse. Joe leaned against one of the ticket machines. The snow was falling so heavily now that they looked at the train through a shifting white curtain. *Not a bad thing*, Vera thought. People would blame the weather, not them, for disrupting the Metro system.

She listened while he described the journey from town, the packed train, the lippy youths and the pissed businessmen. She didn't take notes at this point. Notes stopped her concentrating. She needed to picture herself in the carriage, listening to the banter.

She waited until he'd finished talking. 'All good-tempered then? Nothing that could have led to a Christmas moment of madness? The victim hadn't made a fuss about kids swearing or putting their feet on the seats?'

'Not that I saw or heard. It was packed in there, but if there'd been any sort of row, I'd probably have noticed. Even when the train stopped and we all had to get out, nobody kicked off.'

'What do we know about the victim?' This was Vera's favourite moment in an investigation. She was nosy, loved digging around in another person's private life. Perhaps, she was forced to concede, because she had no personal life of her own.

'Only what we could get from her Metro pensioner's pass. She was carrying a handbag, but in it there was nothing but a purse, a set of house keys and a hankie.'

'Money in the purse?' *There were druggies*, Vera thought, *who'd stab their granny for the price of a fix. But probably not in the Metro in the late afternoon.*

'Fifty quid and a bit of change.'

Not robbed then. 'So what do we know about her?'

'Her name's Margaret Krukowski and she's seventy years old. An address in Mardle. One, Harbour Street.' Joe had stumbled over the surname.

'What's that? Russian, Polish?'

Joe shook his head. What would he know? 'She was nearly home,' he said. 'Only one more stop on the Metro and she'd have been safe.' Vera thought he was the most sentimental cop she'd ever known.

'Did you see where she got on?'

'Aye, Gosforth.'

One of Newcastle's posher suburbs. A long way from Mardle in terms of class and aspiration.

Joe guessed what she was thinking. 'More Gosforth than Mardle, from her appearance,' he said.

Vera thought about this for a moment and wondered where people would place her in the social order of things, if they saw her. Bag lady? Farmer?

'We'll go then, shall we?' she said. 'See if anyone's at home waiting for Margaret Krukowski.'

They sat for a moment in the Land Rover outside the house. The Harbour Guest House. A wooden sign beside the front door, the letters almost obscured by snow.

'We bring the kids here sometimes, to the Mardle

Fisheries,' Joe said. 'A treat. It's supposed to be the best fish and chips in the North-East.'

Vera had her own memories of Mardle. Hector bribing some boatman to take them out to Coquet Island in the middle of the night. Lights still on in the warden's house at one end of the island. Music and noise, some party going on there. Her terror that they'd be discovered, while Hector was caught up in the chase for roseate terns' eggs. He'd always loved the risk. She thought he'd been motivated more by the danger than by the obsession that led him to steal and trade in rare birds' eggs.

'Well,' Joe said. 'Are we going in? I've got a home to go to.'

She nodded and climbed out of the vehicle, trying to remember if the guest house had been here when she'd been a kid. She remembered the street as run-down, almost squalid, but that had been more than forty years ago. She rang the bell.

The woman who answered was about the right age to be the victim's daughter. Late thirties, early forties. Curly black hair and brown eyes, the colour of conkers, a pleasant, almost professional smile. She reminded Vera of a nurse. When Vera introduced herself, she stood aside to let them in. 'Is there some problem?'

When the police turned up at the door people felt either guilty or scared. Vera couldn't work out which the reaction was here. She followed the woman to the back of the house, into a warm lounge furnished with heavy furniture that would have seemed out of place in a smaller room, and they sat down on plush, velvet sofas. There was an upright piano against one wall, music on the stand, and against another a sideboard with decanters and bottles of spirits. Vera thought a tot of malt whisky was just what she needed after hanging around on a cold Metro station, but she knew better than to say anything. The curtains had been drawn and the place decorated for Christmas, with holly and sprayed silver pine cones along the mantelpiece and tall red candles on the occasional tables. It looked like a Victorian drawing room.

The lounge was empty, but there was a tea tray on a small table. The presence of the tray seemed to bother their hostess. She kept glancing towards it apologetically. Joe followed them and took a seat by the gas fire.

'Nice place,' he said. 'Cosy.'

The woman smiled and seemed to relax a little.

'Could you give us your name, please?' Joe again.

'Dewar.' The woman had her back to Vera now. 'Kate Dewar.'

The door opened and they were interrupted by a large, bald man with a pleasant smile and an easy manner.

'Hello,' he said. 'More guests, Kate? More waifs from the storm?' He turned so that his smile included Vera and Joe. 'You're very welcome.' It could have been *his* home. 'Would you like tea? I'm sure there's plenty in the pot, and Kate will bring more cups.'

'These aren't guests, George. These are police officers.' Was there a warning in the words? *Watch what you say.*

'Ah,' he said. He stopped for a beat and looked round awkwardly. 'I'll be in the way then. Don't want to intrude. I'll take the tea to my room, shall I?' Picking up the tray, he walked out without a backward glance. Vera thought she'd have been too curious to do that. She'd have asked if she could help, found some excuse to hang around and find out what was going on.

'A guest?' She nodded towards the door.

'George Enderby, one of my regulars.'

'And Margaret Krukowski? Is she one of your regulars? Only she's given this as her address.'

'Margaret? Is she ill? Is that why you're here?'

Vera sensed relief in the voice and wondered what else the woman might have to fear from a visit from the police. 'Margaret does live here then? A relative, is she?'

'Not a relative. A friend. And an employee, I suppose. She helps out in the house. We run the place together.' A flashed smile. 'I couldn't manage without her.'

Vera leaned forward and kept her voice gentle. 'Margaret Krukowski's dead,' she said. 'She was stabbed in the Metro on her way home from town this afternoon. I need you to tell me all about her.'

Chapter Four

Vera wondered, as she sat in the hot lounge, if it was still snowing. If it was, she thought she probably wouldn't get up the steep hill to the house where she'd lived since she was a child, even in the Land Rover. But this would probably be an all-nighter anyway, so there was no point worrying about that.

Kate Dewar was sitting on the edge of one of the heavy sofas, crying. No fuss or noise, but silent tears. Joe Ashworth had provided her with a small packet of tissues. He was like a Boy Scout, Joe. Always prepared.

'How long have you known Margaret?' Sometimes Vera thought it was best to start with simple facts. Something for the person to hang on to, to pull their thoughts away from the shock and the grief.

Kate dabbed at her eyes. 'Ten years,' she said. 'The kids were small. My aunt died – she was some sort of distant relative by marriage. I never knew her, and we lived up the coast. But she'd left me this house in her will. It wasn't a guest house then, but it had been converted into a bunch of bedsits and flats. All tatty. Most empty. Margaret was the only tenant with any sort of lease.' She paused for breath. 'I was bored. It wasn't the best time of my life. My husband worked away a lot. Ryan was already at school, Chloe at playgroup. I thought it would be a project, that Mardle was on its way up and that soon the tourists would arrive. Got that one wrong, didn't I?'

She shrugged wryly.

'At first I thought having Margaret here would be a problem – that she'd, sort of, get in the way.' Kate stopped again and gave a wide and lovely smile. 'But that couldn't have been further from the truth. She was wonderful, and it would have been a nightmare without her. She was like a mother and a best friend all rolled into one. We negotiated a deal. She'd keep her little flat in the attic, rent-free, and help out in the house. And I'd pay her when I could. She's been on a proper salary since the first guests arrived.'

From the corner of her eye Vera saw Joe Ashworth making notes, but she was trying to picture this big house being renovated, the builders in, two women full of plans and ideas for its future, small kids under their feet. That would make you close, and she felt a pang of loss – she'd never had a best friend, no one with whom she could share her dreams. The nearest she had was Joe Ashworth.

'Margaret Krukowski,' she said. 'That's a Polish name?'

'Yes, but Margaret wasn't Polish. North-East born and bred, and from a respectable Newcastle family. She married a Polish seaman when she was very young. Her parents were outraged, but it was the Sixties and she said he was very handsome and a refugee, which made it all the more romantic.'

'What happened to him?' Vera liked this victim already, liked the complexity of her. Joe had said

Margaret looked more Gosforth than Mardle, but she'd taken up with a Polish asylum-seeker and ended up alone in a scuzzy bedsit. Still keeping up appearances, though. Still smart, with the boots and the red lipstick; the long coat that would have cost a fortune new.

'He left her only a couple of years after they married. Ran off with a woman with more money than Margaret had. She said she was heartbroken, but too proud to go running back to her parents. She trained as a bookkeeper and worked for a couple of local companies. When I first knew her she'd already retired. Or been made redundant.' Kate smiled again. 'She was a whizz with figures and saved me from the VAT man a number of times.'

'But she kept her husband's name?' Vera thought that couldn't have been easy all those years ago. A single woman with airs and graces, a strange name and aspirations to style.

'She told me she never stopped loving him,' Kate replied. 'Like I said, she was always a romantic.'

'And your husband?' Vera asked. 'Is he still working away?'

There was a moment of silence.

'No,' Kate said. 'He died. An accident at work in the North Sea. The rigs. He drowned. His body was never found.' And she began to cry again.

Kate led them up the stairs to Margaret's flat. 'As she got older, I asked if she'd like to move to one of the downstairs rooms, but she said this felt like home now and the stairs kept her fit.'

'She was a healthy woman then? Good for her

age?' Despite her new regime and the trips to the pool, Vera was panting, so the words came out in tiny gasps.

'Oh yes. The business is doing well enough now. We have our regular guests and we do some outside catering, but Margaret said she wouldn't think of retiring.' Kate stopped at the door. Joe took out the bunch of keys that the CSIs had found on the body.

'You don't have a master key?' Vera leaned against the wall to catch her breath.

'For all the other rooms, but not this one. I offered to keep one in case of emergency, but she never seemed keen. The cleaner never went in here, though I'd have been happy for her to service it with all the rest. Mags liked her privacy.'

'Did she have any visitors?'

'I was invited in for afternoon tea occasionally,' Kate said. 'Lovely. Always something a bit special. Sometimes smoked salmon from the fishery, on little pancakes. Sometimes a fancy cake she'd baked herself. Once a bottle of pink champagne because she said she had something to celebrate. I never saw anyone else come in to see her.'

She hovered on the landing, obviously wondering if she was expected to go into the room with them.

Vera reached out and touched her shoulder. 'That's all right, pet. We can take it from here.'

Kate nodded and turned back. Joe Ashworth waited until she was halfway down the stairs before trying a key in the lock. There were three keys. Vera wondered about the other two – one was probably for the front door of the guest house. What about the other? Joe pushed open the door.

The flat was, as Kate had said, very small and built into the roof, so one wall was hardly three feet high and joined a sloping ceiling, with three dormer windows looking out over the harbour. There were two main rooms, with a tiny bathroom carved out of a corner of the bedroom. But still it managed to have style. The kitchen, which was also the living room, had a dark polished wood floor with a rug that glowed with colour – blues and greens. Under one window an old desk and a curve-backed chair. A small chaise longue covered with grey velvet. A sink, oven and fridge, separated from the rest of the room by a scrubbed pine table. Most of the pans hung from hooks in the ceiling, and the wooden spoons and spatulas stood in a green glazed pot on the second windowsill. The full wall was all shelves, with books, neatly arranged, interspersed occasionally with pebbles, pieces of driftwood and shells. It was a dark room, because the windows were so small and the walls were thick, but rich and jewel-like, lit only by a lamp on the desk and a spotlight in the kitchen.

'No telly,' Joe said. Vera could tell he was shocked. He opened the door to the bedroom, eager to see if the television was there. They stood in the doorway to look in. This room was carpeted in pale green. There was a three-quarter bed covered by a handmade patchwork quilt, and chests of drawers on each side of it. A narrow wardrobe. All the furniture had been painted white. No clutter, no dirty clothes. The shower room was spotless.

'No telly,' he said again. Perhaps that was the only entertainment he and Sal had in the evenings and he couldn't imagine life without it.

'We'll get the search team in first thing.' Vera walked to the window and looked out. It was still snowing, but the flakes were smaller again. She was glad she wouldn't be the one to pull open drawers and work through Margaret's underwear. She was nosy, but this would have seemed like a terrible intrusion.

Joe was looking at the shelves. 'Only one photo.' He didn't pick it up, but pointed to it. The picture was of a couple. A wedding photo. She was in a simple white mini-dress, with fake fur on the hem, white knee-length wet-look boots, a short fur jacket, and she was holding a bouquet of gold and white freesias. The dark-haired man was in a suit with wide lapels, a buttonhole pinned to one of them. In the background, a church door.

'Is this her?' Vera asked. 'Is this Margaret Krukowski and the Polish love of her life?'

'Oh yes, this is her.' The answer was immediate and unequivocal. 'Our victim has the same mouth and the same cheekbones.' She saw that Joe couldn't take his eyes off the photograph.

'A bonny little thing.' She kept her voice light. Nobody had ever called her bonny.

'She's beautiful,' he said and then he gave a little laugh, as if recognized how silly he was being, because he was drawn to a photograph that was fifty years old. But still he continued, 'That's a face that men would kill for.'

Chapter Five

On the middle landing Kate took her mobile phone from her pocket and phoned Stuart, her lover. The first real relationship she'd had since Rob had died on the rigs. Stuart was more at home in the hills than in a house, but he could play the sax like a dream, and now she was haunted by thoughts of him. There was no reply and she left a message. 'Please give me a ring.' Walking down, Kate wondered how she would tell the kids that Margaret was dead. They'd known her for most of their lives. She'd been their babysitter and they'd treated her like a gran. Ryan still spent a lot of time with her. This year, with Stu on the scene, and with Kate full of new plans, they'd already had to adjust to change. Kate slowed her steps to give herself time to compose the words and realized she had no idea what her children's reaction would be. They'd grown up and away from her and she could no longer trust her judgement where they were concerned.

George Enderby must have heard her steps, or perhaps he was listening out for her, because the door of his room opened and he stuck out his head.

'Everything all right, Kate?' His voice seemed genuinely concerned. Then a little embarrassed. 'Sorry, I didn't mean to pry.'

'Margaret's dead.' She felt suddenly light-headed and leaned against the wall.

'Oh, I'm so sorry!' He started out into the corridor before realizing that his door would swing shut and lock automatically behind him. Then he made a strange little hop, holding the door open with one foot, but leaning out towards her. 'I didn't know her well, but I never thought of her as an old woman. Was it something sudden? A heart attack?'

'She was murdered,' Kate said. 'Stabbed on the Metro on her way home from town.' Again it seemed as if the world was spinning around her. She sat on the bottom step and put her head in her hands.

George disappeared briefly and she saw he was reaching inside for his key; then he was sitting beside her with his arm around her shoulder. She could smell his aftershave and the sweetness of the biscuit he'd just eaten. Cinnamon and ginger. Kate wondered how different things would have been if Rob had been as kind as George Enderby. She sat for a moment, enjoying the physical contact, and then she pulled away gently. 'I have to tell the kids.'

'Of course,' he said. He stood up and gave her his hand to help her to her feet. 'If there's anything at all I can do to help, please do tell me.' And he vanished back into his room, as if he thought his presence might be contributing to her distress.

In the basement Ryan was in his bedroom. She heard the sound of his computer. Some game about monsters and the end of the world. Chloe was sitting at the table with a pile of books at one side, scribbling into a jotter. She seemed pale and tired.

'Ryan, come in here. I need to talk to you both!'

'Okay.' There was no sign of him, though. And that was Ryan all over. He always agreed with her and then went his own way. Chloe had turned in her seat and saw that her mother had been crying. 'What is it?' The words accompanied by a brief look of distaste, the teenage default response to parents behaving differently. Then she registered that this was serious and not an overreaction to a domestic drama. She was on her feet. 'Mum, what is it?' And, as Kate started to cry once more, Chloe shouted to her brother and this time he did emerge from his room. He stood looking at them with a kind of helpless confusion, as if women were a different species and it was safest not to intervene.

They shifted the textbooks onto the dresser and sat round the table. Chloe fetched a bottle of wine from the fridge and opened it with an ease that would have had Kate worried in different circumstances. She poured Kate a large glass. 'Tell us what's going on.'

'Margaret's dead.'

'How?' It was the first time Ryan had spoken. They looked at him.

'I mean how did she die? An accident? She was fine this morning when I was on my way out.' He frowned and again Kate was reminded of Robbie.

'She was murdered.' Kate thought this sounded like a refrain, the chorus of one of those songs Ryan played on his iPod. Shouted noise. If she repeated it often enough to all the people she needed to tell, perhaps she would believe it. She looked at the kids. In both faces she thought she saw a flash of excitement, before disbelief and distress took over. Murder was the stuff of stories. She imagined they'd both be on their phones to their classmates as soon as she released them from the table. *You'll never believe what's happening in our house* . . . For a while they'd have a vicarious celebrity, the popularity they both seemed to seek.

'Why would anyone want to murder an old woman like Margaret?'

Kate looked at Chloe and thought she had lost weight recently. Had Kate been so wrapped up in Stuart and this strange infatuation that she'd been neglecting her children?

'I don't know.' Kate paused. 'I never thought of her as an old woman. She had too much energy.'

'Where was she killed?' It seemed that Ryan needed details to satisfy his curiosity. She suddenly saw him almost as a stranger. He was a good-looking boy; he'd be a heart-breaker. She'd seen him round Mardle with attractive girls, but he'd never introduced them. Neither of the kids ever brought friends back to the house.

'On the Metro apparently. On her way home from town.' Kate looked at him. 'Did she tell you where she was going when you saw her this morning?'

He shook his head.

'Only I expect the police will want to know.'

'The police?' The question asked with studied indifference. But of course he wanted to hear about the investigation. More snippets of information to stick on Facebook.

'They're in Margaret's room. That's how I know that she's dead.'

There was a silence. 'Poor Margaret,' Chloe said. 'Where is she? I mean, where's her body? Will there be a funeral?'

'I suppose the police have organized a post-mortem. And that there'll be a funeral eventually. I don't know how these things work.'

I expect I'll have to organize that, Kate thought. *Who else would do it?* Then it occurred to her that she would have to discuss it with Father Gruskin, a man she'd never liked. She felt suddenly very hungry. 'I'll get a casserole out of the freezer. We still have to eat.' It was a relief to get to her feet and leave the room for a while.

She was on her second glass of wine and laying the table for supper when the two detectives turned up at her flat. She'd thought she'd seen the back of them, at least for the day. She'd supposed they would let themselves out of the house. Now they stood in the dark basement corridor and she could tell they were about to make more demands.

'You'd better come in.'

'Sorry to bother you again.' But Vera Stanhope was smiling and Kate thought she wasn't sorry at all. 'We'd like to get in touch with Mrs Krukowski's family and her friends, but we can't find an address book in her flat. Perhaps you can help.'

Kate led them into the kitchen. Ryan and Chloe had vanished back into their rooms. Like shy animals, they usually avoided adult company. Chloe would be working again. Ryan might be listening at his door. He was an observer, and she'd caught him eavesdropping before.

'Margaret never mentioned family,' Kate said. The casserole was whirring around in the microwave to defrost. She wished Stuart would arrive. The oven pinged. 'As I told you, there was a breakdown in relations when she married. I don't think she ever saw them again. Her parents would probably be dead now, though I can't remember her going to their funerals.'

'No brothers or sisters?'

'None that I know of.'

'Did she ever tell you where she grew up?' Vera Stanhope had settled herself at the kitchen table. She was so big that she seemed to take up all the space there, and to be so comfortable that Kate could imagine her staying all night.

'Gosforth,' Kate said. 'One of those grand terraced houses not far from the High Street.' She saw a glance flash between the two officers and thought the information might somehow be significant.

'What about friends, then?' Vera asked. She looked up at Kate. 'She'd lived in Mardle for a long time and she doesn't seem to have been a recluse, your Margaret. She must have had friends, even if they didn't come to visit her here.' Vera smiled. 'Friends other than you, I mean.'

Kate thought about that. Margaret had never seemed to feel the need for friends away from Harbour Street, but she didn't want the detective to think Margaret was some sort of loner or loser.

'I think most of her social life away from here revolved around the church,' she said. 'You should ask the priest, Father Gruskin.'

'And where will I find him? Is there a Catholic church in Mardle?'

'He's C of E. Priest of the church over the road. St Bartholomew's. But that's what he calls himself.' Kate could hear the antipathy in her own voice and wondered if the detective would pick up on it. Instead

Vera made a show of looking around the room, at the pile of school books on the dresser and the music stand in the corner.

'How old are your children now?'

'Chloe's fourteen and Ryan's just sixteen.'

'Could we speak to them, please? Nothing formal, just a quick chat here in the kitchen, to find out when they last saw Margaret. Joe here can ask the questions. He's got bairns of his own, similar sort of age. That's right, isn't it, Joe?'

The good-looking sergeant smiled. 'A bit younger,' he said. 'Sometimes they behave like teenagers, though. Not a stage I'm looking forward to.'

So Kate had no choice but to call the kids in, although by now all she wanted was food and more wine. It felt like some sort of conference, all of them round the table, everyone a bit tense and serious. But the children did her proud. Ryan answered the questions politely and even Chloe gave the detectives her full attention. 'Tell me about Margaret.' That was how the sergeant started off. The kids stared at each other, and in the end it was Ryan who answered first.

'She was lovely,' he said. 'When we were little she'd take us out. And I still liked spending time with her.'

'Doing what?' the detective asked.

'She was into good causes,' Ryan said. 'Sometimes I'd help her collect. Rattle the collecting boxes outside the supermarket.' He paused. 'Old ladies like me, and they were always willing to give.' Kate thought that was true, but it wasn't the whole story. Ryan felt safe with Margaret. When he was younger she'd sat with him through the nightmares.

And then Chloe chipped in with a story of her own, about Margaret taking them to the theatre in Newcastle, their first trip to a grown-up play. 'She knew about stuff. Plays and films. Most Saturdays when Mam was busy she'd take me to the library. She encouraged me to do well at school. "Women can be anything they want." Didn't she say that all the time?'

Kate nodded.

'What about now?' Joe Ashworth asked. 'Now that you're older. Were you still close?'

A pause.

'We didn't spend so much time with her,' Chloe said. 'But we knew she was there. If we needed her.'

'I still helped out,' Ryan said, 'but not so much. I've got this part-time job at the boatyard now.'

They had never considered of course that Margaret might have missed their company or their confidences. That the older woman might have needed *them*. Kate thought adolescents were the most self-centred people in the universe.

The sergeant was moving on to more detailed questions. 'Did you see Margaret today?'

'I did,' Ryan said. 'I saw her on my way out to school.'

'Where was she?'

'She was clearing the tables in the guests' dining room after breakfast. There were only a couple of people staying last night and they'd already left by then. She saw me through the open door and shouted out to me to have a good day.'

'Where do you go to school?' The policeman leaned back in his chair. Kate thought he looked tired.

'Mardle High,' Chloe said. 'It's just over the Metro line.'

'The local comprehensive,' Kate added, wondering again if they would have done better at a different school, somewhere with smaller classes. If she'd continued in her career, perhaps she'd have afforded it.

Vera interrupted then, a question directed to Kate. 'These guests? You'll have their contact details?'

Kate could tell the sergeant was used to her butting in. 'Of course. Claire Gordon was on her way to Edinburgh to collect her son from university. She's a regular, lives in Hertfordshire somewhere, and stays the beginning and end of every term to break her journey. The other was Mike Craggs, Professor Craggs. He's a marine biologist at Newcastle Uni and he always stays here when he's doing fieldwork. Claire left early. The weather forecast had said there might be snow and she wanted to be on her way. Mike's always out of the house before anyone else, when he's working.' Kate wondered if this was more information than the inspector needed, if she was coming across as a nosy landlady. But Vera Stanhope nodded and seemed pleased.

'And you?' Joe turned to Chloe. 'Did you see Margaret today?'

'No,' she said. 'I left the house before Ryan. I didn't see her at all.'

Then the detectives stood up and Kate thought they'd finally go away, so that she could eat supper, drink the wine and think about Margaret in peace. She wanted to check her phone to see if Stuart had called her back. But still, it seemed, they wanted more from her.

'That chap we met earlier,' Vera said. 'He's a regular, is he?'

'Oh yes.' Kate smiled. 'George comes once a month and stays for two nights. Then again for another night when he's finished working in Scotland. He's regular as clockwork.'

'I wonder, then, if we might have a word with him.' Vera smiled too, apologetically. It was as if she knew that Kate wanted to be rid of them. 'Then I promise I'll leave you in peace.'

But Kate thought there'd be little peace in Harbour Street until this was all over. Until they knew who'd killed Margaret Krukowski.

Chapter Six

Following the women down the corridor and up the stairs, Joe Ashworth was troubled by a sense of déjà vu, a feeling that he'd met this family before or conducted a similar interview on a previous occasion. It was as irritating as when a word was on the tip of his tongue, but he couldn't remember it. Perhaps something about the kids – polite enough, but wary and watchful – reminded him of his own children when they had something to hide.

They'd arrived at Enderby's room and the man had the door open almost as soon as Kate had knocked. It was clear that the detectives wouldn't be invited in, though. Enderby seemed pleasant and rather shy, but also experienced at getting his own way.

'The lounge would be best for a chat, I think, don't you, Kate? I'll switch on the fire again and make it cosy. And I'll bob down to the kitchen and make us some more tea, if it wouldn't be too much of an imposition. No need for you to do anything.'

So that's where the interview took place, in the impressive lounge with its gleaming dark furniture and smell of beeswax polish. Enderby lit some of the red candles and switched off the main light, so Joe almost expected him to take their hands and call up the dead, as if this was a séance.

Kate Dewar had returned to her own flat. The three of them drank tea and ate biscuits and sat for a minute watching the gas flames. While they'd been waiting for Enderby to bring in the tray, Joe had pulled back the curtains to look out of the window and seen that the snow had stopped. The sky was clear now and there were stars, a huge white moon. Still he replayed the interview with Kate Dewar and her family, wondering what he'd missed, what had been so familiar.

Vera was asking the questions and already there seemed to be an understanding between her and Enderby. She wasn't exactly flirting, but there was a sense that they could get on. He was charming, Joe could see that. People didn't usually make an effort to charm Vera, and Joe thought she was flattered by it.

She smiled now, over her cup, dunking her third home-made biscuit into the tea. 'So what brings you to Northumberland, Mr Enderby?'

'George, please.' A wide, easy smile. 'Work, I'm afraid. I keep promising myself time in the county to explore properly, but my wife thinks anywhere north of the Wash is wild and uncharted territory, and I spend so much time away from home that I wouldn't want to come up on holiday without her.'

'And what is your work?'

'I'm a rep for a publishing company. Almost an endangered species, but I'm one of the few survivors and I hope I can hang on until I retire. And I do love it.' He stared wistfully into the fire. 'I read, you see. It's an addiction. Not a requirement for the job, though. In fact, almost a hindrance in some ways. Hard to press a title onto a reluctant bookseller when you think it's crap yourself. But I've built my contacts now. Sympathetic buyers. Managers in some of the big retail chains, owners of a smattering of lovely indies. I understand what will work best for them.'

'An odd time of year to be selling books, I'd have thought.' Vera spoke with that same light, almost flirtatious tone. 'The stores will have their Christmas stock by now, surely. This time of year wouldn't you all want to be back in London? Office parties. Sloping home early to fill the kiddies' stockings.'

Enderby leaned forward, his voice earnest. 'Actually, Inspector, I don't really *do* Christmas. It sends me into a panic. I was glad to escape. And of course I have the new season's titles to present.'

'Of course.' A silence.

'Why do you stay in Harbour Street when you come north?' She set down her cup on the low table beside her. A sign that she was taking the conversation more seriously now. 'It's hardly convenient for the motorway.'

'But it *is* very restful, and I like it here. I found it through the Northumberland Tourism website five years ago and have been using it ever since. I have an aversion to bland and anonymous hotels, and Kate is an efficient and welcoming landlady. She looks after me very well.'

Joe thought that he was talking too much. Any one of those reasons would have been sufficient.

'You knew Margaret Krukowski?'

'Of course,' Enderby said. 'She was a lovely woman.' He paused. 'They made a great team, she and Kate. I do hope Kate has the strength to carry on alone. But perhaps she will have other plans now.'

'Did you ever chat to Margaret?' Vera looked directly at the man. 'It seems to me that you're someone who takes an interest in people, that you might have engaged her in conversation over the breakfast table.'

'Oh, you know, the usual pleasantries.' Enderby reached out for the teapot.

'And what did you find out about her?'

'Surprisingly little! She was always friendly, but somehow guarded. As if it had become a habit to keep her life secret.' He gave a sudden charming smile. 'I make up stories about people. Fantasies. Perhaps because I read so much. Sometimes I think I might write a novel of my own.'

Joe felt as though he had lost the thread of the conversation now, with no real idea what Enderby was on about, or how it could be relevant to the investigation, but Vera seemed to be keeping up. 'And what was your story for Margaret Krukowski?'

'That she'd been a spy left behind when the Cold War ended. Given a new identity.' He smiled again and his face lit up. 'Quite ridiculous, of course, just because she had a Polish name! I've always allowed my imagination to run away from me.'

Vera smiled too, but it was the tight, rather disapproving smile of a teacher who is starting to lose patience with a favourite pupil.

'We'll stick to reality then, shall we? After five years you must know something about the woman.'

'I fear the reality was rather more mundane. Margaret Krukowski was articulate, intelligent and well read. Attractive still, for her age. Mardle seemed an odd place for her to have landed up. I could have imagined her in a rather nice flat in Tynemouth or Jesmond. But I assume she had no money. She was a good cook – these biscuits will have been hers, and she baked rolls and pastries for breakfast. She was a regular church-goer. Given to good causes. She cost me a fortune in raffle tickets for every charity from the lifeboat association to the Red Cross.' He paused. 'I did wonder if she'd once been a victim of domestic abuse. One of her charities was a women's refuge, and she seemed more devoted to that than to any of the others. I came up specially a couple of weeks ago to act as Father Christmas for its winter fair. She was a very persuasive woman and very committed to that particular cause.' He stopped short. 'Sorry, Inspector, take no notice – I'm telling myself stories again. Rambling.'

Joe thought that was the way Vera Stanhope worked too. She was always making up stories throughout an investigation. Only she called them theories.

'Did she ever mention her family?' Vera was back to specifics.

Enderby paused for a moment and stared into the fire. Joe couldn't tell whether he was trying to remember or playing for time.

'No,' he said. 'I don't think the subject of family ever came up. Women of that age usually have somebody, don't they? Grandchildren or great-nephews or -nieces. They bring out the photos at the least excuse. But not Margaret. She mentioned her ex-husband from time to time. Rather a rogue, by the sound of it. A rogue and a chancer.'

Joe was wondering what Vera had made of the comments about lonely old women, but if she was hurt by them she gave no sign.

'Had she seen him at all since they separated all those years ago?'

Enderby laughed. 'Oh, I don't think so. Much easier to convince oneself of a passion for a memory than for the reality. Really I think the man disappeared from her life entirely. According to Margaret, it was as if he vanished from the face of the Earth.'

'When did you last see her?' Vera was facing the man again.

'At the beginning of the month. The last time I was staying here. I can check the date in my diary, if you need to know exactly.' He sat back in his chair and everything about him seemed relaxed and helpful.

'You didn't see her today at all?'

'I'm sorry, Inspector. I can't help at all about today. I only arrived just as it was getting dark. Kate will tell you. She let me in.' He stretched and yawned.

Vera seemed almost to be asleep. The room was very warm now. Joe looked discreetly at his watch. At home the youngest children would be in bed. He wished Vera would move things on. It was obvious this man had nothing else useful to tell them. Even though the snow had stopped, it would be a nightmare getting back. And it seemed that even Enderby was losing patience, because he coughed gently.

'If there's nothing else I can help with, Inspector . . .'

'Of course.' She smiled at him. 'I was just weaving stories of my own.'

Enderby stood up. 'I'm starving, actually. Rather

tasteless to be thinking of one's own creature comforts at a time like this, but I had an early start and I didn't stop for lunch because I was hoping to get here before the weather set in. I was going to pop out to the Coble for a bite.' He looked at them. Vera too was struggling to her feet. 'Will news of the murder have got out, do you think?'

'Oh, I expect so.' She straightened her skirt, which was tweed and frayed slightly at the hem. 'Nothing the local media like better than a good murder.'

Enderby bent to turn off the gas fire. He switched on the light and blew out the candles. 'I'll be here for another night, and then again on my way south from Scotland.' He took a wallet from his jacket pocket and pulled out a card. 'Here's my mobile number. Do get in touch if you think I can help at all.' He picked up the tea tray, hesitated and then set it down again. 'Perhaps I'll leave it here. I expect Kate wants to be on her own with the children. If Stuart hasn't come along to look after her.'

'Stuart?'

'Ah, Kate's new man. We were all delighted that she'd found someone at last. About time, we thought.'

He gave them a last, self-effacing smile and walked out of the room.

Joe expected Vera to follow, but instead she walked across the carpet and leaned against the piano, bending to touch the tapestry covering on the stool.

'What did you make of him?' The words came out as a sharp bark that surprised him.

'I don't know. He seemed pleasant enough.' Joe looked at his watch again, less discreetly now.

'Telling the truth, do you think?'

'Aye, I can't think of any reason why he should lie.'

'We need details of Kate Dewar's new boyfriend,' Vera said. 'Someone new in the house.'

He nodded. And suddenly he knew what was familiar about the scene in the kitchen. 'That woman,' he said. 'Kate Dewar. She's Katie Guthrie, the singer.'

Vera looked blank.

'You must remember. She was big when I was young. A young singer-songwriter. Had a hit with "White Moon Summer".' He paused and was dragged back in time. He and Sal had done their courting to that song. He thought of one long summer, intense and charged. Parties on the beach, and conversations lasting into the early hours. It seemed that they were hardly the same people today. Despite himself, he hummed a few lines.

'You're wasted in the police service, Joe Ashworth, with a voice like that.'

He was never quite sure when Vera was taking the piss. 'Aye, well,' he said. 'Our Jessie takes after me.'

'So our Kate Dewar was famous?'

'For a couple of years she was a real star,' he said. 'And then she fell out of favour. Or fell out of sight. Seemed like almost overnight.'

'What must that be like?' Vera was speaking almost to herself. 'To have all that fame and influence, and suddenly you're nobody.'

Joe wondered if she was thinking about her own retirement and how she'd cope with that. He didn't answer and there was a moment of silence.

'What next then?' She looked up at him, a challenge, as if she'd set him a test.

'Talk to the priest,' he said. 'She might have confided in him about her family – what really went on in the marriage.'

'Confession, you mean?' She gave a little chuckle.

'I don't know.' Joe was confused. He'd grown up in a Methodist family, and Methodists didn't go in for that sort of thing. 'More just a chat, I was thinking.'

'And he might know about the women's refuge.' Vera was almost talking to herself now. 'That might be a motive, do you think? An abusive bloke, too much to drink, blaming our Margaret for the fact that his lass finally found the guts to leave him.'

The gas fire hissed as it cooled.

Vera turned towards him. 'I suppose you want a lift home?'

'Aye, if that's okay.' That was a relief. He'd thought she'd keep him out all hours and suggest a drink on the way back to talk things through.

There was a pause. 'Look,' she said. 'Do you mind getting a taxi? It's stopped snowing now and they'll have the gritters out, so you should get back okay. Put it on expenses. Pop down to the flat and get the details of Kate's new man on the way out. I'd like to stick around in the town for a while.'

'You want me to stay too?' Usually she did want him to.

'Nah.' A wicked grin. 'You get back to Sal and the bairns. I don't want to be in her bad books again. Besides, Holly's on her way.'

Chapter Seven

Vera watched Joe Ashworth drive away in his taxi. She could tell he was torn and that he'd almost have preferred to be standing out in the cold with her. It was so easy to wind him up that really there was no sport in it. She shouldn't torment him. There was a light in St Bartholomew's Church and for a moment she was tempted to go inside and ask for the Father Gruskin mentioned by Kate Dewar. But she was starving and could never work properly when she was hungry.

It was so cold that she was gasping for breath and, talking to Holly on her mobile, she could see spurts of vapour coming from her nose and mouth; caught in the street light, it almost looked as if the steam had been turned to ice.

'Where are you, Hol?'

'Liaising with CSI, Ma'am, just as you told me.' Classic Holly, tart and chippy at the same time.

'Can you make it over to Mardle? Joe's gone back to the bosom of his family and I could do with a hand. I'll be in the fish shop close to the harbour. Shall I order anything for you?'

'No thanks, Ma'am, I've eaten.' And she would have done. A Tupperware box full of salad leaves and an apple. No saturated fat for health-conscious Holly. 'I'll be there in twenty minutes.'

Vera walked on down the street, drawn by the smell of frying fish. A woman, big and blowsy in laddered tights and a short skirt, stumbled out of the pub. Vera thought she'd catch her death. From inside someone shouted at the woman, the words indecipherable, but the tone abusive and faintly amused. Vera felt a stab of sympathy for her. Underfoot the freezing snow squeaked.

In the Mardle Fisheries Vera took a seat at a table – more than half the space was set out as a restaurant. It felt good to walk past the queue at the takeaway counter, to have a waitress approach her immediately for her order. Vera wondered if class was so ingrained in England that even here in a Mardle fish shop she was tainted by it, if feeling slightly superior was a natural – if guilty – pleasure. Inside it was warm, condensation running down the windows, a television with some daft chat show on in the background. The waitress came with a tray. Tea in a pot, bread and butter on a china plate, the batter crisply thin and the haddock soft. *Oh yes,* Vera thought, *this is class!*

Holly arrived just as Vera had finished the meal. She was skinny and stylish, even now, dressed for the weather. Was it possible to get a designer parka? If so, Holly was wearing one. She sat opposite her boss, wiped the table in front of her with a paper napkin.

'Have they finished at the crime scene?'

'They've taken the body to the mortuary.' Holly had a southern, educated voice. Not her fault. 'And the train back to a shed in Heaton. Billy Wainwright says it's a nightmare. So many traces and footwear prints.

They'll be in there for a few days yet. Maybe longer. But at least the Metro line's clear. They'll reopen it later this evening if there's no more snow.'

'She's an interesting woman, our victim.' Vera leaned back in her seat. 'Married a Polish guy straight out of school. Divorced a couple of years later and since then seems to have lived alone. Given to religion and good works, apparently. Stayed rent-free in a guest house just up the road here, in return for helping out in the place, but it seems to me she's more like one of the family. The landlady is Kate Dewar, a widow with two teenage kids and a new bloke who doesn't live in.'

'Not a natural victim then.' Holly had some sort of electronic gadget on the table and was typing into it.

Vera resisted the urge to ask what was wrong with an ordinary notebook. 'No.' The early-evening rush was over and the chip shop was quieter now, the queue had dissipated. Vera got to her feet. 'Come with me.'

'Where are we off to?' Holly turned off the device and slid it into her handbag.

'We're going to see a priest.'

There was still a light in the church and when they pushed the heavy door it opened, though the building seemed empty inside. It smelled of damp and mould and incense, and the same furniture polish as had been used in Kate Dewar's house. Vera wondered if Margaret Krukowski had cleaned in here too. If so, they'd need to look for another member of the congregation to take on the domestic chores. Here there was no Christmas decoration, and the only colour came from a stained-glass window over the altar.

'Hello! Anybody home?' Churches always made her feel irreverent.

There was a scuffling noise ahead of them and a dark figure emerged from a door to their left. Vera thought this was probably the ugliest man she'd ever met. He was younger than she'd been expecting, perhaps in his early thirties. Black hair, black caterpillar eyebrows, thick lips that moved, even when he wasn't speaking, and narrow eyes. A large and shambling Mr Bean. He should be a stand-up comedian. He'd just have to walk onstage and there would be horrified, rather nervous laughter.

'Yes?' He was wearing a black cassock with a black cloak over the top. A man who liked his uniform. There was nothing welcoming about the way he approached them.

'Father Gruskin?' She didn't wait for him to answer, but flashed her warrant card in front of him. He squinted at it as if he was short-sighted. 'I'm afraid I've got some bad news about one of your parishioners.'

He took them into the vestry, where it was warmer. A Calor gas heater hissed and the fumes from it caught in the back of her throat.

'Yes?'

'Perhaps you'll have heard already,' Vera said. 'There was a murder on the Metro early this evening. The victim was Margaret Krukowski. I believe she was one of your regulars.'

He stared at them with horror, before collapsing into a chair at a plain wooden table and putting his face in his hands. 'I can't believe it.' It seemed to Vera that he was genuinely distressed and she felt a brief moment of sympathy for him. 'What have we come to, when a fine old lady is murdered in public?' He was posh, but local. Brought up in the city, Vera decided. Coddled. He looked as if he could do with a walk in fresh air.

'You knew her well?' Holly was sticking her oar in, but at least the priest looked up and answered, and he hadn't responded to Vera's comments.

'She attended regularly and she was always willing to get involved,' he said. 'These days most churches only keep going because of the efforts of elderly women. My father was a clergyman and I grew up in a parish in the city. It was much the same even then.' So there was a family tradition of dressing up in frocks.

'We're trying to trace her family.' At least Holly wasn't fidgeting with the electric gadget, but was giving the man her full concentration. 'Can you help with that at all?'

'I don't think I can. She lived over the road in the Harbour Guest House. Perhaps Mrs Dewar would know. They were almost like family. Margaret used to bring the children to Sunday School.'

They sat for a moment in silence.

'Margaret worked as a volunteer with you?'

'Yes.' He seemed preoccupied. Vera wondered if he was trying to rearrange the cleaning rota, to think of another old woman to take Margaret's place. At last he gave his full attention to the matter. 'Yes, at the Haven.'

Vera decided it was time for her to take over. 'The Haven is a refuge for battered women?'

Again, it seemed that a simple answer was beyond him. 'No, not really. It's a hostel for homeless women. Some of them might have left home because of domestic abuse, but we care for any woman in trouble who needs accommodation. Some have been in prison, some have been in care.'

'And it's run by the church?'

'It's run by a charitable trust. I'm one of the trustees, along with a senior social worker and a local accountant. But, as a church, we support the project. Financially, practically and with our prayers. Margaret worked miracles with some of the women. She became a surrogate mother to them, I think. They'll miss her very much.'

'Can you think of anyone who might have wanted to hurt Margaret?' The fumes from the gas fire made Vera feel light-headed, almost faint.

'Of course not!' The response was immediate. 'This couldn't be the action of a rational person, Inspector. This was an evil and random act of violence. A sign of the times.'

'Did she have any close friends among your congregation?' Holly's tone was respectful, and again he answered her in a more considered way. He faced her so that his back was turned to Vera.

'Close friends? No.' He hesitated and then seemed to choose his words carefully. 'A church is a community of different personalities. Of course we should treat each other with Christian charity, but we're only human.'

Vera interrupted. 'And get a bunch of women together and you have cliques and bitching. Must be a nightmare!'

He turned to her and for the first time he smiled. 'It's not always easy.'

'Did Margaret belong to any one group?' Vera again. The stuffy atmosphere in the small room was oppressive. She'd prefer to be out in the clear, cold air, and she wanted to move the conversation on.

'No,' the priest said. 'She hated the gossip and kept herself rather apart. That's what I mean when I say she had no close friends. She was always perfectly pleasant and played her part fully in the life of the church, but I don't think she confided in anyone.'

'Not even you?'

'No.' This time the smile was a little sad. 'Not even me.'

'And this hostel. The Haven? Where can we find it?'

'It's the former rectory.' This time Gruskin's smile was tight-lipped, even resentful. 'In different times it might have been my home, I suppose. When the status of the clergy was rather different. Even in my father's day the parish priest lived there. But now it's hard to justify such a large house for a single man, and the diocese lets it to the charity at a reasonable rent. It's a little way out of the town. That's where the main settlement was, before commercial fishing took over from farming.' He gave a sigh and Vera thought he would have been much happier as a Victorian priest, living in the big rectory, mixing socially with the gentry and delivering sermons to the peasants in the back pews.

'You won't get there tonight,' he said. 'There's not much of a road and in this weather . . . The women always grumble about the isolation. I'm not sure it's the best place for them to be.'

Outside it was quieter. The chip shop had closed and all the curtains in the Harbour Guest House had been drawn. The snow was covered with a hard sheen of frost. Gruskin shivered. For a long while he didn't move. Vera thought he must be freezing, with only the thin cloak over his shoulders to keep him warm. At last he set off down the pavement away from them. When Vera turned to look at him she saw that he was talking into a mobile phone.

Chapter Eight

Malcolm Kerr stood at the bar in the Coble. Behind him four elderly men were playing dominoes, rowing about the kitty or whose turn it was to go to the bar. It seemed to Malcolm that the same four men had been sitting at the same table, always arguing, since his father had first brought him to the pub. Their squabbling voices and the screaming of gulls had made up the background music of his life.

Nothing in this place has changed for thirty years.

Except tonight Malcolm was drunk and he couldn't remember the last time that had happened. Maybe when Fat Val was the landlady and he was young and fit and a bit of a firebrand. There was a painting of Val over the bar and she stared out at him reproachfully. She'd had a son called Rick, sly and weaselly, and remembering the two of them, Malcolm felt a sudden pang of guilt. He carried guilt around with him like extra pounds round the belly and he was so used to it that often he didn't notice it. He wasn't sure that he could blame the drink for that. These days he wasn't usually a heavy drinker – he'd stop in the Coble most evenings after working in the boatyard. Have a couple of pints. Read the *Chronicle*. Watch *Look North* on TV if there was no sport on the set. Then take himself back to his little house in Percy Street – all that he could afford after the divorce.

But tonight he'd lost count of the drinks he'd had. Beer first and then red wine, when his bladder wouldn't take pints any more. No spirits, though. He was proud that he hadn't moved on to the Scotch. And proud that he was still standing.

The only conversation he'd had was with Jonny the barman, and to jeer at the old slag, Dee, as she wandered through the pub trying to bum drinks or pick up punters. *God*, he thought, *you'd have to be desperate.* Another moment of pride, because he hadn't sunk to that.

Then through the drunken fug he was aware of a buzz of conversation behind him. Sudden animated voices. A name he recognized, even though it wasn't pronounced properly. He turned to confront a middle-aged couple. He knew them vaguely by sight, thought he might have been at school with the man, but couldn't trawl a name from his memory.

'What did you say?'

'There's been a murder.' The woman was scrawny. She'd taken off her jacket and was wearing a pink V-necked top. He could see vertical wrinkles between her breasts. 'It stopped the Metro.'

'Nah,' Malcolm said. 'That was the snow.' He reached out for his glass of wine, saw in the mirror over the bar that it had left stains like fangs at the corner of his mouth, and wiped them away with the back of his hand. His fingers were callused and grimy, though he'd washed before leaving work.

'There was a murder.' The woman's voice was high-pitched and carried across the bar. The room went quiet as everyone listened and she revelled in the attention. 'Wor lass is married to one of the community support officers, and she just texted us. It'll be on the late news.'

'Did they tell you who got killed?' But Malcolm thought he knew already.

'She lived just up the road here.' The woman's excitement was obvious. Malcolm thought if she were given the chance to view the body, she'd be there in the mortuary. Staring. Drooling almost. 'They called her Margaret. She had a strange second name.'

'Krukowski.'

'Aye, that's it!' She looked at him with more interest now and something like respect. 'Did you know her then?'

He paused for a moment and pushed himself away from the bar. 'Once,' he said. 'A long time ago.' He stood for a moment to get his balance and then he stumbled out into the cold.

In the street he had to stop again to steady himself by leaning against an overflowing bin. The fish shop was dark and the road was quiet. Suddenly his head was full of memories and pictures: a sunny day on the boat out to Coquet Island, a woman in a long floaty skirt and sandals, a wine glass in her hand and laughing. A group of people standing outside the Coble to have their photo taken. Then the flames of a fire licking across wood like a snake's tongue, and the smell of smoke and tar.

It occurred to him that he could knock at the door of the guest house and ask snooty Kate for news of Margaret, but the cold had sobered him sufficiently for him to realize that wasn't a good idea. He'd catch

Ryan in the morning and get the information from him.

He walked towards the illuminated Metro sign. The priest, Peter Gruskin, was walking in the opposite direction, and for a moment Malcolm wondered where he was going. Surely not to the pub? But as Malcolm turned down the alley towards Percy Street, he saw that the man had changed direction and was following him, walking so quickly that the black cloak swung behind him, making him look like a huge, swooping black bird. Gruskin looked so odd – so unlike a human – that Malcolm felt a moment of unease and was tempted to run for home like a child frightened by imagined monsters. But the priest took the footbridge over the Metro line towards the town and Malcolm continued on his way. The alley had the bulk of St Batholomew's Church on one side and only one light at each end, so his shadow was thrown ahead and then behind him on the hard-packed snow. Malcolm was taken by an overwhelming need to relieve himself and, looking quickly around, pissed where he stood against the spiked fence that separated the Metro line from the path. He thought he heard voices at the Metro end of the alley and, embarrassed, turned away quickly and hurried home.

Inside the house it was almost as cold as in the street, and this was a damp cold that clawed into his bones. In the living room he switched on the light and the gas fire and saw the room as if for the first time. *Soulless. This place is soulless.*

It had the same patterned carpet that had been in the place when he'd bought it, a mock-leather sofa and a glass-topped coffee table. A television.

I've worked my bollocks off for fifty years and this is all I have to show for it.

And a decent boat, he thought, and at least that notion gave him a brief moment of comfort. The *Lucy-May* had been worth fighting for, and Deborah hadn't got her hands on that. He switched on the set, thinking he would catch the late local news. Still standing in his coat, he found that the earlier memories were spinning round his head again: fractured light on the water, bouncing onto the face of a young woman laughing. The warm planks of the deck on his back, and terns overhead weaving weird shapes in the sky. Then the whiplash sound of snapping wood and the gunshots of sparks as the fire took hold.

As he waited for the news to come on, Malcolm shook his head to dispel the pictures that crowded his head, and went to the window to shut the curtains. It came to him that he would never again see Margaret Krukowski walk down Harbour Street on her way to church or the Metro, her back straight and her eyes fixed ahead. Her mind full of charity and good works. She could make no more demands. He wasn't sure whether the thought pleased or dismayed him.

Chapter Nine

They stood outside on the pavement. Vera stamped her feet. An attempt to keep warm, but also to wake herself up.

'What shall we do now?' Holly would never be the first one to call it a day. Her working life was spent persuading her colleagues that she was less of a wimp than the rest of them. 'Do you want to try this hostel?'

'Nah,' Vera said. 'We'll go tomorrow when the weather's better.'

'Well then?' Patience had never been one of Holly Clarke's virtues.

'Get off home,' Vera said. 'You live in town, don't you? The roads should be okay. Briefing in the morning, eight o'clock sharp. Paul Keating is planning the post-mortem at ten.'

'What will you do?' More curiosity than concern. The whole team thought she was mad to live in her father's house at the top of a hill, regularly cut off by snow and floods.

'Ah, don't worry about me, Hol. I'll find a bed for the night.'

They walked together to the end of Harbour Street, surprised on the way by the sound of a train pulling into the station. The Metro system was open again. Everything was back to normal.

Vera stood in the street and watched Holly drive off. She was tempted by the light and the warmth of the Coble, could taste the fire of a whisky sliding down her throat. But a woman on her own in a pub in Mardle would attract attention. She might not be dressed like the big lass in the fishnet tights, but folk would stare and wonder all the same.

On impulse she walked back to Kate Dewar's guest house. Her Land Rover was still parked outside, the windscreen now covered with ice. The lock was frozen and she had to tug on the handle to get the door open. In the back was her bag. A change of underwear and a toothbrush and toothpaste. She always kept it with her, just in case.

She knocked on the door. No reply. She knocked again and this time she heard footsteps. Kate Dewar appeared. Behind her stood a man. He was older than Kate, in his late fifties or early sixties, dressed in a checked shirt and a sweater. A grey beard and a weather-beaten face. Vera looked at her watch. Nine-thirty.

'Oh, it's you.' Kate's voice was a mixture of irritation and relief.

'Why, who did you think it might have been?'

'I've had the press on the phone. The Newcastle papers.'

Of course, Vera thought, *the death of an elderly woman wouldn't be sufficiently glamorous for the nationals.*

'I've switched off the phone, but that's not brilliant

for business.' She seemed close to tears, the petty inconveniences pushing her near the edge.

'Of course,' Vera said. 'It's about business that I'm here. Your business. I wonder if you have a bed for the night? Full rate, of course. I'd need an early breakfast. Only I live halfway up Cheviot and I don't fancy trying to get home in this. It's always ten times worse away from the coast. I'd be very grateful.'

And suddenly Kate clicked into professional mode. 'Of course. Come on in. Room six is free. Can I get you some tea in the lounge?' Talking just a little too quickly and glancing at Vera every now and again, thinking there might be something more sinister behind the apparently simple request.

Vera didn't answer immediately. She leaned against the door and stretched out her hand round Kate towards the man. 'I'm Vera Stanhope. Good to meet you.'

'This is Stuart Booth, my fiancé.' The woman's face lit up with a huge beam. She looked like a teenager in love for the first time. Vera tried to think if *she'd* ever felt like that.

'Then good to meet you, Stuart.' Vera smiled. His handshake was dry and firm. 'You know what I'd really love? It's been a bugger of a day. A real drink. Don't suppose you've got a licence?'

'A residents' licence? Of course.'

Vera beamed at her. 'Then I'll have a large Scotch. And why don't you two come and join me. I expect you could use a drink – the day that you've had.' She pulled off her wellingtons and padded into the lounge in her stockinged feet, leaving Kate and Stuart no choice but to follow. She sat in one of the leather chairs, waited for Kate to pour the drinks and then held her glass in both hands and looked at them. 'How long have you been together then?'

They looked at each other. 'About a year.' Stuart's voice was northern, but not local. Yorkshire?

'Stuart teaches at the kids' school.' Kate looked at him as if he was some sort of miracle, as if she could hardly believe that he was real.

'How does that work? Must be a nightmare to have your teacher turning up and telling tales to your mam.' Vera set the glass on the arm of the chair.

'None of us finds it easy. And, really, I'd never tell tales.' He had a way of speaking slowly that was very precise, as if he was considering every word. He took Kate's hand.

My God, Vera thought, *they* are *like a pair of teenagers*.

'You knew Margaret Krukowski?'

'Of course,' Stuart said. 'She was like one of the family.' He gave a shy smile. 'She was going to give Kate away at the wedding.'

'You've planned your wedding then?' Vera was tempted to ask why they'd bother, but held her tongue.

'Well, we've fixed a date.'

'When did you last see Margaret?'

'At the weekend.' He looked at Kate for confirmation and she nodded. 'The kids were out and we invited her down for supper.'

'You don't live here then?'

'No,' he said. 'I stay over sometimes, but as you said, Chloe and Ryan find it awkward. We think they'll find it easier to accept when we're married.'

There was a silence. Stuart slid his arm around Kate's shoulder. Vera felt uncomfortable, as if she were intruding, and thought the kids must feel like this all the time.

'What do you teach, Stuart?' Small talk had never come easily to her. It was one of the few things that she and Hector had had in common. She thought the man sitting opposite might struggle with it too.

'Music,' he said. Then, as she made no comment, he added, 'I run the county youth orchestra too. And the jazz band.'

Vera gave a bright little smile. 'That'll be one of the things the two of you have in common – the music.' She turned to Kate. 'My sergeant said you were a star at one time. What made you give it up?'

'Oh, you know. Family commitments. Kids.' Kate shook her head as if she was embarrassed to talk about it.

'But I'm persuading her to rebuild her career.' The man's voice was earnest and it was almost as if he wanted Vera's approval for the new venture. He stroked Kate's hair, and the charge of intimacy made Vera feel awkward again. She said she'd take a second drink and some tea to her room.

The bedroom was well furnished and comfortable and looked out over the street. Vera sat at the window with her tea and her whisky, and when the glass was empty she topped it up from the bottle she kept in her bag. Also for emergencies, like the toothbrush and the clean knickers.

She thought about Margaret Krukowski, who had

lived in this house for years. What had kept her in Mardle? Poverty, or a kind of lethargy? Perhaps she'd got used to the place and couldn't face a change. And she'd liked this family, Vera decided. Liked watching the kids grow up and feeling that she was part of Kate Dewar's life. A part of something. She might have been a self-contained woman, essentially private, but she hadn't wanted to be completely alone. So what had Margaret made of Stuart Booth, who was closer in age to her than to Kate? Had she thought her life would change when Kate married?

Why had she been killed? Why now, on a snowy afternoon, when everyone was full of Christmas spirit? Why had she been stabbed? Vera was reminded of an old news story: a spy or a dissident stabbed with the end of an umbrella, the tip containing some lethal and secret poison. She'd thought at the time that the incident was ludicrous. There were easier ways to kill people, and this had smacked of little boys playing adventure games. Then she remembered George Enderby's fantasy that Margaret Krukowski was a spy left over from the Cold War, and she thought she could see what had triggered his imagination. The exotic Eastern European name, of course, but also the sense that this was a private woman who carried secrets with her.

Share your secrets with me, Margaret Krukowski. Help me to find your killer.

Vera stood up to go to the bathroom. Looking at her watch, she saw that it was eleven o'clock. She'd been sitting here for more than an hour. She pulled back the curtain and looked outside. Closing time at the Coble, and a scattering of drinkers were making their way back to the town centre. There was a light on in the church. As she watched, the lights went out and the door opened. The priest emerged, still clothed in his black robes.

What have you been praying for, Father? Margaret Krukowski's immortal soul? Or your own?

The police station at Kimmerston was freezing. The snow had brought down the power lines and cut off the electricity overnight. The power was back on now, but the timer was out and the heating had only just come on. They sat in their jackets, wrapped up in scarves and gloves. A good night's sleep and a full English breakfast had Vera feeling on top form.

She stood before the whiteboard. There was a recent photo of Margaret Krukowski, donated by Kate. It had been taken when the woman hadn't been expecting it. She was standing at the table in the basement kitchen, a biscuit cutter in one hand, and she'd looked up at the camera at the last minute. Her expression was startled and amused. Vera had also brought Margaret's wedding photo from the guest house. Sometimes she thought that the younger members of her team considered older people a different species. Close to death anyway, so not worth the same effort. Not like a child or a teenager. They would never say that, probably would not even think it consciously, but Vera hoped this picture of a young and beautiful woman would jerk them out of that mindset. *Once she was young and just like you.*

'Margaret Krukowski. Stabbed on the Metro yesterday afternoon. Apparently without anyone seeing –

though the Metro was so busy that's not as impossible as it seems. People would have heard if she'd screamed loudly, but probably not a moan. Nightmare scenario, but this time we're lucky because there was an expert witness on hand throughout. That's right, isn't it, Joe?'

Joe smiled. She thought all his bairns must have slept well and he'd had a good night. He and Sal were getting on at the moment and that always improved his mood. 'I was in the same carriage,' he said. 'But a few rows away from her. And the place was jammed. You know what it's like just before Christmas and the rush hour.'

She nodded. 'All the same,' she said. 'Give us what you remember.' She listened as he told his story again and listed the characters he could recall. There were no omissions and no elaboration. He was a good witness. She'd trained him well.

Vera went on. 'We have a nightmare forensically. So much material that it'll take them weeks to work through it. The one blessing is that it'll keep Billy Wainwright busy throughout the holiday period. Office parties get him over-excited, and he's too old for that kind of carry-on now.'

There were a few sniggers. Crime-scene manager Billy enjoyed his reputation as a serial adulterer.

'Most important actions for today: some folk who were on the Metro have already come forward. It was the four-thirty from Newcastle Central Station and it was stopped by the weather at Partington. Margaret was in the first carriage. We need a media release asking everyone else who travelled on the same train to get in touch. Then we'll put together a plan showing where people were sitting or standing and what they saw.' She looked out at her audience. 'Holly, that's for you. Do the press conference. A broadcast request on BBC's *Look North*, if we can manage it. Contact the press office and tell them what we need. Then you take charge of the responses that come in, get a floor plan of the seating arrangements and see what you can put together.'

Holly preened, and Vera patted herself on the back: she was getting better at handling her DC. Holly would love to do the television and would be good at collating the passenger information. If Vera had asked her just to do the paperwork she'd have sulked for a fortnight. Getting her team onside was a piece of piss. Who needed management training?

'Next. What was Margaret doing in Gosforth? We think she grew up there. Did she have family still living in the area? We've checked the records and her maiden name was Nash. Charlie, see what you can track down. She might even have a parent still alive, given the age we all live to these days. Can we check with the Department of Work and Pensions and the care homes in the area? She never talked about her family to folk in Mardle, but the one thing we do know about Margaret is that she was intensely private. She might have been in Gosforth to visit her relatives.'

Charlie nodded. Vera noticed that he was tidier these days. When his wife first left him he could have passed for one of the homeless guys who hung around Kimmerston bus station. She could be less than tidy herself, but she was never dirty. Well, not often. She wondered fleetingly if he'd found himself another woman or if he'd just come to terms with being left to fend for himself. She'd always thought he missed having his laundry done more than he missed his wife's company.

Vera paused for breath. It was getting light. A bright, icy gleam shone through the window directly into her face and made her squint.

'The other thing we know is that Margaret was given to good causes,' she continued. 'All sorts of good causes, but especially a charity called the Haven.'

'That place for fallen women in Holypool Village.' Charlie looked up from his mug of coffee.

'Fallen women?' It was Holly, her voice a horrified shriek. 'What century are you living in?'

'I was being ironic.' Charlie slid her a grin.

Vera thought that something had definitely happened in his life. He'd never have talked about irony before. 'How do you know about the Haven?'

'I arrested a young druggie once. No room in the cells, and I didn't think she was fit to let out onto the street. Seemed to me she might be suicidal. Social services suggested I took her there.'

'Joe, will you check out the Haven? You're good at social work, when you put your mind to it. If Margaret was a regular volunteer she might have made friends with the staff, confided in them about family, relationships. And it's possible she made an enemy of one of the women. Gruskin said they were vulnerable. Anyone with a history of mental illness, given to paranoia and violent episodes? Or an ex-offender with some sort of axe to grind.'

Joe nodded and scribbled down the address.

Holly lifted her hand. 'If there are victims of

domestic violence there, Margaret could have been targeted by a male partner.'

'So she could, Hol.' Vera was pleased that at least now there were lines of enquiry, but she still thought the centre of the investigation lay in Harbour Street. She leaned back against the desk and shut her eyes against the sun. 'And the owner of the guest house, Kate Dewar – formerly known as musician Katie Guthrie – has a new man in her life. Stuart Booth. No record, not even a speeding ticket, but let's see what we can find out about him. Track down any former partners. Any history of violence? And we'll need to chat to the head of the school where he teaches.

'The rest of you: we've set up interviews with the folk who were on the train and who've already been in touch. Treat them nicely, but be aware that any one of them could be the killer. So no dismissing the smart guy in the suit because he doesn't seem the type. We need to know where they were sitting or standing, and if they saw anything unusual. Margaret's hard to pin down socially and she could have mixed with all sorts. We're especially interested in the people who got on at Gosforth. Did any of them see Margaret on the platform, or notice which direction she walked from to get there?'

Charlie coughed. 'Ma'am?'

'Yes?' She lifted an eyebrow.

'Don't the Metros have CCTV these days?'

'Usually, but the one in our train wasn't working.' She gave them a wide smile. 'We're chasing up the reason. So we're dependent on old-fashioned policing. And before anyone asks, there was CCTV outside the station, but the snow was so heavy that it was impossible to see anything.'

She waved them back to their desks. 'If anyone wants me, I'll be with Prof. Keating at the post-mortem.

Chapter Ten

Kate Dewar had hardly slept. Stuart had gone home soon after Vera Stanhope had left for her room. 'I've got all the end-of-term reports to finish,' he'd said. 'And the kids will want you to themselves.' She'd almost asked him to stay, but didn't want to force the issue. He could see that she was upset, and he wasn't sure how to help her. Her sadness would discomfort him. He was never very good at talking about feelings. He'd been on his own for so long that it was as if he'd had to learn a new language. And he was a kind man. She saw that the nature of Margaret's death had touched him, even though he hadn't known her for long.

It wasn't fear that had kept her awake in the night. She wasn't expecting Margaret's killer to break into the house and murder them in their beds. She might have been haunted by fancies like that – she had a vivid imagination – but somehow the presence of Vera Stanhope, solid and implacable, had made the idea seem quite ridiculous. Instead, more subtle anxieties kept her awake: the business, the family, how she would arrange a suitable funeral for Margaret. She lay on her side, rigid with tension, checking her bedside clock every hour. It seemed as if she'd only just fallen asleep when the alarm went off.

Usually she served breakfast from seven, but when she'd checked in Vera had asked if she might take it early: 'Cereal and toast will be fine. I don't want to put you to any trouble.' There had been a wistful edge to her voice, though, and Kate hadn't had Vera down as a healthy eater, so she'd had bacon and sausage under the grill just in case, eager to please. She'd always been eager to please – part of her problem. If she'd gone into her marriage deciding what *she'd* wanted from the relationship, instead of trying to guess what would make Robbie happy, perhaps things would have worked out better.

She'd certainly made Vera Stanhope happy. The woman had cleared her plate in minutes and beamed. 'I'm supposed to be watching what I eat these days, but no harm in a treat once in a while, eh?' There'd been no more questions about Margaret. No mention at all of the murder. The inspector had paid her bill in cash and, when Kate had offered her a receipt, she'd waved it away. 'Not the police service's fault that I live out in the wilds. Can't really get this one on expenses.' Then she was out of the door with a little wave, and Kate had felt inexplicably bereft. A repeat of the sensation that had overcome her when she'd realized that Margaret was dead.

George Enderby arrived in the dining room at eight on the dot. He might like to come across as a free spirit, but Kate had noticed that he was a great one for routine. A pot of coffee and poached eggs on brown toast. The order was always the same. She was clearing his dishes when the kids left the house for school. Through the window she watched Ryan idling up the street, his heavy bag weighing down one shoulder. No hurry to get to his lessons. He seemed more eager to help Malcolm Kerr out in the yard these days than to get to class. Chloe left a few minutes later. Further up the street she was joined by a lad Kate didn't recognize.

'Where are you off to today, George?' She turned her attention back to the room. His wheelie suitcase of books was already sitting at the bottom of the stairs.

'Into Newcastle.' He smiled a little sadly. 'A challenge. It's hard to get booksellers interested in our titles for spring when everyone's mind is on Christmas.'

'That police inspector stayed last night. She couldn't get home because of the weather.'

'Oh?' He was suddenly interested. She thought, now that the shock had worn off, they were all interested in Margaret's death. It was like a television drama. Even the kids, who had been pleasant and careful with each other the evening before, seemed back to normal, sniping and bickering.

'She left an hour ago. She didn't say anything about the investigation, of course. I suppose they have to be discreet.' Kate wiped crumbs from a neighbouring table with a napkin into her cupped hand.

'Yes,' George said. 'I suppose they do.'

Later, when the house was quiet and tidy, she sat on the sofa in the kitchen and dozed a little; a new folk band recommended by Stuart was playing in the background and the voices sounded somehow like waves on shingle, blurred and soporific. She was shocked by the ringing on the doorbell. The detective had said that some officers would be in during the morning to search Margaret's room. This was a piece of information she hadn't passed on to George Enderby. His eagerness to discuss Margaret's death had seemed a little tasteless to her, and unlike his usual courtesy. Now she supposed that the search team must be here and she rushed to let them in. She didn't want Father Gruskin and his coven of elderly admirers to see a group of uniformed officers on the doorstep. Rumours spread like wildfire in Mardle.

But there were no policemen in the street. Instead it was Malcolm Kerr, the boatman. Sometimes Ryan helped him out in the yard for pocket money, and from her son she'd picked up snippets of gossip about his divorce, and the move from the big house in Warkworth to the ex-council place on Percy Street. His skin was very grey. He'd shaved badly and his eyes seemed yellow and bloodshot all at once. Because he'd stepped back onto the pavement their faces were on the same level and she noticed the whiff of stale alcohol on his breath.

'Malcolm.' She didn't invite him into the house. Although she didn't know him well herself, he had a reputation for being an awkward customer – taciturn, always moaning. Her first thought was that Ryan had done something to annoy him. She'd always thought Malcolm liked having him hanging around the yard, but Ryan had become a mystery to her.

'It's about Margaret,' he said. 'Can I come in?' And he quickly moved up the steps towards her so that her immediate reaction was to move out of his way before he knocked into her. Then he was in the house. She took him into the guest lounge, because it was nearer the front door; somehow she felt better speaking to Malcolm if she knew she could escape. Something about this man, intense and frowning, scared her. His yard had been on Harbour Street since before she'd moved in, for many years, she believed. He was a fixture like the church and the pub. He'd taken over from his father as boatman to Coquet Island and he'd been coxswain of the lifeboat until recent years. Stalwart of the town. Grumpy, but reliable. She'd never really taken any notice of him. Now she wondered if he was suffering from some sort of mental illness.

'What do you want, Malcolm?' He was a good distance from her in a corner by the fire. She kept her voice calm. It was important not to make him angry.

'It's about Margaret.'

'If you know anything about Margaret you should tell the police.' She added, a sudden inspiration: 'They'll be here soon. They want to search her room.'

'Can I see it?' The words fired from his mouth like a shot. It was as if they'd formed themselves without his thinking about them.

'What do you mean?'

'Can I see her room? Where she lived?'

'Of course not!' She was less scared now than exasperated. He seemed rather old and confused, sitting in the high-backed chair, his hands on his knees like a resident in a care home. 'I don't have the key and, besides, it's private.'

Then she saw that he was crying. Large round tears rolled down his cheeks. It occurred to her that he was so unused to weeping that he didn't know what to do with them. She pulled a paper handkerchief from her pocked and walked across the carpet to give it to him.

'I didn't realize you were such friends,' she said, more gently.

He took the tissue and dabbed at his face. 'Margaret Krukowski worked for me. A good while ago. My father was still alive and we had an office on the yard then. She kept our books, sent out the invoices, answered the phone in the office, took the bookings.'

'Ah,' Kate said. 'I didn't know.' She thought there were lots of things she didn't know about Mardle. Her children belonged to the place more than she did. Ryan especially picked up things at school. Secrets about other families. Rumours about the businesses in Harbour Street. Stuck in this big house, Kate learned very little and Stuart took no interest at all. He seemed entirely self-contained and only needed his music and her. She got her gossip second-hand, through the kids and from overheard snatches of conversation in shops and cafes.

'Things got tough.' Malcolm was talking almost to himself. 'We had to let her go. And there was a fire, so we lost the office too.'

'I'm sorry.' What else was there to say?

He stood up suddenly and the power of his movement, the size of him, frightened her again, so she backed away from him.

'The funeral,' he said.

'I don't know when that will be,' Kate said quickly. 'I suppose we have to wait for the police to release her body.'

'But I'd like to help,' he said. 'Whatever needs doing.'

She saw that he was close to tears again. 'I'll let you know. Really.' She walked towards the door, hoping he would follow. He made his way after her, but stopped at the foot of the stairs and looked up. For a moment she was scared that he'd become unpredictable again, that he'd clamber up the stairs towards Margaret's room. She had the sense that he had been in this house before and knew his way around.

Kate was going to mention it: *You must see a difference in the place.* Because really there was no comparison to the way it had been before she took over, and he hadn't been in the house recently, had he? Margaret had never taken visitors to her room. But before she could speak, Malcolm turned and almost ran down the steps to the pavement. It was as if he'd been chased away. He lifted his hand to wave goodbye to her, but didn't turn round and didn't stop walking.

Kate shut the door and locked it, then returned to the kitchen. The music was still burbling as if nothing had happened, and she felt for a moment as if the encounter with Malcolm Kerr was the subject of the song. Vera Stanhope had left her business card on the breakfast table when she'd got up to leave. 'Just in case you remember something that might be useful.' Kate took it from the dresser and held it between her fingers. And then on impulse she reached for her phone.

'No matter what it is,' Vera had said. 'It's the trivial things that make the difference.'

Kate felt like a child again. The good girl at the front of the class, wanting the teacher to like her. Eager to please. She told Vera that Malcolm had been at the house and that Margaret had worked for him and his father.

'I had the feeling,' Kate said, after Vera had listened patiently to her explanation, 'that they were more than friends.'

Chapter Eleven

Vera had never been bothered by post-mortems. Dead people couldn't hurt you; it was the living you should be frightened of. Paul Keating, the pathologist, was from Belfast. He was a religious man, taciturn and dignified, and a great golfing friend of crime-scene manager Billy Wainwright. Vera wondered what the two men could talk about on the course or in the bar after the game. She sometimes thought they would have nothing in common except the dead.

The mortuary was even chillier than usual and she wondered if the electricity had cut out at the hospital overnight too, as it had in the freezing police station, because of the heavy snowfall. The woman lying on the table certainly looked cold. Frozen. Vera wasn't squeamish, but she wished they would cover her with a blanket.

Keating was talking, recording his first impressions. Vera listened to his words, but she was thinking that Margaret was good for her age: not a lot of spare flesh except for a little fat around the waist, and the woman still had cheekbones to die for. Vera remembered Joe's admiration of the young Margaret in her wedding photograph and felt a familiar itch of jealousy. *She* hadn't been much admired even when she was twenty. Joe obviously liked thin lizzies; his Sal was all skin and bone.

Keating paused for breath and she took the opportunity to ask the question that had been troubling her from the start of the investigation. 'I don't understand,' she said, 'how nobody noticed. A Metro packed with people. She'd have screamed, wouldn't she? Joe didn't hear her, but he was at the other end of the carriage. There would have been blood.'

'No,' Keating said. 'There was hardly any blood. Not enough for anyone to notice.' With the aid of an assistant he rolled Margaret onto her side. 'She was stabbed by a knife with a very thin blade. Long and thin. She'd have felt it, but more as a discomfort than any real pain. A pin prick. Then, if the subcutaneous fat closed over the wound, there would have been hardly any external bleeding. She'd have died before she or anyone else realized what was happening.'

Vera wondered if that was a good way to die. Just before Christmas on a busy train, surrounded by excited bairns and adults full of beer. She could think of worse ways to go.

'So he knew what he was doing?' she said. 'The murderer, I mean.'

Keating shrugged. 'Either that or he was lucky.'

'She was stabbed from behind?' Vera couldn't see how that would work. The woman was sitting down. Joe had described in detail how she'd taken the one empty seat in the carriage. So how could she have been stabbed in the back?

'Definitely from behind.'

He continued to make his report, but Vera was running that image over and over in her head. Margaret, well dressed, stepping from the snowy platform into the train, finding a seat and leaning back against it. Vera created scenarios to explain the knife wound in the back, the sharp blade piercing the cashmere coat. Perhaps Margaret was being followed from Gosforth and was stabbed while she was still standing. But if that was the case, why had the killer waited to make his attack until she was in a crowded train? A dark and quiet suburban street would surely provide a better opportunity. Or perhaps Margaret had turned in her seat to look out of the window as the train pulled into a station and the killer had taken a chance then. In either case the murderer could have left the train at any stop between Gosforth and Partington. They'd assumed that Margaret had been killed close to the final stop, but if death had crept up as unobtrusively as Keating had suggested, that needn't have been the case.

Keating's words had been running as a background to her thoughts and she noticed a sudden silence.

'What is it?' She was jerked back to the present, to the freezing mortuary and the stink of human waste.

'Our victim was ill.' Keating stood for a moment, frowning. 'Bowel cancer. I found these indications on the liver. The disease had spread from the bowel.'

'Treatable?' Vera wasn't sure how that could possibly be relevant. The woman hadn't stabbed herself in the back. This hadn't been a desperate and very public suicide.

'Perhaps. No sign that it has been, though.'

'Maybe she'd only just been diagnosed.' Vera was talking to herself, running through the possibilities. More scenarios. More stories. 'I'll need to trace her GP.'

Thinking it was unlikely that Margaret had been visiting an outpatient clinic the afternoon of her death. There were no major hospitals close to Gosforth Metro station.

Outside, the sun was shining, but it was still very cold. Kids had made a slide of the pavement and Vera nearly went arse over tit. She checked her phone, wondering if she'd missed anything important during the post-mortem, and immediately it began to ring. She didn't recognize the voice at first and it was only a few seconds into the conversation that she realized she was speaking to Kate Dewar. Vera listened as the woman described the arrival at the guest house of Malcolm Kerr.

'He ran the bird trips out to Coquet Island.' Vera remembered a thin young man, gauche ashore, but agile on the boat. 'With his dad.'

Kate was obviously surprised by the interruption. 'His father died years ago.'

'And he seemed in a bit of a state?'

'The way he talked about Margaret,' Kate said, 'I had the feeling that they were more than friends.'

Parking the Land Rover in Harbour Street, Vera almost felt as if she were coming home. Kate must have been looking out for her, because the door was opened immediately. 'You don't mind if we chat in the kitchen?' she asked. 'Only I've got baking in the oven.'

Vera followed her down to the basement, pleased that they wouldn't be sitting in the highly polished lounge, which reminded her, she suddenly realized, of a funeral parlour or an elaborate chapel.

'He'd been drinking,' Kate said. 'Last night, if not this morning. I could smell it on him. Everyone knows he likes a pint in the Coble of an evening, and a couple of cans if he's working in his shed, but I've never known him drunk. Not even when Deborah left.'

She'd switched on the filter coffee machine and the water was dripping through the grounds, filling the kitchen with its smell.

'Deborah?'

'His ex-wife.' Kate opened the oven and pulled out a tray of shortbread. 'This won't be as good as Margaret's.'

'Maybe you won't have to bother with baking, if you hit the big time with the music again.' Vera squinted across at her. She couldn't understand what was going on with this music thing. Was it just a dream, encouraged by Stuart Booth, or were there concrete plans?

'Aye', Kate said. 'Maybe. Though I'll not hold my breath. It's a precarious business. Stuart's not one for wild dreams, either.' She smiled, though, and Vera thought that secretly she was excited by the whole package – the music and the man.

'When did Malcolm and Deborah separate?' There was nothing Vera liked better than this talk about the personalities on the edge of a murder. Gossip, but legitimate because it was work.

'Five years ago? Something like that. Deborah had invested in Malcolm's business and he was forced to buy her out. They had a nice house up the coast at Warkworth at one time, but he had to sell it to pay her off. He lives in a poky little ex-council place in Percy Street now.'

'Is that in Mardle?'

'Yes.' Kate poured the coffee. 'Just behind the church.'

'Did you ever know that Malcolm and Margaret were close?' Vera eyed up the shortbread, but it seemed that Kate was going to leave it to cool.

'No, but I didn't know Margaret had worked for him at one time, either. In the office, he said. It must have been before we moved here.' She paused. 'Margaret never mentioned it and Malcolm doesn't have an office now, just that eyesore of a shed.'

There was a moment of silence and then Vera asked, 'Do you have a health centre in Mardle?'

The question came out of the blue, and Kate obviously thought she was mad. 'Yes, just over the Metro line towards town. A new place close to the high school.'

'Handy.' Vera drank the coffee. 'Is that where Margaret's GP was based?'

Kate thought for a moment. 'I don't know. Isn't that weird? We lived in the same house for all those years and I don't know where she went to the doctor. Perhaps because she was never ill. I suggested that she have a flu jab once. Everyone in the town was going down with it. But she wouldn't. She said she'd never liked needles.'

'Had she seemed herself in the last few days?'

This time the response was quicker. 'Actually, not really. Not as sharp. She was a bit preoccupied, wandering around in a kind of a daze. I asked her if anything was the matter, but she said she just had a few things to sort out.'

That obsessive privacy again. All those secrets. Oh, Margaret Krukowski, what did you have to hide?

Outside, there was an odd milky light. Thin cloud obscured the sun and Vera thought she could smell snow. She decided that as soon as it started, she'd head for home. She needed a night in her own bed and a chance to think things through. Her neighbours would have cleared the track by now and would make sure she got out in the morning. It was lunchtime. There were school kids queuing up at the chip shop, some only in their uniform sweatshirts, seeming not to feel the cold. She thought she caught a glimpse of Chloe Dewar with some boy, but she couldn't be certain. Teenage girls all looked alike to her.

Kerr's boatyard was surrounded by tall spiked railings, and you got into it through double wooden gates. Trawling back through her memory, Vera thought they'd met the men here, that night she'd gone with Hector on his raid of roseate terns' eggs. Then they'd gone to the harbour and into a boat. Not the tripper boat, the *Lucy-May*, but a small boat with a powerful outboard. She tried to picture some sort of office, but nothing came. The gate's padlock was open, but the gate had sunk on its hinges now and she had to lift and push it against the snow to get inside. There was no immediate sign of Kerr, but a track through the snow led to a shed made of planks and corrugated iron, and that was where she found him. It had one small window, so grubby that it was hard to see inside, but she made out a shape slumped in a battered armchair and she tapped on the glass. There was no movement and for a moment her imagination ran wild. Another murder. Or a suicide. Plenty of tools to stab a woman with, in a place like this. And knives to slash your wrists with, if the guilt got too much.

She knocked on the glass again, this time more fiercely, and Kerr stirred in his chair, then got to his feet. Before he had the chance to come out to her, she opened the door and went inside.

It felt suddenly very warm. There was a tiny wood-burning stove in the corner and the place smelled of smoke and sweat. He'd drunk too much and slept too little. She recognized the signs.

'Who the fuck are you?'

'Vera Stanhope,' she said. She didn't mind the question. She could be like a bear with a sore head too with a hangover. 'Detective Inspector.'

'Stanhope.' He repeated the name as if he recognized it.

'Aye, I think you knew my dad.' She thought Hector must have worked with this man over a number of years. Kerr wouldn't remember the name after just one outing. Where else had he taken Hector in his rubber dinghy? What other eggs had they stolen together?

'My God, you're Hector's daughter.' The man spluttered, halfway between a cough and a chuckle. 'A cop. He'll be turning in his grave!'

Vera shifted a pile of old boat magazines from a stool and sat down. 'Margaret Krukowski,' she said.

He sank back in his chair and stared ahead of him. 'What about her?'

'She used to work for you?'

'That was a long time ago.' He was wary now,

determined to give nothing away. Vera wondered what else he had to hide from the police, besides the raids out to the island nature reserve. Dodgy tax and VAT returns almost certainly. Black fish? Smuggled fags and booze?

'I'm only interested in the murder,' she said. 'Anything you can tell me about Margaret will help.'

'She worked for us years ago, about the time that I knew your father. The business was better then. We still took trippers out to the island, but there was fishing too. And charters. We had a proper little office in the yard then, a kind of wooden Portakabin. Margaret was hardly more than a kid. A posh kid, looking for work. My dad took her on because he thought she'd sound good on the phone. Classy.'

'Was she married?' Vera asked.

He hesitated. 'I never knew much about her private life.'

'Hey, Malcolm man, who're you kidding here? A bonny thing like that. You a young man in your prime. You'd have remembered if she was single or not.'

He looked up and glared at her.

'I told you,' Vera said. 'I'm only interested in finding out who killed her. Seems to me you might have an interest in that too.'

'I think she might have been married.' He paused. 'Some foreign seaman. It didn't last long. I think she only did it to spite her folks.'

'Did he knock her about?' Vera put the question as if it were the most natural one in the world.

'What makes you think that?' The same anger and the same suspicion.

'According to the priest, she volunteers in a hostel for homeless women. I wondered if there might be a connection. That's what my job's all about – making connections.'

'Nah,' he said at last. 'I don't think he hit her. Margaret loved the bones of him. She was young and daft, and he was all good looks and romantic gestures. They were happy enough, I think, until he got bored with having no money and ran off with someone else.'

'Did you fancy your chances with her when he went away?' Vera looked beyond Kerr to the small window. A few snowflakes melted on the glass and slid towards the frame.

He shook his head. 'She'd never have gone for a local lad when she was thinking she might get Pawel back.'

'That was his name?'

'Aye.' Reluctantly Kerr spelled it out.

'When did you last see her?'

He hesitated. 'Yesterday morning. She was on Harbour Street, walking towards the bus stop on the corner.'

'Did you speak to her?' Vera thought this was like drawing teeth.

'Only to say hello. I passed her in the street. I was coming here. I had a charter booked for one of Mrs Dewar's guests.'

'Who would want to go out on the water in weather like this?'

For the first time he gave a real smile. 'A mad professor. They call him Mike Craggs. He works at the university as a marine biologist. He's researching water temperature, and I take him out to the island for a couple of hours every fortnight. I think he samples the mainland coast too.'

'What time were you back in the harbour?'

Kerr shrugged. 'Late afternoon. The weather forecast was bad and the Prof. wanted to get home. It hadn't started snowing then, but it was almost dark.'

'And what did you do after that?' Vera kept her voice patient. This was a conversation, not an interrogation.

'I went home for a bit. I was frozen and I needed a hot bath and some warm food. Then I went to the pub.' He looked up, challenging her to ask for details, but she didn't bite. She could ask at the Coble what time he turned up there.

'Why were you so upset when you heard about her death?' Vera's voice was low and gentle. 'Had you become friends, like, over the years?'

He leaned forward, wrapped a cloth around his hand so that he wouldn't burn himself, opened the door of the stove and threw in a piece of driftwood. 'Nah,' he said. 'Nothing like that. But I suppose she reminded me of my youth.' He paused again. 'Good times.'

Chapter Twelve

Holypool was just a couple of miles inland from Mardle, but Joe Ashworth felt as if he was in a different world when he approached it, a world to which he aspired. He'd always liked the village and occasionally imagined himself living in the small development of new executive housing just behind the pub. On either side of the narrow main street there were stone cottages with long, narrow front gardens. In the summer there would be birdsong. The sun and the overnight traffic had cleared the street, but there was enough snow left on the roofs to make the place look like something from a Christmas card that his nan might have sent.

In his head an ear-worm, the song 'White Moon Summer' that had made Katie Guthrie famous. The melody swam in and out of his consciousness throughout the drive and he remembered himself and Sal, hardly more than bairns, and that month when they'd both finished their exams and nothing mattered except each other and their plans for the future.

The Haven was based in a house set away from the road, hidden by trees and surrounded by farmland. There was a wooden gate across the drive and, as Joe got out of the car to open it, he heard dripping water – melted ice falling from the branches. The drive was potholed, the pits filled in places with ash and shale, and he had to drive slowly. He wondered what the residents made of the place. He thought most of them would be from the city and that this must seem like the end of the known universe to them. At night how would they cope with the dark and the quiet? Even he shuddered at the thought of it. A bank of cloud covered the sun. He emerged from the trees and pulled onto a flagged courtyard, surrounded on two sides by the stone house and on the third by a series of almost derelict outbuildings.

A woman in jeans and a sweater appeared from an open wooden structure that might once have been a rickety garage. She was pushing a wheelbarrow full of logs and set it down to stare at him. She watched without moving as he got out of the car to approach her. He felt uncomfortable because he couldn't place her. Was she a client or a worker? He was happier when he could give people a label.

'Can I help you?' The words gave no clue to her status. The accent was indeterminate and the voice slightly hostile. Wary at least. Joe stared back, trying to work out if he'd seen her before, if she might have been one of the people in the Metro the afternoon of the murder. There was no spark of recognition. After a brief glimpse of so many people perhaps that was unlikely.

He was about to ask for the person in charge when the door to the house opened and a golden Labrador bounded out, followed by a middle-aged woman. The woman was short and round and wore a purple cord skirt and a brightly coloured hand-knitted cardigan that made her look fatter than she really was. There were wellingtons on her feet. She called back the dog, which was bouncing towards Joe.

'Sandy, come back here.' She was Scottish and her voice sounded as if she was laughing.

Then she repeated the words that had been spoken by the younger woman. 'Can I help you?' They were friendly, but demanded an answer.

Joe stayed where he was. He'd always been suspicious of big dogs since one had jumped up and nipped him on his first day of school. Something else for Vera Stanhope to tease him about. He introduced himself.

The Scottish woman smiled easily. 'I assume you have some ID? We're always a bit wary about strange men turning up at the Haven, aren't we, Laurie?'

The young woman sniffed. 'No need,' she said. 'He's a pig. I can smell them a mile off.' She bent to the handles of the wheelbarrow and pushed it around the side of the house.

Joe waved his warrant card towards the older woman.

'Come in out of the cold,' she said. 'We'll put on the kettle. And it's almost lunchtime, if you'd like to join us.'

It wasn't very much warmer inside the house. There were stone flags on the floor of the hall too, and he had to climb over a clutter of boots, a child's tricycle and a big old-fashioned pram. The hall was wide and high and in one corner there was an enormous Christmas tree decorated with handmade paper chains and foil stars. The woman led him past it and into an office furnished with an elderly desk, a sofa so low in the middle that it was almost on the floor, and a couple of kitchen chairs. 'I should introduce myself. Jane Cameron. I run this place, for my sins.' Then she left him where he was and disappeared. He heard her shouting into the distance for someone to be a sweetheart and bring through a pot of coffee. Then she was back, and her personality seemed to fill the room and warm it. He thought he'd never met anyone quite like her.

'Now, Sergeant Ashworth, why don't you tell me what this is all about?' She'd perched on the desk and he was on the sofa, so she was looking down at him. He had the sense that she was giving him her undivided attention.

'You have a volunteer called Margaret Krukowski?'

'Yes.' She frowned. 'What's happened?'

'You didn't see the local news last night? Father Gruskin didn't call to tell you?'

'I haven't heard from Peter in the last few days and we didn't see any television last night. The electricity went off between six and eleven. All very dramatic. We made do with candles and a big fire. The women moaned, but actually I think they enjoyed the drama of it. By the time the lights came back on we were all in bed.'

'Margaret Krukowski was murdered,' Joe said. 'We're talking to everyone who knew her.'

Jane Cameron stared at him. Suddenly she seemed older, paler. 'I don't believe it. Who would want to kill Margaret?'

'That's why I'm here,' Joe said. 'I thought you might be able to help with that.'

There was a tap on the door and the woman he'd seen previously came in, carrying a tray with a pot of coffee, a plastic bottle of milk and two mugs. On a plate were some biscuits similar to those he'd already eaten in the guest house in Harbour Street. So Margaret had baked here too. Laurie set the tray on the desk. She looked at Jane and noticed the change in her. 'Are you okay?'

'Yes.' Then Jane realized that the woman was worried. 'Really, I'm fine. We'll come through and explain. Just give us a few minutes.'

Laurie looked furiously at Joe Ashworth, as if she blamed him for Jane's distress, and left the room.

Jane poured coffee, offered milk and sugar in a distracted way. 'I'm sorry,' she said at last. 'I can't take this in. Margaret seemed indestructible. She had more energy than anyone I knew. And we'll all miss her here so much. She was very much part of the family. She even brought Kate's children along with her sometimes. She still does occasionally, if we're running a special event. We had a winter fair a couple of weeks ago to raise some cash and Kate and the kids came along to that.' She gave a tight little grin. 'We're always strapped for money here. Always under threat of closure, and these events never seem to make as much as I hope.'

'Tell me about the Haven.'

'It's been running for about twenty years. I've been here for all that time, and Margaret started volunteering soon after I arrived. It's a place for women who need somewhere safe to stay on a temporary basis. Not just a refuge for victims of domestic violence, but women with problems of addiction, or who need support after leaving care or being discharged from psychiatric hospital or prison. We can take the kids of residents too, though we don't have any staying with us just now.' She looked up and smiled. 'I was working as a senior social worker in the city and took a six-month sabbatical to set the place up. I never left. A cop-out perhaps, but much less stressful in some ways. But it's a chance to work intensively with people and to build a community. I still stay in touch with ex-residents. We have reunions sometimes – loads of them turned up to the fair. It's brilliant to see what some of the women have achieved. I'll be here until I retire now – it's my life's work.' She smiled to show that she didn't take the thought, or herself, too seriously.

'And you live here?' Joe wondered what that must be like. Sal thought he gave every spare minute to his work. *Your soul belongs to the fat woman.* But Jane Cameron could have no escape from hers.

'I've got my own flat,' Jane said. 'The women are usually pretty good at respecting my privacy. And I have friends in town – they put me up when I need a break or a bit of culture.'

But no family of your own? No partner? Vera would have asked, but he couldn't bring himself to put the question.

'You must have problems over the years,' he said. 'Abusive husbands. Dealers. Pimps. Coming here and causing trouble.'

'All of those,' she replied. 'We've built up a very good relationship with the community police officers, who turn out to help when needed. But there's been no hassle recently. And there was no reason why anyone would target Margaret. She was a volunteer and her style was unobtrusive. She befriended the women once they arrived here. She had nothing to do with persuading them to come in the first place.'

Joe drank his coffee. 'I'll need to talk to your residents. Margaret might have confided in them, told them if anything was worrying her.' He looked up. 'She didn't mention anything of that sort to you?'

Jane shook her head. 'I learned from the start that Margaret was very private. She didn't talk about herself. If anything, I was the one who confided in *her*. I'll miss her.' She paused. 'Though when she was last here she did say that she'd like a chat sometime, that she could use some advice. I was busy and asked if next week would do.' The social worker looked up, horrified. 'I should have made time for her. All those hours she gave to us and I couldn't squeeze a few minutes from my schedule. But she seemed okay about the delay. At least, she said she was.'

'And you have no idea what she was concerned about?'

Jane shook her head sadly. 'Why don't you come and meet the others. Margaret might have talked to one of them. It's almost lunchtime and you can join us. I warn you that they'll be extremely upset. As I said, Margaret was like a family member. More like a mother or a grandmother to them than a volunteer. You can be sure that none of our residents killed Margaret.'

'I'm sorry,' Joe said. 'I can't rule anyone out at this stage.'

She gave a sudden wide smile. 'Not even me? Of course I appreciate the importance of an open mind, but really on this occasion it would be foolish to pursue that line of enquiry. As I said, none of our residents killed Margaret, Sergeant. The weather was so foul yesterday that nobody went out at all. They were here all afternoon. I can vouch for that.' She looked up at Joe, challenging him to contradict her, but he said nothing.

The residents were sitting in a large and untidy kitchen. It was warmer there – heat came from a chipped and grubby Aga. Children's paintings were stuck on the walls, the corners distorted with age. The dog had curled up in a basket near the stove. Mince pies cooled on a wire tray on the bench. Joe recognized Laurie, who'd been carting in the logs, and there were five others, ranging in age from a teenager – skinny and nervy with a pale, angelic face and long curly red hair – to an elderly woman who was stirring soup on the hob.

'This is Sergeant Ashworth, girls, and he's come to talk to us. I've suggested he join us for lunch.' Jane put rolls onto a plate and took a tub of margarine from the fridge.

Laurie was laying the table and looked up. 'What does he want?'

Joe stared back at her. 'Margaret was murdered yesterday.' He thought he might as well get this over. The soup smelled good, but he couldn't imagine sitting at the table with them, putting questions while they all ate. Vera might be an expert at cosy chats. He preferred a proper formality.

Nobody moved. It was as if they were struggling to take in the news. He saw tears running down the cheeks of the old woman by the stove as she stirred the pan. The girl with the long, red hair was frozen like a statue.

'Why the fuck would anyone kill Margaret?' It was Laurie, so tense and angry that Joe thought she might be capable of murder. Jane put an arm around her shoulder and held her very tight, part comfort, part restraint. Laurie continued, looking round the room: 'Well? She was amazing, wasn't she? Everyone here adored her.' She stared at Joe. 'You can't think we had anything to do with it?'

'I think you might be able to help us find her killer.'

There was silence in the room. Outside it seemed suddenly very dark and a gust of wind blew a branch against the window. Jane moved away from Laurie to switch on the light.

'Let's eat,' she said. 'You know how Margaret liked good food. We can eat and remember her, and tell Joe everything we know about her.'

So despite his intentions and the flurries of snow that threatened to cut him off from the outside world, Joe found himself sitting at the table, sharing a meal with seven women, listening to their memories of Margaret Krukowski.

It seemed that the nervy teenager, Emily, had arrived at the Haven two months before. 'Margaret seemed lovely, but I didn't really know her. We went for a walk one day, but that was just me moaning and her listening. You'd be better to talk to one of the others.' She didn't look at him when she spoke. Her voice was soft and well educated, and Joe wondered what she was doing living in a hostel. Didn't she have parents who would care for her? She looked as if she should still be at school. On one occasion her sleeve slipped back as she ate her soup and he saw cuts on her inner arm. She was a self-harmer. Hardly older than his Jessie.

The elderly woman who'd made the soup seemed either deaf or to live in a world of her own. She continued to cry, but her expression remained blank, and made him unsure whether this was grief for Margaret or a manifestation of chronic depression. Laurie spoke most, turning to the others occasionally, to check that they agreed with her. Jane didn't interrupt them.

'There are other volunteers, but they all have their own agendas. Like they're religious, or they want us to be grateful to them because they've dropped in a few kids' clothes. Or they want to get a job in social work, and helping out here looks good on their CV. But Margaret had none of that shit going on. She was here because she wanted to be, and she liked us and she wanted to make things better for us. By doing simple things like baking a cake for someone's birthday. Or more complicated stuff like sitting in on supervised access, so that some of us could get to see our kids without a social worker having to be there all the time.'

'When was the last time you saw her?' Joe thought this was all very well, and Vera would be interested, but now he needed some facts.

'The day before yesterday.' This was Laurie again, looking round before she answered to make sure she'd got it right.

'How did she get here?' This time the question was directed at Jane Cameron and she answered.

'On the bus usually. Sometimes I picked her up, if I was going into town. But she was quite independent. She had her bus pass, she said. She might as well use it.'

'And her last visit?'

'Someone gave her a lift.' Laurie jumped in before Jane could answer. 'I was working in the garden and a car dropped her off at the gate.'

'Did you see the driver?' Joe thought this was significant. Kate Dewar hadn't mentioned bringing Margaret to the Haven, and any other contact might be important.

Laurie frowned. 'No. They didn't get out of the car. But it was a silver Golf. Not a new one. X-reg.'

'Are you sure?' Joe never noticed cars and, in his experience, women were even less likely to be aware of them.

'Oh yes, Sergeant.' For the first time Laurie grinned. 'I'm an expert. All my previous offences have been vehicle-related.'

Jane invited him to stay for tea and mince pies, but he looked out of the window at the snow still covering much of the ground and said he should leave. He'd just stood up when Laurie spoke again. 'Someone should make sure that Dee knows Margaret is dead.'

'Dee?' Now all he wanted to do was get out of this place. In this weather the countryside held less appeal. He wasn't sure he'd want to live in Holypool after all.

'Dee Robson, one of our former residents.' Jane walked with him past the Christmas tree and into the hall so that they wouldn't be overheard, and they continued the conversation by the front door. 'She never settled here. Not her fault perhaps. She has minor learning difficulties that were never picked up at school, a chaotic childhood.' Jane gave a brief grin. 'We have very few rules here, but Dee broke every one of them. Booze, men, aggression – you name it. In the end the other residents forced her out. But Margaret developed a special relationship with her and continued to mentor Dee even when she left. She didn't judge her. I'm not quite sure how Dee will cope without her.'

'Where does Dee live now?'

'In Mardle, in a flat in Percy Street.' Jane opened the door. 'You will get someone to tell her, won't you Sergeant, and check that she's okay? She'll have a social worker. Some poor soul trying to keep her safe.'

He nodded and wondered why Jane's charity didn't run to *her* telling Dee about Margaret's killing. Outside it seemed a little milder and the snow was now soft and damp. As he turned back to the house he saw Emily, the pale teenager, staring back at him through an upstairs window. He was reminded of a children's fairy tale, a princess imprisoned in a tower.

Chapter Thirteen

Vera had found a cafe in the centre of Mardle on the other side of the street from the health centre. A new place with a hissing coffee machine and fancy buns. She'd already been into the medical centre and had been told by an unhelpful receptionist that Margaret Krukowski wasn't a patient and that she couldn't tell the inspector if, or where, Margaret had been treated for cancer. Vera drank tea and ate a sandwich, feeling virtuous because she chose wholemeal bread. When she finished eating she got Holly on the phone. 'I need to track down Margaret's GP. Can you sort that for me, Hol?'

And Holly, still mellow because she'd be all over the local media, agreed without a murmur.

Now the lunchtime rush was over and nobody seemed to mind Vera sitting there. The floor was swimming with slush brought in on people's boots. She was waiting for Joe Ashworth and found herself grinning, wondering how he'd got on in the women's refuge. Had they eaten him alive?

He came in, his collar turned up against the weather. He always looked smart. A call-out at four in the morning and he'd turn up with a freshly ironed shirt and a suit. Something to do with the Protestant work ethic? Or a wife with nothing better to do than look after her man? Vera called for a fresh pot of tea and a couple of scones and ordered her thoughts back to the matter in hand.

'Anything useful?'

'Aye, I think so.' Joe poured tea. 'Margaret worked at the Haven the morning before she died. Somebody gave her a lift there. One of the women saw her get out of the car.'

'But didn't see the driver . . .' Vera knew Ashworth. He'd not have been able to save the good news, if he had any.

'I wondered if it might have been the priest,' Joe said. 'The church is involved with the place.'

'Aye, maybe.' But Peter Gruskin hadn't mentioned it and he didn't seem the sort to hide his good works.

'The lass did see the car, though. Old silver Golf. X-reg.' Joe cut open his scone and buttered it tidily. Vera had already eaten hers. 'She's an ex-offender car nut. Done for TWOC, driving without insurance, reckless driving. So I reckon she knows what she's talking about.'

Vera tried to remember if she'd seen a car like that in Harbour Street, but it didn't ring any bells. George Enderby, the publisher's rep, would drive something newer and more efficient. She'd always supposed that the Renault parked outside the guest house belonged to Kate Dewar. 'Check out what Gruskin drives.'

'There's another woman they think we should talk to.' Joe wiped the crumbs from his fingers with a paper napkin. 'Dee Robson. I've checked her out too. A record that goes back twenty years. D&D. Soliciting. Shoplifting. Lives in a flat in Percy Street, but mostly to be found in the Coble drinking away her benefit, when she can't find a punter daft enough to buy her a drink.'

'I think I saw her.' Vera remembered the woman in the fishnets, and the jeers that followed her out of the pub. 'What could Margaret have to do with her?'

'She used to stay in the Haven and Margaret befriended her. Still acted as a kind of mentor, once Dee got thrown out of the refuge for getting pissed and taking men back to the place.'

'Margaret was ill,' Vera said suddenly, realizing she hadn't yet shared this information with Joe. It had been playing on her mind since the post-mortem, and even as she'd been listening to him. 'Possibly terminally ill. Bowel cancer. Paul Keating thought she might not have survived very much longer anyway. I'm not sure if she'd seen a doctor. But if she knew . . . She was religious, wasn't she? Maybe there was an idea of setting her affairs in order.' She slapped her hands on the table in front of her. 'I need to know where she'd been before she got onto the Metro that day.' She stood up suddenly.

'Where are we going?' He hadn't finished his tea.

'To see Dee Robson. Alcoholic and occasional sex worker.' Vera stamped across the wet floor to the counter and ordered a bag of cakes to take out.

The snow in the street had turned to a grey mess and it was drizzling, rain mixed with sleet. The flat was in a Sixties box, built at the end of a street of 1930s houses, and Dee lived at the top on the third floor. It wasn't as grim as an inner-city tower block, but there was graffiti all over the stairwell and the inevitable smell of piss and damp concrete. The door looked as if someone had recently tried to batter it in. An over-enthusiastic client or something more sinister? Joe knocked. Nothing. Vera banged on the door with the palm of her hand and shouted, 'Come on, pet. Let us in. We're not here to hurt you.'

There was a movement behind the door, but still it didn't open. Vera pulled Margaret's keys from her bag and tried the one they hadn't yet identified. The door opened. *One mystery solved, then.* Dee Robson stood just inside, legs apart, braced for a fight. When she saw Vera she spoke with loud and righteous indignation.

'Hey, lady, you can't just let yourself into my home!'

Vera took no notice and looked around her. If she hadn't known better she'd have thought the flat was derelict. There was the same smell as in the stairwell. Mould grew where the walls and the window frames met. There was no carpet on the floor, which was sticky underfoot. Through an open door she saw the bedroom. Here there was a stained rug and a double mattress covered with a shiny pink quilt. In there Dee must entertain the men, so desperate or so drunk that they'd been persuaded home with her.

They stood for a moment in the hall, staring at each other. 'Well?' the woman demanded. 'Who the fuck are you?' She was wearing tracksuit bottoms and a hoodie and it smelled as if she'd been sleeping in them for days. She hadn't cleaned off the make-up of the night before and the mascara had run down her cheeks. She'd been crying.

'You've heard about Margaret,' Vera said.

Dee nodded. 'They were talking about it in the

Coble last night. Then it was on the news this morning. You're the police.' Not a question.

She wandered into the living room and they followed her. Again the floor was bare. A Formica kitchen table stood against one wall, with two plastic stools at each side. There was an easy chair, the shape of springs visible through the orange fabric, and in the corner on the floor stood a small flat-screen television.

'Margaret gave you the telly.' Vera nodded towards it.

'Aye. She said she didn't watch it much anyway, and I'd have gone crazy on my own in this place without one.' Still the woman was wary. 'I didn't nick it, if that's what you're thinking.'

'We're here to ask about Margaret. She was your friend, and you might be able to help us find out who killed her.' Vera kept her voice gentle.

Joe Ashworth was hovering just inside the door as if he was worried he might catch something. He must have been in hundreds of scuzzy houses since joining the police service, but the way some people lived still horrified him.

Just wait until your Jessie becomes a student. Vera gave a quick secret smile.

'Have you got tea, Dee?' Vera asked brightly. 'Milk? I'm gasping for a cuppa and we've brought cakes. I never go visiting empty-handed.'

The woman looked at her as if she hadn't understood a word.

'Off you go, Joe. Kettle on. And if you can't find what you want, nip out to the shop. Dee and me are going to have a chat.'

'There's milk!' Dee seemed suddenly to come to

life. 'Margaret brought it with her when she came to visit. She always brings milk. She knows I forget.'

'When did she last call round?' Vera asked. She landed on a stool. Dee took the easy chair. In the kitchen there was the sound of a tap being switched on. Joe would be scrubbing the mugs.

'Yesterday lunchtime. She said she was on her way into town.'

'Did she say where she was going?' Vera tried to imagine the elegant, well-dressed woman Joe had described from the train, sitting in this room, drinking tea from the stained mugs and talking to Dee.

'No, just that she had business to sort out.'

Vera supposed that could mean anything. A visit to a solicitor? An accountant?

'How did she seem?' Vera asked. 'Quiet? Upset? Angry?'

But Dee just shook her head, as if another person's feelings were beyond her.

Joe came in then, carrying the tea. Vera put the bag of cakes on the table and tore open the paper so that Dee could see inside. Joe looked at the stool, but chose to lean against the door instead.

'And before that,' Vera prompted, 'had you seen Margaret recently?'

'Last week.' Dee's mouth was full of cream sponge. Joe looked away. *Fastidious*, Vera thought. *That was the word to describe him*. 'We went shopping in town.' She seemed suddenly excited, and Vera thought sadly that the trip into Newcastle could have been the highlight of Dee's month.

'Margaret took you shopping?'

'Aye, she said I needed a proper jacket or I'd catch

my death. The church has a fund. Mostly for the lasses at the Haven – extras they might not be able to afford – but Margaret said there was no reason why I shouldn't get some of it.'

'Why did you leave the Haven?' This was Joe, not able to help himself, accusing. He'd bring back the workhouse, given half a chance.

Dee muttered something that Vera could only just make out, about being stuck in the middle of nowhere, and a cow called Jane who picked on her.

'Tell me about going shopping,' Vera said.

Dee's face brightened again. 'We went in on the Metro. Had our dinner in a caff. I had fish and chips. Margaret only wanted a sandwich. We bought the jacket in New Look. Dead smart.' She launched into a description of the coat. Given any encouragement, she'd have brought it out to show them.

Vera allowed her a couple of minutes, then interrupted. 'Was it just shopping? You didn't go anywhere else? An office? Or perhaps Margaret met someone she knew?'

A pause. Great concentration. 'She didn't meet anyone, but she saw someone.'

'Tell us what happened, Dee.' Vera reached out for a vanilla slice. 'No stories, mind, just the truth.'

'We were walking down Northumberland Street and there was this man on the other side of the road. Margaret told me to wait where I was and she ran after him. But he was faster than her and she couldn't catch him up.'

'What did he look like, this man?' Vera wasn't sure how much faith to put in Dee's account. She certainly couldn't imagine the woman in a witness box. And a vanilla slice was tricky to eat without a plate and a knife. She turned to Joe. 'Is there a knife in the kitchen? I'll have cream all over me if I don't cut this.'

Dee shrugged. 'Don't know. I didn't really see him. I wasn't looking. He just ran off when Margaret saw him.'

'He was young, was he? If he ran fast?'

Dee thought again. 'He was faster than Margaret, but she was an old lady. Most people would be faster than her.'

'And you can't tell me anything at all about him?'

'Like I said, Margaret just ran across Northumberland Street, shouting for me to stay where I was. She wasn't gone very long. I asked her who the guy was, but she wouldn't tell me. I thought we might stay out for our tea, but she said it was time to go home.' Dee looked at her. Panda eyes over the rim of her mug. 'Margaret was out of breath after running. I thought for a minute she was going to die.'

Ashworth came back with a kitchen knife and Vera cut the cake into bite-sized pieces. Nobody spoke. Footsteps clattered down the stairs outside the flat. Below a door banged shut.

'Where were you yesterday afternoon, Dee?' Vera kept her voice quiet, almost uninterested. No pressure. 'After Margaret left you.'

'Out.' Her mouth shut tight like a trap.

'We just need to know, Dee.' Vera leaned forward towards her. 'No one's going to be cross if you were in the Coble all afternoon. None of our business. But we need to know.'

'I was in the Coble,' Dee said. 'Then I met someone.'

'A man?'

She nodded.

'Where did you go with him? Did you bring him back here?'

'We went to his place.'

'And where was that?' Vera thought the woman was mad. A danger to herself. She allowed some of her anxiety through: 'You shouldn't go off with men you don't know, pet. It's not safe.'

'I did know him. At least I've seen him about.'

'And his name?'

'Jason.' Dee was behaving like a sulky child. 'I'd never heard his second name. And I don't know where his place was.'

'Somewhere in Mardle?'

'No. We went on the Metro. I can't remember.' She looked up and suddenly seemed very young. 'I was a bit pissed.' She paused for a beat. 'He bought me a ticket!' As if that made everything all right.

'Where did you get out?' Vera asked. 'Which Metro station?'

'I don't know! Somewhere on the way to town.' As if, once away from Mardle and its immediate surroundings, she was in alien territory. Vera realized that she probably couldn't read.

'And afterwards,' Joe said, 'what happened then?' He'd pushed himself away from the door to join in the conversation. Dee looked at him properly for the first time and appeared to like what she saw. After that her replies were directed at him.

'I came back. Spent some of the money he'd given me. Bought some chips and went back to the pub.'

'Did he come back with you?'

'Nah!' She was indignant. 'I thought that was the idea, that he'd spend the evening with me, but he just let me out of his flat and I had to find the Metro station myself. It was snowing. Fucking freezing.'

'What time was that?' Joe asked.

'Dunno. It was dark, though.'

'And you came all the way to Mardle on the Metro?' Joe asked the question; Vera held her breath.

'Nah, the train stopped at Partington. Because of the weather. We all had to get out and get the bus. It took ages to come. Total fucking waste of time for a few quid.'

'Which carriage were you in, Dee?'

She looked at Joe as if he was mad. 'What?'

'On the Metro? Were you near the front or the back?'

'I can't remember! Why?'

'Because that's where Margaret was stabbed,' Vera said quietly. 'On the Metro that was stopped by the snow.'

'I didn't see her!' Dee turned to her, horrified. 'If I'd seen her I might have saved her.'

Chapter Fourteen

Holly tracked down Margaret's GP to a practice in Gosforth. An efficient receptionist said that Margaret had visited a couple of times in the last month, but not on the afternoon of her death. If they wanted more details they'd have to make an appointment to come into the surgery and talk to the doctor. When Holly rang Vera to tell her, expecting at least to be thanked for her efforts, the boss only seemed disappointed.

'Oh well, it can't be helped, but I really need to know what the woman was doing in Gosforth yesterday.' There was a pause before Vera added, 'How's it going there otherwise?'

'I think the press conference went okay, but I'm going bog-eyed here, boss. It's a nightmare trying to collate all the info we've got through so far, but I'm pretty well up to date. I don't think we'll get another surge of calls until after the six-thirty news.'

It was already late afternoon. After the buzz of the press conference Holly had spent the next couple of hours in the police station, plotting names onto large pieces of graph paper. She'd tried to map the location of passengers in the Metro carriage electronically, but in the end it worked best to spread the graph paper over a double desk, each large square marking either a seat or a space. Still there were gaps. Some of the people Joe had remembered – the smooching kids and the partying businessmen – had failed to come forward. Other passengers had seen Margaret get onto the train at Gosforth, but hadn't noticed if she'd been followed onto the platform.

There was a moment of silence on the end of the line, so Holly wondered if she'd get a bollocking again for complaining. She felt every contact with Vera Stanhope was like an approach to a large and unpredictable dog. You never knew whether it would lick you to death or take a chunk out of your leg.

'Do you want a break from the desk work?'

'I wouldn't mind!' Holly regretted the words almost as soon as they were spoken. The trouble with Vera was that she took advantage. Holly might be sent off on a wild goose chase that had no relevance at all to the investigation.

'Have a word with Professor Michael Craggs,' Vera said. 'I can't see him as any sort of suspect, but he's on the edge of the investigation. He stays regularly at the guest house where Margaret lived and worked, and he might be able to provide an alibi of sorts for Malcolm Kerr.'

'And who's Kerr?' Again Holly wondered if she might have missed something, some detail of the briefing, and waited to be yelled at for not paying attention. Vera always made her feel like a school kid.

'Sorry, Hol. I should have explained. Kerr's a boatman. He has that scruffy yard close to the harbour and lives in Percy Street, just behind the Metro line. Margaret Krukowski worked for him when she was a young woman. Kerr turned up at Kate Dewar's place this morning in a bit of a state. She had the impression that he and Margaret might have been lovers. Anyway, he claims to have been out collecting samples of the North Sea with Craggs when Margaret was stabbed. So check out the alibi, but see if Craggs can tell us anything new about our victim too. At the moment we still have no family and no close friends, and the professor has been a regular at the Harbour Street guest house for years.'

Holly replaced the receiver, shell-shocked, because she'd had an apology from the boss, and checked out the number for the university. She was told that the professor wasn't in the building today, but was working with a group of undergraduates at the Dove Marine Laboratory in Cullercoats. She collected a pool car and set out for the seaside.

Cullercoats was on the coast south from Mardle, a pretty cove between the wide sweeps of beach at Tynemouth and Whitley Bay. On the front a couple of restaurants and a wine bar looked out to the sea. In the summer it was a place for eating and drinking at tables on the pavement, watching the kids play on the beach. Holly had spent happy evenings in the village with friends. Now, as the light was fading and cold rain blew in from the sea, it was grey and dismal. She parked in a side street and crossed the main road that followed the coast. A light marked the end of the pier. The occasional car splashed through the icy puddles, but nobody else was out.

The laboratory was a red-brick villa with a modern extension, built almost on the beach. Inside, the students were calling it a day, pulling on outdoor clothes and packing equipment into bags. Craggs was a gentle Lancastrian in his sixties. Holly thought he looked too old and heavy to be clambering around in small boats. She found the group in a small room kitted out with lab benches and metal stools and he stood at the front, calling goodbye to the young people, wishing them a happy Christmas. Holly felt a pang of regret. She'd been a graduate entrant into the police service. She'd enjoyed her time at university. Perhaps, after all, she'd have been better suited to life as an academic. Then reality kicked in: *Nah, you'd have been bored rigid.*

He looked up and saw her. 'Hello! Anything I can do?' He was friendly and sounded genuinely helpful. But Holly seldom found older men unfriendly. They were flattered by the attention of a young, attractive woman, even when they discovered what she did for a living. Now the room was clear of students and she identified herself.

'What's this about?' No anxiety. He turned to glance at a row of test tubes behind him.

'You haven't heard about Margaret Krukowski?' But perhaps, after all, it wasn't so hard to believe. The students wouldn't be interested in the death of a woman who would appear to them impossibly old. They'd be gearing up for the end of term – this was obviously their last seminar before leaving for the Christmas holidays – and the main preoccupation for everyone seemed to be the weather. And even now Craggs seemed focused on his research. He moved his attention to the microscope on the table in front of him as if he longed to get back to it. He frowned. 'Kate Dewar's Margaret? No. What's happened?'

'She was murdered,' Holly said. 'Yesterday afternoon. Stabbed while she was in the Metro on her way home.'

She'd expected an expression of grief, horror. Even strangers seemed to think a response was needed when they heard of a violent death. But Craggs's reaction seemed dramatic. The colour appeared to drain from his face and he sat suddenly on the stool by his side.

'Poor Margaret. What a terrible way to die.'

'You knew her well?'

He took a while to answer. 'I've been researching in the waters off Mardle since I was an undergraduate, and I've stayed at the guest house in Harbour Street at least one night a month since it opened. Kate and Margaret felt almost like a second family. Kate must be devastated. Even now that she has a new partner, I'm not sure how she'll cope there without Margaret.' A pause. 'Do you know who killed her? I'm not sure how you think I could help.' He sat with his elbows on the bench. Holly saw that his blue rib-knit sweater had been neatly darned. There was a splash of something that might have been egg on the front of it. He looked like an absent-minded professor from children's stories.

'We're talking to all the regulars at the guest house.'

'Of course.'

'When did you last see her?' Holly took a seat herself. They faced each other across the bench. There was a background smell of chemicals and something organic.

'At breakfast yesterday. She cleared my table as usual.'

'How did she seem?'

'Just as she always seemed.' Craggs played with his wedding ring, turning it on his finger. 'Polite, helpful, cheerful. I had an early breakfast because I had a full day ahead of me. If there were other guests, they hadn't appeared by the time I left.'

'You didn't have any impression then that she was upset or anxious.'

'No, but then I probably wouldn't have noticed. We don't often notice the people who look after us, do we? Though we'd miss them if they weren't there.'

Holly thought he was a strange man. She wondered if he was quite as sharp as a modern professor should be. She couldn't imagine him fighting his corner with university politics or pulling in overseas students prepared to pay high fees. 'We're having problems tracing her family,' she said. 'Did she mention anyone to you?'

Again he took a while to consider before he answered.

'All the years that I've been staying at Harbour Street I only once had a real conversation with Margaret. She had a flat upstairs and rarely came into the visitors' areas except for work. But one evening we came into the house together. She'd crossed the road from the church, I think, and I was chilled after a day on the water. I invited her to join me for a drink, and we sat together in that dark, gloomy lounge.' He paused. 'I probably talked about my work, my family. I've been married for forty years and have grandchildren of whom I'm ridiculously proud. Happy people can sound very smug, and I thought suddenly that she wasn't happy at all. That the quiet efficiency was a show, and underneath there was a terrible desperation. I asked her about her husband. Did she ever see him? "Oh no," she said. "He's long gone." Then she said something very odd. "Secrets are all I have left." I didn't ask her what she meant. I could see that she wouldn't tell me.'

Holly made detailed notes. Some of it didn't mean much to her, but Vera had been in the guest house and it would all mean more to her. She turned back to the professor. 'You spent yesterday with Malcolm Kerr?'

'Yes. He took me out to Coquet Island. My research is into water temperature and how small changes can have an impact on microorganisms and therefore affect things further up the food chain. We collected samples. It's meticulous work – some might say tedious. It took until the middle of the afternoon.'

'You don't have a student to do the fieldwork for you?' Holly had once gone out with someone doing a PhD, who was always complaining about doing the donkey work for his supervisor.

Craggs gave a little laugh. 'I'm what you'd call a control freak. I like to be in charge of my own data.' He continued to twist the ring on his finger. 'Besides, I enjoy being on the water. That was what drew me to the subject in the first place. A passion for ecology and for open spaces. I'm due to retire next year. I'm not quite sure what I'll do with myself. Write a book, perhaps, like all retired academics.'

'You must know Malcolm Kerr well then?'

'We've certainly spent a lot of time together since I began the research. I started working with him when I was doing my Master's, and his father was in charge of the business then. Malcolm was a bit of a tearaway in those days and could lose his temper in a second. He came in a couple of mornings with a black eye after scrapping with other lads in the Coble.' Craggs smiled. 'He settled down, as most of us do when we find a good woman, and it's only recently that things have gone wrong for him. His wife left and he lost his house and doesn't get to see his children much. Started drinking more than was good for him. Some days he's been turning up for work looking as if he's slept in the clothes he was wearing. He lost his job as coxswain of the lifeboat because the crew thought he'd become unreliable. He's still an excellent boatman, though.'

Holly wondered if any of this was relevant. 'What time did you and Kerr get back to Mardle yesterday afternoon?'

'Three-ish. I'd hoped to be out longer, but the weather forecast was awful. Originally I was going to spend another night in Harbour Street, but I decided to get home. We live in the Tyne Valley and it's a bit of a trek.' He looked at his watch again. 'I'm sorry, I really should get there now. It's the grandchildren's school play, and I promised that I'd be back in time for that.'

Holly walked to the door with him and waited for him to lock up. His vehicle was a dirty 4x4 parked on the slipway. By now it was dark. 'What car does Malcolm Kerr drive?' The question casual and last-minute, as if it didn't really matter. Joe had mentioned that Margaret had been dropped off at the Haven in an old car, the day before her death. Showing off with perhaps the one piece of concrete information that they'd had all day. Holly knew that

Joe would check with DVLA, but it'd be good to get the information before he did.

Craggs paused for a moment, his hand on the car door. 'A battered old Golf. His wife got the new Toyota. That was another source of bitterness.'

In the darkness Holly grinned. Margaret had been driven to the Haven in a Golf. 'How come Malcolm Kerr got such a bad deal out of the divorce?'

She sensed, rather than saw, the shrug. 'Something to do with the fact that her new man is a lawyer?' He paused, as if wondering if he should go on. 'Or that she once accused Malcolm of hitting her.'

'Had he hit her?'

Another shrug. 'I don't know? Perhaps. He's not the most stable of men. With a drink inside him, he might be capable of it.'

Back in her car Holly phoned Joe Ashworth and Vera, but neither of them was picking up. She felt a stab of the usual paranoia about Joe and Vera – that they were a team and she was deliberately excluded – but tried to ignore it. She left a message for each, saying that she thought she'd traced the identity of the person who'd dropped Margaret at the Haven on the day before her death. Even inside the car she could smell food cooking in an Italian restaurant nearby and felt suddenly hungry, but refused to give in to temptation. It was easy to put on weight during a major inquiry – most detectives lived on a diet of takeaway pizzas and chocolate – and soon she'd be home for Christmas, and her mother would feed her up too.

She drove back to Kimmerston. In the police

station colleagues were in a meeting room gathered around a television set, waiting to see the coverage of the press briefing. She arrived just in time for the opening titles and there was a cheer when there was a shot of her at the top of the programme, plus lots of ribald comments when it was over. Holly thought she'd handled it well. She'd come over as professional and hadn't given anything away. As soon as the piece on the press conference was over, the phones began to ring.

Chapter Fifteen

Vera and Joe stood in the entrance of the flats in Percy Street waiting for a shower to pass. Across the road someone was playing a CD of Christmas songs, so loud that the music spilled out onto the street. The Pogues followed by Slade. Vera wondered what Dee Robson would do on Christmas Day, and if Father Gruskin would be a good Christian and invite her into his home. The notion was so unlikely, so incongruous, that it made her laugh out loud. She shook her head to dismiss it and then decided that the old ladies in the congregation would be fighting among themselves to give their priest Christmas dinner.

'What do you think?' Joe stamped his feet and put his hands in his coat pocket.

'I'm not sure our Dee will manage on her own without Margaret to support her.' Vera knew that wasn't what he'd meant. 'Poor lass. Perhaps the Haven would take her back. We should give social services a ring.'

Joe looked impatient. Perhaps he thought her sympathy for Dee misplaced; the woman had disgusted him. 'What should we do now?'

'The evening briefing, then I'm going home.' Suddenly she felt tired and old. 'I need a hot bath and an early night in my own bed.' She looked at him hopefully. 'Fancy calling in for a quick bite on your way back to the family? There'll be something in the freezer. Joanna dropped in a lamb casserole last week. Their own meat. It'll soon heat through. And it'll give us a chance to talk about the investigation in the warm.'

He stood for a moment, his hands in his pockets. 'It's not on my way home. And your house is never warm.' But she could tell he was weakening.

She drove ahead of him and had a fire lit before he arrived. The casserole had already been in the microwave and was now in a pan to finish it off. She knew he'd smell it as soon as he walked through the door. There were bottles of Wylam beer on the table under the window. She'd grown up in this house in the hills. Her mother had died here when Vera was still a child and she'd nursed Hector, her father – the man who still taunted her from the grave – until his death. The house was impractical and mucky, but she knew she'd never move. She hoped that she'd die here too.

In the kitchen she reran the briefing in her head. It had been Holly's show. She'd been full of the information that Malcolm Kerr drove an old Golf and that he'd been back in Mardle at around three o'clock. Kerr had no alibi for the murder, then. And if he had given Margaret a lift to the Haven, he'd lied to Vera when he said he'd not seen her to talk to recently.

Joe came in without knocking. Vera nodded towards the beer. 'You could have just the one to keep me company.' Another ritual. Joe and her hippy neighbours were the only people who ever came into her house. She always offered them beer.

They ate the casserole with spoons from bowls on their knees. It was too cold to eat at the table away from the fire. A loaf stood on a board on the coffee table between them. They drank the beer straight from the bottle. Vera opened a second before they started discussing the case. Joe cleared the crockery into the kitchen – she would have left them on the floor. He came back shivering. 'You don't need a fridge out there. Have you never thought of getting central heating?'

'Maybe when I retire. No point when I'm never here.' Hector had thought central heating sapped a person's strength.

'So,' she said. 'Margaret Krukowski. How far have we got?' She thought this was the happiest she could be. An intricate case and a beer. And someone to share her ideas with: Joe Ashworth, whose wife had ambitions for him and who could move with promotion at any time. Was it only possible truly to enjoy something if you knew there was a danger that it might be taken away?

'Margaret Krukowski.' Ashworth repeated the name like the chorus of a song. 'Kept herself to herself. Why? Because she valued her privacy or because she had something to hide?'

'George Enderby, that rep who stays at the guest house, thinks she was a spy during the Cold War.'

'Nah!' Joe shook his head. 'This is domestic, isn't it? Personal. Or some random, delusional crazy on the train. Not political.'

'Aye,' she said. 'I think you're right.' But she didn't believe in the random loony theory, either. He'd been right first time. This was personal.

'We know that Malcolm Kerr, the boatman, hasn't been telling us the whole truth.' Vera had liked Kerr. She could understand his drinking and his desperation. But she disapproved of witnesses who weren't straight with her. 'He drives a Golf that matches the description of the car that dropped Margaret at the Haven. And he got back to Mardle earlier than he told me. The discrepancy in timing could have been a genuine mistake, but there was something going on between him and Margaret. Why not tell me that he'd given her a lift that day, otherwise?'

'Should we bring him in?' Joe finished his beer and set the bottle on the floor. 'He might be a bit more forthcoming in a formal interview, under caution?'

Vera thought of the man she'd met in the shed in the boatyard. In the bare interview room of the police station he'd be angry and frightened and he would shut down completely. And she didn't want lawyers involved at this stage. 'Let's leave it for a day,' she said. 'I'll try him again on home territory.'

They sat in silence. Vera wondered if she needed anything else to drink and decided against it. 'I'd like you to go and see the priest,' she said. 'Peter Gruskin. Margaret was a regular at the church and he's a trustee at the Haven. He didn't take to me. Maybe he just doesn't like strong women. If there was anything going on between Margaret and Kerr, there'd have been gossip in a place like Mardle. He'd have heard about it. All those old women bitching as they made tea and polished the silver. Make it clear to him that he's doing no favours to Margaret by keeping her secrets now.'

Joe nodded.

'And we'll send Holly into Kate Dewar's, shall we?' Vera felt that she was on a roll. 'She'll be a fresh pair of eyes in the place. I can't remember when George Enderby was leaving. If he's still there, she can talk to him too.'

Joe nodded again and held his hands to the fire. He shot a look at the clock that stood on the mantelpiece. Hector's clock, which had always been there.

'Off you go,' Vera said, making a shooing motion with her hands. 'I'm ready for a bath and my bed. I'll catch up with you at the briefing tomorrow morning.' She got to her feet.

Joe seemed almost reluctant to leave, but he stood up too. 'Holly's press conference will have been broadcast again tonight on the late local news. Perhaps something will have come out of that.'

She gave a little laugh. 'Our Holly as the face of Northumbria Police. She'll love that.' She opened the door to see him out. The rain had stopped and the sky was clear. The stars seemed very bright.

At the briefing the following morning Vera felt full of energy and ready to spread goodwill around the team. 'Holly had a very productive meeting with Mike Craggs, Professor of Marine Biology at Newcastle University. She filled us in yesterday about Kerr's car and the time that the boat got back into Mardle, but I've been thinking that I'd like a more general overview of the conversation.'

Holly got up to take centre stage at the whiteboard, and Vera thought that the young woman was loving this – it was what she was made for, to stand in front of a team and spread wisdom and light. *If I had any sense I'd be grooming* her *for stardom, getting* her *ready for promotion. Then they might leave Joe here.*

Vera thought that she could never be that cunning, when Holly's words suddenly caught her attention. 'Repeat that, would you, Hol?'

Holly looked up, startled. 'Prof. Craggs said that the only time he had a real conversation with Margaret was one evening in the lounge at the guest house. He'd bought her a drink. They were on their own and Craggs asked her about her husband. She said he was long gone and told him that all she had left were secrets.'

'Margaret Krukowski and her bloody secrets.' Vera wondered if there *were* any secrets. Perhaps Margaret spoke about the past like that just to make herself interesting. Perhaps they were the fantasies of a lonely, elderly woman. She looked up. 'Sorry, Hol. Carry on.'

Holly seemed taken aback. Vera thought it was good to surprise the team with a change of tone occasionally. 'After the press conference was shown on television yesterday evening, we had more calls from people who were on the Metro. A few could remember being in the front carriage. There was one guy who was in the group of businessmen Joe remembered. They'd all been to a Christmas lunch. The witness didn't see anything, but he's given us some more names to check. And the lasses, who Joe saw with their boyfriends, got in touch through their parents. They're from St Anne's, that posh school in Jesmond. They got out at Gosforth and they didn't notice Margaret Krukowski.'

'Thanks, Holly. Good work. Get someone round to take a statement from both.'

Holly beamed.

Good God, Vera thought. *Is this all it takes to keep the team happy? A bit of praise?* She thought Holly was like the scruffy collie that belonged to her neighbours. All it needed was a bowl of food at the end of the day and a pat on the head from its owners. She nodded for Joe Ashworth to get to his feet, to talk about the Haven and Margaret's relationship with the women there. And all the time Vera was trying to get inside the head of the victim. Elegant, from a smart family, yet content to live alone in a tiny flat in the roof of a guest house in a rundown coastal town. Hadn't Margaret wanted more than that? If not a family of her own, then work to satisfy her. Vera couldn't imagine life without her work. It was what defined her.

She realized that Joe had finished speaking and that the team was staring at her. She stood up, still feeling somehow that she was standing in Margaret's narrow shoes, balancing on the small heels. She shook her head to clear the image.

'Anyone heard of Dee Robson? Probable alcoholic and sex worker?' Charlie raised a hand and nodded wearily. Vera continued. 'She lives in the flats on Percy Street. Margaret met Dee when she had a short stay at the Haven and had been keeping an eye on her ever since. Dee was in the Metro when Margaret was killed. I don't see her as a murderer, and she looks so distinctive that someone would have mentioned her by now, if she was in the same carriage. But it's another link and we need to check. Dee claims to have been with a bloke in his flat that afternoon. Charlie, put the word out and see if we can trace him.'

Charlie nodded, even more wearily.

'Holly, I want you in Mardle again. Have a chat to Kate Dewar. She spent all those years living with Margaret and I can't believe she knows as little as she says. Maybe she thinks she's protecting the woman's memory in some way. Joe, you do the priest. Same thing. Charlie, I know the CCTV on the platform at Gosforth Metro station was covered by snow, but see if we can find a trace of Malcolm Kerr's Golf anywhere en route from Mardle to Gosforth that afternoon. Craggs said that they got in from Coquet Island at three-ish, so Kerr would have had plenty of time to drive there, to get on the train after Margaret. And he'd have needed to go back later to pick up his car. No Metros were running, so check local taxi firms.' She paused for breath. 'And while you're at it, let's see if we can find out where Dee got onto the train. Either her knowledge of geography away from Mardle is non-existent or she's playing games with us. If you can look at CCTV for earlier in the afternoon you might also find the man she was with.'

They got up and started to wander out. Vera called Holly back. They stood alone in the big briefing room. 'Before you head out to Mardle, Hol, do me a favour. Give social services a ring and ask them to check on Dee Robson. I can never talk to them for more than a minute before I lose my temper.' Which was something to do with the way they'd trusted Hector to look after *her* when her mam died. 'Margaret used to keep an eye on Dee, and I don't think the poor lass will manage in that flat on her own. She's a danger to herself and her neighbours.'

Holly looked as if she thought the inspector was a little bit mad, but Vera was used to that. 'A favour, Hol,' she repeated, losing patience. 'Is that okay?'

Holly nodded and left the room without speaking.

Chapter Sixteen

It was the last day of the school term. Non-uniform day. Chloe left home first in a long black sweater and jeans. Ryan looked super-cool in the jacket he'd bought with his last wage packet from Kerr. Kate thought the boatman must be paying him too much, but liked her son's style. She saw him as he was on his way out and asked quietly if it was a good idea to wear it to school. 'You might lose it, or it could get damaged.'

He responded with one of his volcanic outbursts. 'For fuck's sake, Mam, get off my case. I'm not a kid. I can decide for myself what I'm going to wear.' The sudden temper reminded her of Rob and for a moment she shrank from him. Then he saw that he'd scared her and was smiling and apologetic. 'Look, nobody at school would steal anything from me, and I'll look after it.' He kissed her before he went through the door. *Teenagers*, she thought. *They're like toddlers with hormones.*

The house was quiet. The only visitor booked in before Christmas was George Enderby for one night on his way south from Scotland. Kate Dewar felt lighter, somehow frivolous, as if she'd shed a burden of responsibility. And she had to admit that Margaret's death had something to do with that. She'd loved Margaret to bits of course, and had depended on her, but after the first shock of knowing that she was dead, she realized how much she'd cared what Margaret thought. She'd always felt that Margaret was judging her. About the way she ran the guest house, the way she was bringing up the kids, even the way she dressed. Her relationship with Stu. Nothing was ever said, but she'd wanted Margaret to approve. If Ryan slipped out of the house without saying where he was going, if there was a complaint from a visitor about something to do with their stay at the guest house, or if Chloe had one of her strops, Kate's first thought was for Margaret's reaction. *What would she make of it?*

Now Kate felt wild and silly. She wondered if she could phone up a couple of friends and suggest they go out for lunch. A trip to Newcastle, an Italian meal, too much wine. She imagined herself staggering back on the Metro, too tipsy to care if Chloe was working herself to death. Stuart would be out at an end-of-term dinner with his colleagues tonight and she wouldn't see him until the morning. But the first friend she tried had sounded as if Kate was quite mad. 'Newcastle? The week before Christmas? It'll be a total nightmare. Besides, I'm rushed off my feet.' So Kate felt deflated again. Perhaps, after all, she should be sensible. She should do the Christmas preparation. Bake mince pies for the freezer. Ice the cake. Wrap some of the kids' presents while they were out of the way.

Still, the sun was shining and the frost on the roof of Malcolm Kerr's shed made the building look almost festive, so Kate decided that at least she could leave the house. There was a new place in Mardle, an ice-cream parlour and coffee shop, which had opened with the same optimism as had lain behind her own decision to develop the guest house. At least she could get a decent coffee and a pastry to celebrate her mood. And give some support to the new venture. Perhaps Mardle would see a change in its fortunes and tourists would arrive at last.

She was on her way out. She opened the front door and there on the step was a young woman. The visitor definitely wasn't from Mardle. She was stylish. The boots and the haircut were expensive. Kate felt untidy and rattled by the shock of almost walking into the woman.

'I'm sorry.' *Why do I always apologize?* 'Can I help you?'

The woman introduced herself – another detective. Even today there was to be no escape from Margaret's death.

Kate felt flustered. 'I was just on my way out. Since we heard about the murder I seem to have been trapped in the house. And it's the kids' last day at school. My last day of freedom.' Because although this newcomer, this Detective Constable Holly Clarke, was young and smart and obviously didn't have children, Kate thought that she might understand.

'Where were you off to?' The woman stepped back onto the pavement to give her space, and Kate felt that she had more room to breathe.

'Just for a coffee.' Kate gave a shrug. 'That's about as exciting as my life gets.'

'Tell me about it. And I could *murder* a latte.' Holly

seemed to realize what she'd said. 'Ooh, sorry!' But by then they were both giggling, like schoolgirls, as they walked up the street towards the town.

The new cafe had giant espresso machines and trays of home-made cakes and pastries. The realist in Kate thought that it wouldn't last more than six months in Mardle, but its novelty value meant that it was full now.

'What do you fancy?' Holly asked. 'My treat.' She'd already shepherded Kate towards a table in the corner. The room echoed with the sound of conversation and the machines behind the counter. Kate knew she was being offered cake in return for information, but still she didn't care. It felt almost as if she'd found a new friend.

'How can I help you? I suppose this is about Margaret?'

'Hey, no rush! Let's enjoy this first.'

And instead of asking about Margaret, Holly began talking to Kate about *her*. The woman was full of questions, chatty and gossipy. She wanted to know about Kate's time as a musician, the stars with whom she'd worked, the nightmare of touring. She asked how Kate had come to be running Harbour Street in the first place; about the kids and then about Robbie. 'How did he die?' Looking up from her latte with an interest and sympathy that Kate hadn't expected.

In the bubble of the warm room, Kate began to talk about her marriage. She said things that she'd never even discussed with Margaret, though she'd sometimes suspected that Margaret had guessed what the relationship was like. 'Robbie was a Scot. From the west coast. All dark hair, flashing eyes and Gallic passion. I was still in the music business then and we met at a gig.' She paused, expecting more questions from Holly, questions about Margaret, but none came and Kate continued. 'It was a lovely venue, an arts centre in the Borders. Intimate, you know. I started chatting to Robbie in the bar afterwards.' And she relived the scene in her head: the smoky bar and Robbie Dewar, the handsomest man in the room, walking towards her as if in slow motion, like a scene in a really soppy movie. She'd been chatted up by fans before, but Robbie had charmed her with an old-fashioned courtesy. He'd made her laugh.

They'd spent the night together in her hotel room. She'd thought it would be a one-night stand – after all, she had no plans then to settle down – but two days later he was knocking at the door of her parents' house, tidy in a clean shirt, carrying a bunch of roses, asking if she'd like to go out for a meal. Kate broke off in the middle of the story to look up at Holly. 'He drove sixty miles that day just to spend an evening with me and drove back sixty miles at the end of the night.'

'Wow!' Holly smiled. 'Romantic or what?'

And Kate agreed that it had been. 'I was bowled over by him. Most men only seemed interested in my music. The money. Or managing my career. Robbie liked my singing, but he was too proud to live off me. He wanted to be the provider.'

'So you stopped singing?' Holly looked up, and Kate could tell that she was shocked. This woman wouldn't let any man get in the way of *her* career.

'Not straight away.' Kate was defensive. How could she make this modern and confident young woman understand? 'And when we were first married I was happy to take things easy for a bit. I loved the business, but it was tough. The travelling. The pressure of media stuff. I missed the performing, though. That response you get from an audience. Stuart, my new bloke, set up a gig for me in a little theatre in Whitley Bay a month ago and it was fantastic to be onstage again. Addictive.'

She paused, remembering the event. A middle-aged audience who'd still remembered her hits, who'd got to their feet and cheered a couple of bars into the intro. Who'd queued up afterwards to buy the new CD that Stuart and a couple of his friends had helped her to produce.

But Holly was still waiting for the end of the story.

'When we had the kids I couldn't tour any more and the bookings dried up. It's a fickle business. You're quickly forgotten.'

'Couldn't your husband do some of the childcare?' Again Holly looked at her as if she were mad. 'Or you could have hired a nanny.'

'Robbie was an engineer,' Kate said. 'And that was before the time we talked much about work–life balance.' She smiled at the idea of Robbie managing two small kids in the morning. Breakfast and the school run. Of Robbie joining in with 'Wheels on the Bus' at the toddlers' group, making small talk about breastfeeding and house prices with the other parents.

'So you just gave it all up? All your ambitions and your dreams?'

'Not consciously. They just kind of slipped away. And I loved Robbie. I thought it was admirable that he wanted to care for us.'

She paused. Now she was coming to the difficult part of the story. She could just stop there, of course. It was none of this detective's business after all. What did Kate's private life have to do with the murder of Margaret Krukowski? But after all these years she wanted to tell it – she'd started now.

'Then Robbie was made redundant,' she said. 'The firm he'd been with since he was an apprentice got taken over and they laid off most of the skilled workers. He had a bit of redundancy money, but we knew that wouldn't last long. My manager offered me a UK tour – something gentle to remind people I was still there. When I talked about it to Robbie, he lost it. Absolutely refused to consider the idea. It was a crazy time. He was so unhappy. He'd walk out of the door and not come back until a couple of days later. And I wondered if he was turning up on another lass's doorstep, in a clean shirt, carrying a bunch of flowers.' She stopped because she was running out of breath, and because she was afraid that she might cry in front of this immaculate young detective.

'When did you move to Mardle?' Holly asked.

'Then. This aunt I'd never heard of died, leaving me the house on Harbour Street. It seemed like the most wonderful piece of luck. A place of our own and the chance of a steady income. I remortgaged to do the renovations. I thought Robbie might be excited too. He might see it as a possibility.'

'But it wasn't his thing?' Holly had chosen a cake for herself, but it lay untouched on her plate. She gave Kate her full attention.

'He told me he'd got a job on the rigs. A couple of his mates were there already. And I thought it might work. Two weeks on, two weeks off. And it would give me a break when he was working away. It's hard to describe what he was like when we were here. He was so restless and he had so much energy, but it was destructive. Like it wasn't the sort of energy that got walls painted or the house cleaned. He just prowled like a lion in a cage.'

'It sounds as if he might have been depressed,' Holly said.

'Yeah? Well, I think I was depressed too.' Kate paused for a moment. She knew what she wanted to say, but couldn't quite find the words. In the end she continued in a rush. 'Do you know what I felt, when the news came that Robbie had died in an accident offshore? Relief. I thought I wouldn't have to worry about him any more. I wouldn't have that constant anxiety when he stamped around the house, shouting at the kids.'

'Was he violent?' Holly asked the question as if it was the most natural thing in the world. And for a detective perhaps it was natural. Her working day would be spent with people who kicked off at the least provocation.

'Sometimes,' Kate said quietly. 'When he had a drink inside him. I mean, he never broke any bones, but he could lash out. Not with the kids, but sometimes with me.' *And the children saw.* She pictured them, white, terrified, backed into a corner in the sitting room, watching. Ryan's nightmares had started about then. The nightmares and the wandering. 'It was more that he was unpredictable. You never knew from one day to the next what sort of mood he'd be in.'

'I can see why you'd be relieved that he was dead

then.' Holly sounded perfectly matter-of-fact. And finally she cut a corner off the cake. She looked up. 'Did Margaret know he had a temper?'

'I don't think she ever heard us arguing.' Thinking back to that time when they'd first moved into the Harbour Guest House, Kate found that she was feeling tense and cold. It was remembering the big house and the kids, and dreading the days when Robbie would come back from the rigs. 'And I didn't know her so well then. But she'd have picked up that there was an atmosphere. One day she said to me: "You're a different woman when Robbie's away."'

'Would you have divorced him if he hadn't died?'

Kate thought Holly probably didn't have anyone serious in her life. Otherwise she wouldn't ask these questions as if there was one simple answer. 'I'm not sure,' Kate said in the end. 'Even when he was angry and restless I felt sorry for him. Responsible. As if he was another kid. And partly I *was* responsible. If he hadn't hooked up with me, if I hadn't dragged him to Mardle, perhaps he could still have had the life he always wanted. The perfect wife and kids, the happy family.'

'You didn't consider going back to the music, once he was dead?'

Kate thought about that and tried to answer honestly. 'I'd lost all my confidence,' she said. 'I sang for me and the kids. Taught them to play the piano. But I thought all I was good for was to be a guest-house landlady. Until Stuart came along and persuaded me otherwise. There was no pressure, but he let me believe in myself again.' As she said the words they sounded like the worst sort of cliché, too cheesy even to use in a song, but still she thought that they were true.

They sat for a moment in silence. Holly stood up. 'I'm going to have another coffee. Want one?'

Kate nodded.

Then the talk was all about Margaret, and Kate couldn't decide whether she was pleased or sad about that. 'Did you get the impression that Margaret had been in an abusive relationship?' Holly asked. She was very serious now.

Was that what I had? An abusive marriage? Again Kate thought that it wasn't possible to sum up a relationship in one phrase.

'No, I thought her husband had been the love of her life. Why do you say that?'

'Because she had a special sympathy for the women at the Haven.' Holly seemed surprised that Kate had asked. The informal chat had turned into an interrogation. 'And she seemed to recognize what you were going through, didn't she?'

'I suppose she did.' But Kate thought it wouldn't have taken personal knowledge to see what was going on with her and Robbie.

'What about Malcolm Kerr? His wife claims that he hit *her.* Did Margaret ever say anything to suggest that Malcolm might have been violent towards her too?'

'No!' The whole tone of the discussion had changed and Kate felt that she'd been misled, conned somehow by the expensive haircut and the pretence of friendship. 'I don't even know if they were an item. I just told your inspector that Malcolm was upset when he turned up at the house yesterday.'

'You hadn't seen them together recently?' Holly

finished her coffee and pushed away the plate with the half-eaten pastry.

'No!

'He never gave her a lift in his car, for example?'

'I never saw them together.' Kate heard her voice rising in pitch. 'Not in the street. Not in a car.' She got to her feet and started walking towards the door. How could she have been so stupid as to have trusted this woman? To have thought that they might be friends.

Holly followed her and they walked together back towards Harbour Street, the atmosphere quite different now. There was no schoolgirl giggling over tasteless jokes. Instead, an icy silence. Outside the guest house they stopped.

'And Stuart? How did he get on with Margaret?'

'Fine! They got on well together. They had lots in common – a love of music. The countryside. But they didn't really know each other. They only met occasionally when we invited Margaret to have supper with us.' Kate sensed she was talking too much and shut her mouth tight. No way was she going to invite the detective into the house.

'So Margaret didn't know Stuart before he came here to visit you?' Holly was pulling her car keys from her bag. This was her last question.

'No! Of course not! How would she?' But even as she was speaking, Kate was remembering the first time she'd introduced Margaret to Stuart. It was in the summer, an unusually fine day and she'd put lunch in the small garden at the back of the house. Chilled white wine and cheese and salad. She'd called up to Margaret: 'Come down and meet the new man in my life.' Margaret had walked out onto the patio and Stuart had stood to meet her, and for a moment Kate had been sure there'd been a mutual jolt of recognition.

Chapter Seventeen

Joe Ashworth pushed on the door of the church and was surprised when it opened. It was midweek and weren't all churches locked these days because of a fear of theft and vandalism? But it seemed that he'd walked into the middle of a service. Inside a scattering of elderly women sat on the front pews. They all turned and stared, curious. The priest was kneeling with his back to them and continued to read a prayer. The women turned back to the front and joined in a response. The priest's voice was deep and musical. Joe took a seat at the back and waited. They stood. A skeletal woman with fingers like claws began a tune on the organ and they sang a hymn. Very slowly. Stopping occasionally to allow the music to catch up. Again the priest's voice rose above them, carrying them along. The music stopped and they dropped to their knees for a moment of private prayer, before pulling together their belongings and turning to chat. The service, it seemed, was over. The women disappeared into a door to the left of the building and Peter Gruskin swept up the aisle towards Joe.

'I'm sorry to have interrupted.' Joe introduced himself.

'It's the Mothers' Union.' The priest nodded

towards the door through which the women had gone. 'They meet every month and we always start with a short service. They'll be having coffee and mince pies. The last session before Christmas.' He sounded wistful and Joe had the sense that he resented being kept away from the pies.

'I'll not keep you long.'

Gruskin sighed and sat on the pew next to Joe. Under his cassock he was wearing black cord trousers and old-fashioned black shoes. The men were of a similar age, but had nothing at all in common. Joe saw that there was a hole in the priest's sock, near the ribbing, and he wondered what it must be like to live alone in a place like Mardle, with only elderly women to keep you company. Because Joe was sure that Gruskin was single.

Through the open door came the high-pitched chatter of women's voices, the clink of teaspoons against crockery.

'I suppose you're here about Margaret Krukowski,' Gruskin said. 'There were two women detectives the other day. I told them everything I knew then.'

'Sometimes' – Joe chose his words carefully – 'it isn't just about what people *know*.' He paused. 'It can be useful to hear what people think, or guess, or suspect. Usually we wouldn't encourage idle gossip, but in a case like this, that sort of unconfirmed suspicion can make all the difference.' He turned in the pew so that he was looking at the priest. 'Do you understand what I'm saying?'

There was a moment of silence, the background hiss of a tea urn.

'There was some resentment in the parish because

Margaret kept herself to herself,' Gruskin said at last. 'It was viewed in some quarters as a kind of snobbishness. She spoke differently from the rest of the congregation and didn't have the shared experiences. I suspect that people made up their own stories to fill the gaps.'

'And what sort of stories were those?'

'There was an implication of a somewhat colourful past.' Gruskin shifted uneasily. Joe thought the priest had found the stories exciting. Perhaps he'd even encouraged them, or elaborated on them in his imagination when he was alone. There was something very creepy about him. 'Male friends. You know.'

'Did Malcolm Kerr ever feature in these tales?' Joe thought he was even starting to sound like Gruskin now and rephrased the question. 'Were there rumours that Margaret and Kerr had been lovers?'

Gruskin looked horrified. 'I'm not sure that the gossip was that specific.'

'Have *you* heard rumours about a relationship between Margaret and Kerr?' Joe was starting to lose patience. He could see why Vera had been so irritated by this man.

'There were probably rumours about a relationship between Margaret and every man in Mardle.' The priest was being waspish now. 'My congregation thought she was stand-offish and proud, because she spoke with an educated accent, read books and refused to get involved with their gossip. They could be cruel.'

'But specifically about her and Kerr?'

'Yes, there were those rumours. The relationship was supposed to have caused the breakdown of Margaret's marriage. I don't believe it. Margaret still spoke of her ex-husband with great affection.' Gruskin gave a small smile. 'Of course that was long before my time here. I would have been a baby. But Mardle people have long memories.'

'Margaret was seen in Kerr's car the day before she died,' Joe said. 'He took her out to the Haven. Was he in the habit of giving her a lift, do you know?'

There was another silence. Joe had the impression that Gruskin was surprised by this information. 'I really don't think so,' he said at last. Joe waited for him to continue. 'I offered to take her out to Holypool on a number of occasions, but she always refused. She said she preferred to use public transport.'

'Did you know that Margaret was ill?' Joe paused for a beat, but Gruskin didn't reply immediately and he continued. 'She had bowel cancer.'

The Mothers' Union party was getting into full swing. The voices were louder and there was a burst of laughter.

'No.' Gruskin stared out towards the altar. 'I wish she had confided in me about that. I might have been able to help.' But his voice was petulant and Joe thought the priest resented Margaret's obsession with privacy as much as his parishioners had. He would have been able to do nothing to help her.

They were interrupted by the elderly organist. She carried a tray, with two cups of coffee and a plate of mince pies. Her progress up the aisle was as slow as the tempo of her music.

'No need for these, Ida,' Gruskin said. 'I was just coming to join you. I think Sergeant Ashworth has finished now.'

'Not quite.' Joe took the cup and a pie from the plate the woman held. 'There are just a few more questions.' He waited until she had disappeared before he continued the conversation. In that time Gruskin ate two pies, very quickly and with a glum concentration. 'I wanted to ask you about Dee Robson.'

'You think she might be involved in Margaret's murder?' The priest looked up sharply and seemed almost relieved.

'No, there's no question of that. She's on the edge of the inquiry. A possible witness. I understand that she was asked to leave the Haven. I wondered if you could explain why.'

'Ah,' Gruskin said. 'Deirdre Robson. An unfortunate woman, with limited intellectual capacity. We couldn't keep her at the Haven, though. Not after the incident. Jane Cameron, who runs the place, made that quite clear and the trustees supported her judgement.'

'Perhaps you could tell me exactly what happened.' Joe spoke sharply. Now that Gruskin had been given something to eat he seemed prepared to sit and chat. Joe found the atmosphere in the church oppressive and wanted to be away.

'She had cards printed at one of those machines in the Metro station. Advertising her . . .' Gruskin paused for a moment '. . . services. Using the Haven's address and telephone number. They appeared all over Mardle. Jane was bothered by unsavoury phone calls at all hours of the night. A couple of men even turned up in cars, mistaking the place for . . .' He paused again.

'A brothel?'

'Quite.' Gruskin blinked rapidly. 'Dee was already

on a final warning, after turning up at the house drunk. We contacted her social worker and asked that he find somewhere more suitable.'

Joe thought of the bleak flat on Percy Street. That didn't seem suitable accommodation for anyone. 'But Margaret kept in touch with her.'

Gruskin sniffed. 'She didn't take it as seriously as we did. She even questioned whether Dee would have been capable of having the cards printed, and suggested that one of the other women might have had a tasteless joke at Dee's expense.'

'What did you think?'

Gruskin shrugged. 'Jane seemed to find Dee a disruptive element within the Haven. She is the professional, she lives there and has more experience than the rest of us put together. I felt that we had to trust her judgement. It was clear to me that the woman would have to leave.'

'When did this happen?' Joe had disapproved of Dee Robson, but he wished that this priest would show a more Christian attitude to a sinner. The man's ruthlessness made him uncomfortable.

Gruskin considered for a moment. 'Six weeks ago.'

'Did Margaret tell you that she was continuing to visit Dee?'

'She made no secret of it. She was angry about the way the trustees dealt with it, actually. I wondered if she would stop volunteering at the Haven. Her relationship with Jane became rather strained.'

Ashworth thought back to his meeting with the women in the Haven and with the warden. Jane wouldn't have mentioned Dee Robson at all, if one of the others hadn't suggested that she should be informed of the murder. He wondered if the smiling and competent Scotswoman had something to hide. Perhaps she'd simply been embarrassed to have fallen out with one of her volunteers, just before she was murdered. He stood up. 'Thanks.'

The priest walked with him to the door. 'I hope this matter is cleared up quickly,' he said. It was the middle of the day, but outside it was so gloomy that already the street lights had come on. 'It's unsettling for us all.' Then he disappeared quickly back into the church.

Joe Ashworth stood for a minute. The light was on in the basement kitchen of the guest house. Kate Dewar sat on a stool holding an acoustic guitar. Her head was turned away from the window, so she didn't see him. He wished that he could hear what she was singing. He would have loved his own personal performance of 'White Moon Summer'.

Ashworth arrived in the high school during the lunch break. Kids were screaming around the playground and through the corridors, excited because it was the end of term, and everywhere there was the smell of fried food and cheese sauce. The receptionist was fierce. 'The head doesn't see anyone without an appointment.'

Joe was tempted to bark back, Vera-style, but kept his temper. He couldn't imagine what it must be like to work in a place where there was no escape from children. He would never have admitted it, especially to Sal, but by the end of their two-week summer holiday in Cornwall he'd been longing to get back to work.

They'd rented a small cottage that looked idyllic in the brochure, but it had rained for four days on the run and there'd been sod all for the kids to do. Now, after explaining that he was investigating the murder of Margaret Krukowski, he smiled apologetically. 'It is rather urgent.' The woman scurried away without a word.

The head teacher was small and bald and had a face that gave away nothing of what he was thinking. 'I'm not sure how I can help you, Sergeant, but of course I'll do anything I can.'

'You'll have heard of the murder.' The office was on the third floor and looked down over the playground. The dark clouds gave a strange sense of dusk.

'Of course. Two of our students lived in the same house as the victim. She was almost part of their family. I've asked their class teachers to keep an eye on them. They'll obviously be upset.' The teacher looked up at Ashworth. 'I assume there's no question that they're involved in the crime.'

'Would you be surprised if they were?'

There was a moment's hesitation, but when he spoke his voice was unequivocal. 'Astonished. Chloe is an outstanding pupil. She has ambitions for Oxbridge and has every chance of getting there.' He paused. 'We all feel that she puts too much pressure on herself. Sometimes I wish she were a little less driven. Adolescent girls can make themselves ill . . .' His voice tailed away. 'Ryan's less academic, and I know that his mother has concerns about his progress. Comparisons are always being made with his sister. There have been a couple of unexplained absences, but I don't think he has plans to go into the sixth form, so we're reluctant to make a big issue of it. It's tough for boys growing up without a man in the house.'

An electronic bell rang and children skittered across the playground and into the building.

'But there is a man in the house now. At least, there soon will be.'

'Ah, you're here about Stuart.' The man frowned. 'Of course there's been talk in the staffroom about that relationship.' He paused. 'We didn't make the connection about Mrs Dewar's musical past until she performed in the Whitley Bay Playhouse recently. Stuart persuaded some of us to go along to support her and it was a great evening. The students have never heard of Katie Guthrie of course, but for people of our age she's rather a celebrity. We're glad that she chose Mardle High for her children.' Joe thought that the head had been a bit star-struck too.

'So there was a lot of gossip about the relationship?'

The head gave a little smile. 'Well, this is the first sign Stuart's ever shown that he might tie the knot. Some of the female teachers have tried to persuade him over the years, but he's always been wary of settling with anyone. The idea that he's taking on a wife and stepchildren has fascinated us all, because it's so out of character. The romance has become Mardle High's very own soap.'

'We're asking about anyone who knew Mrs Krukowski,' Joe said. 'Routine. You'll understand. Has Mr Booth been at Mardle long?'

'As long as the school. It was built in the Eighties and he was one of the first intake of staff. He's been head of music for the past fifteen years. He's talking about retiring to support Kate in her career, and we'll miss him. He's given himself heart and soul to the kids. Not just the timetabled lessons, but all the extracurricular stuff. Music, of course – the choir and the wind band – but he's keen on the great outdoors too. He leads our Duke of Edinburgh Award scheme. It's rare these days to find a teacher with such passion for his work.'

'He's passionate about Kate Dewar too?'

The head smiled. 'Apparently so.'

'Was he in school the afternoon of the murder?'

The man raised an eyebrow. 'Checking alibis, Sergeant?' He was suddenly more alert. Tense.

'As I said, sir. Routine.'

The teacher turned to the computer on his desk to check the electronic diary. 'That was the evening of our Christmas concert. Stuart didn't leave the building all day. He taught in the afternoon and then took the kids for a final rehearsal before the performance. I remember it because of the snow. We wondered if we should cancel, but most of our students live within walking distance, so we went ahead anyway.'

He looked up from the computer and Ashworth sensed that he was disproportionately relieved that his colleague was in the clear. Perhaps that was the natural response of a head teacher who was anxious about his school's reputation. Or perhaps he had a suspicion that Stuart Booth might be capable of murder.

Chapter Eighteen

Malcolm Kerr's yard was shut up, the big wooden doors padlocked. Vera was about to wander back to his house when she saw him walking past the fisheries towards the harbour, a dark figure dressed in oilskins and boots, recognizable by his stooped back. She hurried to catch him up.

'I wanted a word.'

He stopped. It seemed he'd been engrossed in his thoughts, because he hadn't heard her footsteps behind him and she'd startled him. 'Well, you can't. I've got work to do.'

She looked at his eyes and thought he hadn't drunk so much the night before and had managed some sleep. He was truculent, but more human. 'Where are you off to?'

'Prof. Craggs left some of his equipment in the water off the island. He didn't want to pick it up the last time we were out because of the weather. I said I'd come and get it the first chance that I had.' He carried on walking.

The boat was already tied up at the harbour wall and ready to go. Not the *Lucy-May* that carried the trippers around Coquet Island in the summer, but a small open boat with an outboard at the back. A newer version of the vessel that had carried her and Hector out to the island years before.

Vera looked down at it. It seemed sturdy enough. 'Room for a small one?'

He stared at her as if she were mad. 'You want to come out with me?'

'Why not? You'll not be long, will you? And like I said, I need a word.'

He chuckled. 'Taking a bit of a risk, aren't you? If I'm a murder suspect, I could pitch you out between here and Coquet, and nobody would know. And, whatever I say, you've got no corroboration. It'd never stand up in court.'

She looked at him for a moment. Of course he was right and it was a daft thing to do. 'Ah, I'll risk it.'

She carefully lowered herself down the metal ladder fixed to the wall and into the boat. Gravity helped. She hoped the tide was on its way in and that the water would be higher when they returned. Then she wouldn't have so far to climb up. The boat wobbled when she stepped in and she had a moment of panic, imagining herself tumbling into the freezing brown water. Kerr fished a buoyancy jacket from under the back seat and threw it to her and arranged a plastic cushion for her in the middle of the boat. 'Don't move. The weight of you, you'll have us over.' He tugged on the starting rope and the engine coughed into life.

There was quite a different perspective on the town from the water. A monochrome vision like a black-and-white film. She could see the backs of the buildings on Harbour Street. The women in the fisheries were getting ready for the lunchtime rush, carrying white plastic buckets of prepared potatoes from an outhouse at the end of the yard. The guest house looked rather grand from here, the narrow windows symmetrical and the grey stonework as solid as a fortress. There was a small garden between the house and the shore. Beyond, the tower of St Bartholomew's dominated. She felt like a voyeur, a peeping Tom looking at the world from a hiding place. Though they were hiding in full sight.

'Why did you lie to me, Malcolm?' They were outside the harbour wall now and there was a slight swell on the water. She'd always been a good sailor and was untroubled by it. 'You said you hadn't had any contact with Margaret recently.'

'I haven't!' But he sounded like one of the young scallies she used to round up as a junior PC, all bluster and swearing.

'Come on, Malcolm man. You were seen dropping her off at the Haven the day before she died.'

He didn't reply immediately and the only sound was the rasp of the engine and gulls screaming.

'Look, man, talk to me. This is about as unofficial as it gets, in a bloody boat in the North Sea.' *With me looking like the Michelin man in a bright-orange life jacket.*

'We were friends,' he said. 'I was probably the only real friend she had round here.'

'Lovers?'

He shook his head sadly. 'A long time ago. Not recently. Not many times even then.' He paused. They were halfway across the stretch of water that separated the island from Mardle. 'And we didn't meet much as friends when I was still married. She knew what I felt about her and thought she'd get in the way. She said that it wouldn't be fair to Deborah. She was kind enough when I was getting divorced, but she made it clear there was no chance of us getting together again.'

'Is that what you wanted?' They were close enough to the island for Vera to make out details. The warden's house and the muck on the cliffs where the seabirds had nested. She tried to remember more details of the trip she'd taken there with Hector to steal birds' eggs all those years ago, but all that came back was the sense of foreboding and the dreadful certainty that they'd be caught. 'You wanted more than friendship, even now?'

'I adored her from the first time we met,' Kerr said. 'I should never have married. When I lay next to my wife I was dreaming of Margaret.'

Vera wondered what that would be like and decided it was probably easier to adore a fantasy heroine than a real woman.

'But you'd spent time together again recently?'

'She'd just found out that she was ill,' Kerr said. 'She wanted to tell someone. Not Kate and the kids. She thought they'd get too upset.'

'She told you that morning before you dropped her off at the Haven?' Vera had to turn in her seat to see his face.

He nodded. 'She asked if I fancied going for a walk. We went to the beach at North Mardle. It was freezing and we had the place to ourselves, apart from a couple of dog walkers miles off. Then the sun came out.' Vera could see that in his head he was back on the beach in the winter sunshine walking beside the woman he'd known since he was a young man. Had he taken her hand? Put an arm around her shoulder?

'She had cancer,' Vera said.

'I said I'd look after her. Whatever she needed.' He was almost in tears. 'She said she had to sort a few things out. Affairs to get straight. "I'll need you to help me with that, Malcolm."' He smiled. 'Of course I hated the thought of her being ill, but I loved her involving me, making me part of her life again. So we'd be together in a way, even if we didn't have very long.'

'Did she say what she needed to sort out?'

But Malcolm didn't answer immediately. They'd reached a red buoy close to a rocky outcrop of the island. He cut the engine and tied the boat to a metal ring on the rock. The boat swung and he reached out to haul in the rope attached to the buoy. The water was very clear here and Vera watched the object slowly emerge. He lifted it, dripping, into the body of the boat. A weighted metal plate covered in sand. Vera's attention shifted briefly from the investigation.

'And what did you say is in there?'

'A sediment monitoring plate. The Prof. needs it for his research. I said I'd bring it in, in case there's a storm over the holiday.' He slipped the knot from the ring and pushed the boat away from the rock. 'He's a good man, the Prof. I don't mind doing him a favour when I can.'

'Why didn't you tell me you'd met Margaret when I talked to you yesterday?' She was exasperated. 'We could have saved all this carry-on – half my team having you down as a murderer.'

'I was scared,' he said.

'You said you'd been in touch with Margaret since your divorce? Did you approach her?'

He shook his head. 'She knew how I was fixed. It was up to her. She contacted me about Kate Dewar's lad.'

The boat was moving back towards the shore. Spray blew into her face and she could taste the salt on her lips. 'What about him?'

'He was getting into bother. Skipping classes occasionally. Nothing serious. That house full of women, Margaret thought he could do with some male company. She asked if I could find any work for him around the yard.'

'And you said yes?'

There was a pause. The strange, dark sky was pierced briefly by one arrow of bright sunlight. 'If she'd asked me to swim naked three times round the island, I'd have said yes. I loved her.'

'How do you get on with the boy?' Vera wasn't sure that kind of passion was healthy. It embarrassed her that Kerr was prepared to talk like that. As if he had no self-control or pride. Much safer to move on to a discussion about Kate's son.

Kerr seemed to consider for a moment before answering. 'I never have any bother with him. He's just one of those lads who don't like school. He's kind of restless. You see him walking the streets at all hours. Too much energy for school work.' He was bringing the boat round the harbour wall now and the sunlight had disappeared as suddenly as it had arrived. The water was calmer. 'Ryan was a bit cocky when he started, but he settled down once he realized I wasn't going to stand any messing. He wants to make something of himself, and I'm glad of the company.' He paused as if that was a confession. 'When I was his age I'd already been working full-time for a year.'

'You never fancied staying on and getting an education?' Because Vera thought that Kerr was more intelligent than he'd seemed to her at first. Margaret wouldn't have taken up with a stupid man, even briefly.

'Never got the chance.' Even now this obviously rankled. 'My Dad needed cheap labour in the family business.'

Vera turned back to face him. 'Just like mine.' They grinned.

With an easy move he had the boat next to the ladder in the wall. It occurred to her that he'd done this so many times that he'd manage it with pinpoint accuracy even with his eyes closed.

'Your friend the professor said you were back in Mardle by three o'clock the afternoon Margaret died,' Vera said. She took off the life jacket, but stayed sitting. 'Where did you go when you got in from the water?'

'The Prof.'s wrong about the time. You know what these academics are like. Not fit to be let out in the real world. It was later than that. Nearly dark.' He took her hand to help her to her feet and then leaned across her to grab one of the rails to hold the boat steady. She hoisted herself onto the ladder, aware of how close to him she was. When she got to the top and looked back, he had the engine running and the boat on its way back to its mooring. He waved at her and she waved back.

*

As she walked along the wall to Harbour Street, the pavement felt uneven under her feet. Even after such a short trip she could still feel the motion of the boat. The smell of frying fish in the chip shop almost tempted her inside, but she carried on past. She phoned Holly.

'Did you get hold of a social worker to check up on Dee Robson?'

'I spoke to social services. Her key worker's a guy called Jim Morris.'

'And?' *Sometimes, Holly Clarke, you really wind me up.*

'There's absolutely no chance that anyone will get round to see her before Christmas. And there'll just be a skeleton staff on over the holidays. Emergencies only.'

Vera switched off the phone without answering. For a fleeting moment she considered inviting Dee home with her for Christmas. Her neighbours, Joanna and Jack, wouldn't judge the woman. They'd all sit round the table in the farmhouse, drinking too much and eating Joanna's fabulous food, and if Dee flirted with Jack they'd just laugh. But Vera knew that it wouldn't do to have a suspect in a murder inquiry as a temporary lodger. She grinned as she imagined Joe Ashworth's outrage if she suggested it.

She phoned Holly again. 'Have you got the number of that hostel, the Haven?' Holly, as efficient as ever, found it within seconds. Vera had to keep her talking while she got into her car and found a pen. 'Just repeat that number again, Hol, would you?'

Her call was answered by someone with a motherly voice and a Scottish accent. Vera explained who she was.

'Inspector, how can I help?'

Vera explained that she was anxious about Dee Robson. 'She's an important witness. She's spent quite a lot of time with Margaret Krukowski recently. She has a very chaotic lifestyle and, without Margaret's supervision, I'm frightened that she'll just disappear.'

There was silence on the other end of the phone.

'I wondered if you might put her up at the Haven, just over the holidays. So we know where to find her, if we need to interview her again.' Vera could tell she was wheedling and hated it. She'd never been good at asking for favours.

'I'm sorry, Inspector, we've just taken another emergency resident. I'm afraid that we have no vacancies.' The phone went dead.

Out in the street, Vera looked briefly into the Coble, thinking that Dee might be there. It was still early and almost empty. In the bar a couple of elderly men played dominoes. There was no sign of the woman, and Vera knew better than to look in the lounge. That wasn't Dee's territory. On impulse she went into the fish shop and bought two haddock and chips to take away. Even wrapped in paper and in a carrier bag, the smell walked with her down the alley between the church and the Metro line.

She walked quickly up the concrete stairs of the flats, feeling the strain on her legs from when she'd climbed the ladder at the harbour. *Eh, Vera, pet, you'd best catch this killer quickly or there's a danger that you'll get fit.* She knocked at Dee's door, but didn't expect an immediate response. When they'd turned up there before, the woman had checked who was on the doorstep before letting them in. There could be a man from the council in the corridor wanting his rent, or some irate wife. Dee had at least some notion of self-preservation.

But the door opened when Vera hit it. She stayed where she was and shouted in. 'Are you there, Dee? It's Vera Stanhope. I've brought fish and chips.'

Still no reply. Vera set the carrier bag on the floor in the corridor outside and went in, noticing again the stain of damp on the wall by the door. The living room was empty. The empty paper bag that had held the cakes she'd brought as a previous peace offering still lay ripped on the table.

'Dee, are you there?'

The bedroom door was shut and Vera listened before going in. Not through embarrassment, but because she wanted to know what to expect before she burst in on Dee Robson at work. Silence. Vera opened the door. In the bedroom Dee lay on the mattress staring at Vera. She was dressed for work: short skirt and white lacy top, shiny white plastic shoes. Glitter blue eyeshadow and pink lipstick slightly smudged. There was a kitchen knife in the side of her neck. It was the knife with which Vera had cut the custard slice the day before.

Blood had pooled under her head and her neck, a dark background to the very pale skin. Her skin was icy blue, except where her bare legs touched the mattress, and there it was dark, almost purple. The flesh looked like plastic. Vera was reminded of a big blow-up doll. The woman had probably died not long after she and Joe had visited the previous day.

Vera went to the hall to make the phone call. She smelled the fish and chips and was almost sick.

Chapter Nineteen

Kate was waiting for George Enderby to arrive. She wanted to book him in quickly because Stuart would be here soon. She was already excited, listening for the sound of Stuart's key in the door. They had plans. The Metro into Newcastle for an afternoon of culture – a new exhibition at the Baltic on the river and a stroll round the Laing Art Gallery. Then dinner. Stuart had a mate from the Ramblers' Association who'd opened a restaurant near the cathedral. 'Nothing pretentious,' Stuart had said. 'But decent enough, and he could do with the support. You know.' Stuart didn't have many mates, but he was loyal to them. She liked that. She thought he'd be loyal to her.

And afterwards they had tickets for a concert in the small hall of the Sage. A Danish poet and a musician from the Faroes. 'It'll probably be awful,' Stuart had said, 'but if we don't go we might miss something important.' He was full of surprises. She'd never have thought he would go for something so experimental. It seemed to Kate that her world had shrunk with her marriage to Robbie and it was as if she was being given a second chance to explore it. They'd get the last Metro home and Stuart would stay over. She was daydreaming about that too. Since Rob had died all she'd had were daydreams; now there was flesh and skin, touch and taste. Some days it seemed that thoughts about sex swamped her brain, leaving room for nothing else. Maybe that was why she'd become such a crap parent and why she felt so little grief at Margaret's murder. Had her infatuation for Stuart left her heartless and cold?

In the past there would have been no problem about leaving the guest house. Kate would have asked Margaret to let George in and show him to his room. Margaret would have made his tea and left it in the lounge, just as he liked it. She'd have kept an eye out for the kids too. Today Ryan was out and probably wouldn't get back before Kate and Stuart. She never knew where he was. Sometimes he just wandered around the neighbourhood, marking the boundaries of his world. Even as a small child, if anything had upset him he'd walk miles, backwards and forwards from Margaret's flat at the top of the house to the basement. Chloe was at the kitchen table, her nose to the laptop and the pile of books higher than ever. But she had her phone on the table next to her and Kate saw her attention stray to it occasionally, as if she was willing it to ring. She knew what that was like.

'It's the start of the holidays,' Kate had said, trying to keep her voice light. Stuart never said anything, but she could tell that he thought she nagged the kids too much: Chloe for working too hard and Ryan for not doing enough. 'Give yourself a break!'

But there was some competition apparently, run by a national science magazine, and Chloe thought it would look good on her CV if she won. So that was her project for the holiday. When she had a project she thought of nothing else. Except, apparently, the call she was waiting for, as her eyes moved again to her phone. They looked dark and bruised and Kate thought she'd been up all night brooding. About the project or about some lad? Kate wasn't sure which would worry her most.

The doorbell rang and George Enderby was standing there with his wheelie suitcase full of books.

'Me again. The proverbial bad penny.' He gave her a hug and kissed both cheeks as he always did. Then he stood back to look at her. 'You're looking very smart. Going anywhere nice?' She blushed and, though there was no hint of reproof in his words, she felt guilty. Should she be going out enjoying herself when Margaret was so recently dead?

'Just into Newcastle with Stuart.'

'Well, good for you! Don't worry. I can see myself up to my room.' He seemed tired too. His overcoat was crumpled and the jollity in his voice was rather forced. She supposed that perhaps he hadn't received many orders for the novels he loved.

'I'll put some tea in the lounge,' she said. 'Though the biscuits aren't up to Margaret's standard, I'm afraid.'

They smiled sadly at each other. 'I'm sure they'll be delicious,' George said. He began to take off his gloves and added, as if it were an afterthought: 'Any news about that? Have they caught the killer?'

She was already on her way to the kitchen and turned back to answer. 'I haven't heard anything. There seem to be police in the town whenever I go out. They're knocking on all the doors and asking questions.'

And as if in response to his query there was the noise of sirens in the street and they looked at each other, sharing a frisson of anxiety.

Stuart was late, so she was starting to panic, to wonder if she should call him. He was usually obsessively punctual and she was the one who made *him* wait. And now, with Margaret's killing, she thought that he would make an effort to be on time because he'd know that she would worry. Then he was there. He had let himself in, and she heard his footsteps coming down the stairs to the basement. He was so tall that it seemed minutes after seeing his feet before his head appeared. He was wearing a brown leather jacket, very old and beaten-up, and jeans. It was what he always wore when they went out to town. A scarf was his only concession to the weather. Nearly sixty, but he looked good. Cool.

'Sorry!' His hands turned up in a gesture of contrition. 'I don't know what's going on in Mardle this afternoon. The traffic's a nightmare.'

Then he put his arm around her, very easy and natural, and she wanted to reach out and touch his face because she thought he was so beautiful, felt the pull of wanting him in her guts. If they'd had the house to themselves she'd have suggested staying here instead of going into town.

'Hi, Chlo? Everything okay?' He'd already pulled away from Kate and had his hand lightly on Chloe's shoulder, looking down at her work.

'Yeah, well, you know.' Chloe stretched. 'I don't

know how much detail they want. What do you think?'

He sat down beside her and leaned in to give his full attention to the laptop, and Kate felt jealousy, bright and sharp like the prick of a needle. *She never talks to me like that. Does she think that I'm too stupid to understand?* And, immediately afterwards: *Does he find my daughter more attractive than me?*

She left them chatting and went to see George, who was lingering over his tea. 'Are you okay?' She thought he looked ill, still wrapped up in his overcoat. She bent and turned up the fire.

He turned on his performer's smile, the one he must use to charm publishers and booksellers. 'You're so kind to me, Kate. This is like a second home. You do know that?' He smiled wistfully and she thought he was regretting the old days before Stuart had come into her life, when she would sit and drink with him all evening and listen to him talking about his magnificent wife.

Newcastle was full of people and friendly. They walked arm-in-arm between the art galleries, crossing the Tyne by the Blinking Eye Bridge. Then on to the restaurant. Kate could smell the leather of Stuart's jacket and the city, sweet and enticing, all around her. Mardle only smelled of salt and fish and seaweed, and there was no adventure in that. The restaurant was tiny and cramped and they sat in the window, looking out onto a steep cobbled street. Stuart joked with his friend, the owner, about the background music and ordered a bottle of wine. Then he took her hand across the table. The candle threw odd shadows across his face and for a moment she felt that she was sitting with a stranger. There was a heady excitement in that too.

'I'm so sorry about Margaret,' he said. 'I know you were close.'

She was disappointed. She'd hoped for something more romantic. At least a declaration that he was as obsessed with her as she was with him. She was sick of talking about Margaret, sick of the drop in her stomach every time the realization hit her again. She just wanted to forget about it. Move on.

'It was dreadful,' she said. Kate didn't quite know how to explain out loud how she felt. 'I don't want to sound callous, but in a sense I have more options now. I can think of selling the house, for example. I know we've talked about it before, but really it would have been impossible when Margaret was still alive.'

'A new start,' he said. It was almost as if he was talking to himself, playing with the words, turning them into a riff.

'Yeah.' She found that she was grinning.

'I could take early retirement,' he said. 'I've been teaching for long enough.' He poured more wine. His face was flushed.

'What would you do?' She couldn't imagine him as a pensioner, weekly walks in the hills, watching television in the afternoons, though the thought of him being free during the day when the kids were out of the house excited her again.

'I'd manage your career – properly, not just the odd gig, like at the moment,' he said, suddenly serious. 'We'd get you writing again. Performing. If you sold the Harbour Street house we could get somewhere smaller in town – a new start for the kids too, a better school. See if we can persuade Ryan to stay on for A levels.'

She thought that he'd been thinking of this for a while. 'Are you saying that we should move in together straight away?'

'If we can find the right place, why not? We'd get something decent if I sold my flat too. A new start.' Repeating the words again. He'd never talked about moving into Harbour Street with her, though she'd dropped plenty of hints. It was as if the building itself – so public when it was filled with guests – put him off.

'I'd love that,' she said. 'Really.'

'Then I'll give the head my notice tomorrow. He'll need a full term.' And so, it seemed, the decision was made.

He went to the counter to pay his friend and there seemed to be a flurry of anxiety for a moment. She wondered if he'd forgotten his cash or his credit card, but when she asked him he said it was nothing. A photo that he kept in his wallet seemed to have gone missing. She hoped he'd kept a photo of her, though she couldn't remember him taking one. She didn't like to mention it again because he seemed so put out to have lost it, and by then they were out in the street and on their way to the Sage.

When they returned from Newcastle, George must have gone to bed because the lounge was empty, the curtains drawn against the dark. Kate was buzzing.

The concert had been so awful that it had been funny and the audience had shared the experience like a joke. In the end it was as if they'd all been present at a really special gig, with the small hall at the Sage warm and intimate, and they'd all wandered out talking and laughing about it like old friends. The last Metro home was full of partying drunks, but everyone was good-natured. A policeman got on at Haymarket and stayed on the train; someone said that had happened every night since the murder. They'd got the seat right at the front, so the lights of the approaching stations rushed at them and Kate felt as if it was a fairground ride, as if she was about ten years old.

Both kids were home when they arrived back. Ryan hadn't long got in; it was raining and his jacket, thrown over the banister at the bottom of the stairs, was wet. Kate and Stuart had had a couple of drinks in the interval to keep them going through the second half of the gig and Kate was still not entirely sober. She felt very happy, in a tipsy, emotional way. Both her children were safe at home and she had this wonderful new man and her future seemed exciting.

The kids were in the basement sitting room in front of the television.

'There's been another murder,' Ryan said as soon as they were in the room. 'They were talking about it in the Coble.'

For a moment she didn't take in what he'd said. She knew he went into the Coble occasionally, but she didn't like it. Stuart had once said in his dry, practical way: 'Boys that age are going to drink anyway. Better that they do it in the pub where there are other adults around.' Her worry, which she'd never discussed with

Stuart, was about where Ryan got the money from for drink. She gave him an allowance, but would that run to pub prices? She knew Malcolm Kerr paid him, but Ryan always seemed to have cash. Deep down she was anxious that he'd started thieving. It was as if she had a stranger in the house. She remembered the small, affectionate boy who'd held her hand when they walked to the park, but this stylish young man bore no resemblance.

Then the shock of another killing hit her and her concern about Ryan seemed petty.

'What did you say?'

Ryan seemed sober, but hyper, and he repeated the words with a kind of repressed excitement that made her feel ill.

Stuart seemed not to notice the boy's reaction. 'Do you know who the victim was?'

'Some woman,' Ryan said. 'She drinks in the Coble and lives in Percy Street. Dee Robson they call her.'

Kate recognized the name and remembered that Margaret had talked about her. One of her waifs. *Dee needs someone to look after her, and all they can do is call her names.*

'We're waiting for the late local news.' Chloe was wearing the same black knitted jumper as she'd had on for school; it was too big for her, and she seemed to disappear inside it. She was drinking a mug of tea.

There was a strained silence. Kate was quite sober now, but she couldn't find anything appropriate to say.

'I'll put the kettle on,' Stuart said at last. 'Anyone else want a brew?'

But nobody answered because the local news came

on the television and there were the flats in Percy Street, with blue-and-white police tape stretched around the lamp posts, and scientists in white suits and masks making their way to the door. Even Stuart paused on his way to the kitchen to watch.

Chapter Twenty

Joe Ashworth found Vera still standing outside the flat in Percy Street when he arrived, as if she'd been fixed there since calling in the murder, waiting for him to arrive. He knew that she'd be upset. Something about Dee Robson had moved her. She could be as callous as hell, but occasionally she connected with a witness and, when that happened, she would move heaven and earth to help them. The objects of her pity were usually loners, clumsy, despised. And fat, Joe thought, grinning to himself despite the situation. Much like Vera herself.

'What do you think happened?' It was cold. A draught blew up the stairwell. He knew that the last thing she'd want would be sympathy.

'She must have been killed not long after we came to see her.' Vera was standing with her hands in her pockets. There wasn't much room there and his elbow brushed against her arm.

'A customer?'

'She was dressed for work, but still wearing her knickers. No evidence that sex had taken place.'

He could tell that she'd already thought this through. 'It could still have been a punter,' he said. 'We know that she wasn't much good at risk assessment.

She went off with that guy Jason, without knowing where he lived.'

'The link with Margaret Krukowski is just a coincidence, do you think?' Vera gave a sharp little smile. 'That's some elephant-sized coincidence.'

'What then?' He was losing patience. If Vera Stanhope had a theory, why didn't she just tell him? Why play games?

'Dee Robson knew something about Margaret's killer,' Vera said. 'But she didn't know that she knew. Otherwise she'd have told us when we saw her yesterday.' There was a pause. 'Or maybe she was smarter than anyone thought.'

'Blackmail?' Sometimes he knew the way her mind was working. 'She kept the information secret so that she could make money from it.'

She gave a slow clap. 'Well done, that boy.'

'You think that she'd have been capable of that?' He couldn't see it. He didn't think Dee had been bright enough to make the connections, and he'd been convinced by her performance the day before.

'She was desperate,' Vera said. 'An alcoholic, living like this – there'd be an incentive to get money any way she could. Maybe Margaret said something to her when they last met. Something so obvious that you wouldn't have had to be Einstein to work out who'd killed her.'

There were footsteps on the stairs and Billy Wainwright appeared. He looked grey and ill.

'You okay, Billy?' Joe disapproved of Billy's lifestyle choices – the string of young lovers seemed undignified for someone of his position – but couldn't help liking him.

'A bit of a hangover. Nothing a good night's sleep won't cure.' He was already in the scene suit and was putting on a mask, so the words were muffled.

'I thought you were so busy with the crime scene in the Metro there'd be no time for partying.' Vera's words were sharp.

'All work and no play . . .' Joe could tell by his voice that he was grinning. 'You could do with a bit of play yourself, Vera.'

'Just go in there and do your work, Billy. Tell me who killed these women. Find some fibres or spit or fingerprints, and link the two investigations. That would be a good start.'

He realized that she was serious, gave a mock salute and went into the house. Outside came the sound of sirens. 'The cavalry,' Vera said.

Joe couldn't face standing here for much longer, watching Vera tear herself apart with guilt, but bottling it all up inside. 'What do you want me to do?'

'Knock on some doors, Joe. Start in the flats and then move down the street. Dee would have been an object of interest. There might even have been a campaign to get her shifted. She was hardly a model tenant. Let's hope there's a busybody somewhere who's made a note of the comings and goings. I've sent Hol back to the station to coordinate calls from the public.' When he paused she continued angrily. 'If it's not beneath your dignity as a sergeant, sometime today would be good.'

He put up his hands, a gesture of surrender, and walked away. When she called him back he thought she was going to apologize for being so sharp. But she handed him a greasy carrier bag. 'Get rid of these, will you? Fish and chips. They'll be cold by now.'

He started at the ground floor and worked up. Two flats on each floor, six lots of tenants. Mid-afternoon and the week before Christmas he expected most people to be out, but he was 50 per cent lucky. The first door he knocked on had a handrail outside and a ramp to the front step. A tiny elderly woman with a walking frame opened the door. She had shining white hair permed into tight curls. He showed his warrant card.

She stepped aside and let him in, sat him in front of the gas fire and chatted while she made tea. She couldn't have been happier to see him if he'd been Santa. 'It gets a bit lonely,' she said. No self-pity. 'Though I get out to the over-sixties on Thursdays, and that's always a laugh. Our Christmas party tomorrow.'

'I'm here to ask some questions.' He sat with the tea and a plate balanced awkwardly on the arm of the chair. She'd insisted on him getting the Battenberg out of the cake tin.

'About that woman who was killed on the Metro?' She poked her head forward, eager for information. 'The one with the foreign name. I remember her when she was a lass. Always a bit full of herself and stirring up the lads. Ricky Butt had his eye on her at one time, and Val threatened to bar her from the Coble.'

'Ricky Butt?' The woman obviously wanted to chat and she reminded Joe of his nan.

'Oh, this won't have anything to do with him.' The

woman shook her head. 'Val was the landlady of the pub for years, but she's long gone, and he left Mardle when he was still a boy.' She smiled. 'Sorry, pet, you're not interested in me wittering on. How can I help?'

'There's been another incident,' he said.

'Oh?' Eyes wide with curiosity.

'Dee Robson. She lives on the top floor. Do you know her?'

'Oh, that one! Peggy Jamieson lives next door, and her life's a misery. Banging up and down the stairs at all hours. Men knocking. She told the police and the council, but nothing happened.' She paused. 'Not Dee's fault, mind.' She tapped the side of her head. 'I knew her mam and she was a bit daft too, like. Though not as bad as Dee.' A thoughtful pause. 'They used to lock up people like that in asylums.'

Ashworth couldn't tell if she approved or disapproved of the notion.

'Dee's dead,' Ashworth said. 'We think she died in her flat yesterday. Did you hear or see anything unusual?'

The woman shook her head regretfully. 'I was out all day yesterday. My daughter took me back to hers for my dinner.'

He stayed for a few more minutes and had another slice of cake. Vera wasn't the only one with compassion.

The next inhabited flat was on the second floor. A woman in her early thirties with a toddler clinging to her legs. She didn't ask him in.

'I've already talked to you lot about the woman that was stabbed on the Metro.'

'Did you know Margaret Krukowski?'

'Nah, but when they showed me her picture I realized I'd bumped into her on the stairs a couple of times. She was on her way to the flat upstairs. I told them that.' The toddler began to grizzle.

'Perhaps we could go in and talk about it,' Joe said. 'We don't want the bairn to get cold.'

The flat was exactly the same in layout as Dee's, but there was carpet on the floor and it was furnished. In the living room there was a box of brightly coloured plastic toys. The television was on. *CBeebies*. The woman was called Jodie and she didn't like cops.

'You're here on your own with the bairn?'

'Only since you put my man inside.'

Here, then, he was unlikely to be offered tea and cake. 'Dee Robson . . .'

'What about her?' Jodie was very thin, with a ratty face and narrow eyes.

'She's a neighbour.'

'The social set her up in that flat upstairs. All the old biddies in the block want her out.' She put the child on the floor and he pulled a train from the toy box.

'And you?'

She shrugged. 'Live and let live.'

'You weren't worried that she was attracting unsuitable men into the flats?'

The woman gave an unpleasant laugh. 'Have you met her? How many men do you think she attracts? Those too drunk to get up the stairs. She hangs out in the Coble because the locals feel sorry for her and buy her drinks. She might have done a bit of business a few years ago, but now she's just a laughing stock.'

'Are you in the same line yourself?'

She laughed again. 'I'm a reformed character. Check my record.'

'Dee's dead,' he said. 'We think she was killed sometime yesterday afternoon.'

'Poor cow.' She scooped the child into her arms and held him tight, kissing his hair. 'She was as mad as a snake, but she didn't deserve that.'

'When did you last see her?'

'I haven't seen her for a few days, but I heard her yesterday. Her flat's above mine and the ceiling's like cardboard. Usually there wasn't much noise. The telly, but I have it on most of the time anyway.' She sat on the sofa with the child still in her arms and watched the children's presenter pretending to be a lion.

'But yesterday you heard something,' he said. 'People shouting? A row?'

She shook her head. 'Nothing like that. Music. Could have been on the telly, but very loud. I'd put Alfie down for a nap and I was worried she'd wake him up. I banged on the ceiling with a broom handle and it stopped. She must have gone out then, because I heard her on the steps outside.'

'But you didn't see her?'

Jodie looked horrified. 'Oh my God, you think it was the killer going past the door?'

'It's possible,' Ashworth said. 'What time was it?'

She shook her head as if time didn't mean anything to her. 'I didn't see anything. I mean, I didn't look out of the window.'

He left her sitting with her son on the sofa and staring at the television.

*

Peggy Jamieson was expecting him and knew who he was. Her friend on the ground floor must have phoned her, and anyway by now the neighbouring flat was swarming with people and the blue-and-white tape was across the corridor, blocking her way to the stairs. Ashworth bobbed underneath it, nodded to the PC who was standing guard, and knocked on the door. There was no sign of Vera. Peggy opened the door and immediately started talking. She was short and round, and the stairs must be a trial to her.

'They never should have put that woman to live there. She couldn't look after herself.'

Her flat was spotless and it glistened. There was a view from the living-room window over the top of the Coble and to the harbour. Behind the pub a man carried a crate of empties into the yard. Joe let her talk for a while.

'How long has Dee Robson been there?'

'About six weeks. But long enough for me to know it wasn't going to work out. Staggering back drunk at all hours. Men. And I could see when she opened the door that it was an absolute pigsty in there.' The state of the flat seemed to bother her more than Dee's habits.

'How many men?'

'Well, I didn't see *that* many. But I'm not always in. And I'm not as nebby as some.'

Joe thought Dee's reputation had arrived at Percy Street before her, and that Jodie's assessment of her ability to attract customers was probably accurate. He wondered about Jason, who'd taken Dee on the Metro on the day of Margaret's death. Had he been very drunk? Very desperate? Certainly he'd dumped her as soon as he'd sobered up. Joe smiled at Peggy. 'Were you here yesterday?'

'Aye, all day.'

'Did Dee have any visitors?'

'You were in there,' Peggy said sharply. 'You and a fat woman. I saw you from the window.'

'We could have been going to any of the flats.' Joe thought this was just the sort of witness Vera had been hoping for.

'You could,' she said, 'but you didn't.'

'And after us?'

She shook her head. 'Then it was *Countdown*. I don't like it so much since the old presenter died, but I still watch every day.'

'Did you hear anything?'

'No.' He could tell she wished that she could help. 'There's the stairwell between the flats and my hearing's not as good as it used to be. Just as well. The things that used to go on in there.'

He stood up. He wished Peggy had said that she was sorry Dee was dead. Even Jodie had expressed some sympathy. Then he thought that Dee had caused the elderly woman nothing but nuisance and he was getting as soft as Vera.

Chapter Twenty-One

Vera waited until the scene was secure and then she ran down the stairs. Running didn't come naturally, and halfway to the first landing she paused to rest and shouted back to the constable on duty, 'Tell Sergeant Ashworth that I've gone to Holypool and I'll catch up with him later.' She was so breathless that she wasn't sure if the words had carried far enough for him to hear.

She drove straight past the Haven on her first attempt to find the place. She'd never gone in for satnav – more trouble than it was worth. By now it was late afternoon and the countryside surrounding the house was in shadow, so it was easy to miss the entrance. Vera could see why Dee hadn't settled in the Haven. If she'd felt she was in alien territory a couple of Metro stops from Mardle, this would be way outside her comfort zone. This was wide, flat coastal country, where the wind blew straight from Scandinavia and only the Cheviots broke the horizon inland. Vera parked the Land Rover in the courtyard next to a blue minibus and tried to calm her thoughts. She'd been swept here on a wave of righteous indignation, angry on Dee's behalf, but now she had to decide how she should play the meeting. She was still thinking when there was a rap on the window. She opened the door.

The woman was plump and cheerful and Vera recognized the voice from the earlier phone call that she'd made to the Haven. 'Are you lost? Do you need directions back to the village? This is a dead end, I'm afraid, even though some maps show a way through.'

'I'm not lost.' Vera climbed out. Again she felt the stiffness in her knees. And they said that exercise was good for you. 'I'm exactly where I wanted to be. You've already met my colleague, Joe Ashworth.'

'And you are?' Jane Cameron was on the defensive, but her smile didn't shift.

'Eh, pet, I'm his boss, Vera Stanhope. We've already spoken on the phone.'

'And I explained that we have no vacancies at the Haven.' The response was sharp. This woman wasn't accustomed to having her judgement questioned.

Vera waved her hand. 'No need to worry about that now.'

'You've found other accommodation.' Jane sounded relieved. 'That's good.'

'No need for other accommodation,' Vera said. 'Dee Robson's dead.'

They talked in Jane Cameron's office. The house seemed unnaturally quiet. 'What have you done with your women?'

'Most of them are in town. Last-minute Christmas shopping. We don't keep them locked up.'

'How did they get there?'

'We've got a minibus. I gave them a lift to Mardle

Metro. They'll ring when they want picking up.' Hostility prickled between them. Joe would say they were two strong women marking out their territory, but Vera thought it went deeper than that.

'I found Dee Robson in the flat that the social found for her when you chucked her out.' Vera went first. 'Lying on her back with a kitchen knife in her neck. Blood everywhere.'

'And you blame me for the murder because I wouldn't take her back here?'

'Nah,' Vera said. 'She was already dead when I called you.' She narrowed her eyes and made her voice quieter. 'I blame you for throwing her out in the first place. Did you really think she'd manage on her own in the big bad world?'

'Not my responsibility.' Cameron leaned across the desk towards the detective. 'My responsibility is to this place and to the existing residents. Making it run smoothly. As a therapeutic community, helping the women find their feet before moving on to take more independence. One of our residents is a teenage schoolgirl, who fell in with the wrong crowd, was bullied and tried to kill herself. The last thing she needed was Dee Robson pissed and shouting in the middle of the night, or men turning up in taxis looking for pretty young things to abuse. Dee was never going to be independent. I took her in against my better judgement as an emergency placement. I knew we wouldn't be right for her and she wouldn't be happy with us. It was never meant to be a long-term arrangement, and the social worker knew that.'

'But once he'd got Dee into the Haven, he stopped trying to find somewhere more suitable.' Vera was starting to understand how it had worked. The judicial system played games of shifting responsibility too. Like pass the parcel: the one supervising the offender when the music stopped was left to carry the can.

'Of course. From that moment *his* client became *my* problem.'

They grinned at each other, a sudden moment of contact. Vera could understand why Jane had been reluctant to take Dee Robson back, even for Christmas. A lazy social worker would heave a sigh of relief, and Jane might never get rid of her again.

'I thought social services would come up with a better solution,' Jane said. 'And I've felt guilty since I heard that they'd dumped her in a flat with no support. But we couldn't keep her here. And if I made any contact with her, I'd be landed with the responsibility for her. Margaret thought I was a monster and that I was just washing my hands of Dee. She brought Dee along to our winter fair just a couple of weeks ago. Making a point.' She paused. 'Come into the kitchen and I'll make some tea.'

This sounded like a peace offering and Vera followed. 'We think she was killed yesterday afternoon,' she said. 'Can you account for all your lasses?'

'I'm afraid that I can't.' Jane put teabags into a big pot. 'I wasn't here. But they're not great ones for walking and they'd have to get to the end of the track to catch the bus. I doubt they went very far.'

'And where were you?' Vera eyed the tin of biscuits as Jane Cameron opened it. She hadn't had lunch.

'I was summoned to a meeting with Peter Gruskin. He was panicking about Margaret's murder and how the publicity might reflect on the trust. He's always looking for an excuse to shut us down. In the past it's been about money. We're operating on very tight margins here. Now he thinks he's got a better reason.' She paused. 'But I won't let that happen. For some women we're the only place they can be safe. Later I met up with some friends in Jesmond. We went to the pub, had something to eat and too much to drink. What you do at this time of year, I suppose. I got the last Metro to Mardle and then a taxi home. Laurie was still up. She's pretty sensible as long as you keep her away from cars, and she said everything had been fine.'

'What do you make of Gruskin?' Vera was on to her second biscuit and was already feeling more human. Hunger always made her crabby.

'He's not very comfortable around women, unless they know their place.' Jane grinned again. 'Fine if they're cleaning the church or listening to his sermons with rapt attention. Otherwise, forget it. Only child with a doting mother and a clerical father who acted like God. Single-sex school where he was probably bullied.' She paused. 'Sometimes I wonder if some men become pricks because they're bullied, or if they were bullied because they were pricks in the first place.'

Vera chuckled and thought this woman wasn't so different from her after all. They were in the same business. Clearing unpleasantness from the streets so that respectable people could continue their daily lives in blissful ignorance.

'I'm sorry,' Jane said. 'I shouldn't be making light of this. Two women dead, and both with connections to the Haven. Are we looking for a man who doesn't like women? I don't mean Peter Gruskin – there are still lots like him around, and I don't see violence as his thing – but someone with a deep, psychological hatred of single women.'

Vera didn't answer immediately. She thought that this room was quite similar to her kitchen at home. Bigger of course and probably cleaner, but she felt at ease here. She had the sense that if she stayed here long enough, talking through the case with this woman, she might come to a conclusion. She wondered what her boss would make of that as a case-management strategy.

'I don't know,' she said. 'Maybe that has something to do with it.'

In the office the phone rang, obviously amplified throughout the rest of the house because it sounded very loud. Jane got up to answer it. Vera took another biscuit, then on impulse a couple more, which she put in an evidence bag and into her pocket.

When Jane returned she was halfway into her coat. 'That was the girls. They need a lift home. Do you want to stay here and talk to them? You'd be very welcome.'

Vera shook her head and got to her feet. 'I'm not supposed to do the hands-on stuff. Strategic planning, that's my role. Not what I came into the job for, though.'

'Like me.' Jane was walking through the house to the front door. 'If I'd stayed in social services I'd have been promoted away from the front line years ago.'

At the vehicles Vera paused. 'Will you talk to the residents? They trust you, but most of them will have reasons to dislike the police. Any bit of gossip . . . And I'll send someone round tomorrow to do a more formal interview.'

'The lovely Joe?'

'Aye, why not?' Vera had the Land Rover door open, when she turned back to Jane. 'Tell your women to keep safe, eh. No wandering around Mardle on their own.'

Jane nodded and drove off. It was dark now and the headlights of the minibus swung across the damp farmland all the way to the road.

The team came together for the evening briefing in Kimmerston police station. More photos on the white-board. Dee Robson's body. *No dignity in death and not much more when she was living*, Vera thought. The only photo they'd found of her alive was with Margaret Krukowski, taken in a booth, both women grinning. Margaret thirty-five years older, but still more attractive. *Poor lass. I know how that feels.* Perhaps it had been taken on their shopping trip into Newcastle. They'd found the picture in Dee's purse, along with four pounds thirty in loose change.

Vera looked out at the team. There was no sign of Joe Ashworth, but it was time to make a start. 'So what have we got? Two women. Both isolated. Connected through the Haven, where Margaret had been a volunteer, and through geography; they lived two minutes' walk from each other in Mardle. And by the fact that they were on the same Metro when Margaret was killed. How significant is that? Did they *both* see something that led to their deaths? Or did Dee recognize Margaret's killer? Thoughts anyone?'

She looked out into the audience. They seemed

sluggish and unresponsive. Holly raised a tentative hand.

'Hol?'

'Apart from the geography they don't have much in common, do they? I mean Margaret was an educated woman. Why would she choose to spend her time with someone like Dee?' The disdain was obvious and Vera wanted to yell at her. *Do you think Dee Robson wanted to live like that? Do you really think she had a choice?* But Holly was right, and this wasn't the time to teach her the facts of life.

'Good point, Hol. Any ideas?'

'Krukowski was a Christian. Getting down with the sinners.' Charlie, trying for a laugh and missing the mark.

'Why not?' Vera said. 'We don't come across them very often, but there are some good people out there.' The door opened and Joe slid in at the back. 'Anything for us, Joe?' To show him that she'd registered the fact that he was late.

He grinned and her heart gave a little leap. *Ah, my Joe, my little teacher's pet, what have you got for me?*

'I've been chatting to the guys manning the phones. A few bits of information in the last couple of minutes.'

'Well, don't keep it to yourself, man.'

'Jason, the guy who took Dee Robson back to his flat on the afternoon Margaret died, has just got in touch. He saw a picture of Dee on the early-evening news. Had to wait until his girlfriend went out to her mam's before making the call.'

'And?' Vera was almost hopping with impatience.

'Corroborates Dee's story. He'd just been made

redundant from a place in the Mardle industrial estate.' Joe looked at his notes. 'Mardle Foods. They make own-brand cakes for the supermarkets. His shift finished at one and he headed for the Coble with the sole intention of getting pissed. Achieved the aim big-style. Somehow allowed himself to be picked up by Dee and took her home. Realized it wasn't such a good idea when he sobered up a bit, and he bundled her out of the flat before his girlfriend got back. Later that evening he carried on drinking with mates, who can vouch for him.'

Vera nodded. She'd always believed Dee and she couldn't see how that got them much further forward. *Ah, Joe, you shouldn't have raised my hopes like that.* But Joe hadn't finished.

'We know where Margaret Krukowski went the afternoon that she died.'

She beamed. She should have had more faith. 'Well, put us out of our misery!'

'To see a Mr Edwin Short, who has an office in Gosforth High Street. He's been away for a couple of days – a city break in Barcelona. Not short of a bob or two, Mr Short.' Joe looked up and grinned. 'He's a solicitor from the firm Medburn, Liddle and Short. Margaret Krukowski went to see him because she wanted to make a will.'

Chapter Twenty-Two

They caught up with Edwin Short at home because Vera was too impatient to wait until his office opened the following day and she swept Joe along with her. The only parking space was at the end of the street and they walked along the grand Edwardian terrace, catching glimpses of the affluent domestic lives inside: a specky lass practising the violin; a woman laying a table for dinner, carefully polishing glasses and silver before setting them on a dark wood table; an elderly gent with his eyes closed listening to something classical on the radio. Vera thought that Margaret must have lived in a street such as this as a child.

Edwin Short opened the door to them. He was a gentle, courteous man in his late fifties, silver-haired and smart except for a pair of leather slippers with a hole in the toe. He took them into a living room with a high ceiling, an open fire and shelves of books, and offered them sherry. Vera sensed that Joe was a little overawed by his surroundings. The British class thing getting in the way again.

'Did you know Margaret Krukowski well?' She took the glass, which looked tiny in her huge hand. Sherry wasn't really her tipple, but Joe was driving and it didn't do to be impolite.

'Our firm acted for her family,' Short said. 'I met her parents, although they were already elderly when I knew them. My father was a lawyer, set up the practice, and I followed in his footsteps. He knew the couple better than I did, of course.'

'Tell me about them.' Vera leaned back in her chair.

'James Nash was a businessman. His family had a chain of butcher's shops in the North-East. He sold out just at the right time, before the supermarkets took hold, and after that he played at property development. He was cautious, though. Nothing too risky. When he died he was a wealthy man. His wife was a traditional home-maker. Margaret was the only child.' He looked at Vera. 'Is this relevant? Do say if I'm rambling.'

'Not rambling at all.'

'The family fell apart when Margaret married against their wishes. All quite ridiculous, of course.' Short shook his head. 'You have to let your children make their own decisions. My father thought it would all blow over, but Nash was a stubborn man and it seems that Margaret took after him. They never made up the quarrel. I don't think they met again.'

'What happened to all the family money?' Joe interrupted.

'It didn't go to Margaret. The couple died when they were very frail and elderly, and much of the inheritance disappeared in care-home costs. They'd given us power of attorney and we administered their affairs. What remained went to a cancer charity.'

'Did you inform Margaret of their death?' Joe asked.

Short shook his head. 'I assumed she was still living in Poland. That was what her parents had told my father, when he was still dealing with them: that she'd gone with her husband to start a new life there. She wasn't a beneficiary and, after all this time, it seemed too complicated to track her down.'

'And all the time Margaret was in a flat in Harbour Street in Mardle. I wonder if she visited them in the care home.' Vera realized that she'd finished the sherry and she set the glass on a small table.

'You'd have to check with the staff. Certainly she never got in touch with me to find out where they were living. As I said, until she phoned the office to make an appointment, I assumed that she was still living abroad.'

Vera was baffled by this. Margaret Krukowski had been a good woman, a church-goer, yet she'd seemingly made no attempt to find out what was happening to her elderly parents, who'd lived only half an hour away from Mardle. They'd stayed at the same address until they'd moved into residential care, so it would have been easy for her to find them. Margaret didn't seem like a woman who would hold a grudge for fifty years. After all, her parents had been right about her husband. He'd deserted her after a couple of years of marriage. Had pride been her sin then? Had *she* led them to believe that she was happily settled in Poland, because she didn't want to admit that she'd been wrong, or had *they* spread the story to explain her disappearance?

Short continued. 'Margaret got in touch with me out of the blue a week ago. I must admit that I was intrigued. I'd heard a lot about her, at least about the rift with her parents. I only had time to see her the day that she died. We were flying to Barcelona that evening and I tried to put her off until my return, but she insisted. "I don't know how long I have," she said. So I went into the office specially to meet her.' He leaned forward in his chair. 'She was an impressive woman. Articulate and attractive. She said that she was dying and that she wanted to order her affairs. I asked if the cancer might not be treated. There's been so much progress in medical matters. But she said she wasn't interested in fighting the disease. She had no desire to prolong her life.' Vera thought she could understand that. She wasn't a woman who stood on her dignity, but she'd hate hospital, the tests and the poking about, tubes and needles. It was the only reason she was making an effort to get fit.

'Margaret was here to make a will?' Joe Ashworth, wanting things clear and tidy.

Short nodded. 'I asked about the value of her estate. She said that there was no property. "I didn't take after my father, Mr Short. I never felt the need to accumulate houses." But there was a little cash on deposit and, as she had no family, she wanted to make sure that it found a good home.'

'You drew up the will for her then?' Vera had a sudden realization of her own mortality, followed by a moment of panic. What would happen when she died, to the house that she still thought of as Hector's, to the little cash *she* had on deposit? Perhaps she should make an appointment with this quiet and courteous man and make arrangements of her own. But how would she divide up her belongings? It seemed even more of a challenge than buying a Secret Santa Christmas present for a member of her team.

Short was talking. 'No. Apart from one complication, it was all quite straightforward and she was eager to complete the business with one visit, but because of that complication I persuaded her to wait until I returned from my holiday.'

'Can you tell us the proposed terms of the will?'

'In the circumstances, of course. We agreed on the wording, apart from one bequest. Margaret Krukowski had fifty thousand pounds in fixed-rate bonds and ISAs with the North of England Building Society. She intended to leave ten thousand to her friend Kate Dewar,' he looked at handwritten notes on his lap, '"an investment in a musical talent". Ten thousand was to go to a charity for homeless women called the Haven, and ten thousand to "my old friend Malcolm Kerr, in gratitude for his help and support over the years". And the remaining cash, twenty thousand pounds, to . . .' he paused '. . . Deirdre Robson. I understand that she was your second murder victim. I got in touch with you as soon as I heard.'

For a moment Vera didn't speak. Ideas and questions were spinning around her head. Fifty thousand might seem a modest sum to the lawyer, but it was considerable for a woman who'd spent the last twenty years as a glorified chambermaid and kitchen assistant. And ten thousand might be enough to save the Haven from closure. She wondered if Margaret had talked to Jane Cameron about the bequest. If she'd had second thoughts when Dee had been asked to leave the hostel.

Short went on. 'The complication was the bequest

to Miss Robson. The money wasn't to go to her directly, but to a third party to administer the money on her behalf, to befriend and assist her, and to provide additional funds to supplement her benefits. It wasn't a usual clause in a will, and I explained that I'd need to check the wording.'

'Had she chosen this friend to look after Dee Robson?' Vera wished Margaret was still alive so that she could discuss all this; Vera would have applauded the woman's generosity and common sense.

'It was another of the beneficiaries, Malcolm Kerr.'

Vera wondered what all that was about. Malcolm was hardly the most reliable of Margaret's acquaintances. Perhaps she'd hoped that responsibility for Dee Robson would stop him falling apart through grief and self-pity.

Short was continuing to speak. 'I wondered if she'd asked Mr Kerr if he was willing to take on the role. It seemed to me rather an onerous task. She said that she'd discussed it with him in general terms. I said that she should get his specific and formal agreement to the arrangement before we drew up her will.'

'How did you leave matters?'

'That she would talk to Mr Kerr and ask if he'd be willing to meet me. We'd even made an appointment.' Short turned away and Vera thought that even after such a brief contact, he was mourning the death of a woman whom he'd admired.

'What happens to the money now?' She saw that Joe was keen to get home. He knew this was unofficial overtime and wouldn't go on his expenses sheet.

Short gave a sad smile. 'We try to find her next of kin. No children and no immediate family, so it won't be easy. Certainly none of the friends she'd hoped to help will benefit.'

They sat in Vera's Land Rover to discuss the conversation. The street was quiet. 'Well, that doesn't help much.' Vera fished in her pocket for the evidence bag and offered a biscuit to Joe, who shook his head. 'Some of the people we might have considered suspects had every reason to keep Margaret alive. If they knew what she was planning, of course.' A young couple, their arms around each other, walked down the pavement towards them. They stopped under a street light and kissed.

'Where did she get all that money?'

Vera thought about that. 'If she'd been frugal, she might have saved a bit when she was working for Malcolm's father. Left on deposit for all those years, it could have grown into something substantial.'

'Why wouldn't she spend it, though?' Joe couldn't get his head round that one. 'Why live in that tiny flat when she had the deposit for a bigger place of her own?'

Vera shook her head. 'Maybe she just liked it where she was, being part of Kate Dewar's family.' She looked at her watch. 'You'd best get on home. Sal will be making wax models of me and sticking pins in.'

He had his car door open when her phone rang. It was Holly, her voice triumphant. Vera listened. 'Well done, Hol. Brilliant work!' And she could sense Holly beaming on the other end of the line.

'What was all that about?' Joe pretended lack of

interest, but she could tell that he was desperate to know.

'Holly, showing a bit of initiative. George Enderby, one of the regulars at the Harbour Guest House, the publisher's rep . . .'

Joe nodded.

'He told us he was on his way to Newcastle for work, then to Scotland to visit a couple of independent bookshops there,' Vera said. 'And that tonight he was staying in Mardle again on his way home.'

'And?' Curiosity was getting the better of Joe and making him shirty.

'He's a publisher's rep all right. One of their longest-serving employees, apparently. Very highly thought of. But he's not at work this week. He finished last Friday for his Christmas holidays.'

'So what's he doing in Mardle?'

Chapter Twenty-Three

They were at the early-morning briefing and the focus was on George Enderby.

'Why would Enderby come north to stay in Harbour Street if he's not here for work?' Vera was pacing up and down in front of the whiteboard. Since Holly had come up with the information, Vera had been worrying at the notion. She couldn't see the man as a killer, but couldn't imagine why he would lie. She looked around the room. Most of the team were bleary-eyed and untidy. No energy. She'd dragged them in early. 'What do we know about him? Holly?'

'Nothing,' Holly said. She was still sharp and smart. 'No record.'

'Have we got him on CCTV?'

'A possible sighting of him walking down Harbour Street towards the Coble with another guy on the day that Margaret died, but it's just a back view from the Metro, so it's hard to tell.'

Vera wondered if Holly had been to bed or if she'd been in the station all night. 'Do we know where he is now?'

'He checked into the Harbour Guest House yesterday. I phoned in the evening and got Chloe, Kate Dewar's daughter. Apparently he asked if he could stay an extra night, so he's not scheduled to leave until tomorrow. I've asked the team canvassing in the area to keep a lookout for his car, in case he changes his mind.'

Vera thought about that. 'Okay. So why would Enderby want to hang around in Mardle if he's the killer? Why not get away from the place as soon as he had the chance?'

Charlie raised a hand. 'Some killers do haunt the crime scene. They get a thrill out of watching the investigation.'

Vera could imagine that. Enderby with his spy stories, watching the action playing out in front of him, thinking that he could outwit the police. She paused and came to a decision. 'Hol, you carry on the good work here. Any connection between Enderby and Margaret or Dee, we want to know about it. He told me that he supported Margaret's good causes with cash. Did he help out more directly, go to the Haven or meet up with Dee Robson at any time? Let's make some connections. Joe, you're with me.'

'Where are we going?'

'To the Coble. If Enderby was heading in that direction the day Margaret died, that's probably where he ended up. Let's go and see.'

The pub was closed. Outside a scattering of cigarette ends on the pavement and, even from where they stood, the smell of stale beer. Inside a tiny woman was pushing a Hoover across the floor. It was as big as she was. Vera banged on the window, but the woman didn't hear until she turned off the machine. She shook her head and pointed to her watch. Vera held up her warrant card to the dirty window and eventually the door was unbolted.

'Do you run this place?'

'Nah, I'm just the cleaner.' She was nervous. Vera suspected she was paid cash in hand and still claimed benefit.

'Who does?'

'Lawrence. He lives in the flat upstairs.'

'Well, give him a shout, pet. Then you can get on.'

'I'll unlock the door and you can go up yourself.' She was as skinny and shapeless as a ten-year-old girl. Nicotine on her fingers, and Vera could tell she was desperate for a tab. She'd be outside on the pavement smoking as soon as she'd got rid of them.

She led them through the lounge bar to a back corridor and took a string of keys on a chain from her apron pocket. Vera was reminded of a prison officer at locking-up time.

Lawrence was up, but only just. He was wearing jogging bottoms and a vest and his feet were bare. Vera had knocked on the door at the top of the narrow stairs, Joe standing behind her. The landlord was probably expecting the cleaner, a demand for payment or for new dusters.

'Who are you?' A giant of a man, but somehow gentle with it. Vera would have sworn like a trooper, if strangers had turned up in her home at this hour of the morning. He stood back to let them in. The room looked out over Harbour Street and onto the water.

'Were you in the bar on the night Margaret Krukowski was murdered in the Metro?'

'I was working early on,' he said, 'but not when the

news first came through. The other bar staff had come in by then and I was up here, taking my break.'

'Quiet, was it, early on?'

'Yeah, dead. Snow had been forecast and everyone was keen to get home.' He leaned against the windowsill and turned to look out into the street.

'So you'd remember anyone in the bar that evening?'

'Early on, like I said. Not later. The Metro closed down and folk couldn't get into town, so they all piled in here.'

'George Enderby,' Vera said. He didn't respond straight away, so she continued, 'He's one of the regular guests at Kate Dewar's guest house.'

Lawrence nodded to show that he knew who they were talking about. 'Aye,' he said. 'He was in that afternoon with a mate. Older. Kind of scruffy.'

'Malcolm Kerr?'

'Nah!' Lawrence said. 'He was in later, and he had a skinful. I didn't know the other man.'

'Was Dee Robson in then too? We know she was in sometime that afternoon. She picked up a guy called Jason. Then she was back later in the evening.' Vera remembered seeing the woman coming out of the pub, tottering on her heels, bowled along by the jeers.

Lawrence thought for a minute. 'I don't think she was in at the same time as the men. They were on their own in the lounge.'

'What were they talking about?'

Lawrence shook his head. 'No idea! There was music and they were in the far corner. When I went to collect their glasses they shut up.'

'But you'd have got some impression of their

mood,' Vera said. 'It'd be instinctive, wouldn't it, picking up the atmosphere in the pub. Keeping an eye out for trouble.'

Lawrence gave a little chuckle. 'Those two would be no trouble. A couple of old gadgies, sitting over a pint. But one of them was upset. At one point he was crying.'

'Which one?'

'The one you were asking about. George Enderby.'

Then Vera's brain was buzzing. Because George couldn't have been crying for Margaret Krukowski. At that point she was still alive, making her way to the solicitor's office in Gosforth, to talk about her will. Perhaps she'd talked to George and told him that she was dying, but then there'd be no need for the man to have lied to the police. And he'd still have had time to drive to Gosforth, to follow Margaret onto the Metro and to have killed her. Then plenty of time to collect his car and drive back to Harbour Street, arriving in the guest house just before Vera and Joe had turned up. But he'd been so charming then, so confident and pleasant. Not the demeanour of a man who'd just committed murder. Or that of a man who'd sat in a pub earlier in the day crying.

'You really don't know who the other bloke was?' This was Joe, getting impatient, while she was staring out of the window lost in thought.

'I've seen him about in Harbour Street,' Lawrence said. 'He goes out with Malcolm Kerr in the boat to the island. Some sort of research.'

Mike Craggs, who'd also lied. He'd said he drove home to the Tyne Valley as soon as he got back from Coquet Island.

Vera thought that Enderby and Craggs were stupid men. She couldn't see them as killers, so why hadn't they told the truth? Unless this was a great conspiracy and all the suspects were in it together. She smiled at the thought. She was back to Enderby and his fantasies, his wild fictions. 'Thanks. You've been very helpful.'

Lawrence didn't ask anything about the investigation. She liked his gentleness and his lack of curiosity. He'd make a better priest than Peter Gruskin. 'I'll show you out,' he said and padded ahead of them, his bare feet splayed and huge like a bear's.

Downstairs it was quiet. The cleaner had moved into the toilets. In the lounge there was a painting of a fat old woman. She was leaning forward with her elbows on the bar. It wasn't a brilliant painting, but it gave an impression of someone strong and eccentric.

'Who's that?' Vera nodded towards it as they passed.

'Val Butt.' Lawrence smiled. 'She managed this place for years. I took over from her. She was quite a character. A fierce lady. People still tell stories about her.'

Out in the street the morning was moving on. Women were already in the fisheries preparing to open for lunchtime. Vera phoned Holly. 'Tell me you've found another connection between Margaret and Enderby.' Looking up the street, she could see that his car was still there. Why was he staying two more days, instead of only his usual one? Perhaps he was one of the ghouls who found a murder investigation exciting, who travelled from crime scene to crime scene like a rock-star groupie.

'Nothing of any real importance. As we already know, he went along to the winter fair at the Haven a few weeks ago. He'd donated some books for them to sell and acted as their Father Christmas. According to the woman in charge, he spent a fortune on raffle tickets and whenever he won a prize he put it back on the stall.'

'Did you get a list of residents who were staying there then?'

'Of course.' Holly was still full of herself after making the discovery about Enderby. 'The same bunch as are there now, apart from an emergency admission, a woman who'd been beaten by her husband. She's since got an injunction and is back in the family house.' She paused. 'Dee Robson was there for the afternoon too. Margaret took her along for a treat.'

Vera remembered Jane Cameron's words. *Not just for a treat, but to make a point.*

'Boss?' Holly still on the line and impatient.

'See if you can track down Professor Craggs,' Vera said. 'We need to talk to him too.'

She switched off the phone and started up Harbour Street. Joe Ashworth followed and caught up with her, so they were walking side by side. 'You can't really think that Enderby and Craggs planned the murder?' He thought she was mad.

'They've lied to me,' she said. 'Both of them.'

'People lie to the police for all sorts of reasons.'

'But they shouldn't.' She stopped abruptly to catch her breath. 'They shouldn't lie to *me*.'

Chapter Twenty-Four

Kate was drinking coffee in the kitchen with Stuart when there was a knock at the door, so loud that she jumped and felt an irrational surge of fear. They'd had a lazy morning. George Enderby had come to the dining room for breakfast as usual and then had disappeared. The kids were out. The house was still and quiet; it rarely was, and she thought that in the future their life could be like this, peaceful and easy. Then there was the knock at the door and Stuart looked up from the newspaper on his lap, frowning. 'Shall I go?'

But he seemed so settled there, and a little elderly in the harsh light of a working kitchen, so she got to her feet and kissed his forehead as she went past him and felt the skin very dry on her lips.

She looked through the hall window before opening the door and saw the fat detective and her sidekick standing outside.

'Sorry to disturb you, pet. Do you mind if we come in?' And by the time Vera Stanhope had finished the words she was inside the house, the younger man trailing after her. Kate wondered how that must make him feel, always in the fat woman's shadow.

Vera stood in the hall, rubbing her hands against

the cold, as if they'd been waiting outside for hours and not just a few minutes.

'I was wondering if we could get breakfast,' she said. 'I mean, we'd buy it of course. We'd have to. These days even a freebie fry-up might be taken the wrong way. Bribery and corruption.'

And she flashed a bright smile, so Kate wondered if this was the only reason for the visit – if they'd disturbed her perfect morning just to make them bacon and eggs. Or if this was some kind of weird joke. She remembered the rush of adrenaline when she'd heard the banging on the door and felt angry. The cheek of the woman! It was hard to believe this was happening – the strange woman invading her house and demanding breakfast. But then it was hard to believe that two women had been killed in the town.

Vera was still talking. 'You're not on your own, are you? I thought you still had guests staying.'

'Only George,' Kate said. 'George Enderby.'

'Ah, I thought I saw his car outside. We wouldn't have disturbed you if we'd thought you were planning to take the day off.' She walked further into the house, looking round her. 'Is Mr Enderby around?' She made the question casual, but Kate could tell it was important.

'He went out,' Kate said.

'Oh?' Still the pretence that it didn't really matter. 'But his car's still there.'

'He got the Metro into town.'

'Did he say where he was going?' Vera's eyes were sharp as tacks and there was no mention now of Kate cooking breakfast for her. It seemed that was just a pretext to get through the door.

'Some library? Something about getting a fix, a visit to a proper place for books to be cherished, before he heads south tomorrow.' George had mentioned it at breakfast, but Kate hadn't taken much notice.

'The Lit & Phil Library?'

'Yes!' Kate thought the inspector must be some sort of witch to have guessed that right. 'How did you know?'

'It's where book-lovers hang out.' Vera flashed her another smile. 'And the lonely and the slightly mad. I should know. I'm a member myself.' Another pause. 'Can you show Joe here into Mr Enderby's room? I need to get back to work.'

Kate hesitated. She found it hard to stand up to the fat detective. 'But I can't do that. It's an invasion of his privacy.'

'It's your house, pet. Give us permission and we don't need a warrant.'

They stood for a moment staring at each other, and finally Kate gave in. She didn't owe George Enderby anything and, if he was involved in these murders, then it was her duty to help the police. She wondered what Stuart would make of it. Surely he would agree too. And perhaps there'd always been something a bit odd about the man, something a bit unsettling.

Kate went into the kitchen to fetch her keys and, when she returned, Vera Stanhope had disappeared. It was hard to imagine that such a big woman could move so quickly or so lightly. The sergeant followed her up the stairs and waited in silence while she opened the door. She thought he would send her away, but he nodded for her to go in first. Perhaps he needed her there as a witness. Kate hadn't been in to make up the room yet, but it was tidy as always, the duvet folded back to air the bed, the cup on the tray next to the kettle.

George's holdall was open on the floor in the corner. It seemed that he hadn't really bothered to unpack this time, and that was unusual. Normally he hung up his work shirts and his jacket as soon as he arrived. *'If you're a salesman, Kate, first impressions count.'*

Standing next to it was the wheelie suitcase in which George carried his samples. The sergeant laid it flat on the floor and unzipped it. Inside she saw some jeans and a heavy jersey, a pair of walking boots and a waterproof jacket.

'But where are the books?' Kate couldn't help herself.

'What books?' The sergeant looked up. He was still kneeling on the floor. He frowned a little.

'He carries books in the suitcase. Samples to show the shopkeepers.'

The detective said nothing. He began opening the drawers, but all George's clothes were still in the holdall. Joe Ashworth emptied that carefully, laying each item on the bed, but it seemed there was nothing of interest to him. He looked in the bathroom, before turning back to Kate. 'That's been very helpful. Thank you.' His face gave nothing away. She wanted to ask if they thought George was a murderer.

'I have children,' she said. 'A daughter. Is it safe to let Mr Enderby stay here tonight?' She could hear the hysteria in her own voice.

There was only a moment of hesitation before he replied. 'We have no evidence against Mr Enderby. We think he can help us with our enquiries.'

She didn't find that reassuring.

At the bottom of the stairs the detective held out his hand and thanked her again. He could have been one of her paying guests.

Stuart was still in the kitchen. He'd heard Kate come down the stairs and already had the coffee machine on again. 'What was all that about?' He didn't look at her as he asked the question and she couldn't tell how curious he really was.

'The police. They wanted to look inside George's room.'

'Did you let them?' Now he did turn to look at her.

'Yes.' She wondered now if she'd been a coward not to stand up to them. 'If it helps find the killer . . .' Her voice trailed away.

'You think George could be the murderer?' Stuart waited for her to answer and she saw that this wasn't an idle question. She recognized the teacher in him. He'd use the same tone standing in front of his class. *Is that really how you think that piece should be played?* He seemed unusually serious.

She took his question seriously too. 'No,' she said at last, because despite her earlier misgivings and the hesitation in the detective's voice, it was impossible to think of quiet and gentle George Enderby hurting anyone. She'd seen him open a window to allow a wasp to escape. 'What reason would George have for killing Margaret? And he'd have hardly known Dee

Robson. Unless she'd tried to pick him up in the Coble.'

'What do you mean?' Stuart frowned.

'Dee was always trying to pick up men in the Coble. The locals knew her and just made fun of her.' Kate couldn't help an awkward smile, as she thought how embarrassed George Enderby would be by such an encounter. Polite and awkward, but terrified too.

'Are you saying that Dee Robson was a prostitute?' The coffee had stopped dripping and he poured a mug for Kate. She saw that he was shocked. She had never thought of him as a prude.

'I suppose I am. Not a very good one, though.' She gave a nervous smile. 'An amateur, not a professional.' Then she thought the attempt at humour was in poor taste. The woman had just been killed. She slid a look at Stuart, but if he disapproved of her flippancy he didn't show it. He seemed lost in thought.

'What shall we do for the rest of the day?' She imagined a walk in the hills. The kids had said they'd be out until the evening, so there was no danger they'd be in the house alone with George. She and Stuart had talked about doing a part of Hadrian's Wall. Then perhaps lunch in a pub. A real fire and home-made broth. Suddenly she was desperate to escape from Mardle and Harbour Street.

'I'm sorry,' he said. 'I think I'll be a bit tied up after all.' She was expecting an explanation, but he still seemed preoccupied. He jumped to his feet as if he had a sudden impulse to escape from *her*. At the bottom of the stairs he stopped abruptly. 'Can I come round again later?'

'Of course!' It came to her now that the strange

behaviour had a logical explanation: he was going into town to buy her Christmas present. That was why he was being so secretive. 'You know you can come here at any time.' And she turned her head to kiss him.

Left to herself in the big house, Kate felt that things were slipping out of her control. She wished now that the children were still at home, that Ryan was back from Malcolm's boatyard and that Chloe hadn't disappeared into town with a mysterious friend. She wanted everyone here, where she could keep an eye on them. Where they'd be safe.

Chapter Twenty-Five

Joe crossed the road so that he couldn't be seen from the Harbour Guest House basement and wondered what he should do next. He assumed Vera had gone into town on the trail of George Enderby. She'd probably dragged Holly or Charlie along with her, a corroborative witness if the case came to court. He tried phoning her, but the call went straight to voicemail. Joe was still standing there dithering, phone in his hand, when the door of the guest house opened and Stuart Booth emerged. He hesitated and then looked back at the house. Joe expected Kate Dewar to follow, but the man closed the door behind him and remained there for a moment. Dithering too. They formed mirror images of each other on both sides of the road. Booth seemed to come to a decision, before making a dash across the street to join Joe outside the church.

'I wonder if I might talk to you, Sergeant. I have some information; it might be relevant to the murder of Margaret Krukowski.'

Joe was in a pool car and he drove Booth to the police station in Kimmerston. Vera might have done it differently, had some informal chat over tea or beer or chips. But Joe wanted this done properly – the man's words recorded. Driving to Kimmerston, he felt a tingle of excitement. It occurred to him that the man intended to confess to murder: Booth was so still and so serious.

In the car Booth didn't speak. Joe turned occasionally to sneak a look at him and saw that he was staring out of the window, very tense. The muscles in his face were set hard. Joe had come across men like him in rural Northumberland. Hill farmers and shepherds, with few words. Tough, sinewy men. It was hard to imagine Booth as a musician. Joe had looked him up, and Google said that jazz was his thing. Perhaps that was when he *did* relax, and he could picture the man then in a basement bar playing saxophone, head tilted back, eyes half-closed, wrapped up in his music.

'What instrument do you play?' The question came without thought.

Booth didn't turn away from the window to answer. 'At school, whatever they need me to. Piano for assembly, recorder to start the little buggers off. But for pleasure, the alto sax.'

Joe was pleased that he'd guessed right.

In the station Joe got Booth coffee from the staffroom, in a mug, not the cardboard cups they usually gave to witnesses. One of Vera's tricks. Holly had gone into town with Vera in search of Enderby, so Charlie sat in, the silent man, the observer, while for once Joe took charge of the discussion. They sat in an interview room and their words bounced off the gloss-painted walls and seemed to rattle like hail from the ceiling.

He asked if he might record their discussion and Booth nodded.

'So, Mr Booth, you said that you have some information about Margaret Krukowski.'

It took Booth a while to speak. Perhaps he was expecting the officers to ask him direct questions.

As he waited, Joe looked at him, taking in the details. His clothes. Denim jeans and a checked shirt and knitted sweater. Those sturdy trainers that could act as walking boots. Booth was wearing a green fleece too, though it was warm in here. He wouldn't be a man to feel the cold, but it would have taken movement to get it off, and still he wasn't moving much. A face moulded by the weather, and eyes like slate.

'Margaret Krukowski was a prostitute,' Booth said. 'Not recently, as far as I know, but years ago. I only just discovered – when Kate said it – that Dee Robson was a sex worker. And suddenly it seemed important.'

Sparks were firing now in Joe's head. *So we're not looking for a man who hates women, but a man who hates prostitutes.* He wondered what Vera would make of the news, then thought she might not be surprised that church-going Margaret had once worked in the sex trade. The boss had said from the beginning that they needed to uncover Margaret's secret.

'How do you know that, Mr Booth?'

He took a deep breath. 'Because I used her services. Regularly, over a number of years.' Joe thought the man would stop there, but he continued to speak. Joe thought that a priest taking confession might feel like he did now – curiosity flecked with embarrassment and distaste. Booth continued: 'I was a newly qualified teacher, awkward, shy. Needing a relationship, but not sure about how to get one. A kind of joke with the other musicians. One of them gave me her number.' Even now he seemed to be blushing at the memory. 'I got drunk one night and phoned her.' He paused. 'She didn't call herself Margaret, of course, and never mentioned a second name.'

'What did she call herself?' The room was on the ground floor, and outside there was the background rumble of traffic.

'Anna,' he said. 'She told me she was Polish, but I didn't believe that. Her accent was English. Perhaps she thought the story would make her seem more exotic.'

'She married a Polish man.' Joe felt an urge to stand up for the woman, despite her chosen profession. 'So it was almost the truth.'

'Well, of course she never told me that she'd been married.'

'The marriage didn't last long,' Joe said. 'Only a couple of years.'

'I was probably with her longer than her husband.' Booth leaned back in his chair and shut his eyes. The notion seemed to give him some satisfaction.

'Where did she live?'

'Where she was living when she died.' He opened his eyes again. 'That flat in Harbour Street. The house was very different then, but her rooms were always clean, pleasant. You'd walk up the stairs past the sound of kids grizzling and the smells of cooking, and then you'd go into her place. Everything calm and warm. Like going into a different world. I went for that, as much as for the sex. The escape from reality.'

'She worked from her home?' Joe was surprised by

that. All the working girls he knew were fiercely protective of their privacy.

'I think she'd looked into the possibility of finding a place to operate from, but she said she'd been ripped off. She'd rather trust her clients than the sharks who preyed off sex workers. And there weren't many clients. We paid well. She was worth it.'

Joe was suddenly intensely curious about what had gone on between these two people. Despite himself, he imagined them in the attic room in Harbour Street, the shy young teacher and the slightly older woman, who was taking money for sex. He found himself wanting details. Perhaps Booth guessed what he was thinking because obliquely he answered the unspoken question.

'Anna was amazing.' He paused. 'I counted the days until I could see her again. Though, looking back, I suppose it wouldn't have taken much to please me. I was young and awkward and she was older and more experienced. Kind. And there was the thrill of the illicit. I never told anyone about the encounters, not even the friend who'd passed on her name. I loved the fact that our meetings were secret, that the next day I would walk into school to be a respectable, responsible teacher and nobody had any idea what I'd been doing the night before.'

'Why did it stop?' Joe asked. 'I take it that it *did* stop?' He couldn't imagine this man in his late fifties climbing the stairs to see Margaret when Kate wasn't looking.

'I found a girlfriend, Sergeant. Not someone I cared for as I do about Kate, but someone to sleep with. That was less exciting than the visits to Harbour

Street, but it seemed more appropriate. And as I got older I lost my courage. I was scared someone would see me. I couldn't have stood it getting out that I used the services of a prostitute.'

'Did you ever meet any of Margaret's other clients?' The thought came to Joe quickly. A sudden flash of hope.

Booth shook his head. 'No. As I say, I think we were a select bunch. Margaret presented a respectable face to the world too. A couple of times I saw the back of a man disappearing down Harbour Street in the gloom as I came in. But no faces. Nothing that would be of any use to you.'

'When did you realize that Margaret was still living in the same house?' Joe thought Stuart seemed almost relaxed now. The relief of sharing his secret had eased the tension.

'Not until Kate introduced us. A sunny lunchtime in the garden. When I found out that Kate lived in Harbour Street I was intrigued. It seemed some sort of omen when it turned out to be the same house. Perhaps I was hoping to regain that youthful excitement. And I have captured it, in a way, though the house was unrecognizable. She'd talked about Margaret, the friend who helped her in the kitchen, but of course I didn't make any connection. The woman I'd known was called Anna, and I'd last seen her more than thirty years before.'

'But you recognized Margaret?'

'Oh yes, immediately.' He leaned forward across the scratched table to make a point. 'She was still a very beautiful woman.'

'And did she recognize you?'

He thought for a moment before answering. 'I think she did. I hope so. I had the sense that she was giving Kate and me her blessing. We never talked about our former lives, even on the few times that we found ourselves alone.'

Joe drove Stuart back to Mardle. He was glad of an excuse to leave Kimmerston and, like Vera, he thought that Mardle was the centre of the investigation. There was still no conversation. Booth directed him to a small development on the edge of the town, a conversion of farm outbuildings where he had an apartment. The place was on the west side of the town and Joe thought that it would be just a short walk across open fields to the Haven. When the car stopped Booth stayed still for a moment and turned to Joe, wanting reassurance. 'I suppose this makes me a suspect. Because Margaret could have told Kate about my past, I do have a motive of a sort.'

Joe wasn't sure what to say. 'We keep an open mind,' he said at last. 'We always do. Everyone who knew Margaret Krukowski is a potential suspect. But we're grateful for the information. It's been very useful.'

Stuart frowned. 'Do you think I should tell Kate? I suppose if there's a court case it might come out. It would look better if I told her now.' He paused. 'I did wonder if she'd guessed that I knew Margaret. I'd kept a photo of her in my wallet. Margaret gave it to me as a memento when I told her that I wouldn't be visiting her any more. It's gone. I thought perhaps Kate had found it, but rooting through other people's possessions isn't her style. It must just have fallen out one day.' He stopped suddenly and seemed terribly sad that he no longer had anything to remember Margaret by.

In theory Joe was a great believer in honesty in a relationship. Though there were certainly things in his past that he'd never discussed with Sal. But this was a murder investigation, and information was power. He imagined Vera's face when he passed on the news, and thought it gave *him* power too. At least it would earn him a few brownie points. 'We'd rather you kept this to yourself for the moment, sir.'

Relieved to be let off the hook, Stuart flashed him a sudden bright smile, and got out of the car.

Chapter Twenty-Six

Vera stood outside the Georgian symmetry of the Lit & Phil Library in Newcastle city centre, waiting for Holly, and letting her mind wander. Passengers from Central Station swept past her and cars screeched at the lights, but Vera was lost in thought and took no notice. Two women. Margaret Krukowski, bright and smart, born into affluence and wanting to set her affairs straight because she realized that she was ill. Dee Robson, one of life's unfortunates, someone who'd needed looking after from the moment she was born, though until Margaret had come along, nobody had bothered much. They were linked by geography, living close to each other, on the seaward side of the railway line, and they'd both travelled on the same Metro train the afternoon of Margaret's death. As had Joe Ashworth. And his daughter Jessie. Vera wondered if it had occurred to Joe that he and Jess might be in danger too. Perhaps it was just as well that he had so little imagination.

Holly appeared, fighting against the crowd, still immaculately made-up. They went inside and stood at the bottom of the grand stone stairs.

'Do you know the Lit & Phil?' Vera was a member. Hector had brought her here for lectures on birds and bugs. A love of the building was one of the few things she'd inherited from him.

'Of course. Brilliant, isn't it?'

Of course she knew the library. Holly had no areas of ignorance at all. Or so she thought.

'Apparently Enderby's inside. He left Harbour Street straight after breakfast and told Kate he was coming here. Let's see what he has to say for himself.'

They climbed the stairs to the library on the first floor and opened the door to a room flooded with light from the glass domes. The walls were made of books. There was no immediate sign of Enderby either at the reading tables close to the door or at the hatch where coffee was served. The members looked up briefly, but took no notice. The library assistant behind the desk gave Vera a wave. Holly seemed surprised that her boss had been recognized – the Lit & Phil wasn't the inspector's natural habitat.

Scouring the room for Enderby, Vera felt a rising panic. Perhaps the man was cleverer than they'd thought and had misled Kate. Perhaps he was on a train south. She looked round the corner into the other leg of the L-shaped room. Still no sign of him. Ignoring Holly, who was trailing behind her, Vera returned to the desk.

'George Enderby,' Vera said. 'Big guy. Balding. From the south. Loves his books.'

'Ah, George.' The library assistant smiled fondly and Vera saw that the man had worked his charm on her too. 'Yes, he came in as soon as we opened. He's one of our southern members. You'll probably find him in the Silence Room. He prefers to read in there.'

Vera told Holly to stay where she was and went

through the door at the back of the room and down the stairs. The heavy door shut out the sounds of the library. There was the gurgle of a cistern in the distance, otherwise a dense quiet. Vera paused outside the Silence Room. A moment of superstition, as close to prayer as she'd ever get. *Let him be there.* She opened the door.

It was a square room with no natural light. Silent. Of course. Talking wasn't allowed. Even a cough provoked tutting. At first it seemed empty, but bookshelves jutted into the room at right-angles to the walls, forming small alcoves, and she couldn't see into those from the door. In one a middle-aged woman typed furiously on a laptop. In another was George Enderby, leaning forward with his head on the small card table, as if he were asleep.

The rules of silence were entrenched from childhood and she couldn't bring herself to speak. She came close to him. He was still in his overcoat and must be very warm. She tapped him on the shoulder. For a brief moment there was no reaction and she had the wild thought that he might be dead. Another victim. Then he woke with a start. In his shock he seemed about to talk and she put her finger to her lips. She motioned for him to follow her and left the room.

They used one of the upstairs rooms for their discussion. Vera had liked Enderby when they'd first met, but had felt even then that he was playing games. All that talk of stories, of Margaret Krukowski as a spy. Now she watched him drink coffee and let him sit in silence, the tension building. He was used to words and didn't cope well with quiet. He spoke first, as she'd known that he would.

'This is very pleasant, Inspector, but I was surprised to see you, I must admit.' The shy, boyish smile. 'Clever you, to track me down! To what do I owe the pleasure?'

'Did you know Dee Robson, Mr Enderby?' A question sharp like sleet on the skin. He hadn't been expecting it.

He paused. 'That poor woman who seems to live in the bar of the Coble? I've seen her there of course, and heard the cruel comments.' He hesitated again. 'I've bought her a drink once or twice. I always sit in the lounge, but passing through the bar, you know, I've felt sorry for her. Perhaps it's because she was one of Margaret's good causes that I always felt obliged to be kind.'

'You haven't heard that she's been murdered?' Holly asked the question, and Enderby turned towards her and seemed startled by the intervention. It was as if an impertinent child had interrupted a conversation between adults.

'No,' he said slowly. 'I didn't go into the Coble last night. I had a large lunch before I got back to Harbour Street and managed with a sandwich in my room. How would I have heard?'

'I need to know why you lied to us, Mr Enderby.' Vera leaned forward across the table. The room was very warm. There was no response. The man stood up and took off his coat, folded it carefully on the back of his chair.

'Well, Mr Enderby?' Vera was at her imperious best. 'Why the porkie-pies?'

'I don't quite understand, Inspector.'

'You told us that you were in the region to sell

books. But as far as we can tell, you haven't been near a bookshop since you arrived. So would you like to tell us what this is all about?'

He seemed to collapse from inside. Vera had the inappropriate thought that he was like the shiny bag inside a box of wine once all the booze had been drunk. All the gentlemanly politeness had been a protection from the world and, now that it wasn't working, he was empty. She thought he might cry, but instead he looked up with a quiet desperation. 'I didn't kill anyone,' he said.

'So why all the lies?'

'You wouldn't understand. *I* don't understand.'

'Try me.'

There was a silence. Vera thought he was taking time to compose one of his stories, but in the end the words came out as an unfiltered stream. It was the same pleasant voice, but she sensed this conversation was personal, not his usual performance.

'I was lazy at university – not intellectually lazy, you know. I always found time for work. But emotionally. Can you be emotionally lazy?' He looked up at them, but didn't seem to expect an answer. 'So there was this girl in our tutor group. Pleasant enough. Good-looking in a staid, country-rose sort of way. And she seemed to fancy me, so I thought, why not ask her out? She was from a good family, so my parents liked her. And I didn't *dislike* her. It was all very easy, and I could give my energy to my books and at the time that mattered more than anything.' He paused and took a breath. 'After university we sort of drifted into marriage. I knew I didn't love her or anything like that, but everyone expected it and it would have been very unkind, you know, to dump her once we seemed to have got engaged. So I just went through with it. As I explained, a sort of emotional laziness. Or cowardice. Perhaps that would be a better word.' He stopped again. Vera poured him some coffee. She could see that Holly was wondering where this was leading. She was itching to tell the man to get to the point, but knew better than to interrupt in front of Vera.

George Enderby continued. 'And it all seemed to be working out for the best. Diana didn't need to find a job. Money was never a problem for us. She'd inherited from a wealthy grandmother. Horses were her thing: dressage. She's really very good. She only just missed out on an Olympic place a few years ago. I do admire her. We both wanted children, and that was a disappointment. When it never happened, I mean.' He broke off and stared out of the window at the traffic queuing in the Westgate Road.

'That's the background,' Vera said. 'And all very interesting. But it doesn't quite explain why you're in Northumberland pretending to be at work.'

'Diana's left me.' They expected another torrent of words, but he paused again and then spoke more slowly. 'I suppose I just felt the need to run away, and this is where I feel most at home.' He put his head in his hands again. 'I considered leaving her a few times. The relationship was never entirely satisfactory. So why do I feel so dreadful? So hurt.'

'Male pride,' Vera said briskly. She was curious about this strange marriage and would have liked to know more. Had the couple shared a bed, for example? Had they had sex once they'd decided there'd be no children? But she supposed that was hardly relevant to the inquiry and might be considered intrusive. 'We need to know where you were when you were pretending to be at work. Where were you yesterday, Mr Enderby?'

'When poor Dee Robson was killed, you mean?' He seemed shocked that she still considered him a suspect after he'd bared his soul to her.

'And before that, when Margaret Krukowski was stabbed.' Vera thought George had slid through life using his charm to protect him. Now he had to face the consequences of that emotional laziness. Or cowardice.

'I wasn't even here then,' he said. 'I was driving up from London. I arrived just before you, if you remember.'

'No!' Vera almost shouted the word. 'No more lies. You were in the Coble in the afternoon. The landlord remembers you.' She began running through the possibilities in her mind. George Enderby trailing Margaret to visit Dee, then onto the Metro to Gosforth. He would blend in very easily with the respectable residents of the smart suburb. Then following her back through the snow, his hand on the knife's handle in his overcoat pocket. 'Did you kill Margaret Krukowski?'

'Of course not! The idea's ridiculous. Why would I kill Margaret?'

And that was the central question in the case, Vera thought. *Why would anyone want to kill Margaret Krukowski?*

'Where were you yesterday?'

He shrugged. 'Is it really relevant? Or are you

accusing me of killing Dee Robson now too? The idea is quite preposterous.'

'No, Mr Enderby. It's preposterous to refuse to answer my questions. Especially after you lied to me previously.' She leaned forward across the table again, so that she was almost touching him. 'Or perhaps you'd prefer to come with us to the police station. The custody suite might provide a suitable escape from your domestic problems.'

This time he answered immediately. 'I spent the night before last with a friend who lives in the Tyne Valley. It wasn't planned. Nothing was planned. But when first I arrived, the day that Margaret was killed, Kate presumed that I was working and that I'd follow my usual routine. Two nights here, one away and then back for a night. I didn't want to explain.' He looked wistfully out of the window. 'I hoped that it would carry on snowing and I'd be stranded in Mardle.'

'And the name of the friend?' But Vera thought she already knew. The heart of this investigation was Harbour Street and all the characters in the piece were linked by the place.

'Michael Craggs.' Enderby looked up and smiled. Vera thought that smile was a habit, a reflex, like a nervous tic. 'He's a marine biologist, based at Newcastle University. I met him in the guest house in Mardle. He's a regular there when he's on the coast for research. I always envied him actually. He seemed to have everything – a perfect marriage and a perfect family, satisfying work. I envied him so much that I wanted to dislike him. But nobody could dislike the Prof.'

'And how did that work?' Vera asked. 'The invitation, I mean. Did you just phone him up? *I'm pretending to the world that I'm still happily married. Give me a bed for the night so that I can hide.*'

'There was no need to phone him.' Enderby looked up at her. 'He was here in Harbour Street, the afternoon I arrived. The afternoon of the snow.'

The afternoon of Margaret's murder. There was a pause. Vera wondered if he understood the implication of his words. Perhaps he was deliberately pointing them towards Craggs as a possible suspect. Enderby was beginning to irritate. He was slippery and selfish.

The man continued. 'Mike was walking up the road to collect his car when I drove up. He asked me how I was. I said: "Shit actually." He must have realized that I was pretty desperate. He took me to the Coble and bought me a drink and said I could stay with him any time.' He gave a brief, brittle smile. 'I didn't fancy it much. I wasn't really in the mood for happy families. But I didn't want to explain to Kate that Diana had left me.' He paused and Vera sensed that another confession was on its way. 'I've always had a bit of a crush on Kate, actually. I was about to declare my love when Stuart appeared on the scene. I never could get my timing right. So I asked the Prof. if I could stay the night with him when I was supposed to be in Scotland.'

Enderby looked up as if he was expecting another question, a comment at least, but Vera was thinking about Professor Mike Craggs, who'd known Margaret, who'd drunk occasionally in the Coble and so would have known Dee Robson. They'd assumed that he'd driven straight home when he left Malcolm Kerr on the afternoon of the first murder. Certainly that was the impression he'd given to Holly when she'd spoken to him at the Dove Laboratory in Cullercoats. So what was the man doing in Harbour Street later the same day? How had he spent the intervening hours?

'You had a jolly evening, did you?' Vera said. 'That night in the Tyne Valley, when we thought you were selling books in Scotland. You and the Prof. and his wife?' She'd never quite trusted happy families. Joe always thought her cynical. He still kept the faith.

'Mary Craggs wasn't there.' Enderby seemed to have lost interest in the conversation, perhaps because it was no longer about the drama of his wife deserting him. 'She was babysitting for one of their children and had stayed over. But yes, it was very pleasant, thanks. The following day I had a wander around Hexham. A beautiful town. And then I made my way back to Harbour Street. This morning I caught the Metro into town. I've always loved the Lit & Phil and it's helped, having the time and the peace to think things through. One more night and I'll be ready to drive home and face the world.'

'That's your plan, is it?' Vera wondered what facing the world entailed. Perhaps Enderby would have to come to terms with the fact that he'd no longer have access to his wife's money, that there'd no longer be a big house in the country. Perhaps that was why he was so upset now. He'd despised the woman, in a vague and patronizing way, since he'd married her. Vera wondered why it had taken her so long to leave him.

'Yes,' he said. 'That was the plan. Diana said that I could stay in the house until after Christmas, but I'll have to start looking for somewhere of my own.'

What will you find? An attic bedsit. Like Margaret Krukowski.

'We'll have to check your story with your wife, of course.' But Vera thought this time he was telling the truth, or as close to the truth as he could bear to get.

Chapter Twenty-Seven

Early afternoon and Vera was back in Kimmerston. An emergency meeting of the core team to discuss the new information. She had picked up a message from Joe when she'd left the Lit & Phil. He hadn't given any details, but she'd sensed his excitement. They were squashed into her office, and the smell of onions and garlic came from the pile of empty pizza boxes stuffed into her wastebin. Holly looked as if she was about to retch.

Vera was perched on her desk. She preferred to look down onto the rest of them.

'So, Joe, let's have it again.'

'Stuart Booth said that Margaret worked as a high-class hooker out of her flat in Harbour Street. She wasn't greedy. She had a few well-paying clients. But she *was* a prostitute.' He frowned.

Vera thought that he was feeling let-down. He'd believed in Margaret the saint, the embodiment of womanly virtue. 'And Booth was one of her customers? Didn't he think he should come forward earlier with this information?'

Joe shrugged. 'He's in a new relationship. He'd hardly want it made public, would he? It was only when he found out that the second victim was in the same business that he thought we should know.'

'Very public-spirited,' Vera said. 'Or very clever.'

'You think he's lying?'

'People do, pet. He's got a motive, hasn't he? If he's found the love of his life at his age, the last thing he'd want is Margaret Krukowski spoiling it for him.' Vera spotted a smear of melted cheese on her sweater and tried to scrape it off. 'Let's dig around in the past of Mr Booth and see what else we can find. Charlie, that's the rest of your day taken care of.'

The new, happier Charlie didn't even pull a face.

'And it would be useful to track down other people who knew Margaret all those years ago.' Vera wasn't sure what to make of the new information about Krukowski, couldn't make up her mind if it was relevant or a distraction. 'Any suggestions?'

'An old lady, a neighbour of Dee's in Percy Street, talked about one of Margaret's admirers.' Joe looked up from his notes. 'A lad called Ricky Butt. He'd be in late middle age now, but he might remember her. His mother was landlady at the Coble.'

Vera remembered the portrait over the bar. 'Check that out too, will you, Charlie? See if you can get an address for him.'

'How did you get on with George Enderby?' Joe was impatient. Now that they'd finished eating he thought they should be working, not sitting around chatting. The Protestant work ethic again.

'Hol, what did you make of him?' Holly sulked if she didn't get her share of the limelight, and it was only fair that she should get a chance to express her opinion. *She'd* discovered that Enderby had been lying to them.

'I thought he was a bit pathetic actually. He didn't even like his wife, so why make such a fuss when she decided to leave him?' Holly stretched. Vera thought she was too young to feel the real pangs of isolation. It wouldn't occur to her, so youthful and healthy, that she might die alone.

'Is Enderby a potential murderer, do you think?'

'Well, he had opportunity, didn't he? If you check the timeline, he was in Mardle early enough to be on the Metro with Margaret, and until we check his alibi with Craggs we only have his word for it that he was away from the area when Dee Robson was killed.'

'Motive?'

A silence. 'He's weird, right?' Holly said. 'And he hates women.'

But Vera knew that wasn't enough. 'You don't remember seeing him on the Metro, Joe?'

'Nah, but it was packed. Doesn't mean he wasn't there.' A pause. 'In the wheelie suitcase, the one he usually carried books in, there was a change of clothes. Waterproof jacket, jeans, boots. Worth taking them in for testing? Just in case of blood spatter. Be interesting to see his reaction when we ask, anyway.'

'So it would.' The room was warm and Vera suddenly felt sleepy. It was time to get outside for some fresh air, or she'd end up snoozing, her head on the desk. Like George Enderby in the Silence Room. Time to get the team moving.

'Hol, I want you out at the Haven this afternoon. I told Cameron that Joe would go, but I want you to do it. Did any of the women know about Margaret's past?

This new information helps us to understand why she was so sympathetic to Dee Robson, doesn't it? And the girls wouldn't tell us, unless we asked. That thing about speaking ill of the dead. See if anyone knew Margaret before she started volunteering. They're all local people. And I'd be interested to hear what you make of Jane Cameron and the women.' She paused for breath. 'Joe, you take on Professor Michael Craggs. He misled us too. Why was he still in Mardle that afternoon when he told Holly he'd headed straight back to Hexham? Do a bit of digging today, and first thing tomorrow go and see him at home. Take Charlie with you. He could do with a day in the country after being chained to his desk for days.'

Charlie gave her a grateful smile.

'You see Craggs as a suspect?' Joe was sceptical. He'd always been taken in by the educated classes.

'Why not? He lied to us. And he's the right age to have been one of Margaret's customers. And as the head of a happy family, he had a lot to lose if she decided she wanted to go public about her past. Knowing that she was dying might have made her want to set the record straight.' *Which might have made Margaret feel better*, Vera thought, *but would have been cruel to the people around her*.

'What about you, boss?' Holly. 'What are your plans?' As if it was any of her business.

'I'm going back to Mardle.' She didn't elaborate and they knew better than to ask.

The rest of the afternoon Vera paced around Mardle, unable to settle, getting her thoughts into some sort of order. The knowledge that the church-going charity worker had sold her body for money had already changed the way the team saw the investigation. Changed the way they saw Margaret. There was a danger that suddenly the investigation would become simple for them. They'd be looking for a killer of prostitutes. The case would be reduced to that.

But Vera thought the information only made the murders more complex and subtle. There was the relationship with Malcolm Kerr, for example. Had he known how Margaret earned her living? Surely he must have done. And how had that worked, when he was so obviously in love with her? *He's protecting her honour even now*, Vera thought, though she failed to define the relationship. Then: *Who else knew?*

For some time she'd been unaware of her surroundings and only now realized that she was outside the high school. Ugly brick and concrete, with a fence that made it look like a prison. Bars on some of the windows too. Presumably an attempt to stop vandalism, but they made Vera want to hurl bricks. This was the outside limit of the boundary to the case. A profiler would make a map and put pins in it. *This is where all the major players live. Except for the Haven*, Vera thought suddenly. The old rectory was out of the town, but it was at the heart of the case too. Many of the people involved in the case had been there on the afternoon of their winter fair. Margaret had wanted to discuss a problem with Jane Cameron. Her illness or something else? Could one of the older residents have been in the same business and recognized her? Vera would have liked to go to the Haven herself. She would have been patient with the women, teasing out their memories. But how would Holly develop as a detective if Vera never gave her the chance to go it alone?

She turned and headed back towards Harbour Street, her flat shoes beating a rhythm on the pavement. At the Metro she stopped and turned up the alley to Percy Street. The CSIs were still in Dee Robson's flat. The crime-scene tape twisted outside looked strangely festive against the grey building. Vera knocked at Malcolm Kerr's door. No answer. Almost without pausing she turned again, carried along by the same beat, the same thoughts rapping in her brain.

Past the guest house. The day so dark that the light was on in the basement kitchen and the domestic scene inside played out like a soap opera for passers-by. Kate Dewar at the table, ladling soup from a bowl. *God, I'm hungry*, Vera thought. And beside Kate stood Stuart. Her lover. Had he confessed to his youthful indiscretions, despite Joe asking him not to? *If I could get a good man like that, I wouldn't mind what he'd got up to thirty years ago.* He looked serious, but then he always looked serious. There was no clue to the conversation. No sign of the kids, though, and he'd have sent them away before starting to talk.

It came to Vera suddenly that Hector had come to Harbour Street, at the time when Margaret was operating out of this house. He'd known Malcolm Kerr and had hired his boat to raid birds' eggs. He'd probably been served in the Coble by the fat landlady in the picture over the bar. Had Hector been one of Margaret's clients? Had he slipped through the shadows from the boatyard and let himself into the big house on the corner? Had he knocked on her door?

A sudden detour. A swerve. Across the road towards the church, because Vera heard organ music. Slow and joyless. A half-remembered Christmas carol, murdered by the organist. No accompanying singing, so there was no service. This was practice, perhaps and Christ, did the organist need it!

Vera pushed open the door. Inside it was dark, apart from a light above the organ. The noise stopped with a screech and a very old voice called out, terrified. 'Hello, is that you, Father?' And of course she had a right to be scared because two women had been murdered.

Vera called back. 'No, I was just looking for the priest.'

'Father Gruskin went out.' The woman was still suspicious, but terror was replaced by curiosity. 'What do you want?'

'Do you know where he is?'

'He's out at that place for fallen women.' Spitting out the words. Contemptuous.

Vera wondered how Margaret could have continued to worship here, surrounded by all this spiteful virtue. After all, it was easy enough to be virtuous if there was no temptation. She should know. She left the church, allowing the door to close behind her with a satisfying crash. The noise carried her across the street to Kerr's yard.

The double gates were unpadlocked. Kate Dewar's lad Ryan was sanding the hull of a dinghy; the grating sound of the machine jarred her nerves and prevented him from hearing her. She went up to him and waved in front of his face and he turned it off.

'I'm looking for Malcolm,' she said.

'He's not here.' He smiled at her. 'Sorry.' He rubbed his hand along the smooth hull of the dinghy, almost a caress.

'It's bloody freezing out here,' she said. 'Come into Malcolm's shed for a minute. I could do with a chat.'

He seemed reluctant to leave the boat, but he followed her.

'You enjoy your work don't you?' she said.

'Yeah.' He seemed embarrassed by the admission.

'Any chance Malcolm would take you on when you leave school?' She pushed a charred black kettle onto the top of the stove.

'Maybe.' He paused. 'I'm not sure how that would work, though. I've got plans. I'd want to be the boss. You could make real money out of the place.'

She raised her eyebrows. Money had never motivated her. 'Tea?' She nodded towards the kettle.

'Eh,' he said. 'Isn't that theft?'

'Cheeky monkey.' She couldn't help grinning. 'I don't suppose there's any milk. We'd best have it black then.' She looked up at him. 'Where is Malcolm?'

'He took the boat out. Some guy wanted to go over to the island.'

'Prof. Craggs?' Perhaps she would wait and talk to the academic and save Joe a journey halfway across the county.

'Nah, some maintenance guy. Something to do with the wardens' accommodation.'

'Couldn't they wait until the weather gets better?' Vera sipped the tea. The best you could say was that it was warm. 'There'll be nobody living out there now.'

'Don't ask me! Nobody tells me anything.'

'But you know things, don't you?' Because it seemed

to Vera that this boy was like a sponge. People would talk to him. He'd soak up information and confidences and stray pieces of gossip. 'You've lived on this street for most of your life. You've seen things.'

'I have nightmares,' he said. 'I don't sleep well. And then I walk. Mam hates it; she thinks I'll get into bother out on the streets. And yeah, I see things.'

'And what do you see?' Vera asked. 'What do you see when you're walking down Harbour Street in the middle of the night?' She paused. 'What secrets can you share with me, Ryan?'

He looked up at her, as if he was surprised that she could be so perceptive. He seemed about to answer when his mobile rang. He looked at the caller ID and his face changed and turned blank and hard. 'Sorry,' he said. 'I've got to take this.' He stood up and went outside.

When she followed him a few moments later he had the sander going again. He waved at her in a friendly way, but she could tell that she'd get nothing from him now.

Leaving the yard, Vera decided there was only one option, weighing up all the possibilities: a sit-down meal of haddock and chips in the Mardle Fisheries.

Chapter Twenty-Eight

Holly arrived at the Haven in the early afternoon. A flat landscape facing the sea, and the trees all bent away from the wind. A big grey sky. The house was grey too, stone and square, but crumbling through lack of care. Peeled paintwork on the window frames and gutters with weeds growing inside, slates missing on the roof. A bit of money, though, and it would be a magnificent place. Holly could see it as a smart country-house hotel or converted into luxury apartments. She was a sucker for makeover programmes on television and she read the interior-design mags at the hairdresser's. She wondered why the charity didn't sell the place and buy somewhere more convenient for the hostel in town. They'd still end up with a profit.

She parked next to a black Volvo and, as soon as she climbed out of the car, the wind seemed to blow right through her jacket. Somewhere a dog was barking. She knocked at the door and it was opened almost immediately by a thin girl, hardly more than a child.

'Are you the social worker?' Her words eager, her eyes wide. Her red hair was tied back with a ribbon. She was dressed like a student, but a student with taste and money. Holly would have had her down as a staff member, but she was too thin and too nervy, nibbling now on her nails.

'I'm afraid not.'

'Ah.' The girl backed away from her, disappointed. 'A social worker's supposed to be coming to take me home for Christmas. My key worker's away on holiday. My mother said that she'd give it another go.'

'Any chance I could speak to the person in charge?'

And at that point a plump woman appeared in the corridor. 'I told you she wouldn't be here until five, Emily,' she said to the girl. She could have been talking to an eight-year-old. 'Go and wait in the kitchen where it's warm.' Then she held out her hand to Holly. 'I'm Jane Cameron and I run this place. You must be one of Vera Stanhope's gang. I assume you're here to talk to the residents about Dee Robson.'

Jane reminded Holly of her former French teacher. She had the same good-natured authority and the same confidence that she would get what she wanted from her charges without any fuss. The same sort of Scottish accent. There was a sound from further inside the house and Peter Gruskin the priest appeared. If he recognized Holly he didn't acknowledge her. He was frowning. 'I'll get off then, shall I? I don't think there's anything else we can do at this stage.' He nodded to both women and made his way outside. The wind tugged at his cloak and his hair. They stood watching until he drove away.

Holly followed Jane into the kitchen, where two women were pulling on gloves and boots. 'We were just planning a walk,' Jane said. 'Everyone seems to have been stuck indoors and the weather forecast is dreadful for the rest of the week. We all need a breath of fresh air. Come on, Em. Coat on. I promise you won't miss the social worker.' Jane turned to Holly. 'That is okay with you? We can talk as we go.' And Holly had no choice. There were just three residents – the others had apparently been invited to more comfortable or exciting places for Christmas. The skinny child, Em, an athletic young woman called Laurie, who strode ahead throwing sticks for the dog, and Susan, who was older, grey-haired and who scarcely spoke when they were all together.

At first Jane let the women walk ahead of them and spoke to Holly herself. 'Have you met Peter Gruskin before?'

Holly nodded. She'd thought she would be the one to ask the questions. She felt that she was being dragged along by this assertive woman and had the sense that she was losing control of the situation.

'What did you make of him?'

Holly hesitated. She could hardly gossip about other witnesses.

Jane didn't wait and answered her own question. 'He's a horrible man. The last priest was lovely. Gentle, and the women liked him. Peter finds us incomprehensible. He's anxious that the press will pick up the Haven connection between Margaret and Dee. Is that likely, do you think? He would rather that we just went away.'

'I don't know. We haven't said anything.' They were walking along a footpath that skirted the edge of a bare field. A small flock of brightly coloured finches fed on dead thistle heads.

'What's it like working for Vera Stanhope?' Jane sounded amused.

Holly paused, torn between loyalty and a desire to let off steam. In the end she restrained herself. 'Interesting,' she said. 'Inspector Stanhope is a fine detective.'

Jane chuckled and Holly walked ahead to talk to the women. This route-march might be the only opportunity she'd have, and she had to get something to take back to Vera.

At first Emily had nothing useful to say. She was preoccupied with the prospect of getting home for Christmas. 'My mother thinks it might work this time. We've talked about my going back to school to retake my A levels.' The voice wistful and not very optimistic.

'Where do you go to school?'

'St Anne's in town, but Mummy thinks I might be better at the local comp. Less stress. I'm not sure, though. I think that might be a bit scary. I've never been at a school where there were boys.' She blinked and was quiet for a while. Holly thought this fragile young woman would never survive for a week in a big high school. *Her* parents had saved hard for her to go private. 'Margaret was going to come and visit, to see how I was getting on,' Emily said. She turned to Holly and her voice was pleading. Perhaps she saw Holly as a substitute saviour.

'Did you know Dee Robson?'

'No.' A pause. 'Well, I met her once at the winter fair – she'd come with Margaret – but I had a bit of a panic attack. All those strangers. I didn't really talk to anyone.' And Emily walked on, leaving Holly to follow. She must have realized that Holly wasn't someone who could help her. When Holly caught her up, Emma continued talking about the murders. It seemed that she hadn't spent any time with Dee Robson at the Haven because she'd only been in the hostel for a few weeks, referred from the adolescent unit of the local psychiatric hospital. 'The girls told me about Dee. They always made out she was a bit of a joke. Nobody deserves to die like that, though, do they?' They walked for a while in silence, the only sound the cawing of rooks in the nearby trees and the engine of a distant tractor.

'Did Margaret mention if anything was bothering her?' Though Holly thought the last person Margaret would have chosen as a confidante would be Emily, who was weak and had so many problems of her own.

Emily shook her head. 'You had the feeling that nothing bothered Margaret, that she'd seen it all.'

Laurie knew Dee, though. 'She was one of those lasses who were always around in Mardle. Like people got so used to seeing her making a spectacle of herself that they didn't notice her any more. It's the same with the *Big Issue* sellers. They're there, but you don't really see them.' Laurie swiped at the dead brambles by the side of the path with her stick. 'Margaret thought that some time at the Haven would sort Dee out.'

'But it didn't?'

'Nah. She hated it from the time she got here. I love the countryside, me, but Dee didn't know anywhere outside Mardle.'

'Where did she stay before she came to the

Haven?' Holly hoped that she'd remember all these details when she got back to the station. She was lost without her iPad.

'Prison. She'd got into a scrap with some guy in the Coble and got done for ABH. She was already on a suspended for shoplifting. At the end of the sentence she wanted to go back and stay with her gran, but they'd stuck *her* into a home when Dee was inside. So the probation brought her to us. Jane didn't want to take her, but Margaret persuaded her to give Dee a chance.' Laurie shrugged. 'I could have told them it was never going to work.'

'Did Margaret know Dee from before?' That, after all, was the information Vera had wanted.

'I don't know. Maybe. Or maybe she knew Dee's mother. I think that was it.' Laurie threw the stick for the dog again and it ran after it. Of all of them, she seemed most at home in this place. 'Dee's family have always lived in Mardle.'

They'd turned back towards the house on a different track through the trees, when Holly spoke to Susan. The older woman had been struggling to keep up and Holly had to wait for her. The wind was blowing in the bare branches above them, and because Susan seemed not to hear well, at times Holly had to shout to make herself understood. The others had wandered far ahead.

'How long have you been at the Haven?'

It seemed a safe way to start, but Susan appeared threatened by the question.

'I don't have to move, do I? Margaret said I could stay as long as I wanted. I know it's only supposed to be a temporary arrangement, but she said I was a special case.' The voice surprised Holly. It was anxious, but soft and articulate.

'Had you known her for a long time?'

'Oh yes, we'd been friends for many years.' The woman paused. 'But Margaret was always much stronger than me.' Another pause. 'My nerves have never been very good. And now my memory is going too.' She gave a strange little giggle. 'I'm falling apart.'

Ahead of them the other women had disappeared from view. The wood was all dark shadows.

'Did you know Margaret's husband?' Holly asked.

'Not him, no. He'd gone by the time we met. I knew her other man. The one she worked for.'

'Malcolm Kerr?' Holly was thinking that Vera would love this. There was nothing she liked better than an unexpected connection.

'Is that what he was called?' Susan looked around her vaguely as if she couldn't quite remember where she was. 'I don't recall the name.'

'Were you living in Mardle then?' Holly wished this woman were more reliable. These might not be memories, but Susan's weird imaginings.

'In Mardle? Oh yes. I was living in Harbour Street, in a ground-floor flat. Margaret was in the attic. I had a baby, you know, but they took her away. I wonder sometimes where she might be now. She'd be quite grown-up. But it was all for the best. Yes, I'm sure that it was all for the best.'

'Do you know what Margaret did for a living?'

There was no response. Holly wasn't sure that the woman had heard the question and she repeated it.

But still Susan didn't answer. Instead she started

humming. At first Holly couldn't make out the tune and then she recognized it. She'd had a boyfriend once who was into Nineties music. 'White Moon Summer' by Katie Guthrie.

When the two of them arrived at the house, Emily was back hovering by the front door waiting for the social worker. Laurie had disappeared and Susan shuffled off too, still humming, to a room at the end of the corridor. There was the sound, very loud, of a television game show. Holly found Jane in the kitchen making tea.

'Did you get what you wanted?' The woman turned round. She'd been slicing cake and still had the knife in her hand.

'I'm not sure.' *And what business is it of yours, lady?* Perhaps it was the resemblance to the schoolteacher, but Holly found herself distrusting this woman. Disliking her at least. 'Tell me about Susan.'

'Ah, poor Susan. She has a history of depression and psychotic episodes. In and out of mental hospital. They tried everything from talking therapies to ECT, but I'm not sure there's ever been a reliable diagnosis. She seems quite stable at the moment.'

'Has she been here for a long time?' Holly sat down at the table, took out her iPad and discreetly started to make notes. She tapped out what she could remember of her conversation with the women on the walk. Vera liked these things word-for-word.

'More than two years. We're supposed to provide temporary accommodation in an emergency, and honestly she should be moving on, but it suits her here and I'm not sure that I've got the heart to ask her to leave.'

Jane poured two mugs of tea. 'Where would she go?'

'She said she used to live on Harbour Street in Mardle.'

'Did she? I'm sure she has no family close by. Social services would have checked.' Jane joined Holly at the table.

'She told me that she knew Margaret Krukowski years ago.'

'Really, you shouldn't take too much notice of what Susan tells you.' It was Jane in schoolmistress mode again, patronizing. 'She gets confused, hears things that people say and repeats them, or turns them into a narrative about herself. She'd make a very unreliable witness.' The words sounded almost like a warning.

Then there was a commotion at the door. It seemed that the social worker had arrived early for Emily after all. The girl rushed into the kitchen with her holdall to say goodbye and Jane went out to the car to see her off.

'I hope it works out for her,' Holly said, when Jane returned.

'Aye, well, I'll not hold my breath. Last time her mother could only cope with her for one night and was outside social services with her in the morning, waiting for the office to open. She has problems of her own. A new partner with money, but no time for Emily. This time social services will have closed for Christmas, and I expect I'll have to pick up the pieces.' Jane must have realized that she sounded hard. 'Sorry. Compassion-fatigue. I'm just tired.'

Holly thought that she felt tired too – and she'd only spent an afternoon in the place.

Chapter Twenty-Nine

Professor Craggs lived in a low stone cottage in a village not far from Hexham and the Roman Wall. All the way there Joe Ashworth was thinking that this was a waste of time. A phone call would have done. But Vera was a great one for face-to-face contact. 'It's much easier to lie on the phone,' she'd said before he set off. 'And Craggs has known all the players for a long time. Get his take on the set-up at Harbour Street, and dig a bit further for information on Kerr and Enderby. I know Holly spoke to him, but she's impatient; she doesn't always give people time to get the words out.'

In the end he enjoyed the drive. Charlie fell asleep as soon as they left Kimmerston, and Joe felt he had every right to play his own music. There was a CD of Jessie's choir and he had that on as they approached Craggs's house. He'd chosen the Military Road, built by the Romans. It was straight as the eye could see, following Hadrian's Wall, and there was little traffic. The soaring children's voices suited the wide, empty landscape and were only partly spoiled by Charlie snoring beside him. Joe shook Charlie awake as they drove down the narrow road towards the house, a low cottage that could have done with a fresh coat of whitewash. The professor was in the garden, raking dead leaves from an untidy lawn. He heard the gate and turned round, leaning on the rake, faintly hostile. Joe saw that the man had decided they were salesmen or Jehovah's Witnesses, and he got in first.

'DS Ashworth. Northumbria Police. And this is my colleague Charles Laidler.'

Craggs was big and square, with cropped grey hair. He hadn't shaved today and had holes in his trousers and his sweater. A grey mackintosh was tied at the waist with a bit of binder twine. Stick him on Northumberland Street in town, with a ratty dog, and you'd have him down as a well-fed tramp. Joe thought clothes were important, and he wouldn't have dressed like that even in the garden. The professor and Vera were two of a kind. Maybe she should have driven all this way to do the interview herself.

'How can I help you, Sergeant?' Craggs set down the rake.

'It's about the murders of Dee Robson and Margaret Krukowski.'

'I saw on the television that there'd been another killing. A dreadful business. You'd better come inside. I was going to stop soon anyway. Mary was going to make some coffee. Though I'm not sure if I can provide any useful information.'

The professor left his boots in a rackety porch tacked onto the back of the house. It held seed trays on the windowsill, a couple of fishing nets and a child's bucket and spade. Joe followed him into a long, thin kitchen and on to a living room. There was a table close to a French window, covered with a patterned oilskin cloth and a pile of newspapers. Light came in through the window and fell onto the woman sitting there, but the rest of the room was in shadow. Joe had an impression of paper – books, files, notebooks – on shelves and chairs and on the floor, and of dust. The woman looked up and smiled.

'My wife, Mary,' Craggs said. It was a simple introduction, but Joe could tell that he adored her. She was small and her hair was held back from her face with a comb. 'These men are detectives, my dear, and they want to talk about those dreadful murders in Mardle.'

'I'll make coffee then.' She got to her feet and Joe saw that she wore faded denim jeans and sandals, an Indian cotton tunic in bright colours. She still dressed as she probably had as a student.

Underneath the table there was a box of apples, individually wrapped in newspaper. The room smelled of them.

'You were lucky to find me in, Sergeant. We're quite often on childcare duties in the school holidays.' It was a gentle reproof, a reminder that the detectives had turned up without warning.

'We need to talk to you about George Enderby.' The view from the window was from the side of the house. A small orchard and, beyond it, a high wall of old red brick covered in ivy.

'Ah, poor George. I'm afraid he's got himself into a bit of a state. When I told Mary, she said it was his own fault and that it seemed as if he'd treated his wife appallingly for years, but I can't help feeling sorry for him.'

'You've known him for a long time?' In the distance Joe heard a kettle boiling, cups set on saucers. In a corner Charlie was taking notes.

'That house in Harbour Street had become a

second home for both of us. There was something very appealing about the company there. Kate and her children. Margaret Krukowski, so gracious and welcoming. The regular guests. It won't be the same now of course, but then I fancy it would have changed anyway. Kate has found other interests: Stuart, who seems to have made her very happy, and a renewed enthusiasm for her music. From my own point of view I was rather glad that they were all moving on. It made my decision to retire much easier. Less to miss.'

'Was Margaret moving on?' *She was dying,* Joe thought. *But that's moving too.*

'You know, I think there was a change in her,' the professor said. 'She seemed distracted on my last visit. Somehow disengaged.'

'Could you go through your movements again, for the afternoon that Margaret was killed?' Joe couldn't imagine this man as a murderer, but Vera had found discrepancies in his evidence and she'd slaughter him if he didn't check. 'You were out in the boat with Malcolm Kerr?'

'That's right. Part of my regular fieldwork off Coquet Island.'

'And what time did you get back to Mardle?'

'I told that young woman who came to the laboratory to talk to me.' There was no resentment in his voice, but a kind of resignation. 'It was about three o'clock.'

'And what did you do then?' This was the important question. Craggs had told Holly that he'd driven straight home, but Enderby claimed that they'd met up in Harbour Street later in the day.

'I went to the Dove Laboratory in Cullercoats. I had equipment to drop off there.'

'And then?' Joe leaned forward across the table.

'Then I went back to Mardle. It was a nuisance. It was snowing heavily and I wanted to get home. But I'd left my briefcase in Malcolm's yard – one of those senior moments that seem to happen more frequently these days – and I had an important phone call to make the following morning. I knew I'd need the papers. I have a key to the yard and to Malcolm's shed, so I didn't need to disturb him. And in Harbour Street I bumped into George. He seemed so miserable that I couldn't leave him there alone. We had one drink in the pub. I thought if the snow was really bad I could always stay the night at Kate's. In the end it seemed to have cleared a bit, so I drove home.'

The words came easily. Too easily? Joe wondered if they might have been rehearsed. 'And you invited Mr Enderby to spend a night here with you?'

'Not that night, but two days later, yes. He'd got himself into a state. He's obviously told you that his wife has left him. He'd run away to Harbour Street, still pretending that he was working. Because he couldn't face telling Kate what had happened, I invited him here on the day that he claimed to be in Scotland.'

Mary arrived with coffee and melted discreetly away.

'How did he seem when he was here?' Joe asked.

'Distraught. He drank too much of my whisky and became incoherent. We knew that Margaret was dead by then, of course. Her death seemed to have upset him almost more than his wife's leaving him. We spent a lot of time talking about her.' The professor drank coffee, leaning back in his chair.

Joe thought he was reliving that evening in his head. 'And what exactly did you say about her?'

'That she was a wonderful woman. We couldn't understand why her husband had left her all those years ago. And that there was something mysterious about her.' Craggs smiled. 'George is a romantic, I'm afraid. Perhaps he reads too many novels.'

'Did you ever meet Margaret's husband? If you've been working with Malcolm Kerr for such a long time, you might have come across him.' Joe was struggling to work out the timeline for this. When he got back to the office he'd make a chart with dates.

'No. I never stayed in Mardle in those days. There was no guest house, and Harbour Street was rather disreputable. Most nights there seemed to be fights spilling out of the Coble. I travelled out from Newcastle when I needed to go out to the island.' He paused. 'Of course the Metro wasn't opened until 1980, so I used to drive before then. I had a wreck of a minivan that was always breaking down.' He smiled at the memory. 'Good times.'

'Did you know Margaret Krukowski before the house in Harbour Street became a guest house?' Joe thought the area must have been a small and tight community thirty years ago. There'd be the people living in the bedsits and those working at the fisheries. Even before the Metro came, it would have been cut off from the rest of Mardle by the disused railway track. He wished he had a better picture of the town in those days.

'Oh yes. For a short while she worked as a bookkeeper and receptionist for Billy Kerr, Malcolm's father. Then he decided that he didn't need her. I suppose money was tight. Later we'd see her occasionally in the Coble or walking down the street.' Professor Craggs smiled. 'Always dignified. Always immaculately turned out. Kate Dewar didn't take over the place until about ten years ago, and I've been making regular visits for my research since I was a post-doctoral student. But I'm pretty sure Margaret's husband had left even before that. I always knew her as a single woman.'

Joe had a sudden idea. 'Do you have any photos? I'm interested in what Harbour Street looked like then.'

'Probably. If you think it's important.' He seemed surprised and a little sceptical. Had the detectives come all this way just to look at some snaps? 'I had the camera to record specimens on the island, but I know I took photos of some of the characters in the street too.' He got to his feet and rifled through the drawers of an elderly dresser. Joe was about to tell him not to bother, that it wasn't important, when the professor pulled out an album almost falling apart at the seams. He put it on the table and Joe stood up to get a better look. Charlie stayed where he was.

And there, suddenly, was Harbour Street, familiar but subtly changed, the images slightly faded. A young Malcolm Kerr standing by the harbour wall with an older man and in the background the fisheries building, sparkling and new in bright sunlight. The older man grinning and the younger glaring. On the opposite page a woman was pushing a big, old-fashioned pram down the road past the church. She had a cigarette in one hand and controlled the pram with the other.

'Why did I take that?' Craggs frowned. 'After all this time, I really can't remember.'

He turned the page of the album and there was a group of people posing outside the Coble. Summer. The women in sleeveless dresses and sandals, the men squinting into the sunshine. In the middle Billy Kerr, with a big drunken grin, next to a large woman in a shapeless floral dress.

'I remember that day,' Craggs said. 'Billy's fiftieth birthday.' He pointed to the fat woman. 'That's Val Butt. She was the landlady. And that's her son, Ricky. Local wheeler and dealer. Always seemed to have cash, and none of us knew where it had come from. Flashy. He moved on very quickly. I'd guess that Mardle was too tame for him.'

Joe looked at the image of Ricky Butt, a dark-haired young man, dressed in denim, but his attention was immediately drawn to the woman who stood in front of him. Margaret Krukowski. No longer the young woman of the wedding photograph, here aged in her thirties, but still lovely. On her face a smile that was tense and unnatural, as if she hated having her picture taken.

Craggs turned the page again and this time it was a long shot up Harbour Street, with the big house at the end. Even from that distance it looked as if it was falling into disrepair. And on the same page, Kerr's boatyard. In place of the corrugated-iron shed there was a Portakabin, rather smart, a sign on the door saying *Kerr's Charters*. Joe supposed this was the office where Margaret had answered the phone and booked in customers, before she became too expensive.

'Was Margaret working there when you first knew her?' he asked.

Craggs shook his head. 'No, that was before my time. Soon after this photo was taken, the building they used as an office burned down. Rumours were that it was some sort of insurance scam. It was widely known that the Kerrs owed money all over the town. They'd over-committed themselves buying a new boat. Malcolm's makeshift shed appeared soon after.'

The next page was blank. 'That's all there is,' Craggs said. 'Unless you're interested in seaweed . . .'

Joe shook his head and smiled. He felt that he had a better understanding of the background to the case, but he was here to check more recent movements.

'George Enderby stayed with you the night Dee Robson was murdered.'

'Yes,' Craggs said. 'It must have been that day.'

'What time did he arrive?'

'It was late. Eight o'clock. Mary had left us a casserole and I was starving. I'm used to eating earlier, and I almost started without him.'

So Enderby had no alibi for Dee's murder, either. Joe thought he would achieve nothing more here and moved towards the door.

Mary Craggs must have been watching them, because she appeared again from the kitchen. 'Have you got everything you need, Sergeant?'

'Yes, your husband's been very helpful. Thank you.' Then he reconsidered. 'Might I borrow the photo album, Professor? I'll return it as soon as I've shown my boss.'

Craggs nodded and returned to the house to fetch

the book. Then the elderly couple walked together with Joe and Charlie into the garden and stood, looking over the gate, the professor with his arm around his wife's shoulder, watching until they drove off.

Chapter Thirty

The evening briefing. Outside it was dark and the traffic was heavy. The start of the long Christmas weekend and people making their way south to visit family and friends. Vera had shut herself away in her office and only emerged as the meeting was about to begin. She'd run her fingers through her hair so that it stuck up at the back, but nobody dared tell her.

She stood at the front of the room, with her legs apart, her eyes bright. 'Let's get this cleared up by Christmas, shall we, folks? Then you can all go home to your bairns in time to open the stockings.'

In the room a few sceptical cheers. Vera wasn't known for her family-friendly policies.

'I'll go first, shall I?' Defying them to contradict her. She pointed to the photo of the young Margaret Krukowski on the whiteboard. 'Our first victim. Seventy-year-old woman, member of St Batholomew's Church, committed to the work of the Haven, a hostel for homeless women. From the beginning we wondered if there might be a clue there. Had she been in an abusive relationship? Was that why she'd befriended our second victim, Dee Robson?'

From the back of the room Joe Ashworth thought he'd never seen Vera looking so animated. She seemed ten years younger. He wondered if she'd been at the secret stash of whisky that she kept in her office drawer. Or if she had some information of her own to share with them.

Vera continued: 'But yesterday a witness came forward and has thrown a very different light on the relationship between Dee and Margaret. As you all know now, it seems that there was another connection between the women.'

Vera paused. The room was silent. She looked out at them, and Joe could tell that she was loving the attention. 'Thirty years ago Margaret Krukowski was a call girl, working out of the house in Harbour Street, where she was living when she died. Discreet and classy, despite the neighbourhood. Successful too, because I reckon the money in her savings account probably came from that time. Seems to me that this answers a lot of the questions we've had about this woman. She sometimes talked about secrets and implied that she had a mysterious past. It explains, at least in part, Malcolm Kerr's reluctance to be straight with us. He fancied the pants off her and wouldn't want her memory sullied by rumours that she'd been a sex worker. And it explains her fondness for Dee Robson. I'm assuming Margaret went into business when she was deserted by her husband. And when she lost her office job with the Kerrs. Sad that she preferred selling her body to going to her parents and admitting that she was wrong about him, but she was a proud woman. And it seems that she was in control of her own business. Booth didn't mention that a man was involved. Margaret valued her independence.'

She fell silent and looked around her. Joe wondered if she was expecting a round of applause for her expert summing-up. Holly stuck up her hand.

'How does this move the investigation on, boss? It was a long time ago. How many people still around knew that she was on the game?'

Oh, Holly! Joe thought. *When will you learn? You don't question Vera Stanhope when she's on a roll.*

But Vera must have been feeling generous and today there was no cutting put-down. 'This is still relevant, Hol. Because you're a babe-in-arms you don't understand how the dim and distant can come back to haunt you. Maybe Margaret wanted to go public about her past before she died. To set the record straight. And there were respectable people – ex-clients – who didn't want her to do that.' She paused. 'How did you get on at the Haven?'

'One of the residents there claims that she lived in the house in Harbour Street at the same time as Margaret.' Holly looked at her notes. 'Susan Coulson. She's a bit confused, and was talking about having had a child that was taken away from her. But she did say that she knew Margaret's boss.'

'Okay. That'd be Malcom Kerr. Or his father, Billy. Let's get Malcolm in tomorrow. I can't believe that he didn't know how Margaret was earning her living at that time. He's always seen himself as some sort of confidant. I don't see him as a pimp, though. Anything else?'

Holly looked again at her notes. 'Not from the Haven, but I spoke to Enderby's wife.'

'And?'

'She confirmed that she's left him. Posh Diana has fallen for a guy who runs the stables where she keeps her horses.' Holly grinned. 'He's very fit apparently. She went into some detail . . . And I asked Enderby if we could take the outdoor clothes that he was carrying around in his wheelie suitcase for testing.'

'How did he seem when you asked him?'

'Hurt. "How can you believe that I would do something like that?" He didn't kick up too much of a fuss, though.'

Vera looked around the room. 'Anyone else like to contribute to this investigation? Or is this just a case being run by the women on the team?'

Joe slowly raised his hand.

'Yes, Joe. You and Charlie have had a nice day out in the country visiting our professor.' She pointed to Mike Craggs's name on the board. 'What did you get from him? He was knocking around in Mardle at the time. A young research scientist. Was he one of Margaret's customers, do you think?'

'Craggs admitted that he admired her,' Joe said. 'But nah, I don't think so. He was already married to his wife then, and you can tell that he loves her to bits.' He saw that Vera was about to sneer – any talk of romance and she pretended to puke – so he moved on quickly. 'Craggs did pass on one interesting bit of information, though.'

'Get on with it, Joe man.'

'The Kerrs were in financial difficulties in the Eighties. They owed money all over the town and when the office building burned down, it seemed a bit too convenient. Rumour had it that it was an insurance scam.'

Joe could see Vera processing this and dismissing it as unimportant. He suspected that she'd developed a theory of her own. That would explain her excitement. She was just waiting for the right moment to share it. Still he persisted. 'Margaret would have known the Kerrs' financial position. She kept their books, after all. If she was planning to come clean about the past, maybe she was going to talk about that too.'

'That's petty stuff. I don't think anyone would give a toss so many years later.'

So, Joe thought, *that's put me in my place. Vera might have given the idea at least a moment's consideration.*

She moved forward, a star preparing to step into the spotlight. 'Could the professor tell you anything about Pawel Krukowski, the husband?'

'Nothing. He was already off the scene by the time Craggs got to know Margaret.' Joe was going to offer up the photo album to Vera, but thought that the mood she was in now, elated and carried away with some theory of her own, she would only mock him for implying that it had any significance.

There was a silence. Vera looked out at them, and Joe saw that at least she was gearing up to share her grand idea. 'I don't believe that Pawel suddenly disappeared off the face of the Earth,' she said. 'Margaret could have been hiding more than the fact that she sold sex for a living.' She looked around her and again she seemed to be expecting applause.

'You think that she killed her husband?' Joe thought Vera was entering the realm of fantasy now. Margaret Krukowski wasn't a killer, but a victim.

'I don't know *exactly* what to think at this point.' She glared at him. 'We're telling stories. Creating theories. But tomorrow we need to check some facts.' She was back at the whiteboard and she wiped out a bare patch and started making notes. 'Pawel Krukowski. What's happened to him? I'm betting that he's dead and, if he's still alive and living happily in Warsaw, then I'll be buying the carry-outs for the next five years. Charlie, you take over tracing him. First thing in the morning. Get our European colleagues to help out. Hol, you see if you can find any record of the fire at Malcolm's yard, but don't waste too much time on it.'

She stopped, her hand raised, holding the marker pen. 'This Susan Coulson, did you meet her when you visited the Haven, Joe?'

Joe reeled back his memory and saw a grey-haired woman stirring soup, the tears rolling down her cheeks. He'd thought she was odd, overreacting to the death of a virtual stranger, but if she and Margaret had been friends for more than thirty years that would make more sense. 'Yes,' he said. 'I met her.'

'Chat to her. Away from the hostel, if you can manage it. Jane Cameron's a control freak. It takes one to know one. And I don't want her listening in.' Vera paused again. 'Bring her back to Harbour Street. Buy her a fish-and-chip dinner or a port and lemon in the Coble. See if you can jog any memories.'

'I really don't think she'd be an admissible witness, boss. Any defence brief would eat her for breakfast.' Holly had jumped in again. Joe wondered if she was resenting the fact that her witness had been taken away from her, though he knew Holly would have little patience with Susan, who was old and confused.

Vera kept her voice mild. 'At this point I'm not

worrying about the court case, Hol. I just want to know who killed these two women.'

When Joe arrived home the kids were looking out for him. Sal's parents had taken them to see a panto at Whitley Bay Playhouse and the two oldest were full of it. Michael had been onstage and a clown had pulled a *live* rabbit from his ear. They were full of wonder, even Jessie, who claimed that she was a bit old for magic these days. He wondered how he would cope with her as a teenager, stroppy and defensive, and remembered again the schoolgirls he'd seen in the Metro on the afternoon Margaret Krukowski had died. Simpering and playing up to the boys. It was hard to imagine that they'd ever been excited by a pantomime.

In bed, he found it difficult to sleep. He was planning how he might carry out Vera's instructions to get Susan Coulson away from the Haven. He'd been intimidated by Jane Cameron, and he could hardly kidnap the woman. And something about the picture of the older woman, her eyes streaming with silent tears, seemed very moving to him. He wasn't sure now if she was weeping for Margaret Krukowski or for the child that had been taken away from her. Later he replayed his conversation with Michael Craggs, anxious because he felt that he'd missed something important. The last image in his mind, just before he slept, was of the elderly couple leaning over their garden gate, their arms around each other and waving goodbye to him.

When he woke, it came to him, almost as part of a dream, that he hadn't passed the photo album on to Vera.

Chapter Thirty-One

The next day was clear and frosty and Vera was in Mardle before it got light. It felt like truancy. She should be in her office coordinating the actions, supervising. An inspector's role was strategic. Except that she'd always been seduced by the detail. She told herself she'd be back at the station before lunchtime. It was time to reel in Malcolm Kerr. He'd been playing silly buggers with her, and she hated being taken for a fool.

The first stop was Percy Street. The curtains were drawn, so she assumed that she'd find Kerr in, but when she knocked on the door there was no response. An alley ran along the back of the houses, separated from the gardens by a wooden fence. The street light caught the frost on the overgrown grass and when she went in, there was ice on the concrete path. She banged on the kitchen door and again there was no response. When she tried the handle it was locked.

A man came out of the house next door. He wore an anorak and a Newcastle United knitted hat and matching black-and-white striped gloves. He was on his way to work and he regarded Vera with suspicion.

'What do you want?'

'You don't happen to know where Malcolm is, do

you, pet? Only I can't get an answer.' Her breath came as a cloud in the strange, white light.

He was in a hurry and now he had Vera down as someone official. 'I haven't seen him since yesterday morning.' And he rushed away before she could ask anything more from him. She was tempted to try to get into the house. There'd probably be a spare key somewhere, under a flowerpot or the back doormat, but if Malcolm Kerr was inside sleeping off a hangover she'd be caught in the act of breaking in. Anyway something about the stillness of the house made her think it was empty, that Malcolm was probably at his yard. She imagined him there in his shed, wrapped in an old overcoat, dreaming of the love of his life. He'd have done anything for Margaret Krukowski and Vera thought now that the man could have killed Margaret's husband, or at least helped her to dispose of his body. That was one of the theories she was working on, which had been spinning around in her brain all night. She wanted to get Kerr safely into custody, but without frightening him. The present murders could be the result of fear, she thought. Of a man trapped into a corner and fighting to save himself.

When she arrived at the boatyard it was locked and padlocked. The street behind her was beginning to come to life, but there was no sign that anyone had been into Kerr's secret domain. The hoar frost on the pavement was undisturbed. Now her anxiety increased. She saw Malcolm Kerr as a lost and friendless man with nothing to lose. Bad enough if he'd killed himself. But, again, she thought that he was desperate and that he might try to fight back. She wanted no more violence. She ran through the options for action. She could get a warrant to search his house and the yard. Any evidence was circumstantial and based on the fact that he'd lied to them, but with two women dead it should be straightforward. A phone call to Holly would set the process in train. Still she hesitated. She knew it was illogical, but she had a fellow-feeling for Kerr. She'd known him since she was a child. She wanted the chance to talk to him before he was labelled a killer.

On impulse she walked back to the Harbour Guest House. She saw that George Enderby was eating breakfast in the dining room, at his usual table in the window. She'd forgotten that he'd told her he was staying an extra night. He glanced out and saw her and looked suddenly anxious. *I have that effect on people wherever I go.* She waved to him and smiled, then climbed the steps and knocked on the door. Kate Dewar answered. It seemed that she was in the middle of a conversation and something had made her laugh. She was still smiling when she saw Vera.

'Inspector?' A little wary, but not worried. Vera hadn't seen her so happy. Then she noticed Stuart Booth standing in the shadow just behind Kate. The woman had been talking to him when Vera had arrived. Vera guessed that Booth hadn't told her about his earlier relationship with Margaret Krukowski. Sensible. Vera had always thought honesty was an overrated virtue. Except during a police investigation.

'Is your son in, Mrs Dewar?'

Now Kate was suddenly worried. 'Why do you want Ryan? What's he done?'

'Nothing!' Vera smiled in what she hoped was a reassuring way. 'I'm looking for Malcolm Kerr, who seems to have gone AWOL, and I thought Ryan might have some idea where he might be.'

'The kids are both downstairs having breakfast. We've just finished.'

'Is it okay if I go down? You come along too.'

The kitchen was the warmest room in the house and, after being outside, it felt like walking into a greenhouse. Chloe and Ryan were at the table. It was laid for four, all very proper, milk in a jug and marmalade in a bowl. Perhaps it was running a guest house for all those years that meant Kate couldn't cope with cartons of juice, butter still in its wrapper. Or perhaps she was still trying to impress her lover. Vera was surprised that the kids were up at all. Teenagers in the school holidays – shouldn't they still be in bed at lunchtime? Or perhaps Ryan was planning to work for Malcolm again today.

'The inspector has some questions for you.' Kate's voice was a warning.

Ryan was reading a music magazine and had toast in his hand. He looked up. 'What is it?'

'Malcolm Kerr.' Vera sat down. The toast smelled wonderful and she was suddenly a child in Hector's house again. Toast was one of the few things he could cook well. 'I've been to his house and to the yard, but I can't find him. Any idea where he might be?'

'Sorry.'

'Had you arranged to work for him today?' She couldn't keep her mind off toast, dripping with butter, and the sharp fruitiness of marmalade, spread very thick.

'Yeah, but not until a bit later.'

'Have you any idea where he might be?' This time

she directed the question towards the girl too. She was sitting with her elbows on the table. Vera thought how young she looked, but too serious for a girl of that age. Troubled. Someone else burdened with secrets. A looker. When she was older you might mistake her for that photo of Margaret Krukowski on her wedding day.

The boy shrugged again and his glance slid back to the magazine. Hector would have slapped him for that. *Show a bit of respect, boy.*

Kate Dewar said sharply, 'Answer the inspector, Ryan.' She looked at Vera and rolled her eyes as if to say: *Kids these days. What would you do with them?*

'I don't know where Malcolm is. Really.' He looked at her with a wide-eyed innocence. Vera thought he could be hiding something, protecting his occasional employer. Boys this age, she could never tell what they were thinking.

'Malcolm might be on the beach,' Chloe said.

It was the first time she'd spoken. She rolled her napkin in her fingers, so that it looked like a fat Christmas cracker.

Bloody Christmas. This time of year you can't escape it. Even in your head.

They all stared at Chloe and she went on defensively. 'I've seen him there before. Just walking.'

'Which beach?' Vera kept her tone chatty.

'North Mardle,' Chloe replied as if the answer was obvious. 'He parks by the dunes and then he walks.'

'Ryan?' Vera's voice was sharper now. *So why didn't you tell me? Why leave it to your sister?*

'He goes beachcombing,' Ryan said. 'Sometimes you get wood washed ashore from the Norwegian cargo boats. Long planks that he can use in the yard. He goes early to find the good stuff.'

Vera looked at them both and nodded. Something was going on in this family, a tension between brother and sister, and she didn't understand it. She had no siblings. As far as she knew. So no experience of the way they worked out their differences. She thought it could just be rivalry, both of them wanting their mother's attention and approval. But at their age, shouldn't they be over that? Then she thought of Joe and Holly and decided that some people never grew out of it. She smiled briefly at the idea that her team were like a big, dysfunctional family.

She turned to Ryan. 'Have you got a key to the yard?' There was a possibility that Kerr had been there all night, holed up drinking in his bothy. Best try that before a wild goose chase to the beach.

He nodded and pulled a key from his pocket. 'Do you want me to come with you?' Suddenly he seemed eager to get out of the house. To be walking again? Soaking up secrets?

'Nah, you're all right.' She took the key from him and walked up the stairs to the hall. Stuart Booth was still there, standing awkwardly, not a paying guest, but not part of the family, either. She walked past him without a word.

In the street it was quite light now. She unlocked the padlock and let herself into the yard, the metal sticking to her glove because it was still icy. All the time she was thinking about the family in Number One, Harbour Street. Perhaps they were all still mourning

Margaret and the awkwardness she'd imagined was no more sinister than that.

Kerr's shed was empty and she left quickly, locking the yard behind her. She headed for her vehicle and for the beach. His elderly car was parked in the sandy space behind the dunes and she left the Land Rover next to it. Nobody else was about. She climbed the sand hills, pulling on the marram grass in places to help her up. There were patches of frost in the hollows. More memories of Hector. This time of a trip away, a beach in North Wales with breeding little terns. They'd stayed in a dreadful B&B. Slimy nylon sheets, shelves covered with glass ornaments: cats and rabbits and a row of blue owls with bulging eyes. Hector had flirted with the landlady in the hope of a discount. Then they'd climbed the dunes, Hector with an egg box in each pocket of his long Barbour coat. They'd peered over the top of the dune to find a warden sitting just below them. A young man, frozen because he'd been there most of the night, huddled in a cheap anorak. Hector had pulled her down beside him. 'We'll wait. He'll have been drinking coffee all night to keep warm and awake. He'll soon need a piss.' The words whispered, his face so close to hers that she'd felt his prickly chin on her cheek.

And at last the warden had stood up. By now there were dog walkers at the far end of the beach and he'd jogged past Hector and Vera's hiding place to the public toilets in the car park, deserting his post through embarrassment or a sense of decency. Immediately Hector was on his feet and amongst the tern colony, raiding the nests on the shingle beach. They passed the warden on their way back to their car and he smiled and said hello. Because who could be suspicious of a middle-aged man and an overweight girl.

Back in the present, Vera reached the last sand hill and stood looking down at the long beach. A big orange sun over the horizon, and space that took her breath away. Rolling breakers and the smell of the sea. So much space that it made you dizzy to look at it. And in the distance a stooped figure, dragging a plank of wood behind him. He was on his way back to the car and she waited, taking in the view. She thought Chloe was probably right and he came here often. This was where he'd walked with Margaret Krukowski, discussing her illness.

Malcolm didn't see her until he was at the foot of the dunes. He always walked looking down at his feet, avoiding eye contact with strangers, perhaps. Then he stopped for a moment and looked around him, and that was when he saw Vera. She gave a little wave. She didn't want to appear threatening.

'We need a chat,' she said. Then, feeling hungry again, remembering the smell of toast: 'Is there anywhere we can get some breakfast?' Now that it had come to it, she was reluctant to take him to the police station just yet, to start the formal process that would lead to his arrest.

They ate sausage sandwiches in a greasy spoon on the road out of town. A steaming tea urn and a couple of German lorry drivers at the table by the counter. Vera sat Malcolm near the window.

'Margaret Krukowski was a prostitute,' she said. 'You didn't think it was important to tell me?'

'No.'

Vera thought Malcolm was like a boy who hadn't

quite grown up. 'I didn't want her memory dirtied by that sort of talk.'

'But she *was* a prostitute?' Vera tried to catch his eye, but he was staring out of the window at the passing traffic.

'Not like Dee Robson,' he said immediately. His face was red, indignant. 'Not cheap, tarting herself around the pubs. She had men friends and they paid towards her expenses. She had to live, she said. Once Pawel had left, and my dad let her go from working for us. And she'd always enjoyed the company of men.'

She enjoyed sex, Vera thought, *but you can't bring yourself to say that.*

'You can't have liked it, though.' She leaned forward across the table, where the remains of their breakfast lay. 'The thought of her going with other men. You loved her.'

'But she didn't love *me*.' His voice was so quiet that if she hadn't been so close to him she wouldn't have heard. 'I had to come to terms with that years before.'

There was a moment of silence. The German drivers clattered through the door, letting in a blast of icy air.

'Margaret was going to leave you some money,' Vera said. 'Enough for a decent car, at least. But she was killed before she signed the will.'

'I didn't know anything about that! And I didn't want her money!'

'Did she ask you to keep an eye out for Dee once she was gone?'

Malcolm's gaze slid away from her. 'Aye.'

'And you said you would?' He didn't answer and Vera continued. 'Of course you did. You couldn't deny her anything. Would you have kept your promise, though? Not an easy woman to keep track of, Dee Robson?'

He shrugged. 'I'd have done my best.'

'But now the woman's dead, you don't have to.' Vera wiped the grease from her mouth. 'Must be a relief.'

'I wouldn't kill the woman because she was a bit of a nuisance!' He'd raised his voice and the woman behind the counter was staring.

Vera ignored the outburst and continued. 'Now we'll have to trace Margaret's relatives, because there's no valid will. Her husband. I call Pawel that, because I've looked and I can't find any trace that they were officially divorced.' She looked up and this time she did catch his eye. 'Any idea where he might be?'

He shook his head slowly.

'We're tracing other people who were around at the time,' she said. 'That mother and son who ran the Coble. If you don't talk, there are folk who will.'

He shrugged and still he didn't speak, but this time she sensed something unexpected in his reaction. Pleasure? A certain wry humour? 'Pawel went back to Poland,' he said. 'He found a woman who suited him better and he went back home.'

'If you know anything about his disappearance, and you don't talk, you're playing a dangerous game.' She felt as she had with Ryan at the Dewars' breakfast table: that she wanted to slap some sense into him. Demand some answers. Both knew more than they were letting on. 'You could be charged with murder, man. All these secrets and lies. The truth won't hurt Margaret now.'

He shrugged again, the eternal teenage boy.

'You'll have to come into the station and make a statement,' she said. Not because she thought they would get more information from him – Malcolm was too stubborn for that – but because it was the only way she had to retaliate.

He shrugged once more and followed her in his car back to Kimmerston. On the way she thought that she *would* get a search warrant. Even after all this time there might be traces of Pawel Krukowski in Kerr's yard.

Chapter Thirty-Two

When Joe Ashworth arrived at the Haven there was no sign of Susan Coulson. The house seemed quiet and empty. The road through Holypool hadn't been gritted and he'd skidded turning into the track. Everything was white. Frost on the grass and on every tree and twig. A white mist rising from the low pasture. No tyre tracks marking the frosty drive. Walking to the front door, he saw that there was nobody in the office, but then he noticed a light in the kitchen. Jane and Laurie were at the table, bent towards each other, looking like conspirators. Or lovers. They didn't notice that he was there. He stood watching for a while and then Jane Cameron looked up and saw him and he felt awkward, like a voyeur.

She opened the kitchen door to let him in. 'Well, Sergeant Ashworth, you're becoming a regular visitor.' She poured him coffee and set it on the table. 'We're making a list. Our last shop before Christmas.'

'How many of you will be here?' He couldn't understand how she could bear to spend Christmas Day with these demanding clients. Didn't she have family of her own? When would she escape?

'Laurie, Susan and me. And I've invited a couple of friends from town. We've got lots of space, so they can stay the night. I'm looking forward to it.' Jane gave an easy smile. 'No men to get in the way or make demands.'

'Father Gruskin won't be here?'

'Good God, no.' She seemed horrified by the idea. 'The old ladies from St Bart's will be fighting to cook him lunch. We're planning a proper party.'

'What do you want?' Laurie looked at him. 'If you need to talk to me, be quick, because I want to take the dog for a walk before we go into town.'

'No,' he said. He was surprised, but also faintly amused that she was so bossy. An offender had never spoken to him like that before. 'I don't need to talk to you.'

Laurie stood up and left. He heard her speak to someone in the hall and a dog barked, and then Susan Coulson walked into the kitchen. She was dressed in the sort of shapeless trousers that Vera wore on a bad day, with a baggy jersey across her swollen belly. Her grey hair was pulled back into a ponytail. She was yawning as if she'd just stumbled out of bed. He wasn't sure that she'd recognize him, but she nodded as she put on the kettle for tea. He thought she seemed more composed than she had on their previous meeting.

'There's been a development,' he said. 'A possibility that Margaret's murder was linked to the way she lived a long time ago. I was hoping that Susan might help me.' He looked at the woman. 'Because you knew Margaret then, didn't you? You both had bedsits in Harbour Street?'

She looked at Jane first, as if she needed her permission to answer, and then she nodded. No words.

She squeezed the teabag in her mug, threw it into the bin and sat at the table.

'I wondered if you'd like to go back to Harbour Street,' he said. 'See the house as it is now.'

Still silence. Through the window he saw Laurie in boots and jacket walking with the dog across the grass. Their feet left scuffmarks in the frost. The sun was burning off the mist.

'Would you like me to come with you?' It was Jane, talking directly to the older woman. 'Laurie and I can go shopping later.'

This time Susan shook her head and did speak. 'I'd like to see where Margaret lived,' she said. 'She never offered to take me back there. Perhaps she thought I'd be too upset.' She paused for a beat. 'And I'm sure this bonny lad will take care of me.' For the first time there was a glimmer of a smile. 'My age, I don't need a chaperone.'

Joe didn't talk to her as they drove away from the Haven. He wasn't sure where to begin and he thought he'd wait until they were there. Susan sat beside him in the front seat, looking around her as if she were a tourist. She seemed to be enjoying the trip out, the low sun on her face. Occasionally she would lean back in her seat and shut her eyes, and he wondered if she was sleeping or thinking about the past. As they approached Mardle she sat up and was more alert.

'Tell me about Margaret in those days.' They'd pulled up outside the Harbour Guest House now. Susan was looking around her, but made no move to get out. And at least in the car it was warm and they wouldn't be overheard. 'How did she earn her living?'

The woman turned her head sharply to face him. 'You already know or you wouldn't be asking.'

He wondered now that he could have thought her stupid or slow. 'She was a sex worker?'

'An escort,' Susan said. 'High-class. Choosy. She could have made a fortune, but she was never greedy. And she saved the money. I could never save a penny.'

'Were you in the same business?'

She shook her head. 'Nah, I never had the nerve for it.' Another smile. 'Or the body. I managed on the social. Had a man, until he left me.'

'I'm sorry.' Joe wasn't sure what else to say.

'I wasn't. He was a bastard. But I started taking drugs then. Tranquillizers from the doctor, then anything I could get hold of. Never stopped really. They took my baby.'

He didn't reply. It would have sounded trite to say again that he was sorry.

'But you're clean now? At the Haven.'

'Aye. Still have bad days.' A brief grin. 'And I make the most of them when they happen. I don't want them to get rid of me. If they think I'm well, they might make me leave, set me up in a place all on my own, like they did Dee. I couldn't live like that.'

'You like it at the Haven?'

'Eh, pet, I love it. Always someone about to chat to. A bit like the old days in Harbour Street.'

They sat for a moment in silence. 'Can I see inside? Where Margaret lived.'

'I don't see why not.' He got out of the car, then

went round and opened her door for her. It was still very cold.

She took his hand and pulled herself out, then stood for a moment looking up and down the street. On the pavement opposite, Peter Gruskin let himself into the church.

'Could we go in there first?' She nodded towards St Bartholomew's. 'For old time's sake.'

Joe wasn't sure what the priest would make of them wandering in, but it was a place of worship and it belonged to the community, not to one man. He crooked his arm so that Susan could hold onto it to steady herself as they crossed the icy road.

'Were you a member of the congregation?' he asked.

'I was baptized there,' she said. 'And I went there to grieve, when they took the baby.'

'Was it a boy or a girl?'

'A little girl,' she said. 'I called her Ellen, after my mother. I don't know what her new parents called her.'

'You never tried to find out what happened to her?' Joe tried to imagine what that would be like. To hand over a child when you'd been through the pain of labour and you'd held it in your arms. All those hormones rushing around your body and your mind.

'Nah,' she said. 'It wouldn't have been fair. Besides, they were right. I wouldn't have been able to give her any sort of life.'

She opened the church door, and Joe let her walk ahead of him. Partly because he'd been brought up to think it was gentlemanly to let the woman walk first, and partly because Peter Gruskin spooked him.

He was used to Methodist ministers, who dressed like everyone else, apart from a soft white collar at the neck.

Gruskin wasn't there. He must be in a back room. They sat for a moment in a pew. Joe looked at Susan and almost expected to see her crying again, those big silent tears that she'd shed when she'd heard about Margaret, but she was just staring towards the altar. After a few minutes she stood up and he followed her out.

'It brings it all back,' she said. 'Not the details – I was off my head most of the time and I can't remember much – but how I felt.'

'You said you knew Margaret's boss,' Joe said. They were outside now and the light seemed suddenly very bright and they were squinting against it.

'Did I?' She still seemed preoccupied by the church and glanced back to look at it.

'That would have been Malcolm Kerr's dad, Billy?'

'Aye,' she said. 'I expect that you're right.'

'Was Billy one of Margaret's clients?' It had just come to Joe as a possibility.

'No, pet, I don't think anything like that was going on.'

But he could tell that she was thinking about something else and hadn't put any thought into the answer.

When he knocked on the door of the guest house he wasn't sure how he'd explain their presence. It was opened by Chloe, Kate's daughter. She stared out at them, her arms wrapped round her bony body to keep out the cold. She had big fluffy slippers, just like Jessie's.

'Mum's out with Stuart,' she said. 'I'm the only one here.'

'Susan used to live in Harbour Street in the old days.' Joe found himself talking gently, as if to an invalid. Something about this child was so fragile that he felt she needed careful handling. 'She'd like to see Margaret's room. I've got a key. Is it okay if we go on up?'

'Yeah, fine.' She didn't seem at all curious about the strange woman turning up on her doorstep. Joe supposed that strangers must turn up there all the time, as they did at the Haven. It must be an odd way to live. He thought of his home as being safe from intrusion. Even Vera knew better than to turn up there unannounced.

Susan climbed the stairs to the attic with some difficulty. She was younger than Margaret, but unfit and heavy. At the top there was a sheen on her skin despite the cold.

'The house must look very different,' he said. 'But Margaret always lived up here, didn't she?'

'Aye. She liked to look out to the sea.' A brief pause, then that old spark of humour. 'And she said that if a man couldn't make it up the stairs he was no use to her.'

'She enjoyed her work then?' Joe couldn't get that. A woman as bright and well brought up as Margaret Krukowski enjoying life as a sex worker. Vera always said he should have been born in the nineteenth century, and there was something of the Victorian about him. But deep down he knew that if he'd been around at the time, he'd have been tempted to run up the stairs and knock at her door. He'd probably have paid to spend time with her, to touch her. As he put the key in the lock he almost imagined her inside, ready for him.

Again he stood aside to let Susan in. This time he needed a moment to compose himself. 'Is this what it was like in your day?' He'd arrested prostitutes, but they'd been working out of scuzzy massage parlours, or rundown houses in faded seaside towns. Pimps on the pavements watching from a distance, a perpetual threat to their women not to talk. Those girls had been addicts, rattling for a fix, lank-haired and sharp-featured. Nothing soft or inviting about their bodies or their beds.

Susan walked in and sat on the sofa. 'The kitchen's been done up,' she said. 'But she always had this room nice. I never saw inside the bedroom. She always had the door shut.'

'Did she *enjoy* it?' He repeated the question. Thinking about it again, it wasn't so much the sex that shocked him, but the fact that it had happened here, in Margaret's own space. It seemed like a terrible invasion of her privacy, another example of living on the job. He could see why she'd invited so few people into her home once she'd retired.

'She said it was better than working for a living. And once she'd got herself sorted, her own clients – regulars – I think she did like it. She only ever took on someone new if they were recommended. She never had to advertise.'

'Not like Dee Robson?'

Susan gave a sad chuckle. 'Poor Dee. She was an alcoholic and she enjoyed the drink too much to give up. Every couple of quid was important. And she needed the attention. But she was never a real professional. Not like Margaret.'

Joe sat beside her. 'Did Margaret ever talk to you about her customers?'

'Clients,' Susan said. 'She called them her clients. And no, she never talked about them. She said she was like a doctor or a priest, and what happened in the bedroom stayed secret.'

Joe took another tack. 'Where was your room?'

'On the ground floor. Near the front door. Draughty. And I never got it looking like this place.' She looked wistfully at Margaret's furniture. 'Didn't have the eye.'

'But you'd have seen people coming in and out from there?' Because Joe thought Susan would have been curious. Jealous even. He pictured her peering through stained net curtains, catching a glimpse of Margaret's gentleman callers on the pavement outside.

'Sometimes.' Susan snapped her mouth shut, as if she'd just remembered that this pleasant young man was a police officer.

'It might help us to find out who killed her,' Joe said. 'We think it might have started all those years ago.'

'Nah! That's just daft. Who'd care what happened then?'

'Margaret was dying,' Joe said. 'Bowel cancer. We think she wanted to talk about what happened back then. And maybe somebody wanted to stop her.'

There was a pause. On the roof outside herring gulls were screaming. 'I never knew their names. And there were only a few of them.'

'But you saw them.'

'All respectable,' she said. 'Suits, you know. Shiny shoes.' She leaned forward and lowered her voice. 'Once there was even a vicar. He was wearing a scarf, but when he was leaving it was open at the neck and I saw that white collar they have.'

But not Peter Gruskin, Joe thought. *He'd hardly have been born*. He remembered Vera and her manic behaviour at the briefing the day before, her conviction that Pawel Krukowski was dead. 'Tell me about Margaret's husband?'

'What about him?'

'What was he like?'

It was as if she hadn't heard him again. He wondered if she was lost in her memories, or if this vacant stare was a technique she'd developed to persuade social workers that she still needed to stay at the Haven.

'Susan.'

She turned her head slowly. Her eyes were cloudy and it was as if she hardly knew him.

'Tell me about Margaret's husband. Pawel. The Polish guy.'

'I never met him,' she said. Her head was tilted to one side, as if she was listening to a far-away voice. 'When I moved into Harbour Street he'd already disappeared.'

Chapter Thirty-Three

They had a fish-and-chip lunch in the Mardle Fisheries. Only a few days to Christmas, and the staff wore Santa hats and a crackly version of 'All I Want for Christmas Is You' played on a loop in the background. Joe didn't think he'd get anything more from Susan, but Vera had told him to buy her lunch and, anyway, he thought it would be a treat for her. He'd started to think of her as a slightly batty aunt.

'Were the fisheries here when you lived in the street?' He thought Susan went in and out of reception like a badly tuned radio. Sometimes she listened and understood, and at other times she seemed in a world of her own.

She nodded, her mouth full of chips. 'But only the wet-fish shop and the takeaway. Not a sit-down restaurant.'

'And the pub was there?'

'Yes.' She scrunched up her forehead, a parody of someone thinking. 'The landlady was called Val. She ran the place for years. I don't know what happened to her. She had a son.' Again Susan frowned in concentration, as if remembering the man's name was a sort of test. 'Rick? It might have been Rick. I never liked him. He was cruel to me. Made fun. There's nothing clever about making fun.' She put her hand to her mouth as if she regretted giving so much away and returned to her meal.

Now Joe's mind was wandering. He couldn't see what any of this could have to do with the murder of two women in the twenty-first century, but he imagined the Coble in the 1970s. It would be before all the pits and the shipyards closed. Lads in flared jeans and lasses in hippy skirts. The two small bars filled with smoke and the ceilings brown with nicotine. There would have been more commercial fishing then, and the men would've come for a pint straight from the boats, full of talk of their catch and the weather. What would they all have made of Margaret Krukowski? Perhaps the men wouldn't have cared how she made her living, but some of them would surely have guessed. They'd have seen Margaret's clients, even if they'd been few in number, out of place in their business suits and clerical collars, knocking at the door of Number One, Harbour Street. They'd have been curious. Would they have wanted some of the action too?

'Do you fancy going in for a drink?' he asked. 'For old times' sake?'

Susan shook her head immediately. Perhaps she thought that Rick, the landlady's son, would still be there to jeer at her.

Joe took out the photo album from his inside pocket. 'Do you recognize anyone here?'

She turned the pages slowly, but nothing registered until she came to the photo of Billy Kerr's birthday party. 'That's Margaret! And Billy and Malcolm.'

'Anyone else that you recognize?'

'Val, the landlady.' She pointed to the big woman.

Joe waited for her to point to Rick, the landlady's son, but she shut the album without mentioning him. Again he wondered what exactly the boy had done to upset her. 'Shall we get you back to the Haven?' He wasn't sure what good this was doing. He saw a police van pulling in beside Kerr's yard and wondered what was going on there.

'Aye,' she said. 'But it's been canny, coming back.'

'Not too many ghosts?'

She put on her blank, not-understanding face and didn't reply.

They arrived at the Haven at the same time as Laurie and Jane, and Joe helped to carry in the carrier bags of food.

'How did it go?' Jane caught him, just as he was about to get back into the car. There was something complicit in the question, as if they were two professionals comparing notes on a shared case.

But we're not, he wanted to say. *You're a suspect as much as Susan is.* 'Fine.' He gave a bland smile. 'I think she had a good time.' Then he did get into his vehicle and drove off before she could pry further.

Back in the police station he searched out Vera, found her in the canteen staring into space over a mug of tea. He sat down opposite her. 'What did you get out of Kerr?'

She looked up. 'Not a lot. He's hiding something, but he's not talking.' She paused. 'I've got a warrant to search his yard. It still seems as if Pawel Krukowski disappeared into thin air. And I don't believe in magic.'

'The search team arrived just as I was leaving.'

She looked across the table at him. 'Tell me that you got on better with Susan Coulson.'

'I'm not sure. She lived on the ground floor of the house and saw Margaret's clients coming and going. There weren't many of them. But all respectable men, she said. Professionals. A vicar even. She claims not to know any names.'

'That doesn't get us any further then.' Vera looked up at him and he saw how tired she was. She'd burned herself out with her excitement of the day before. Perhaps she was no longer so convinced by her idea that Margaret had killed her husband.

'Susan mentioned the landlady of the Coble. The woman called Val. And her son, Rick. Val's probably dead by now, but the man might still be around. Do you know if Charlie ever traced him?'

'He hasn't said.' Vera was preoccupied.

Joe persisted. 'There'd have been gossip in the neighbourhood about Margaret. Not something you could keep secret in a place like Harbour Street: strangers turning up at her door.' Joe knew he was throwing Vera these ideas in the hope of cheering her up. 'I thought it might be useful to talk to people who were around at the time, but not involved in the present case.'

'Aye,' she said. 'You're probably right. See if Charlie has managed to get anything on this Rick. He's babysitting Kerr in the house in Percy Street.' But there was no enthusiasm in her words and she got up suddenly and stomped away from him and back to her office. She sat there with her door shut until mid-afternoon, when she left without a word. Joe knew she'd be going back to Harbour Street. The tension of waiting for the search results would be killing her and she couldn't stop herself from meddling.

Charlie answered his phone on the first ring and told Joe to hang on until he found somewhere private so that they could talk.

'How's it going?' Joe could tell from the first response to the call that Charlie was gloomy.

'Well, I can think of better ways to spend the week before Christmas.'

'Have you tracked down that mother and son who used to run the pub in Harbour Street?'

Charlie hardly paused for a beat. 'The Butts? I haven't got anything on the man, but the mother still lives in Mardle. The address is on my desk.' And then he was gone.

Joe got home before the kids were in bed. They had that wild energy that came of being shut in the house all day, too much sugar and too much anticipation of Christmas. Jessie was sulking because Sal had refused to let her go into Newcastle with her friends. 'I've told her that she's too young to go in without a grown-up. It's mad this time of year.' Sal was crotchety and resentful after having to battle the issue all day. He could see that one more push from Jessie and his wife would relent, just for a quiet life. There were times when being a parent was the hardest thing in the world. And being a daughter-in-law too. In a moment of madness Sal had offered to cook Christmas lunch for his parents this year and she was already stressing about it. The fridge was so full of food that it would hardly shut.

He'd got the kids upstairs and poured Sal a big glass of Pinot when his phone rang. Vera. Just wanting to chat.

'How's it going?' He walked into the kitchen so that he wouldn't disturb Sal – there was a series she liked on the telly. She rolled her eyes when she realized it was Vera on the phone.

'They've stopped the search for the night. Seems to me it'll take days to go through all that stuff. And even if there's anything important among all the crap, I'm not sure we'd recognize it.' He could tell that she was exhausted and frustrated. She was losing faith in her ability to see the case to an end. He was tempted to offer to meet her. He wouldn't have minded sitting in her untidy house talking through the strands of the investigation. But as soon as the thought came into his head, he knew it was impossible. Sal would have a fit. The fantasies of Margaret set up in her small oasis of civilization in Harbour Street and receiving her gentleman callers had excited him. Instead he would share a bottle of wine with his wife and they would have an early night. Vera Stanhope could do without him for once.

Chapter Thirty-Four

Kate Dewar tried to drive to the end of Harbour Street to turn around. She always liked her car to be facing the right way outside the house when she parked. But she had to back all the way up the street again, because a uniformed officer waved to show that there was no way through. Outside Malcolm's yard there was a minibus and a van, dozens of police officers in dark-blue anoraks. They were putting up screens so that you couldn't see anything from the road. Blue-and-white tape, like on television detective shows, but twisted upside down and back to front so that she couldn't read what it said. She guessed: *Police. Do Not Enter.* Did that mean Malcolm had been arrested? She shivered at the thought that her son had been working so closely with a killer. Perhaps the investigation was nearly over and life would go back to normal. She and Stuart could continue making plans to move and start their new life.

In the house Chloe was in – she helped Kate carry the shopping down the stairs to the kitchen – but there was no sign of Ryan. She wondered briefly what he was up to, imagined him prowling. *He needs a girlfriend,* she thought. *Someone stable, without too much imagination.* She was sorry Ryan was out; he would have known what was going on in Harbour Street.

George Enderby was in the lounge. He'd helped himself to whisky.

'I put some money on the dresser,' he said. 'I hope that's all right. I spoke to the inspector. She said that I can leave tomorrow, so you'll be rid of me then, Kate.' He gave a lopsided grin and she thought that really he would have liked to stay. Or he wanted her to say that she would miss him.

'We'll miss you,' she said, wondering if there was really any difference sometimes between kindness and desperation to please. 'But Diana will be glad to have you home.'

'Ah,' he said. 'Diana's moved on. She has a new man. Just like you.' Kate wondered if he'd been sitting here all afternoon drinking her whisky, or if he'd been brooding in the lounge bar at the pub, buying drinks in return for company. He didn't seem drunk, but still he was hardly himself.

'Do you know what's going on at Malcolm's yard?' If he'd been in the pub he might have heard the gossip.

'No.' He seemed hardly to care.

Back in the kitchen she put away all the food she'd bought for Christmas.

Chloe was on the sofa in the living room and there was a book face-down beside her. She'd changed into different clothes, though, a pretty top that she usually only wore for going out, and she'd put on eye-liner and mascara. Kate wondered if one of her friends had been round. Chloe called through to her mother, 'Oh, Stuart phoned.' Implying that any call for her mother could have no importance and that she'd only just remembered. 'He said that you weren't answering your mobile.'

Kate stood in the doorway between the two rooms. She was clasping a huge bag of washing powder to her stomach as if it were a baby. 'What did he want?'

'Nothing.' That breezy voice. 'He just said to tell you that he'd called.'

Kate phoned Stuart, but there was no response. She left him a message, saying that she was in. 'Come round, if you're not busy. It'd be lovely to see you.' She thought that the balance of power had shifted between them. In the beginning Stuart had been the eager one, turning up on her doorstep, excited. Now she felt more needy, less certain of his affection.

She couldn't settle and climbed the stairs to the landing close to Margaret's room. From the round window there was a view over Malcolm's yard. It seemed to her that the police officers were searching for something specific. They had their own method, she could tell: meticulous, shifting all Malcolm's gear to one end of the yard. It was almost dark and suddenly the street lights came on and quite clearly she saw Ryan, peering through the railings, trying to see past the screens, along with other rubber-neckers. No doubt there'd already be a photo on his smartphone and he'd have sent it to all his friends. Then he'd move on, pacing the pavement, restless as ever.

Back in the kitchen she tried to phone Stuart again, but still he didn't answer.

Chapter Thirty-Five

Vera would have continued searching Malcolm's yard all night, would have been there on her own with only a torch and the street lights to illuminate the scene, if she hadn't realized that it would look ridiculous. They'd already gathered an audience. Teenage kids and workers on their way from the Metro to the Coble for a drink before heading home. Staff from the fisheries on their fag breaks. Malcolm wasn't there. He was at home, sitting in the bleak living room in the house on Percy Street, with Charlie to keep an eye on him. She felt a moment of guilt about Malcolm, a moment of self-doubt. She didn't have enough evidence to charge him, but the locals would all have him down as the murderer now, even if the search team didn't find anything in the yard. The press had turned out big-style, before the team gave up the operation for the night, and there would be lurid pictures in the papers the next day. His ex-wife had already done an exclusive with a tabloid, telling them that Malcolm had once battered her.

When the search team pulled out they left a PC to secure the yard and another outside Malcolm Kerr's place. She gave Charlie a lift home and they sat for a moment outside his house. There was a light on inside and the curtains were shut. So Charlie *had* found another woman then. Vera thought that maybe she wasn't such a bad detective after all.

'Who is she?' She nodded towards the house. Then, when he didn't reply immediately: 'You're a bit of a dark horse, keeping quiet about a new woman in your life.'

'It's not a new woman. At least, not how you mean.'

'What then?'

'It's my daughter. She finished uni in the summer and couldn't get a job. Couldn't get on with her mother, either. So she's back with me.' He grinned despite himself.

'It's working out okay?' Vera supposed she must have known that Charlie had a daughter, but couldn't remember anything about her.

'Champion!' He grinned again. 'She's doing work experience with an engineering company in Blyth, thinks she might get a real job at the end of it.' He couldn't keep the pride from his voice.

'Good for your lass.' Meaning it really. But Charlie had been a loner like her since his wife had left, and now it seemed that Vera was the only oddball in the team. She couldn't help feeling she'd been deserted, that he'd let her down.

When Charlie disappeared into the house without a second glance back at her, she phoned Joe. She'd have liked to spend a bit of time with him, but she could tell there was no way he'd come out. His lass would want him for herself: mulled wine and carols and crap TV. So Vera drove home and sat alone in the cold house. Drinking like she had in the old days, before she got the doctor's warning. Worrying at the case, not allowing herself to think that they'd find nothing of any importance in Malcolm Kerr's yard; that all that manpower and expense would be wasted and she'd be a laughing stock.

The next day she was first in the briefing room. A hangover, dull like a bruise or an aching shoulder. The team turned up on time. Eager and expecting results, because she'd been so positive the day before.

She stood in front of them and tried to keep her energy level high. 'Hol. Charlie. Any news on our elusive friend Pawel?'

'Not yet.' Holly pulled a face. 'I took it over yesterday afternoon when Charlie went out to Mardle, but civil servants seem to stop working at least a week before a bank holiday. I've got a couple more contacts to try today.'

'That's our priority. The searchers will be back at first light, and if they find anything we need to know what we're working with. We need a date for the last time we can prove that the man was alive.' Vera swept her eyes around the room. 'Charlie, how was Malcolm yesterday? Did you get any sense from him that he's bothered by us digging around in the yard?'

'Nah. He seemed kind of frozen. As if he didn't care one way or another.'

'Joe?'

'I'm going to see the woman who ran the Coble for years. Prof. Craggs has some photos which suggest that they were all friends – the Kerrs, Margaret and the landlady and her son. Maybe Pawel too. Susan

Coulson from the Haven says she knew the others, though she has no memory of Margaret's husband. The landlady's name is Valerie Butt and Charlie's tracked her down to an address in Mardle.' He turned apologetically to Vera, as if he knew he wasn't helping much. He realized that what she needed now was proof that Krukowski was dead. Bones. Teeth. Or a witness who had seen him killed. 'I thought she might remember gossip about Pawel disappearing suddenly. I'm still a bit confused about timings, about when exactly he left the town. Talking to other people might help.'

Vera thought it was a long shot, but she didn't want to put him down again in front of the others. Whatever his shortcomings, he'd always be her favourite. 'Aye,' she said. 'Why not? Worth a punt.'

It was light now and the team would have started in Harbour Street. She was drawn back there. A terrible fascination, because she knew that if nothing was found, her theory would be baseless. If Pawel hadn't been killed by Kerr, or with his help, there'd have been nothing more for Margaret to confess to and no reason for Kerr to have killed her. Vera was certain that Margaret had been keeping a more profound secret than just her profession. Without a body, Vera would have to rethink the investigation entirely. Immediately after the briefing she headed back to Mardle, only telling Joe where she was going.

When she arrived they'd searched most of the yard. There was one rusting hull to get into and Malcolm's shed still to clear. She stood by the fence, feeling the tension coming up from her feet like the cold. She couldn't keep still, but she knew better than to interfere. Bad enough that she was here, keeping them in her sight, instead of letting them get on with it. She'd hate a superior officer watching over *her.* She knew what they were thinking: *Doesn't the woman have any work of her own to get on with?* In the end she could stand it no longer and walked away, telling herself that she wanted coffee, but really just needing to move, the nerves in her body jingling, the muscles in her face tense.

On the other side of the road Peter Gruskin hesitated on the pavement, looking in at the activity outside the yard. She caught his eye and he hurried away. She thought that he was like a crow, hovering over a piece of carrion. A predator on other people's miseries. But then she'd inherited Hector's antipathy to the clergy.

In the smart cafe opposite the health centre she drank black coffee and ate a croissant. It had almond paste in the middle, very sweet, and she felt a rush of energy from the caffeine and the sugar. She knew she should get back to the police station in Kimmerston. That was her proper place. In an office. She should leave the detail to other people. But she told herself it would do no harm to call back into the search site first. They might have found something in the last half-hour. It would be crazy to drive away without checking.

When she arrived at Malcolm's yard there was no sense of urgency. Most of the officers were standing by the fence drinking tea from flasks. Just a couple of men were emptying the junk from the shed. First she felt angry and then sick with disappointment. They'd given up. She bobbed under the tape to join them. Now the shed was empty and there was nothing left but the small stove standing on the bare concrete floor. She went inside and found the team leader there.

He looked at her. Part pity and part derision. 'Nothing.' He was a Scouser and it sounded as though he was spitting the word. 'No clothing dating back to the time in question. Nothing that could have belonged to your man. No sign that anything's been buried, or that the concrete's been disturbed anywhere in the yard.'

'Except in here.' Coffee, sugar and a flash of the new idea made her almost light-headed. No hangover now. 'There was a wooden temporary office here before the shed. Smart; linked to mains services. It was burned down. There was a suspicion that it was an insurance scam. But maybe Kerr wanted to hide a body, hide the evidence of a murder. A fire would give him an excuse to replace the floor. The shed appeared on the same site soon after. Nobody would have noticed, would they? Customers coming into the yard would have thought any work was connected to the fire damage.'

'You want us to dig up the floor in here?' He looked at her as if she was crazy.

'Aye, I do.' She smiled, knowing that she seemed manic, unhinged. 'Humour a mad old woman, eh? All those fit men out there, it won't take more than a few minutes.'

She walked away from him across the yard, her coat flapping behind her. As she emerged from the screen onto the pavement there was the click of a camera. The press were there already then. More predators. She walked up the street to her vehicle and drove back to Kimmerston. Partly because she couldn't stand the stress of watching them: the men with their picks and shovels and wheelbarrows of debris, calling her all sorts under their breath. The waiting would send her blood pressure sky-high. But there was another reason too. She didn't need to hang around because she knew she was right. She was sure of it. Because she felt it in her bones, just as she felt Margaret's guilt – and because nothing else made sense. It would be better for her to be in the office when the news came through, ready to brief the rest of the team.

The call came sooner than she'd expected it. She'd made tea, wandered over to Holly's desk to see how she was getting on and back into her office. She left the door open. Some days it felt like a cell and she needed to let in some air. So the team saw her raise her fist, a sign of triumph and vindication. They saw her beam. And when she strode out to greet them, they had all turned to face her.

'The search team has just found a body under the shed in Malcolm Kerr's yard.' She was fizzing, but tried to keep her voice calm and factual. 'The concrete there is as thin as eggshell apparently. Replaced after the fire in the original building. No details yet. Paul Keating and Billy Wainwright are on their way. But the team leader reckons the skeleton of a male.' Now she allowed herself to look out at them, to bask in their glory. 'A young male.'

There was a round of applause, a few cheers.

'Time to bring in Malcolm Kerr, don't you think?' she said. 'See to it, Charlie.' A moment's pause. She knew that in a performance timing was everything. 'Didn't I tell you this would all be over by Christmas?'

Chapter Thirty-Six

It turned out that Val Butt wasn't as old or as frail as Joe had expected. Prof. Craggs's photograph of the group outside the Coble had been taken in 1975; the date was written faintly on the back in pencil. Margaret would have been thirty-two. Val Butt, large and ungainly, would have been just in her forties, already looking tired and middle-aged, and her son Rick in his mid-twenties. Val would have been hardly more than a child herself when she'd had him, and it would have been hard to be a teenage mother then. Joe tried to take the imaginative leap back to Harbour Street in the year before he was born, but the effort was too much for him. Better to find Val and talk to her.

The woman lived on her own in a single-storeyed miners' welfare cottage in a small estate on the outskirts of Mardle. It astonished him how many of the players in the case still lived in the town, or had connections with the place. It was as if they'd had no ambition, or lacked the confidence to uproot themselves and try life elsewhere. He wondered if Kate Dewar would move away now, whether she and Stuart and the kids would set up home in a new town, make a fresh start. He hoped they would. He wasn't given to strange thoughts, but it occurred to him suddenly that

Mardle was toxic. There was something unhealthy in the air.

He hadn't made an appointment and it took the woman so long to get to the door that he was about to turn away. Then he heard a painful wheezing and the door opened slowly. Val Butt was huge. She was still in her nightclothes, and the pink candlewick dressing gown hardly met around her waist. She walked with the aid of a Zimmer frame and, before speaking, she let go of it with one hand and flicked ash from her cigarette onto the path beyond him. 'Who are you?' Eyes narrowed. *The same look*, he thought, *she would have given the underage drinkers in the Coble, before serving them anyway.*

He introduced himself and showed his warrant card.

'You're here about Maggie Krukowski.' There was a rattle in her voice and she gasped for breath again.

'And Dee Robson.'

'Aye, well. I never knew her.' She backed herself carefully into the corridor. 'You'd better come in. Dee was after my time. I'd have left the Coble before she was a regular there.'

He made a pot of tea on her instruction. 'I'm never my best in the mornings.' She installed herself on the sofa that took up most of the tiny front room, hauling her legs onto a padded stool in front of her. 'The carers are supposed to get here at eight to dress me, but they're always bloody late. Most of them don't speak English anyway.'

'You knew Margaret in the Seventies and Eighties?'

She ignored the tea and biscuits he put beside her

and lit another cigarette. The room stank of smoke and the ceiling was brown with nicotine stain.

Joe put the photo on the arm of the sofa so that she could see it without moving. She picked it up and stared at it.

'That was 1975,' she said, without turning it over to look at the date. 'Billy Kerr's birthday.'

'Nothing wrong with your memory then.' He was genuinely impressed.

'It was the year I took on the licence.' She paused. 'We'd had a place in the West End of Newcastle before that, but it wasn't easy. There was always trouble. It was tough, especially for a woman. The Coble was a step up. A bit more respectable.'

'You were on your own with your son?'

She gave a sudden quick grin and the ghost of a wink. 'On and off. There was the occasional bloke.' She stubbed out the cigarette in her saucer and gulped the tea. 'But always my name over the door. I stayed there until I retired.'

'Margaret Krukowski,' he said. It was time to get to the point.

'Aye, the gorgeous Margaret. She could stop a conversation in the bar just by walking through the door.' There was a niggle of resentment in her voice, which he realized was probably jealousy. Most women would have been jealous of Margaret Krukowski in her heyday.

'You didn't like her?'

'I didn't trust her.'

'Tell me,' he said, remembering advice given by Vera, one night at her house. *Get them to tell you a story. It's all about stories. It might be a pack of lies, of course. But that'll tell you something useful too.*

Val settled back on the sofa and her eyes were half-closed. 'Maggie thought she was better than the rest of us. She hated being called Maggie, and I only did it to spite her. She had a fancy accent and fancy clothes. I said to her once: "We're alike, you and me. Both left by our men to fend for ourselves." The look that she gave me! As if I wasn't fit to clean her boots.'

'Had you seen her recently?' Joe wondered where this story was taking him. He still wasn't convinced that something that had happened almost forty years ago could have any relevance to the present investigation. He didn't believe in the body under the boatyard.

'Nah! I didn't see her much after that photo was taken. There was a falling-out.' She paused, drank more of the tea. 'Things were never really the same after that.'

'What do you mean?' Outside, the postman walked down the street. The last delivery before Christmas, his bag fat and heavy. Val saw him too and watched. A moment of hope or anticipation. But he walked straight past her door.

Val lifted her shoulders, an attempt at a shrug. 'Nothing. Just that she never came into the pub again.'

'What sort of falling-out?'

'How would I remember after all this time?' She glared at him, challenging him to contradict her.

Joe thought she remembered perfectly. 'Did something happen the night of Billy Kerr's birthday party?'

'I don't want to talk about it.' She shut her mouth like a toddler refusing to eat her vegetables and they sat for a moment in silence.

'Did you ever meet Margaret's husband, Pawel?'

She shook her head. Her hair was very fine and she was bald in places. 'He'd long gone by the time we moved to Harbour Street.'

Joe thought that in that case Vera couldn't be right. If Pawel was buried under Malcolm Kerr's yard, he must have been in Harbour Street the night of the fire. 'Are you sure? Our information is that he was still in the region then.'

She shrugged. 'Maybe he was, but he wasn't living with Maggie Krukowski.'

'Was Margaret working for Billy and Malcolm Kerr when this photo was taken?' Joe thought it was hard work, prising information from the woman, and he wasn't getting anywhere. He was wondering now why he'd come. He wished he was at Kerr's yard watching the search team. He'd trained with a couple of the lads and it would have been good to catch up.

Val made a strange choking sound that was half-cough and half-chuckle. 'By the time I knew her she was what you'd call freelance. A professional working woman.' Each word came out as a separate sneer.

'What do you mean?' Joe pretended ignorance.

'She was a high-class slag. Playing with fire. No man to keep a lookout for her. No protection. If she'd been murdered *then*, I wouldn't have been surprised.'

He was surprised by the vehemence of her words. 'You were a woman without a man to look out for you too.'

'I had my Rick. He was a good son.'

But he's left you, Joe thought. A sudden flash of insight. *And he doesn't even send you a Christmas card.*

'Around the time of Billy Kerr's birthday there was a fire at his yard,' Joe said. 'His office burned down.'

She looked at the clock on the windowsill. 'Those bloody carers. They get later every day.'

'You must remember the fire. It would have been a big deal round here then. There was a rumour that it was all an insurance scam.'

'Was there?' She seemed genuinely surprised. 'I never heard that.' Another pause while she fidgeted with a packet of cigarettes. 'It happened the night of the birthday party. Or early morning the next day. Though I think there was talk in the bar about arson, I never believed it. People always like a drama, don't they?'

'You can't help in any way with our investigation then?' Joe Ashworth was losing patience and he wanted to be out of the house before she lit another cigarette. He hated the way the smell got into his hair and his clothes. It made him retch.

'I've never been one for helping the police,' she said. 'Never trusted them, and they do nothing for the likes of me.'

A car with a council logo pulled up outside and two women in pink overalls got out. 'You'd best go,' Val said. 'Unless you fancy helping them to get me into the bath.'

Joe left the house before the carers had their key in the lock.

In the car his phone rang. Vera Stanhope, her voice chirpy. 'How's it going, bonny lad?' She only ever called him that when she was in a particularly good mood or when she was being sarcastic.

'I haven't got much from the ex-landlady of the Coble.' But he knew Vera wasn't listening. She'd phoned to share information, not to get it.

'We've found the body.' Her voice was high-pitched with excitement. 'It was under Malcolm's shed. I think he set the office fire not for the insurance money, but to hide evidence of Pawel's murder.'

Joe didn't say anything. He was thinking that Val Butt had been lying to him. Pawel had still been around in Harbour Street in 1975, when Malcolm Kerr's office had burned down, and she would have known that. Joe thought she'd have known everything that was going on in her patch. She'd have been that kind of landlady. And what had actually happened the night of Billy Kerr's birthday party to trigger a murder? A fight that had got out of hand? Two young men scrapping over Margaret, like dogs over a bone.

'Well?' Vera was indignant. She'd been expecting congratulations. 'Now we have everything: motive, opportunity and a skeleton in the cupboard. Or under the concrete. I've sent them to bring in Malcolm Kerr. He'll talk. No reason not to, when he'll be forced to plead guilty to one murder. We'll have it all wrapped up by teatime, and the drinks are on me.'

'What do you want me to do now?' Joe looked through the window, wondering if he should go back and talk to the woman inside. He didn't like inconsistencies, and why would Val Butt lie about Margaret's husband? What could she have to hide at her time of life? But the carers were already helping her to her feet and leading her towards the bathroom. Her nightdress and dressing gown were caught in the waistband of her knickers and a huge bare thigh was exposed. He decided that old people often got confused and there was nothing to be gained by talking to her again.

'Come back here,' Vera was saying. 'You can sit in on the interview.'

Joe switched off his phone and stood for a moment in the street outside the old folks' bungalows. He had a second crisis of conscience. Perhaps he should knock at the door and talk to Val Butt again, ask her if she knew anything about the body buried in Malcolm Kerr's yard.

But the moment soon passed and then he found himself smiling. When Vera was happy, her good humour was infectious. Why not be a part of the celebrations? He started the engine and set off for Kimmerston. Arriving into the station expecting a party atmosphere, laughter and the inevitable release of tension after an investigation, he found instead that Vera was furious. He could hear her swearing from the bottom of the stairs. She was so caught up in her rant about the incompetent scum that made up the police service these days that she didn't notice him entering the room. He slid in beside Charlie.

'What's going on?' He whispered, but Vera wouldn't have heard a five-piece jazz band in the corner of the room.

'Malcolm Kerr's gone AWOL. They just had one plod on the front door, and Kerr slipped out of the back first thing this morning. She's blaming me, because I told her I didn't think he had any spirit left for the fight.'

'Nah,' Joe said. 'She's blaming herself.'

The room suddenly went quiet and the silence was more terrifying than the storm of noise. Vera was standing in the middle of the room, looking round at them.

'So,' she said. 'Where do we think Malcolm will be hiding? Ideas, please.'

Joe raised his hand. 'Do we know that he's hiding? He'll know that we'll get him eventually. This isn't some gangland boss with a villa in Marbella. Sounds to me like he's broken and depressed, and a cell won't be so different from that place in Percy Street.'

'So what are you saying, Joe?' Vera's voice was so quiet that there could have been just the two of them in the room.

'I'm wondering if there's some unfinished business.'

'Explain, please.'

Joe wasn't sure he *could* explain. He knew that he should have saved this conversation until he'd got Vera on her own. It was never a good idea to question her in front of an audience.

'I still don't see Kerr as Margaret's killer. He loved her, didn't he? I'm wondering if he's got his own agenda. He knows who the murderer is and he's out for revenge.'

'For Christ's sake, man, most of the men I've nicked for battering their wives claim to love them.'

'Aye,' he said. By now he'd lost the train of thought, the faint glimmer of an idea that had made him crazy enough to challenge the boss. 'You're probably right.'

There was another brief moment of silence and then she was issuing orders. 'I want this man caught and brought in within the hour, before we're slated in the press for incompetence. Again. And if we don't get him by the end of the day, I'll be writing the story myself and selling it to the papers. We know he's in that clapped-out car of his. It'll be on CCTV somewhere.' A pause while she glared round the room. 'Well, clear off, the lot of you!' Then there was a flurry of activity and a scraping of chairs. Soon Joe was the only one left.

She leaned against his desk. 'North Mardle beach,' she said. 'I want you to go there. It's where Malcolm goes to think. I'd go myself, but I've got to be here to stand between the shit and the fan.'

Joe nodded.

It was midday. Quiet. Not even a dog walker on the long beach. There'd been no sign of Kerr's old car parked behind the dunes, but Joe had walked through to the shore anyway. Vera had thought the man would be here and usually she was right. But the only figures, right in the distance, were kids chasing a ball.

He phoned Sal from the top of the sand hill, suddenly missing her, thinking that they should bring the children out here sometime over the holidays. They could all do with a blast of fresh air and the sight of the long surf curling onto the beach.

'How's it going?' He knew Sal was wound up about Christmas. She had this dream of how it should be for the family. Everything perfect. And the reality never quite lived up to her expectations. This year she'd be thinking that his parents were judging her too. 'How are the kids?'

'Jessie's gone into town.' Her voice defiant, knowing that he wouldn't approve. He thought his little girl was too young to go into Newcastle without an adult. She went on, 'It's all right. There's a gang of them, some older kids too. Sarah's mother was going to take them in on the Metro and she'll be in town too. Last-minute shopping to do, and just on the end of the phone if they need her.'

'Okay.' Because what else could he say? It had already been decided without him. He stood for a moment watching the low sun on the waves, and then he drove back to Kimmerston.

Chapter Thirty-Seven

Malcolm Kerr sat on the Metro, an inside seat, next to a big-boned woman with a squawking toddler on her knee. The train was packed. The last shopping day before Christmas Eve. Nobody took any notice of him. He was a grey man, old and ineffective. Powerless. *But I'll show them.*

He wasn't sure what he was doing there at first. He'd left the house in Percy Street, not intending to run away, but to get some air. He'd been on North Mardle beach just as it got light, saw the grey dawn in from the top of the dunes and, driving back, he'd had a fancy to re-create Margaret's last steps. He might get a sense of her sitting in the Metro. He knew it was crazy, but then he could feel his mind being eaten away at the edges. It was like mice nibbling at a piece of rotting carpet, leaving his thoughts ragged and frayed.

He saw a face he recognized as soon as he got onto the train, but he hid in a corner and thought he hadn't been seen. It seemed like a sign. Was Margaret talking to him from the grave? Did she want him to run and find a new life for himself without her? Or was there something else she needed from him? In the space by the doors a group of kids stood. They were laughing and he felt a terrible resentment. *How dare they?* Then he realized that they were talking about the murders. He took an instant dislike to the first girl to speak. She was too young for make-up, but was wearing it all the same.

'Your dad's in the police, Jess.' Her voice so loud that everyone in the carriage could hear it. 'Have they caught the killer yet?' The other passengers stared, and perhaps that was what she'd wanted.

The lass Jess seemed younger than the others. Skinny and unsure of herself, but wanting them to like her. Malcolm knew how that felt.

'I was there,' she said with a touch of pride. 'I found the first body.'

Malcolm looked down the aisle at the prying, curious eyes and in his head he was screaming at the girl: *You shouldn't have said that. We didn't need to know.* It was a complication.

All the way into town he peered out into the carriage. Alert. Some sort of hunting dog, aware of every passenger, wondering how he might separate the one he wanted from the crowd.

He thought he was certainly going mad. Lack of sleep. Or forty years of stress. He'd thought he didn't care any more, that he was dead, like the specimens the professor collected in his lab at Cullercoats. Looking fresh and glossy on the outside, but inside hard and frozen. That he was as good as dead, at least. No feelings. No soul. But now he saw that there was a possibility of escape. Of living again, feeling whole, and he felt a moment of hope. That depended on him parting the group and picking off the individual. He felt a sudden rush of excitement, the same brief, destructive excitement that he'd felt forty years before.

He was a reading a copy of the free newspaper that he'd picked up at Partington station and snatched a look over the top of it. Had his quarry seen him? He couldn't be certain and he couldn't take the risk. He shrank back into his corner and his mind slid back, time rewinding, the newspaper a screen between the present and the past.

His father's birthday party. Fifty. The whole street in the Coble, from the minute he and Billy had come in with the boat. A big cheer as soon as they walked through the door. Billy Kerr had always been a hero in Harbour Street. Valerie had organized a cake from somewhere, but by the time they'd come to cut it most of them had been pissed. Then out onto the pavement to take a photograph. Not everyone, of course. Some had stayed inside. There were always people in Harbour Street who were reluctant to appear in photographs.

He remembered in detail what Margaret was wearing that day. A peasant skirt in Indian cotton and a white cheesecloth blouse. Sandals. The fine leather strap tied round her ankle in a bow. Not her work clothes. She dressed up for work as if she was going to an office. Black underwear and a black suspender belt. Sheer stockings and shoes with pointed toes and heels so high you'd wonder how she balanced. Leather and silk. He'd seen her dressing for work once. When he was out in the boat to lift his creels he'd anchored in the bay and peered through her window, using the professor's binoculars. She'd thought nobody was watching, thinking that nobody *could* look into her bedroom, because all there was outside was the sea. Her silhouette had been black against the faint artificial light in the room. She'd stood on one foot, poised as a ballerina, and unrolled the sheer stocking along her other leg. Completely balanced and completely relaxed. *Who are you dressing for, Margaret?* He'd watched her turn, imagined her opening the bedroom door to let in her client. But the angle was too steep for him to see who'd come into the room, or to watch what happened next. He'd guessed, though. He'd run the scene through his mind.

The night of his father's birthday party Margaret had been off duty. She'd made that clear. So it was the peasant skirt and the white blouse, the flat sandals. And she'd been drinking, and he knew she never drank when she was working. She'd let that slip on another of her days off. He'd taken her out to Coquet Island and they'd had a picnic. That day she'd been wearing jeans and a striped cotton jersey, canvas shoes. They'd drunk a bottle of white wine between them and she'd brought sandwiches and home-made cakes. Malcolm had known his father would be furious if he found out – Billy had disapproved of Margaret big-style – but somehow he hadn't cared. It was enough to be lying in the sun beside her and talking. *No work for me tonight. I never drink when I'm working.* Walking down the path to the boat, she'd taken his hand.

The Metro pulled into a station. Malcolm glanced over the newspaper. They hadn't reached Newcastle yet and he didn't think the kids would leave the train until Newcastle. Why would they? What other reason could they have for being here, other than to go into town, last-minute shopping, last-minute fun? And there they were, still laughing and swinging round the pole at the centre of the carriage, behaving like three-year-olds. More people bundled in, but his quarry remained.

He looked out of the window at the flat coastal plain, but in his head he returned to the evening of his father's birthday. A sunny evening, warm, all the heat of the long day trapped in Harbour Street. The middle of the Seventies had brought years of dry summers, of droughts and empty rivers. The seaweed stinking on the rocks in the fierce sun. And that night Margaret had asked him a favour:

'Sort him out, Malcolm, would you? Talk to him. Would you do that for me?'

And of course Malcolm had done as she'd wanted. Like he'd told that fat woman detective, he'd have swum naked three times round Coquet, if she'd asked him.

The rest of the evening had been a blur. Too much alcohol. Tension prickly, like static electricity. A series of images clicked through his memory, like the slides Prof. Craggs used to give his lectures, each one dropping into an old-fashioned projector. The show ended with the fire licking along the floor of his father's office, a bright-orange snake's tongue, fiercely hot. They'd stood with their backs against the railings, watching the varnish on the wooden walls blister in the heat, black and oozing like charred meat. Then the flames had been so high that they'd stood back to watch in wonder, the sparks soaring into the clear sky.

Had that been the first of his sleepless nights? Certainly he and his father had both been standing in their clothes of the night before, when the police and the fire officer had come to sniff around in the morning. Another hot day.

'Arson,' the officer had said. 'No question.' He'd looked at them. 'Any reason why anyone would want to set a fire?' Accusing them with his eyes, but reluctant to go any further than that. More bother than it was worth, and he was a working man himself. If business was bad, he could understand that they might want to claim on the insurance.

'No,' Billy said. 'Unless one of the lads at the party did it. Thinking it was a joke, like.' And that was the story they'd put about. Some of the lads at the party had got a bit wild and leery, and thought it would be fun to set the place alight. And the Kerrs wouldn't make a fuss, because the insurance would come in handy, and they were all mates in Harbour Street, weren't they? Billy had gone into the Coble at lunchtime as soon as the bar opened, spreading the tale. And Billy was a respected man in the town, so the regulars all listened and shook their heads at the foolishness of youth. Val Butt had nodded too, her hands on her ample hips. She understood how these things worked. 'Sometimes these kids are out of control.'

That morning, the smoke in his nostrils, Malcolm had watched from a distance, letting his father take charge, as he always did. Malcolm had never been good at keeping secrets. Had he known even then that the knowledge of what had led to the fire would weigh him down like an anchor, dragging him under, drowning him for the rest of his life?

The train pulled into Haymarket station. Malcolm

watched the other passengers carefully. None of them had seen him. He thought they just *didn't* see the middle-aged or the elderly. He'd wondered if the girls might get out here, at this end of Northumberland Street. The young girls in the group by the door were as flighty as moths, restless and unsettled, but they stayed where they were and it was at Monument station that everyone left the train. Malcolm folded his newspaper in his pocket and followed them onto the escalator and out into the heaving streets.

Chapter Thirty-Eight

Vera blamed herself for Malcolm's disappearance. She should have kept the man in custody while they searched the yard, evidence or no. Now she thought that he was dangerous and desperate. She felt trapped in her office in Kimmerston; she would have preferred to be at the crime scene in Kerr's yard, squeezing early information from Paul Keating and Billy Wainwright. Or out searching for the killer.

Joe Ashworth phoned.

'Tell me you've got something for me.' In her mind she'd seen Malcolm, hunched, walking along the beach, and now she imagined that Joe had him in his car, ready to bring in, ready to talk.

'Nothing.'

She slammed her palm so hard onto her desk that the skin stung. As soon as she replaced the receiver there was another call. Kerr's car had been found at the station car park at Partington. So he'd got onto the Metro and could have taken off from Newcastle Central Station and be anywhere in the country by now. Or he could have taken the Metro to the airport and be anywhere in the world. But Vera didn't see Malcolm as an international traveller. Did he even have a passport? Vera was back on the phone checking, when

Holly knocked at the door. Tentative, but also smug. Vera hated it when Holly was smug.

'Boss?'

Vera waved her in.

'I've tracked down Pawel Krukowski.' Holly sat on the chair on the other side of the desk.

'What do you mean you've tracked him down? He's in a hole in the ground in Mardle. Unless Paul Keating has authorized removal of the remains to the mortuary.'

'No, boss, he's not.' Holly paused. 'He's running a tour company in Krakow, arranging travel to the UK for students and workers. He lives with a Polish woman and they have three kids and five grandkids.'

Vera's mind went blank with panic. 'It could be some other Krukowski.' Knowing that she was clutching at straws and that her whole case was falling apart.

Holly shook her head. 'I've talked to him. He speaks good English. He left the country in 1970. He married Margaret because he thought she was rich. When he found out she didn't have any of her own money, he waited for a couple of years to see if her parents would relent and welcome them back into the bosom of the family. When they didn't, he pissed off home.'

'What was the date of the office fire in Kerr's yard?' Vera kept the panic at bay by demanding facts.

'The fifteenth of July 1975.' Holly could do facts like nobody else in the team.

'The same day as Billy Kerr's birthday.' This was Joe, still in his coat, leaning in through the open door.

'And that's relevant why?' Vera was shouting now. Knowing she'd cocked up and needing to vent her anger.

'Because they were all there, at the Coble to celebrate.' Joe brought a tattered photograph from his pocket and laid it on the desk so that they could all see it. He leaned across and stuck his finger on each of the characters in turn. 'This is Val Butt, landlady. She took over the licence that year, moved to Mardle after some bother with gangs in the West End. That was what she implied, at least.'

'You've spoken to her?'

'I told you I did. I was there this morning.'

Vera sensed the impatience in Joe's voice. Did he think she was losing her grip? Perhaps he was right. 'Of course you did, pet. Go on.'

'That's Billy Kerr.' And Vera could see the resemblance to Malcolm. Billy was more squat, bluff and robust, but the family resemblance was there in the face. 'Mike Craggs, now Professor Craggs, then a post-doctoral student; Malcolm Kerr; Margaret of course. And that's Val's son Rick.'

Vera looked up. 'Have you told me about him before?'

Joe nodded. 'Susan Coulson mentioned him. She said he used to make fun of her.' He paused. 'I had the impression that she was scared of him. I've just checked out his record. He was in lots of trouble as a lad, hanging around with the West End hard men. No convictions since 1974.'

'How old would he be now?'

'Sixty-six.'

'And where's he living?' Vera looked at him.

'No record that he's living anywhere. And no record that he's lived anywhere since the mid-Seventies.'

Silence. In the open-plan office outside there was the murmur of voices.

'And you think maybe he's that pile of bones under Malcolm Kerr's shed.' Vera leaned back against her desk and tried to picture how that would work. Why would Malcolm Kerr have killed the landlady's son. A drunken scrap at his father's birthday party? And what relevance could that have to Margaret Krukowski, forty years later?

Joe Ashworth shrugged. 'Well, we know it's not Pawel Krukowski.'

Suddenly Vera thought that she couldn't stay in the building any longer. She'd start climbing the walls or screaming like a lunatic. 'I'm going to talk to the mother.' She struggled into her jacket and headed for the door. 'You hold the fort here. Let me know if they manage to track down Malcolm.' The last sentence was shouted back over her shoulder as she ran down the stairs.

Vera saw the woman through the window. She was leaning back on a sofa, with her legs propped in front of her, staring at a television. A piece of tinsel strung along the mantelpiece was the only concession to the season. Vera thought *she'd* better start swimming again and lose a bit of weight. She couldn't imagine what it would be like to be old and trapped inside a monstrous body, force-fed crap TV, like Valerie Butt. She rapped on the window to get the woman's attention. Val waved to her to come in. The door was already unlocked. Perhaps she was waiting for someone.

'Another cop?' Val pressed a button and switched the sound off the television. Pictures of smart country houses continued to roll across the screen.

'We've found another body.' Vera squeezed beside her on the sofa. There was nowhere else to sit.

When Val didn't respond, she added, 'Tell me about your lad, Rick.'

This time there was a flicker of interest.

'When did you last see him?' The room was very hot and Vera hadn't bothered to take off her coat. She felt almost faint.

'Ages ago,' the woman said. She paused. 'He had problems. He had to go away.'

'What sort of problems?' Vera pulled her arms out of her jacket, but didn't stand up.

'He got into a bad crowd,' Val said. 'When we lived in the West End. He wanted the excitement. That male-pride thing. He was never one for settling down. That's why we moved out here. I didn't think his mates would find him out on the coast.' She was staring at the television set, at a woman showing off a kitchen the size of her bungalow.

'And did they?'

'I'm not sure,' Val said. 'Things were going on. Maybe he'd just got the bug and wanted to play the hard man, to get a bit of respect in his own right.' She paused. 'Sometimes I think it's worse for the boys. People expect them to be tough. Rick always wanted to seem tough.'

'So people didn't like him.' Vera thought she was getting to the root of the matter now. An idea fired in her head, bounced around the facts, shifted her perspective. 'He was cruel and people were scared of him. He always wanted to be top dog.'

'He was showing off,' Val said. 'Hardly more than a lad when he first got into bother.'

'What happened?' Vera asked. 'The night of Billy Kerr's birthday party? The night of the fire.'

Val lay back in her chair as if she was suddenly exhausted. 'I don't know. Rick was wild that night. Drugs, I think. He was into all sorts.' She looked at Vera. 'You don't want to believe that your kids might be bad. Because it's your fault, isn't it? Who else can you blame?'

Vera put her hand on the woman's fat slab of an arm. 'Tell me.' *Tell me your story.*

'We'd decided to have a bit of a party for Billy Kerr. The boys in the boats organized it. Paid for some food, got one of the wives to make a cake. It was hot. That summer it was hot every day. And from the start of the evening I could tell there would be trouble. There was a kind of tension. You felt there'd be one wrong word and the place would go up.' The woman turned to look at Vera. 'That Margaret Krukowski was at the bottom of it. She wound the men up. All of them. I read about her in the paper when she was killed, and I couldn't recognize her. Some sort of saint. Religious. Spending her time in that place for women with problems. Well, she'd know all about that.'

'Your Rick fancied her, did he?'

'No!' The word rattled like a bullet around the room and then Val continued almost in a whisper, 'If Rick fancied anyone, it was himself. I wondered if he was into men at one time, but there was no sign of that, either. He was a loner. His interest in Margaret was . . .' she paused to find the right word '. . . professional.'

And then Vera understood. 'He wanted to be her pimp.'

'He thought she'd do better with a man to handle things for her.' Val stared out of the window and her words were defensive. 'He'd been knocking around with the gangs in town. He knew how they operated and he saw himself running the same sort of schemes out here on the coast.'

'Did he sell drugs to Susan Coulson?' Vera pictured the man she'd seen in the photo. Dark hair, long over the ears. Hard grey eyes. It triggered another, more recent memory.

'He'd sell his own mother,' Val said. 'If the price was right.' Her voice suddenly bitter. Vera blinked and the pictures in her head shifted again and became firmer.

'But you protected him. You let him operate from your pub.'

'He's my son!' It came out as a wail.

'So that night, Billy Kerr's birthday party.' *Let's get on with the story.*

'That night something was going on. I talked to Rick and told him I didn't want any bother. But you could smell it. The violence. He was twitchy, angry. I wondered if some of the old crowd had threatened him, if he was expecting them to come and get what he owed them.' The big woman closed her eyes briefly. Vera could tell that in her head she was standing behind the bar, pulling pints, cracking jokes, and all the time waiting for her son to ruin all that she'd achieved there. It would take a certain kind of courage not to fall apart. 'Everyone had drunk too much, and it got wild and noisy, folk out in the street. I lost sight of Rick, but I couldn't go and see what was happening. It was dark by then, but steamy hot, like it was a tropical country. You longed for a thunderstorm to clear the air. Or a bit of a breeze.'

Her attention was caught by the television again for a moment. A middle-aged couple with a dog at their feet, standing arm-in-arm outside their dream cottage. A universe away.

'Then we saw the fire in the yard. The flames so high that you could see them from inside the Coble. By then it was gone midnight and I'd carried on selling past closing time, because everyone expects a lock-in when it's somebody's birthday. And I knew the police would come and I'd be in danger of losing my licence, so all I could think of was getting the place cleared.'

Vera wondered how many times Val had relived that scene. But she would never have talked about it before. The way the words came out, Vera could tell that it was new to express the thoughts out loud, and a kind of relief.

'I didn't see Rick again that night,' Val said. 'I thought that he'd made himself scarce. He could disappear like a ghost whenever he wanted to. Police, social security, probation – he seemed to know when they were on their way and he'd be nowhere to be seen.'

She looked at Vera with big haunted eyes. She was preparing herself for a confession. 'I was pleased,' she said. 'I thought: *You piss off back to the city with your gangster friends. Leave me here to make a life for myself.'*

'You thought that was what happened?' Vera asked. 'You thought he'd been involved in starting the fire and he'd run away back to Newcastle.'

'That's what Billy Kerr told me. He came in the next day. Everything quiet then and stinking of smoke. The ruins of the office black and the yard looking like a bombsite. He said that I wouldn't see Rick for a while. "Your boy lost it, Val, and torched my place. I can't have that. I've told him to stay away from Harbour Street. No hard feelings to you, but you know what it's like." And I just nodded. Was that betraying my son? Inside, part of me was singing, because I wouldn't have that stress for a bit. All that time since he was a small kid I was wondering what he was going to do next.'

'Where is Rick now, Val?' Vera still had her hand on the woman's arm. Despite the warmth of the room the skin felt cold and clammy.

'I haven't got a clue.' Another confession. 'I haven't seen him since that day. At first I didn't try very hard to find him. I put a few words out. Nobody was talking. And then I stopped trying. If he didn't want to see me, I didn't feel like making the effort. And it was so much easier on my own, with no other bugger to worry about. I thought I'd hear if he got into real bother.'

'And now?'

'Now he'd be an old man. He might have grandbairns. He'd have calmed down, wouldn't he? I'd like to see him again. A bit of company in my old age. Maybe you could help me look.'

'This body we've found,' Vera said. 'It's old. We think our victim died on the night of the fire in Kerr's yard.'

Val gave an odd little sob. 'You think it's Rick?'

'It's the body of a young man.'

'And all this time I thought he didn't care enough about me to let me know he was okay.' There were tears on her cheek. 'Every birthday I looked out for a card. And I thought: *Sod you, then.* But he was here in Harbour Street all the time.'

'We don't know for sure,' Vera said. 'There'll be tests to do.'

'I know.' Val turned away so that Vera couldn't see her face.

Vera drove to Harbour Street. No real reason except that she couldn't face going straight back to the office, and if there'd been news on Malcolm Kerr somebody would have told her. There was also an itch, the start of an idea, and she needed time to organize her thoughts. This was where everything had started, and this was where she'd find the answer. The street was quiet. The Coble was open for lunchtime drinkers, but the fish shop had already closed for Christmas. There was still activity on the crime scene at Malcolm's yard, but you couldn't see much because of the screens they'd put up to stop ghoulish gawpers. Through the guest-house window she saw Kate Dewar and Stuart Booth in the residents' lounge. She was at the piano and he was leaning over her shoulder pointing at some sheet music. He scribbled on it with a pencil and she turned and ran her finger down his cheek. Vera had parked right outside, but they didn't notice her.

Still sitting in the vehicle, she phoned Holly. 'I need you to check one of the Krukowski witness statements.' And then she called Joe, because she had a question for him too. But he was in a dreadful state and wouldn't listen, almost shouted at her to get off the line because he was hoping for a call. His lass Jessie had got separated from her friends in town, and she'd left her mobile at home and nobody knew where she was.

Chapter Thirty-Nine

Malcom Kerr was still on a mission, but he'd never liked the city and he was almost ready to give up. What business was it of his? He thought he'd just get the Metro back to Partington and pick up his car and drive to the police station in Kimmerston. There was something pleasant in thinking that he might find the fat detective there waiting for him; she'd be glad to see him. He pictured her smiling. She'd make him tea, and might even have a drop of Scotch to put into it. And he'd tell her what had happened. He'd let her take the responsibility. He pulled up his collar against the cold and stood still, so that the crowd eddied round him, like the tide around a rock. All around him was noise. Buskers with amplified music and yelling children and pedlars in his face, trying to persuade him to buy tinsel and cheap plastic toys.

A quiet interview room, just him and the fat woman. Plain painted walls. Nothing to jar the senses. Suddenly that seemed the most attractive thing in the world.

Then the group of young people ahead of him shifted, parted by six jostling youths coming in the opposite direction. It was early afternoon, but they were drinking cans of cheap cider and swearing. Malcolm felt a stab of anger. He wanted to teach them some manners. But he'd been a yob in his time. Worse than a yob. In the following confusion the louts moved on and a single figure was left, uncertain and isolated. The sky darkened. Shards of sleet blew up the street, sharp arrows sending the shoppers into the mall. This was Malcolm's moment of decision. He could give himself up or he could give himself a chance to put things right.

Hesitating, he thought suddenly of the vicar, Father Gruskin. Gruskin had turned up at his house the day after Deborah had left him, offering sympathy and advice. Malcolm thought that Margaret had sent the vicar, because she was worried that Malcolm might do something daft. That he'd kill himself, or kill Deborah's new man. Gruskin had sat in Malcolm's front room and hadn't known what to say. He'd only called because Margaret had asked him to. Another man who would do whatever Margaret wanted him to. He'd muttered a few words and then he'd gone. Vicars should be good men, shouldn't they? They'd make the right decisions. What would Gruskin do now, in his position?

Then Malcolm remembered the way Gruskin had stared at Margaret, watching her longingly as she walked down Harbour Street away from the church. She'd been old enough to be his mother. Older than that even. But still the man had stared with hungry and lonely eyes. Were there no good men in Mardle, then? Did the place only breed liars and thugs?

I'm going mad. My father always said that I should be locked up.

The sleet was heavier now, filling the sky with

pieces of ice, and Northumberland Street was almost empty.

What would Margaret want me to do?

Malcolm looked down the road and saw that there were two people on the opposite pavement now. They walked away from him, one after the other. He hesitated for a moment and then he followed.

Chapter Forty

Joe Ashworth drove home. Sal was almost hysterical and he couldn't get any sense out of her on the phone. All the way there he wanted to yell at someone. At Sal for being so bloody daft as to let their daughter into town, especially with a gang of older kids that he'd never met. At the mother of the kids who'd said she'd keep an eye on them. And at Jessie, who'd pestered them for months to get her own mobile phone and then had left it behind, the one time that she really needed it.

Mostly he was furious at himself. He drove through the empty country roads and began to imagine scenarios. Vera would call them stories. Margaret Krukowski had been killed in the Metro. Dee Robson had been in the same Metro and she'd been killed, possibly because she'd seen the murder or guessed what had happened. And now he realized what hadn't clicked before: that Jessie might have been a witness to Margaret's murder too. Jessie, who was sharp as a knife, with a memory like an elephant's. She'd gone missing and so had their prime suspect, whose car had been found at Partington Metro station. Maybe that was a coincidence, but Joe was so wound up with worry that he couldn't believe in coincidence any more. He pictured his Jessie, in the train with her mates, chatting and laughing because it was nearly Christmas and she was getting her first taste of freedom. He saw Jessie glancing across the train and seeing someone she recognized through the crowd. Someone who'd been on the Metro when Margaret was stabbed. He imagined a flash of contact between them. Then the killer, threatened, following his daughter, and so desperate to escape that he might feel he had to kill her too.

Their estate was on the edge of an ex-pit village and a skein of geese flew overhead from a subsidence pond as he walked up the path. He looked up to watch them, before opening the door. The younger children were in the front room watching a DVD, so he and Sal stood in the small kitchen, communicating in hissed whispers.

'So what happened?' He tried to tell himself that really it wasn't Sal's fault and she'd be feeling even more wretched than him, but he couldn't quite keep the hint of accusation from his voice.

'Sarah's mother didn't realize Jessie was missing until they met up in Blake's for lunch.' Sal was crying now. She'd held herself together for the younger kids, but now she started sobbing.

He took her in his arms and held her tight. 'She'll be fine. You know our Jessie. Sense of direction of a gnat. Remember how she got lost in Boots in Morpeth. Just tell me what happened. Didn't her friends see her wander off?' His voice light and calm – he could be on the stage.

'Apparently they split up into two groups, and each thought she was with the other. It was only when they met up for their lunch that they saw she wasn't there. A couple of the older ones went back to look for her, but they couldn't see her.' Sal reached behind her for a tea towel and dried her eyes with it. 'Sarah's mother thought Jess had just headed home. She phoned, expecting her to be here.'

He didn't say anything, but fumed silently at the irresponsibility of the woman who was supposed to be looking after Jess, and at the carelessness of her friends.

'Your boss phoned,' Sal said. For some reason she never used Vera's name. 'She asked me to email her a photo of Jess. She said they were checking the CCTV in town anyway, and she'd get her people to keep an eye out for Jess.'

Joe thought that Vera's mind must be working the same way as his. She'd already been looking for Malcolm's picture on the CCTV in town. Now she'd get the watchers looking for Malcolm and Jessie together.

'There you are, then,' Joe said. 'They're doing all they can. They'll have her home in no time.' Even as he spoke he wondered if he was really being kind. Perhaps he should prepare Sal for the possibility that their daughter had been abducted. She'd hear soon enough in the media that they'd allowed the suspect in the murder investigation to escape, and then she'd be furious with him for keeping her in the dark. But he couldn't face telling her the truth now. 'Look, I've got to go back to work. I can do more there anyway. I'll call you if I hear anything.' Knowing that he was a coward.

He opened the door into the living room and shouted hello and goodbye to the kids there. They smiled and waved before their eyes returned to the screen. He drove down the road and parked round the corner, where Sal couldn't see him, then phoned Vera's mobile.

'Where are you?' she said. 'Your Sal needs you with her. She's falling to bits.'

'I've just come from home.' He couldn't say that he couldn't bear lying to his wife any more. But he certainly couldn't bear telling her the truth. 'Any news on Malcolm Kerr?'

'I've got men watching his car at Partington,' she said. He wondered where Vera was. He thought he could hear gulls in the background. 'I doubt he'd be daft enough to turn up for it, but I don't suppose he'll be thinking straight now.'

'Do you need me back at the station?' When there was no immediate answer Joe continued, 'I might go into town, see if I can find our Jessie.' He could tell he sounded pathetic, but he couldn't stand hanging around the station, not able to concentrate, jumping every time his phone went, his head full of images of knives and blood.

'Aye, why don't you do that?' Vera said. He thought she just wanted him out of the way. She believed that he wouldn't function properly with his mind on his daughter.

'Don't you care about her?' A bellow. 'A possible witness to a murder, and the suspect on the loose?' As soon as he'd spoken he knew that was unforgivable. The one thing they all knew about Vera Stanhope was that she cared. And she probably had the same pictures in her head as he did.

He thought she was going to let rip with a fury that

would tear him apart, but there was such a long silence on the other end of the phone that he imagined she'd hung up on him in disgust.

'You do what you think best, pet. I'll let you know as soon as I hear anything.' Her voice quiet with pity. And guilt.

He drove back to Mardle, pulled back there by a kind of magnetic field. He had a vague plan to get on the Metro at the end of the line, because perhaps Kerr was fooling them all and was just riding the trains. In the crowds it would be a good place to hide. And the Metro would take him into town, and that was the last place that Jessie had been seen.

His phone rang. It was Sal. His pulsed raced. Jess would be home, safe and well. But Sal only had the same question. 'Any news?' Her voice hoarse and desperate.

'I'm on my way into town,' he said. 'I'll find her. Don't worry.' Before she spoke again, he cut off her call because he didn't need her misery as well as his own, and he didn't think he could pretend any longer that everything was okay.

The Metro car park was full and he ended up stopping in Harbour Street, just across the road from the church.

Passing St Bartholomew's, he tried the door and found it was open. He'd been brought up to believe in a Methodist God of social justice and respectable hard work. His dad had been a lay preacher and had seen evil as exploitation and poverty and the flamboyant decadence of people in the south. Now, Joe couldn't contemplate evil as an almost inevitable result of poor housing or family breakdown. There could be no excuse for a man who planned harm to his daughter. He slipped into the back pew and tried to pray.

Bring our Jessie back safely and I'll do anything you want of me. He tried to think what pact he could make with the Lord, but nothing seemed sufficiently important to set against Jessie's life. There was a deep silence in the church. He was leaning forward with his forehead on his arms, and it was only when he straightened that he realized he wasn't alone. Peter Gruskin was standing in front of the altar looking at him. Joe couldn't face explaining his presence to the man. He stood up and hurried outside.

A shower blew in from the sea. Stinging rain flecked with ice. Further inland there would be snow. The street was almost dark, although it was still early afternoon, but there were no lights in the Harbour Guest House. It seemed like months since he and Vera had first visited there. He remembered walking down the basement stairs, and meeting the woman whose song had been the background music to his romance with Sal. 'White Moon Summer' played in his head again. He realized suddenly that his ignorance had made him responsible for a murder. He wondered if a lifetime of guilt was enough to barter against his daughter's safe return.

Chapter Forty-One

When Joe phoned Vera – ostensibly to ask for news of Malcolm Kerr, but really hoping to be told that his daughter had been found safe and well – the inspector was standing outside the Haven. A flock of black-headed gulls picked over a freshly ploughed field beyond the hawthorn hedge. Vera had ideas of her own about where the investigation might lead.

She knocked at the door of the big house and then went in, too impatient to wait for anyone to answer. Laurie and Susan were in the kitchen as usual and the dog was lolling against the bottom oven of the Aga.

'Where's Jane?' Vera wanted this ended and was in too much of a hurry to be polite. *No more killing*, she thought. It seemed to her that the recent deaths had been a sickening waste. There had been no real reason for them. No adequate explanation. But she knew now who had killed Margaret and Dee, and who had killed the young man in Kerr's yard forty years ago. Joe could have confirmed it for her, but he was caught up with his own anxieties and he wasn't in the mood to think clearly. *No more killing.*

'She's gone into town to catch up with some mates.' Laurie had her standard *I don't cooperate with the pigs* voice.

Vera thought about this. Perhaps she didn't need to talk to Jane now. 'The winter fair,' she said. 'Tell me about it.'

'It was a fund-raiser and a kind of social too. Jane invited lots of the ex-residents back. Kids. A friend of Margaret's dressed up as Santa.' Laurie made it clear she thought this was a waste of time.

'George Enderby?'

'Yeah, that's right. He must have spent a fortune on the stalls. Besides the books he gave away. He'd wrapped them all up in Christmas paper, and we found him a sack so that he could play the part properly.' Her voice softened.

Vera nodded. She could imagine Enderby playing Father Christmas, all jovial and generous.

Laurie continued talking. 'It was sunny and we set stalls out in the barn as well as the house. Invited people from Holypool. They turned out to gawp at us. We had a barbecue, did mulled wine. Susan had been knitting kids' clothes for months and we sold them all. It was cool. Until Em had one of her panic attacks.'

'What happened?' Vera wasn't sure that she had time for this, but thought it might be relevant.

'She just went all weird on us. Said she couldn't cope and she needed to go back to hospital. Jane talked her round in the end.'

'Do you have Emily's address?' This was what Vera had come for. 'She went back to her mother's home for Christmas, didn't she?'

Laurie stared at her, suddenly bristling with antagonism again. 'What do you want with Em? She's not well.'

'I want to stop another murder!' Vera shouted the

words so loud that she could feel the painful rasp in the back of her throat. 'So if you don't mind, lady, I'll ask her a few questions. Quietly and kindly, but needing to get some answers.'

Laurie continued to stare, this time with a little more respect. 'She lives in Tynemouth somewhere. The address will be in the office,' she said. 'On Jane's computer. But it'll be password-protected.'

'Shit!' They looked at each other, a moment of shared communication. If Susan was following the conversation, she gave no sign of it. She was sitting in a low chair close to the Aga, knitting something small and pink. The wool lay in a basket at her feet.

'I can probably find it for you,' Laurie said. 'Not sure it's entirely legal, though, poking around in the system. Hacking into social services.'

'Sod legal!' Vera saw that Laurie was enjoying this. 'Look, I'll take responsibility. Just find that address.'

Laurie grinned and disappeared. In the chair in the corner Susan gave a little smile and continued to knit. She hadn't acknowledged Vera's presence. Was this one of her less coherent days? Or was she pretending to be distant and slow so that she wouldn't be asked to leave the Haven?

'Tell me about Ricky Butt, Susan,' Vera said. 'You knew him, didn't you? He was Val's son and he lived with her in the Coble.'

Susan looked up from her knitting. Her eyes were cloudy. Vera thought she must still be on medication. Vera had read about people becoming addicted to tranquillizers, and Susan had been taking drugs for decades.

'Ricky Butt,' Vera prompted.

'Margaret's boss,' Susan said.

'Was he? Her pimp? He wanted to be.'

'She hated him,' Susan said. 'And so did I.'

Vera had a sudden thought. 'Were you at the Coble the night of Billy Kerr's birthday party?' she asked. 'The night there was the fire at the yard?'

Susan closed her eyes a moment, as if she was making an effort to remember. But before she could speak Laurie bounced back into the room with a scrap of paper in her hand. 'Here's the address,' she said. 'A piece of piss. You should tell them they need better security.'

Outside it felt colder. The wind came from the east and tasted metallic, like ice. Vera's phone went. It was Joe.

'Joe.' Almost faint with hope. If anything happened to his child he'd leave the police service and he'd never speak to her again. And didn't that prove that she was the most selfish cow in the world? A child was in danger, but she could only think about losing the sole person who came close to being a friend. 'Any news?'

'Not yet.'

Vera said nothing. Any words would provoke him to further outrage.

'But I think I know who we're looking for now.'

He gave a name and a reason for believing it. Confirmation. 'Ah, Joe man, great minds think alike.'

'You'd got there already?' Even in his grief she could tell that he had a moment of disappointment.

'Something someone said. You?'

'The same. Then a memory to confirm it. I feel like a fool.'

Another flurry of sleet rattled against the windscreen. It was so noisy that she had to ask Joe to repeat his next words.

'What now?' he asked.

'We go quietly,' she said. 'We need proof this time. No press and no fuss. You just find your Jessie.'

Emily lived in a big house on the outskirts of Tynemouth. It was new and grand, built of raw red brick with porticoes at the front. Through the big living-room window Vera saw a white leather sofa and a flat-screen television. An artificial Christmas tree that almost looked real and a pile of wrapped presents underneath. It came to Vera suddenly that, for Margaret Krukowski, a place like this would be like hell. Much better the life of a call girl operating out of a shabby house in Mardle. And that she still hadn't bought the Secret Santa gift for Holly. She rang the doorbell.

The door was opened by a man in a polo shirt and chinos. The heat spilled out from the hall. Inside he'd need no warmer clothes. 'Yes?' His voice posh Geordie. *A businessman in mufti*, Vera thought.

'Could I speak to Emily, please?' She was aware that she looked even scruffier than usual. No sleep and a hangover, and no time to wash any clothes during the investigation, never mind iron them. She gave what she hoped was a winning smile.

The man looked at her as if she was a tinker selling clothes pegs and didn't bother wasting words on her. Instead he yelled into the house, 'Jackie, there's someone here to see your daughter.'

Your daughter. So he must be the stepfather. And the girl was getting in the way.

He didn't invite her in. Vera stood on the doorstep and waited. Eventually a large woman with an unseasonal tan and a lot of gold jewellery appeared. Her blonde hair was fake, but the tan seemed real. Vera wondered if Emily had been admitted into the Haven to allow the adults to take a holiday somewhere hot.

'Yes?' Emily's mother wasn't as hard as she first appeared. A troubled woman with a nervous tic and a tense smile. A woman who felt obliged to mediate between the two important people in her life.

Just dump him, Vera wanted to say. *There are worse things than being single.* She decided that there were different forms of prostitution. Maybe Margaret's form wasn't the most degrading.

'I think Emily might be able to help me,' Vera said. 'She's not in any bother, but I wonder if we might have a chat.'

'Are you a social worker?'

Good God, do I look like a social worker?

'No, I'm the police. But, as I say, Emily's not in any trouble. I think she might have some useful information.' Vera took a breath. It wouldn't do to scare this woman by rushing her. This was the time for some common politeness. 'How's she getting on at home?'

'Oh, you know. One day at a time.' The woman seemed grateful that anyone was taking an interest.

'But well enough to chat to me?'

Jackie didn't answer, but she stood aside to let Vera in. 'I don't know how we came to this,' she said. 'She was such a good girl at school. Easy. Biddable, you know. We had no idea that she was having problems.'

There was a pause and a moment of honesty. 'I should have given her more time. But I was going through the divorce, and work seemed the only way to stay sane. She was quiet, but she'd always been quiet. And quiet's good, isn't it? Quiet's well behaved.'

Vera was aware of time passing. She was no priest paid to give absolution. 'If I could just talk to Emily, Mrs James . . .'

'Of course.' The tic had returned. Did she think Vera would judge her by the state of her daughter? Perhaps she thought Vera would accuse her of being a dreadful parent because Emily cut herself. And perhaps Joe and Sal thought the world would hate them because they'd let their Jessie have a bit of freedom.

Emily seemed okay, less jittery than when Vera had last seen her. She was a beauty. Her long curly hair reminded Vera of a Pre-Raphaelite painting she'd seen in the Laing Art Gallery when *she'd* been at school.

'Should I stay?' Jackie asked. She seemed still more nervous and keen to do the right thing. She was more tense now than her daughter. Vera thought things might work out for them.

'Why not?' Vera said easily. 'We're just having a chat after all.'

Later, outside in the gloom, she checked her phone. She'd switched it to silent on going into the house. There was a missed call from Holly. She'd left a message to say that CCTV in the Metro system had flagged up Malcolm Kerr earlier in the day, but they'd lost him again. The trains were so crowded now that it was impossible to pick up individuals and there was no sign of Jessie. 'Can you get in touch, Ma'am? We're not quite sure where we should go from here.'

Vera left the Land Rover in Harbour Street and got a lift to North Mardle beach in an unmarked car. A hunch. This was where Malcolm had made promises to Margaret Krukowski, and this was where he came to think. She needed to talk to him before he did anything stupid. The light had almost gone, but the sky had cleared. As the cloud thinned the temperature had dropped, and there were strange white ponds in the bowls formed by the sand at the top of the dunes. Places where hailstones had pooled and frozen. There was a big white moon. Perhaps Kate Dewar would write another song just for the season.

Vera found a vantage point in the dunes. She could see the car park behind her and the beach in front. Further south there were the lights of Mardle town centre and the harbour wall. Out in the bay a boat was moored and on the horizon was a huge container ship making its way towards the Tyne. No sound. Not even of surf on the beach, because there was no wind and the tide slid in like oil. Tomorrow was Christmas Eve and it seemed that everything was breathless, waiting.

Vera's phone pinged. A text from Holly: *Kerr has collected his car from Partington. One passenger.* A name. Which meant, Vera thought, that Malcolm wasn't thinking straight if he hoped to avoid being picked up. More likely, he no longer cared what happened to him. She sent a text in return: *In place. Keep your distance.*

She supposed that she was taking a risk. Perhaps they should pick him up immediately, go in mob-handed, blues and twos. The press and her boss would like that. But she still sensed that Malcolm felt trapped and desperate and had no concern for his own safety. Again, like a mantra or a popular song, the chorus flashed into her head: *No more killing.*

She waited. Nothing. No sound of a car in the distance, and surely they should be here by now if Malcolm had come straight from Partington. It was only a couple of miles away. Occasionally she believed she heard something – footsteps in the frozen sand, or the rumble of an engine – but it was all in her imagination. She was chilled despite her thick coat and her gloves and boots. If Malcolm should appear now, she wasn't sure that she'd be able to move.

The headlights appeared first, sweeping like searchlights over the flat coastal plain behind the dunes, across the reclaimed subsidence ponds where once there had been pits. Vera crouched, because her silhouette might be seen on the horizon against the full moon. The car parked below her. She heard the doors open and shut. Both doors, so there were two people, just as Holly had said. But even in the moonlight it was impossible to make out individual forms. They were just dark shapes. And it was impossible to tell if they were both there voluntarily or if one was the prisoner of the other. There was no other activity on the narrow road leading to the coast. She'd given orders that the officers following should wait on the main road and make their way in carefully on foot. She didn't want to frighten these people. *No more killing.* And she hoped it would all be over before they arrived.

She couldn't see the figures now. They'd started to climb the dunes to the beach and all the shadows had blurred. She strained to listen. Out in the bay she saw the light buoy marking Coquet Island, and again her mind went back to Hector and his raids to collect terns' eggs. He'd trained her well. What better training could there be for this kind of work?

Then she heard the sand shifting and slipping so close to her that she almost felt that she could reach out and touch the walkers. Grunting and heavy breathing: Malcolm out of condition and out of breath, and the frozen air making him wheeze. His companion seemed fitter. Vera waited. Sometimes it seemed she'd spent her childhood waiting, heart thumping. Waiting for Hector or for the police, startled by the noise of sudden wingbeats or heavy footsteps.

Now there was an expected sound: her quarry sliding the last few feet onto the flat beach. And at last she could see them, two dark figures walking towards the water, shadows in the moonlight. Vera shifted her stiff and frozen limbs and began to move. For such a heavy woman she walked quietly. She'd been a heavy child and Hector's jeers had made her conscious of every footstep. *For Christ's sake, girl, do you want us both to end up in prison?*

At the bottom of the dunes she paused. Now she could hear voices. One voice. It was Malcolm, and it seemed that he would never stop or even pause for breath. This was a slow, relentless stream of bitter accusation, a rasping whisper, the voice almost of a lover betrayed. Vera thought he would only stop speaking when the object of his hatred was dead.

And that was when she raised her voice and bellowed too, shining her torch towards them, each word spoken slowly and given equal emphasis. 'No more killing.'

Chapter Forty-Two

Joe finished his phone call to Sal and headed back to Mardle, driving too fast along the icy roads. It was the day before Christmas Eve and the gritters would be on double time, so the council hadn't called them in. He felt responsible for Vera; she thought she was invincible, that she could control any situation with the power of her personality. She could be an arrogant cow, with no sense of danger. He couldn't allow anything dreadful to happen to the boss.

He pulled into the lay-by opposite a petrol station that was putting up *Closed* signs. The roads were almost empty now. Stepping out of the car, he was hit by a sudden cold that took away his breath for a moment. The moonlight made everything monochrome and dreamlike and the shadows were very sharp. He headed away from the road and towards the beach. After a few minutes he heard the sound of an engine, moving down the track towards the car park, and he was close enough to recognize Malcolm's car, the rattling, spluttering sound of it and the shape of the model. There was a bank of bramble and he hid behind that and watched two figures head towards the beach. Joe waited until they were far enough into the dunes not to hear his footsteps and then he followed.

He must have got lost in the strange dunescape, because suddenly he found himself facing the wrong way and looking down towards the main road and the lights of the town in the distance. Perhaps Jessie had inherited his sense of direction. Then he had another moment of panic, imagining Vera dealing with this situation alone. He wished he knew where she was.

At last he reached the highest sand hill and from there he had a view of the beach. The white curve of the softly breaking waves catching in the moonlight. The same two figures, very close, walking towards the water. Did they intend to continue walking, heading towards Scandinavia, until they were killed by drowning or by the cold? Some odd suicide pact.

This was like the set of a black-and-white silent movie. There was no sound apart from the occasional distant rumble of a truck on the main road. It was so quiet that when the words came they were shocking.

'No more killing!' A bellow like a bull elephant.

And he saw Vera, recognizable because of her bulk, moving across the sand at a speed that seemed physically impossible for someone of her size. A giant hovercraft, hardly seeming to touch the ground. And the two companions must have been shocked too, because they stopped moving and watched her running towards them.

Then he was moving too, sliding down the sand, the frozen grains like sandpaper against the skin of his wrists and ankles, trying to keep below the line of the horizon and not make too much noise, because perhaps this time Vera herself might need saving. Even for her, two killers might be too much to tackle.

On the flat, hard sand he stopped and watched.

The moon made a path across the water and over the wet ridged shore. Three figures in conversation. Malcolm Kerr, hunched and broken. Vera Stanhope, triumphant. And Ryan Dewar, the teenage boy who had killed two women and had threatened Joe's daughter. Kerr had his arm around the boy's throat. As Joe watched, Kerr shoved the boy towards Vera and raised his hands in grateful surrender.

Early Christmas Eve and they were in the police station in Kimmerston. Vera and Joe were preparing to interview Malcolm Kerr. They'd leave Ryan until later, once his mother and the lawyer had arrived. Thinking about what Kate Dewar must be thinking, Joe felt sick and sad. Malcolm Kerr had brought *his* daughter to safety. Kate was another grieving parent, but for her there would be no happy ending, no happy families.

Now Vera was in her element, part mother superior and part Mystic Meg, reading the past like a mind-reader. There was a plate of bacon sandwiches on the table between them. God knows where she'd found them at this time of the morning. He could smell the bacon and the coffee and, when he replayed the scene later, describing it to colleagues as an example of Vera working her bloody miracles, it was the smell that remained with him. They'd offered Malcolm a solicitor, but he'd just shaken his head. 'No need for that.' Joe thought he was glad that it had ended like this. Prison wouldn't seem so bad after the soulless house in Percy Street.

'Ricky Butt,' Vera said. 'A horrible young toerag.'

'Ricky was a psychopath,' Malcolm said. Joe might

just as well not have been in the room. All the prisoner's answers were directed at the inspector. Joe was back in his role of observer – Vera's second pair of eyes. 'He liked hurting people. Dealt heroin. Dealt women. We weren't angels in Harbour Street, but we weren't used to that. Not his mother's fault. Val was a bit rough, but her heart was in the right place.'

'And he was making life difficult for Margaret?'

'He'd only been in Mardle for a few months and he was throwing his weight about. He had this attitude. You know, cocky. But cruel with it. Always carried a knife to show he meant business. He said he couldn't have Margaret working freelance on his patch. She should work for him or leave. Or he'd change her looks so that she'd never work again. You could imagine him, his knife on her face. He'd have loved the excuse.' Malcolm's voice was flat and hard. Joe believed every word he said.

'So you decided to sort him out.' Vera wasn't asking a question now, just acting as straight woman, moving the story along.

'I decided to have a word,' Malcolm said.

'The night of your father's fiftieth birthday party. The night that photo was taken.' Vera leaned forward across the table and her eyes were bright. You wouldn't have thought that she'd had no sleep for forty-eight hours.

I asked him to meet me in the yard,' Malcolm said. 'Told him I thought we might do some business together. That was the only language he understood. Business.' Coughing out the last word like an oath. He paused for a moment and then he continued. 'It was hot. During the day so hot that the tar on the road had melted. The heat made everyone crazy. It made me crazy. Butt was just a boy, but he had no respect. No sense of how things worked in Harbour Street.'

'Your dad had a certain position,' Vera said. 'Cox of the lifeboat. It had run in the family. And you had a certain position too.'

Malcolm nodded briefly to show that she'd got that bit right. 'Ricky Butt offered me a cut,' he said. 'He sat swinging back and forth on his chair in the office in the yard. Smirking. Talking about Margaret as if she was shit. "She's got class. Worth a fortune, a bit of class. Bring her onside and you'll get your cut." But Margaret wasn't that sort of woman.'

It was still dark outside, but Malcolm was staring out of the window.

'So you lost your temper.' Vera's voice hardly more than a whisper.

Another pause, then a nod. A brief triumphant grin. 'I hit him. He wasn't expecting it. Not time to get out the knife. He tilted back in his chair and hit his head on the floor. I think that might have killed him. It was a hell of a crash and there was blood and brain everywhere . . .'

Joe thought Malcolm might have meant to continue, to confess to another blow, just to make sure the man was dead, or because he was crazy with the heat and the temper, but Vera interrupted. She raised her hand to stop him in mid-flow.

'Not murder then,' she said. 'Manslaughter, if you didn't mean to kill him.'

Malcolm gave a little shrug to show that he no longer cared.

'Then you fetched your dad and he organized

things for you. Dealt with the mess. Because that's what parents do.'

'He wrapped the body in a bit of tarpaulin and hid it in a rusting old trawler we had in the yard.' Malcolm was obviously still proud of his father, and still a little bit in his shadow. 'Then he set fire to the office. The next day, when the cop and the fire officer turned up, they were only interested in the office. Nobody looked in an old boat waiting to be cut up for scrap.'

Vera nodded. 'And later you were able to bury the body, and you concreted over the grave and built the shed over it. Every day you sat there, you must have remembered Ricky Butt.'

Malcolm thought about that for a minute and then he shook his head. 'Nah,' he said. 'That night felt like a dream. I couldn't believe what had happened.'

'Did you tell Margaret that you'd killed the boy?'

This time the denial was immediate. 'No. I told her we'd frightened him off.'

'But she guessed?' Vera pushed the question.

Malcolm nodded. 'You couldn't get much past Margaret. I told her it wasn't her fault, but she felt responsible, blamed herself.'

Of course she did, Joe thought. And it was guilt that had made Margaret Krukowski who she was. It wasn't the prostitution that had turned her to the church and to helping other women. She hadn't been ashamed of her profession, of the service she provided. It was the knowledge that she'd led to a man being killed.

Vera was moving on, jumping ahead by forty years. 'Ryan Dewar must have reminded you of Ricky Butt,' she said.

Malcolm Kerr didn't seem to hear for a while. It

took him longer to move into the present. He was still remembering a hot summer's night. He lifted his head to look at Vera and she repeated the sentence.

'I didn't want to think that way,' he said. 'I wanted to believe the best of the lad. But yes, he's a psychopath too. Cleverer than Butt, and more plausible. No conscience and no shame.'

'When did you know that he'd killed Margaret?'

'I didn't know. I guessed. Worked it out. It clicked for certain when I saw him in the Metro yesterday, watching those school kids talking about the murderer. He looked full of himself. As if he was a pop star or something. A celebrity. When we had that last walk on the beach Margaret told me that Ryan was . . .' he tried to remember the word '. . . *irredeemable*, and she might have to go to the police. Somehow he'd worked out about her past and was trying to get money from her.' Malcolm looked up. 'Before that, she thought she could save him. Turn him round. Or that we could save him together.'

'You guessed he was trouble, but you still took him on to work at the yard.' Vera leaned back in her chair. For the first time throughout the interview Joe thought she seemed tired.

Malcolm raised his shoulders. 'Margaret asked me to,' he said.

'I know.' Vera gave a very sweet smile. 'And if she'd asked you, you'd have swum three times round Coquet Island.'

He nodded and returned the smile. 'Naked,' he said.

'Oh, pet, I do hope that she was worth it.'

*

On the way out of the interview room Joe paused and turned back. 'You saved my girl,' he said. 'Thanks. Can you tell me what happened? She was a bit confused when they got her home to her mam.'

Malcolm looked up. 'That was your lass? A polite little thing. She was in the Metro chatting to her friends, talking about finding Margaret's body. But Ryan Dewar was there too. I saw him as soon as I got on the train. Fate, I thought. Or Margaret sending me a message. Out of the Metro, your lass got separated from her friends and he was following her. Maybe he thought she'd be able to identify him.' The man paused. He was staring out of the window replaying the scene in his head 'Ryan was chatting to her when I found them. Putting on the charm. Offering to get her home safely. But she'd recognized him and was starting to get scared. There was a community-support officer walking past and I asked her to help get your lass home. I got hold of Ryan – he wasn't going to make a fuss there in the street, with the law looking on – and took him back with me. He thinks he's a hard man, but he's a kid. No match for me.'

'Would you have killed him on the beach if the inspector hadn't turned up?'

Malcolm looked up sharply, but didn't answer.

Chapter Forty-Three

Kate Dewar was on her own in the house when she heard a knock on the door, familiar like the personalized ringtone of a phone. Chloe had said she was out with a friend: Kate suspected a boy, but she hadn't asked. Ryan was away on his wanderings. He'd talked about going into town with some mates and she hadn't seen him all day. Stuart would come along later. Kate opened the door, recognizing the knock and knowing that Inspector Vera Stanhope would be standing outside.

The woman looked exhausted and she didn't have her sergeant with her.

'Come in!' Kate showed her into the lounge. 'Would you like a drink? Whisky?' Because this seemed like an informal visit. It was something to do with the expression on the inspector's face. She seemed softer and more human.

'I'd better not, pet. I'm still working. Maybe you should have one, though, eh?'

And that was when Kate had the first idea that something dreadful was about to happen and that her world would never be the same again. 'What's wrong? Is somebody dead?' Because the policeman who'd come to tell her about Robbie's accident had looked at her in exactly the same way.

Vera shook her head. 'We've got your Ryan in custody. He's been charged with murder.'

'No!' Kate cried. 'He wouldn't. Not Margaret . . . he loved her.' But even as she spoke the words, Kate wondered if they'd ever been true. If her son was capable of loving anyone.

Vera said nothing for a while. She just looked. Then she shook her head again. 'He wanted to make money out of her. He's a great one for money, your Ryan. Money and lasses, and being his own boss.' No judgement behind the words. It was just as if she was listing the facts of the case. And Kate knew that Vera was telling the truth. Perhaps she'd been frightened of hearing this knock on the door since Margaret had been killed. Frightened of hearing that her strange, prowling, angry son was a murderer.

'What happened?' Kate was staring into the other woman's face. Vera had poured her a drink and Kate held it with both hands.

The detective sat down opposite to her. 'Ryan had been thieving,' she said. 'Stealing when he was out on his night-time wanderings. Stealing from Margaret's charity collecting boxes too. I checked with the vicar over the road. The last six months, Margaret's takings had gone down. She made some excuse, but she must have guessed. Had Ryan been stealing from you? From Stuart and Chloe?'

'Sometimes I thought he'd taken money from my purse,' Kate said. 'But he was clever. It was never much at once, and I couldn't be certain.' She thought she wouldn't have been able to admit that to anyone else in the world.

'He stole from your Stuart,' Vera said. 'Maybe not

money, but he took a photograph. A compromising photograph. He used it to try and blackmail Margaret.'

'I don't understand.' Kate drank the whisky and felt it hit the back of her throat. 'What would Stuart have to do with Margaret?' One sip and she felt that she was drunk, that the room was spinning out of control around her.

'No need for you to know the details now,' Vera said briskly. 'Time for that later. Ryan stole from the Haven too. That winter fair they organized for the kiddies. George Enderby was there, throwing his money around like water, and at the end of the day Jane Cameron couldn't work out why they'd made so little. Your Ryan made off with the profits. Dee Robson was there too. She might have had learning difficulties, but she was sharp enough when it came to money.'

'And that's why he killed them? Because of *money*?' It seemed such a mean and pathetic motive to Kate.

'Because of the things that money could bring,' Vera said. 'Power, control, influence. We think he's been dealing drugs too. He's a bit of a bully, your lad. He likes his own way.' She paused. 'Margaret thought she could save him. She felt guilty because of something that happened a long time ago, and she thought if she could persuade your boy to behave well, she'd find some peace. But she was fooling herself. I think she realized that in the end.'

Kate stared at the inspector. These were just words. Sounds like humming in the middle of a song. She couldn't understand what they meant.

There was the sound of a key in the lock. They both looked round and, through the open door, they saw Stuart standing in the hall.

'I've just heard the local news on the radio,' he said. 'They've made an arrest. A juvenile.' He walked towards Kate and held her in his arms. She thought he'd guessed about Ryan already. Nobody was surprised, yet nobody had done anything.

Vera Stanhope stood up and walked towards the door. 'You mustn't blame yourself,' she said. 'You didn't kill those women.'

But Kate knew that in some way she was responsible. And she thought the inspector knew that too.

Chapter Forty-Four

They waited until later in the day to interview Ryan Dewar. 'Let the boy have his beauty sleep,' Vera said. 'He's still a juvenile. Just. We don't want some flash lawyer saying we haven't followed procedures.' Joe hadn't offered to go with her to talk to Kate Dewar and she hadn't asked him.

Vera took the time for a half-hour power nap and a shower when she got back from Harbour Street. There was a change of clothes in her office, kept in case she was called suddenly to court, and she looked unusually smart when she joined Joe in the interview room. She could tell that he was impressed by the transformation. It was another cold, sunny day, hoar frost on the roofs outside the station window.

She hardly recognized Kate at first, she looked so lined and withered. The woman had aged overnight. Ryan was super-cool, lounging across the table, loving the attention. The court case would be a dream for him. All those years of being in his sister's shadow, and now he'd be centre-stage. *What made you different? Losing your dad when you were young? Watching him batter your mother? Or were you just born evil? The shrinks will have a field day.*

Vera didn't talk directly to the boy, but to his

lawyer. Her way of showing Ryan that he wasn't as important as he believed himself to be. 'I hope your client is ready to cooperate, Mr Watson.'

The man nodded. She knew that he had teenage lads of his own. Was he wondering what his sons got up to when they weren't at home?

Now she did turn to Ryan. 'Let me tell you about that day in the Metro, the day you killed Margaret Krukowski. You'd bunked off school at lunchtime again, and gone into town to hook up with a mate and a couple of lasses from the posh school. I bet they thought they were *so* grown-up, going out with a dangerous moron like you. Thief, petty drug dealer and full-time scrote. I spoke to Emily Robertson, who was at St Anne's too, and she knew all about you. You were one of the reasons she ended up in a place like the Haven. She saw you at the winter fair there and she freaked out big-style, asked to go back to the hospital rather than having to face you and your taunts.'

Vera paused before returning to the thread of the story. 'So there you were, playing the lad about town, and who should catch on but Margaret Krukowski.' Vera took another breath, watched the sun edge over the roof of the building opposite, and found that her mind was wandering. She'd be glad to get home. She'd ask her neighbours in for a drink. A big drink. They'd stay up and see Christmas Day in together. She didn't fancy being alone tonight, dreaming of vulnerable women and violent men. Or perhaps Joe Ashworth would be let off the leash for an hour to come back with her.

She turned her attention back to the boy whom she thought of as Ricky Butt reincarnated. 'And she saw you, missing lessons, having lied to your mother again. Maybe that was when she decided she couldn't let it go any longer, that she couldn't save you. You weren't to be her route to salvation after all.'

Vera saw that they were looking at her strangely and, when she continued, her voice was crisp and matter-of-fact. 'Margaret had seen you in town before, of course. There was the day she took Dee Robson into Newcastle to buy her a winter coat. She'd told Dee that the Haven charity would pay for it, but of course that wasn't true. She'd paid for it herself. Margaret was a kind woman. A good woman. She saw you swaggering through town, playing truant, playing whatever game made you money. She knew your mam was worried about you and she chased after you, hoping to make you see sense. And what did you do? You ran away.'

For the first time since she'd started talking Vera looked at Kate Dewar. She was a good woman too. A woman who had wanted to think well of her son. A woman who had hoped for some joy and excitement as she reached middle age.

'Dee Robson saw you,' Vera continued. 'She saw you run off into the crowd. And she was on the Metro the day you killed Margaret. Pissed and hardly aware of anything, but you knew her, didn't you? Everyone in Harbour Street knew the fat slag Dee Robson.'

The boy looked up, almost provoked to speak. There was a moment of silence. Vera changed the subject abruptly.

'Tell me about the photograph, Ryan. The photograph that you stole from Mr Booth's wallet.' Vera knew this would be upsetting to Kate, but at this point her lover's past was less important than getting the boy to talk.

'It was gross.' Ryan's face was red, the picture of righteous indignation. 'Margaret dressed in hardly anything. Stockings. Posing. Like those cards that Dee Robson stuck up all over the Metro station.'

Vera shot a glance at Kate, but her face was blank. Vera thought she couldn't take in this extra information.

'You'd looked in Mr Booth's wallet for money?'

'He had plenty.' Ryan looked up and gave that slow, sly smile. 'He'd have given it to me, if I'd asked. I just couldn't stand the lecture that would've come with it.'

'And you thought the photo would be much more valuable?'

'I was shocked,' Ryan said. 'I wasn't thinking like that. I just took it.'

And brooded about it. And wondered how you could best make use of it.

'You showed it to Margaret.' Not a question. Vera still wasn't sure how this had worked, but she wasn't going to let the boy see that.

'I gave her the chance to explain,' he said. 'That only seemed right.'

'And *when* was that, Ryan?' As if she just needed her memory jogging.

'A couple of nights before . . .' he said.

'. . . before you killed her?'

'I went up to her room,' he said. 'Knocked at her door.'

Vera pictured him slouched against the door frame.

Made cocky by the photo. *Information is power.* But still nervous inside. Still the little boy who'd had nightmares, who'd run away from Margaret in town.

'She let you in?' Vera allowed a little surprise into her voice. 'She liked her privacy.'

'She said that she wanted to talk.' He was less certain now. 'She made me tea.'

'And you showed her the photograph.'

'I put it on the table.' He paused and looked away.

'And she was angry,' Vera said. 'I'd guess she was very angry.'

'She had no right.' His face turned red again. 'She was the one dressed up like a slut. She was the one whose photo was in Stuart's wallet.'

'What did she say exactly, Ryan? This is very important. We need it word-for-word if you can.'

'She said that if I expected her to pay for the return of the picture, I was very much mistaken.' He was a natural mimic and for the first time Vera thought she could hear Margaret's voice. Clear, decisive. 'She said that she'd made allowances for my behaviour. I'd had a tough time. She'd asked Malcolm to give me work and she'd been pleased with my progress there. But this was my last chance. If she caught me thieving or skipping school again, she'd go to the police. She'd tell them that I'd stolen from Stuart and from the Haven, and that I'd attempted to blackmail her.' He broke off and his natural voice returned. 'As if I was bothered. She was a snooty cow. And a tart.'

'What did she do with the photo, please, Ryan?' Because they hadn't found it in her room, but she'd have taken it off the boy.

'She took it from me and burned it.' He sounded

like a sulky toddler. 'She held it over the flame of a candle.'

'So let's move on to the afternoon of her murder, shall we, Ryan? Your friends got off the Metro, and Margaret Krukowski got on. The woman who could land you in the shite big-time. She'd given you one last chance, but here you were bunking off school again. What did she say to you? Whatever she said, it must have been pretty strong, because you followed her to her seat and took out the knife you always carry . . .' *Just like Ricky Butt.* '. . . and when she turned away from you – when she *dared* to turn her back on you – you stabbed her.' Vera had allowed disgust to colour her voice. Kate Dewar was sobbing. She'd probably been sobbing all night.

'Well, Ryan?' Vera insisted. Looking, she saw that he was sitting upright now. Very tense. Reliving the humiliation of being put in his place by an elderly woman. White with anger.

'She didn't say anything. She didn't have to say anything. She looked at me. Kind as if I was a naughty kid. She'd been a prostitute. She had no right to look at me like that.'

'So you killed her.'

'Yes!' Temper constricting his throat, so that his voice was hoarse. He half-rose to his feet and, when he spoke again, he sent a spray of spit across the table. 'I killed her.'

There was a moment of silence in the room, broken only by Kate's muffled cries.

Vera nodded at Joe Ashworth to continue the story. 'I was in the Metro,' Joe said. 'I saw you with the girls, and I hated the way you treated them. It never occurred to me that you were a killer, though. Just a little jumped-up yob, I thought. And that's what you were. A jumped-up yob who thought it was clever to sell drugs to vulnerable kids and stab an old lady to death.'

'You left the Metro at Partington with all the other passengers,' Vera said. 'Hidden by the snow. The Metro bus was waiting and drove you back to Mardle. You got home late.' Vera paused. 'But your mother didn't realize. She thought you'd come in from school with Chloe.'

Kate looked up. 'I heard him come in,' she said. Appalled, as if this tiny example of ignorance made her complicit in his guilt. 'I heard the door and I thought it was just the wind rattling the letter box. It always rattles when the wind's northerly.'

'Did Chloe know?' Vera thought this might be an even worse sin than murder, to involve his brainy sister, to make her choose between sibling loyalty and justice for Margaret. Because she'd feel guilty anyway – the favoured child, the apple of her mother's eye. She had a brief flash of memory: her and the neighbours, and herself in a rare moment of honesty after too much drink, talking about a case when she'd failed; and Jack, wise and gentle, saying: 'Hey, Vera. Just dump the guilt.'

Ryan looked up, suddenly defensive; the anger was spent, but he was still tense. 'I didn't tell Chloe.'

'But she guessed?'

He turned away and said nothing.

Vera nodded to Joe Ashworth. The next part of the story was his.

'When I first walked into the kitchen at Harbour

Street, something was familiar,' he said. 'There was that sense of déjà vu. You were there, sprawled on the sofa, just a school kid in your uniform. I didn't connect you with the lads I'd seen on the train. Then I recognized your mother – I'd been a fan when I was young – and I thought that explained the sensation of familiarity. If I'd remembered properly, we'd have had you in for questioning and the thing would have been over. Dee Robson would still be alive.'

Vera thought that Joe would have to live with that for the rest of his life. Thinking he'd been swayed by the soppy words of a popular song. *Just dump the guilt, pet.* In the end it was Val Butt talking about *her* violent son that had set them on the right trail. Besides, if they'd arrested Ryan on the first day, they'd never have found the body of Ricky Butt under the shed in Kerr's yard. She still wasn't sure what she thought about that, and the consequences for Malcolm. Sometimes perhaps it was better to let sleeping bodies lie. Then she decided that it would be an evil sort of world where a man could kill and get away with it, even if the victim was a toerag like Butt. Besides, this might give Malcolm a bit of peace in his last years. She could imagine him as an orderly in the prison library, catching up on the reading that he'd missed out on as a bairn. Vera thought she might even go and visit him there.

In the interview room the clear winter sunlight was pouring in through the narrow, barred window and Joe was continuing the interrogation.

'Why did Dee have to die?'

There was no response from Ryan. He continued to stare at the scarred table in front of him.

'Because she saw you in the Metro that night? She connected you with the lad who'd run away from Margaret in town? And she'd seen you at the winter fair at the Haven – might even have worked out that you were stealing from them.' Vera pitched her voice a little louder, demanding a response from him.

'She was on the bus that took us from Partington to Mardle. I couldn't take the risk that she might tell somebody, could I?' Ryan looked up now, aggressive again, proud because he'd had the nerve to kill two women, ready to boast. The solicitor touched his arm, a gesture of warning, but Ryan took no notice, and Vera thought the solicitor was as disgusted as the rest of them. Certainly he made no further attempt to stop the boy from talking.

'Talk us through that, would you, Ryan,' Joe said. 'Tell us how you got into her flat.' The voice bland, a schoolmaster's voice. He could have been Stuart Booth. *Talk us through that equation, would you, Ryan?*

'She invited me in.' The boy gave a sudden wild, wolfish grin. 'She was pissed and bumped into me on her way back to Percy Street. 'Offered me sex. Stupid cow! As if I'd ever had to pay for that.'

'Go on.' No accusation in Joe's voice. Vera felt a moment of pride. He was her protégé and he'd learned to control his emotions. He'd been soft as clarts when he'd first come to her.

'The flat was a dump,' Ryan said, as if that was an excuse for what would come later. 'Filthy. She went into the bedroom to change. I mean, just looking at her made me gag.'

'And then?'

'There was a knife on the table in the front room.

A kitchen knife. I wasn't sure if it would work, but I thought it would be safer. Better not to use my knife.'

He flashed a look at Vera. *My God, he wants a gold star for being clever.* She clamped her mouth shut. Best not to reply. He'd like any response better than being ignored.

'But the knife did work?' Joe made it sound as if he was truly interested.

Ryan didn't answer that at first. 'I switched up the telly,' he said. 'In case she made a noise, then I went into the bedroom.' He looked up at Joe. 'The blade was a bit bendy. It took some strength to get it in. But yeah, it worked fine.'

'What did you do then, Ryan?'

'I went into the bathroom and washed. I wiped my fingerprints off the door handles and the handle of the knife. Then I went back to school. I had music and I didn't want Stuart telling my mother that I was bunking off again.'

Chapter Forty-Five

It was midday and they'd finished for the holiday. Stuart Booth had come to collect Kate Dewar. Vera wondered what sort of Christmas there'd be in that house, and if the relationship would survive beyond Boxing Day. Stuart had colluded with Kate to tell her what she wanted to hear: that Ryan wasn't such a bad lad; the boy was misguided and had got caught up with the wrong crowd, but he was sound really. Had anyone in school seen the bullying and the drug-dealing, the petty cruelties? But perhaps nobody had wanted to see. Ryan came from a respectable family, his mam was Katie Guthrie, who had once been famous and would be guaranteed to pull in crowds at the summer fair. Only Margaret Krukowski was anxious, reminded of another cocky young man who'd thought himself above the law. And finally it was the parallel with Ricky Butt that had helped Vera and Joe to find the murderer too.

They stood in the car park outside the station. Vera, Joe and Holly. 'Let me buy you a drink,' Vera said. 'To celebrate. Or come back to mine. I'll shout the cabs to get you home.'

Holly looked shocked. Vera had never invited her to her house before. 'Sorry,' she said. 'I'm spending

Christmas with my folks. It's a long drive and they were expecting me yesterday.'

'Ah.' Vera was pleased really. She suspected Holly would disapprove of the state of her home. 'Joe?'

'Sorry! Sal's got plans.' He raised his hands, a gesture of apology. And to show that he'd have liked to come back with her to talk through the case, but Sal would really go ape if he came back pissed, today of all days.

'Course she has,' Vera said. 'Wish the family happy Christmas for me.'

It was only as Holly got into her car that Vera remembered something. She chased after her, waving. Holly pressed a button and the driver's window opened.

'Shit, Hol, we never did that Secret Santa thing.'

'Nah,' Holly said. 'Never mind. It was never going to work, was it?'

Vera got into Hector's Land Rover and set off alone for the hills.

THIN AIR

The next book in Ann Cleeves' Shetland series – now a major BBC One drama starring Douglas Henshall as detective Jimmy Perez – is out soon.

A group of old university friends are visiting Unst, Shetland's most northerly island, to celebrate the wedding of one of their friends to a Shetlander. But late on the night of the wedding, one of them, Eleanor, disappears – apparently into thin air. It's mid-summer, a time of light nights and unexpected mists.

The next day Eleanor's best friend Polly receives an email. It reads like a suicide note, saying she'll never be found alive. Detectives Jimmy Perez and Willow Reeves are called in to investigate . . .

Turn the page to read the first chapter

Chapter One

The music started. A single chord played on fiddle and accordion, a breathless moment of silence when the scene was fixed in Polly's head like a photograph, and then the Meoness community hall was jumping. Polly had spent thirteen hours on the overnight boat from Aberdeen to Lerwick and when she'd first come ashore the ground had seemed to shift under her feet, and this was another kind of illusion. The music appeared to bounce from the walls and the floor and to push people towards the centre of the room, to lift them onto their feet. Even the home-made bunting and the balloons strung from the rafters seemed to dance. The band's rhythm set toes tapping and heads nodding. Children in party clothes clapped and elderly relatives clambered from their chairs to join in. A young mother jiggled a baby on her knee. Lowrie took the hand of his new bride, Caroline, and led her onto the dance floor to show her off to his family once more.

This was the hamefarin'. Lowrie was a Shetlander, and after years of courtship Caroline had finally persuaded him, or bullied him, to marry her. The real wedding had taken place close to Caroline's home in Kent and her two closest friends had followed her to Unst, Shetland's most northerly island, to complete the celebration. And they'd brought their men with them.

'Doesn't she look gorgeous?' It was Eleanor, crouching beside Polly's chair.

The two women had known Caroline since they were students; she was their voice of reason and their sister-in-arms. They'd been her bridesmaids in Kent and now they were dressed up again in the cream silk dresses they'd chosen together in London. They'd made the trek north to be part of the hamefarin'. They'd followed Caroline round the room for the bridal march and now they admired again her elegance, her poise, and her very expensive frock.

'It's what she's wanted since she first laid eyes on Lowrie during Freshers' Week,' Eleanor went on. 'It was obvious even then that she'd get her way. She's a determined lady, our Caroline.'

'Lowrie doesn't seem to mind too much. He hasn't stopped beaming since they got married.'

Eleanor laughed. 'Isn't this all such fun?'

Polly thought she hadn't seen Eleanor so happy for months. 'Great fun,' she said. Polly seldom relaxed in social situations, but decided she was actually rather enjoying herself tonight. She smiled back at her friend and felt a moment of connection, of tenderness. Since her parents had died, these people were the only family she had. Then she decided that the drink must be making her maudlin.

'They'll be setting out supper soon.' Eleanor had to shout to make herself heard over the band. Her face was flushed and her eyes were bright as if she had a fever. 'The friends of the bride and groom have to help serve. It's the tradition.'

The music stopped and the guests clapped and laughed. Polly's partner, Marcus, had been dancing with Lowrie's mother. His dancing had been lively, even if he couldn't quite follow the steps. He came over to them, still following the beat of the music, almost skipping.

'It's supper time,' Eleanor said to him. 'You have to help put out the trestles. Ian's weighing in already. We'll come through in a moment to act as waitresses.'

Marcus dropped a kiss onto Polly's head and disappeared. Polly was proud that she hadn't asked him if he was having a good time. She was always anxious about their relationship and could tell that her need for reassurance was beginning to irritate him.

The men had set out tables and benches in a smaller room, and Lowrie's friends were handing out mugs of soup to the waiting guests. Eleanor and Polly took a tray each. Eleanor was enjoying herself immensely. She was showing off, flirting with the old men and revelling in the attention. Then there were bannocks and platters of mutton and salt beef. *Bannocks and flesh*, Lowrie had called it. Polly was vegetarian and the mounds of meat at the end of her fingertips as she carried the plates from the kitchen made her feel a little queasy. There was a sense of dislocation about the whole event. It was being on the ship for thirteen hours the night before and spending all day in the open air. The strangeness of the evening light. Eleanor being so manic. Polly sipped tea and nibbled on a piece of wedding cake and thought she could still feel the rolling of the ship under her feet.

When the meal was over she and Marcus helped to clear the tables, then the band began to play again and, despite her protests, she was swung into an eightsome reel. She found herself in the centre of the circle, being passed from man to man and then spinning. Lowrie's father was her partner. He had his arms crossed and braced and the force of the movement almost lifted her from her feet. She'd thought of him as an elderly man and hadn't expected him to be so strong. There was a fleeting and astonishing moment of sexual desire. When the music stopped she saw that she was trembling. It was the physical effort and an odd excitement. There was no sign of Eleanor or Marcus and she went outside for air.

It must have been nearly eleven o'clock, but it was still light. Lowrie said that in Shetland this was called the 'simmer dim', the summer dusk. So far north it never really got dark in June and now the shore was all grey and silver. Polly spent her working life analysing folk tales and she could understand how Shetlanders had come to create the trowes, the little people with magical powers. It must be a result of the dramatic seasons and the strange light. It occurred to her that she might write a paper on it. There might be interest from Scandinavian academics.

From the hall behind her came the sound of the band finishing another tune, laughter and the clinking of crockery being washed up in the kitchen. On the beach below a couple sat, smoking. Polly could see them only as silhouettes. Then a little girl appeared on the shore, apparently from nowhere. She was dressed in white and the low light caught her and she seemed to shine. The dress was high-waisted and trimmed with lace and she wore white ribbons in her hair. She stretched out her arms to hold the skirt wide and skipped across the sand, dancing to the music in her head. As Polly watched, the girl turned to her and, very serious, curtsied. Polly stood and clapped her hands.

She looked around her to see if there were any other adults watching. She hadn't noticed the girl in the party earlier, but she must be there with her parents. Perhaps she belonged to the couple sitting below her. But when she turned back to the tideline the girl had vanished and all that was left was a shimmering reflection of the rising moon in the water.